NO LONGER PR(
THE SEATTLE PL

PRAISE FOR JASMINE ᴏ... ...

Silvera's worldbuilding is exquisite... a rollicking, romantic, riveting ride.

— THE PINK HEART SOCIETY (*THE TALON & THE BLADE*)

A spellbinding urban fantasy.

— BOOK BUB (*THE TALON & THE BLADE*)

DEATH'S DANCER weaves suspense and romance into a story as smart as it is sensual... Silvera deftly choreographs the action using lush depictions of Prague's storied scenery and deliciously dark humor. A thrilling debut.

— CAMILLE GRIEP, AUTHOR OF *LETTERS TO ZELL* AND
NEW CHARITY BLUES

A ... ER PROPERTY OF FEB   1 4 2023
THE SEATTLE PUBLIC LIBRARY

ALSO BY JASMINE SILVERA

GRACE BLOODS

Death's Dancer

Dancer's Flame

The Talon & the Blade

BINDING SHADOWS

TOOTH & SPELL BOOK ONE

JASMINE SILVERA

This is a work of fiction. Names, characters, organizations, events, places and incidents are the product of the author's imagination or used fictitiously.

Copyright © 2020 No Inside Voice, LLC

All rights reserved.

No part of this publication may be reproduced, distributed, or transmitted in any form or by any means, including photocopying, recording, or other electronic or mechanical methods, without the prior written permission of the publisher, except in the case of brief quotations embodied in critical reviews and certain other noncommercial uses permitted by copyright law. Violators subject to punishment by necromancers.

First publication date March 2020

Published by No Inside Voice Books, Seattle, WA

ISBN: 978-0-9976582-6-2

Cover design by The Book Brander

Book Design by No Inside Voice

To mom,

for always knowing

PRAGUE, 1998

TOBIAS WAS fourteen the first time the urge to tear off his clothes and catch small animals in his teeth gripped him. His own screams woke him from the dream of racing through the trees on four legs with moonlight in his fur.

Instinctively, he called out for his brother. "Mark! A m-m-monster's inside me."

"Not a monster, Toby. A beast," Mark offered from the bed across the room.

By the time their mother arrived, Tobias was hysterical. He buried his face in the worn, nubby chenille of her robe and panted.

"You're safe." Her voice curled around the ragged edges of his consciousness as she settled on the edge of his bed. The lilac scent he always associated with her night cream flooded him in soothing relief. "Only a dream."

Her palm, relaxed on his sweaty brow, tingled. She began to sing one of the soft, lilting chants that had soothed all of her four children since birth, ones they would never be able to recall the lyrics to in the morning.

As Tobias drifted again, his brother's voice rose from the darkness. "Not only dreaming anymore, Ma. It's gonna be soon. I can smell him now."

Their mother's sigh turned to the whisper of wind in leaves as dreams swallowed him again. "We'll take him this weekend."

He forgot her words the moment she spoke them.

On Friday afternoon, he tumbled off the tram with Mark and their younger sister, eager for the weekend. They were used to seeing the car parked out front of their building on Fridays. Mom took Mark to the woods at least once a month. Tobias would spend two whole days buried in a book without his older brother giving him a hard time, or their mother urging him to go outside. But his steps slowed at the sight of his own duffle bag in the back of the Škoda wagon.

His parents stood on the top step with his youngest brother between them. Mom shouldered her purse, bending low to give his baby brother a kiss, but her eyes were on her husband. "The performance is at six. Isela has call at four-thirty. Don't forget extra pins for her hair."

"Ich weiß, Liebling."

"I know you know, I just..." Mom stretched up to kiss their father. The kiss went on for too long, as usual. Tobias averted his eyes, his cheeks hot. Mark made gagging noises.

When the two of them parted, their father's face softened into a brief smile before his gaze settled on Tobias. Tobias shivered at the worry in his father's eyes.

"Viel Glück mein Schatz."

Mom and Papa exchanged a final peck before she joined the boys at the lowest step. "You two scalawags in the car. *Jetzt.* Hop along."

Tobias fell asleep on the long drive to the cabin deep in the Šumava forest. Mom made spaghetti for dinner, his favorite, and when darkness fell, she shooed them both outside.

"Everything will be alright," she assured him as they left her a silhouette framed in the light of the doorway. She called to his brother, as always a few steps ahead, "Go easy, Markus."

"Just do what I do." Mark's skin, a brown richer than sun-warmed earth, absorbed the glow of moonlight as he shrugged out of his jeans and socks. "It's easier for them this way."

"Who?" Tobias followed his brother's lead, stripping bare though his skin prickled with goose bumps. Pressure rose in his chest.

The memory of his nightmares returned in a jumbled wave of images and scents. The beast. His heart raced.

"Let that feeling come," Mark murmured, resting a hand on Tobias' still bony, paler shoulder. "It's fun—you'll see."

That promise clutched in the eagerness of his voice, kept Tobias from retreating back into the house. Still, he shivered, refusing to come out of his underwear even when Mark teased. At the sting of raw skin, he looked down to see his fingertips scratching at his own chest as if possessed. The pressure took shape and stretched against the inside of his ribcage.

Mark grinned with too many teeth, all glittering and sharp. "Don't fight him, brother. We're meant for this."

Mark laughed, throwing his head up to the night, the last human sound he would make until dawn. Skin once smooth and brown became furred black. The places between the stars were no rival for the darkness of that tousled fur sprouting in all directions. His face became a snout, and his ears slid back to the top of his head.

Tobias reeled away, but his feet wouldn't hold him. He opened his mouth to scream, and an animal sound came out. He tumbled backward, scrambling in the mud and leaves, away from the juvenile wolf that stood on top of his brother's rumpled clothes.

The beast welled up inside him, flooding his consciousness with scents and sounds beyond his human awareness.

He blacked out just long enough to lose his last grasp of control. The beast inside him surged. When his senses returned, they drowned him. A shocking inner heat banished the night chill from his skin.

What the beast did to his senses was only the beginning. Everything about the way his body moved felt like recovering a forgotten memory. He staggered to his feet—paws—and swung around, backing up in circles until he tripped over his own long legs and landed on his side in the heap of expelled air and lupine whimpers.

The black wolf stood nearby. Mark. Tobias knew him. The same way he knew that what he had become had crawled up from inside his very bones.

He read the black wolf's body as fluently he read Mark's face from growing up together.

Come on, the hunched back and flagging tail ordered. When he barked, it was a clear command. *Get a grip and let's get on with it.*

But Tobias found nothing to hold on to. He managed to get upright after a multitude of attempts the black wolf found comical.

Tobias looked down at his paws and fell over again. He caught a glimpse of his furred tail and tried to flee it. He crashed into brush and trees. All the while, a terrible noise sounded in his ears. The noise of an animal caught in a trap. The trap, his own body. The prisoner, his human consciousness.

His mother called reassurance from the porch. The salt of her tears stung his nose. Tobias wanted to go to her, but the beast held him. When she took a step towards the edge of the porch, the beast bared teeth at her. Mark lunged between them, facing Tobias: head down, ears back, and this time there was no humor in the curl of his tail or the hunch of his shoulders.

Tobias stumbled away, whining.

The first night was a disaster. Mark tried to show him the wilderness around their cabin. They hunted a rabbit in the darkness—well, Mark did—and Tobias would never forget the high-pitched scream it made when Mark's teeth closed on its neck. The black wolf retuned with the limp shape dangling from his jaws. Tobias recoiled, even as saliva flooded his mouth.

A gnawing hunger surged in him as Tobias watched Mark tear open the soft belly and work the carcass with his teeth. Mark tossed the remainder to him. The beast ate, Toby screaming mutely inside.

After that, he surrendered the last of his humanity and retreated into the darkness.

In the morning, he woke on the porch, curled up with Mark as they had in the cradle. Only he was naked and shivering and mottled with what might have been dirt or dried blood. Their mother opened the door, threw out a couple of blankets, and disappeared again. She reemerged a few minutes later with cups of steaming hot cocoa and marshmallows. Mark took his mug, heading inside to the warmth of the fireplace.

Tobias lay where he'd awoken, clutching the blanket around his body and shivering. Smudges of darkness swept semicircles beneath his mother's eyes. She'd never seemed old to him before now.

"We had to wait to see… if…" She offered the cup.

He recoiled.

At the scent of warm chocolate, he vomited on the porch. He sealed his eyes shut against the glimpse of glistening red meat and dark organs, bits of bone and hair.

The second night he tried to fight the change, but the beast overtook him as soon as Mark's paws hit the ground. The beast fought, but he refused to let go of humanity, forcing himself to recall every detail of his bedroom and his books, his siblings and their father.

He slunk to the front door, head and tail bowed. Their mother appeared at the window, her face a question. The black wolf gave a human-like shrug in response. The door opened. She sighed as Tobias slunk past her to the blanket she'd laid by the fireplace. Annoyed, Mark abandoned him in favor of the night forest.

On the way back to the city Sunday afternoon, Mark regaled their mother with stories of his roaming.

"You're so quiet," she murmured to Tobias when they'd stopped to let Mark out to pee.

"W-w-why, Mom?" The words scratched his raw throat.

"I don't know," she said. "We'd hoped—I'd hoped—you just never seemed like you'd change."

"I don't want to," he whispered. "E-e-ever again."

"You have to. I know that much and, if you don't, it will happen on its own, and you will lose control. We survive at the mercy of the necromancers. There are rules about how people like us behave in public. At the first hint of a violation, they can make us disappear, or worse. You understand? And it's not so bad, is it? Your brother—"

"Is a brainless idiot." Tobias choked on the words. "I hate it. I'll never like it. N-n-never."

She sighed. "Don't talk that way about your brother."

She watched Mark trudge back from the woods. "Denying the change makes it more dangerous. You'll come up to the cabin with us every weekend and during school breaks. When Markus says you're in control, full control, you can stay inside and play checkers with me if you want."

"Ma!" he wailed.

"Tobias, some things we don't have a choice about in this life," she snapped with dreadful finality. "At the least, you learn to live with it so you survive. If that's all I can give you, so be it."

Tears choked out whatever reply he might have made. Mark climbed into the car. He avoided looking into the back seat, even though Tobias's wet sobs must have been audible.

Instead, he turned up the radio.

At home, their mother garaged the car, resting for a moment with her palms on the steering wheel and her eyes closed.

Mark touched her shoulder. "Go on in, Ma. I'll get the bags."

She passed a hand over the tight coils of his hair and settled it on his cheek with a weary smile. "Thanks."

When she was gone, Mark shouldered Tobias aside, slamming the doors as he went.

Blinking away tears, Tobias pulled his overnight bag out of the trunk. He passed one forearm under his dripping nose and glared. "I'm telling Dad."

Mark's face hardened. "Who do you think helped pick out the cabin?"

The pat he gave Tobias shoved him backward. Tobias whirled on him, the beast's snarl rising in his chest. Shock stopped him in his tracks. Mark grinned at him, showing his teeth. His eyes glittered yellow for a moment before flashing back to human copper.

"Quit feeling sorry for yourself, you big crybaby," he said with a huff. "And if you say anything to Issy or Chris, I'll kill you. I know where you sleep."

CHAPTER ONE

Fourteen Years Later

Dear Ms. Svobodová,

We regret to inform you —

Barbara should crumple up the letter without subjecting herself to the rest, but she never could resist the urge to finish once she'd started reading something.

—that after careful consideration, your application for the fellowship position has not been selected.

When the blur of tears made reading unmanageable, she reached for a tissue, sending one of the little cartoon pineapples clattering across her desk. She slapped a hand over the small plastic figurine to silence it with a worried glance.

The forgotten office tucked away at the end of a long hall was empty. Situated in the oldest wing of the university library, with the original four-hundred-year-old stone walls, it was cold year-round and occasionally the power went out. She supposed eventually it would be remodeled as a storage closet. At least it was so far down on the priority list for restoration, it was relatively undisturbed by the work efforts that seemed to have turned other parts of the library into a cacophonous obstacle course. Unfortunately, the way things were going, she might still be stuck here in limbo when it finally happened.

By the time the doors opened, she'd composed herself. She tucked her chin, dabbed her eyelashes, and slipped the rejection note back in its envelope under her keyboard. She would take it home and file it with the others. Then she would look over the upcoming fellowships and special research areas and prepare her next application. After five tries, she could almost do it in her sleep.

Her fellow research assistants drifted in, unwinding their scarves and removing their coats. Their break-time conversation lingered like the faint whiff of cigarette smoke.

"...and you heard what he said to Novak when the department objected to his budget request?" The unofficial leader of their little cadre, Edita, was close to defending her dissertation, but still managed to stay on top of all the office gossip. She continued in Czech without waiting for a response, "Absolutely nothing. He just stared, with those eyes."

"Gods, those eyes!" Pale, ethereal Pavlina clasped her hands to her chest and pantomimed a swoon into the rickety chair near the back of the room.

As the newest assistant, she had inherited the worst desk—close to the old window. Undaunted, she arrived on her first day with a stuffed woolen bumper to block the draft and a quilted cushion for her chair, and had, during her tenure, knit an impressive array of scarves, neck warmers and hats for each of them.

The final member of their trio snorted in disbelief. Tall and severely thin, Honza would make an excellent grumpy librarian in thirty years. "Vogel insulted almost every member of the senior faculty, and two of the students on his team have filed complaints. Not a good start for a visiting professor."

"He's so exotic." Pavlina smacked her lips. "I heard his mother is American. He was raised here. You can't tell except for he's so tan and it's the end of winter."

Barbara cringed, her eyes on the plastic figurine in her hand. She knew whispers of speculation about her own background, despite her name, often fixated on her looks.

Pavlina's voice settled into a purr. "We're lucky to have someone of his capability."

"As though we had a choice," Honza grumbled. "Novak lobbied hard for Tesarik and, as glad as we all are that failed, I heard the assignment came down from the liaison to the Necromancer Azrael."

Amazing how a room this cold could still lose a degree or two at the word.

No one knew how many necromancers existed, but when the war had broken out between human populations wielding the power of gods against one another, necromancers were the ones who prevented an apocalypse. An alliance of the most powerful eight had divided the world between them into territories. Now they regulated human interaction with the gods and, under the Peace in Humanity codes, any material deemed a threat by relation to magic was under their strict control.

The Godswar and the Allegiance takeover cast a long shadow over the decades that followed. And though Barbara and the others were too young to remember, they were raised knowing the primary rule by heart: stay away from anything magical. Objects, books, people— anything with the hint of connection to the supernatural had a way of disappearing under the necromancers rule.

Edita tucked her scarf around her throat and lifted her gaze heavenward. "Superstitious git. Azrael's funding is the reason we have renovations...and jobs. His patronage—"

"Ownership." Honza lifted a finger.

"—Has been a boon," Edita snapped. The Necromancer controlling Europe chose Prague as his seat, and the city was the uneasy beneficiary of his interest. "Costs money to keep these old buildings up. And if it brings quality professors here, isn't that our good fortune?"

Honza scoffed. "Have you seen the undead?"

"Zombies?" Pavlina managed both thrill and alarm in a single gasp.

"Undead." Edita sounded the word out as though to a small, stubborn child. "Don't let anyone hear you call them such."

"This Visiting Professor Vogel has two on his team." As the senior assistant, Honza had been the only one of them invited to attend the department briefing where the team assigned to catalog and prepare an exhibit of the newly found items had been introduced. "Spies. They don't breathe. They... volunteered to be turned."

Barbara replaced the dancing pineapple at the front of her desk. Edita's eyes settled on her. "And what do you think of all this, Bara...Bara?"

The Czech diminutive of her name reminded Barbara of her mother. Barbara had been raised on stories of her time at Žižkov University. How much joy would it have given her to see Barbara give her academic pledge?

We'll teach, you and I. The larger hand, tight on her own and chilled with failing circulation. The words slurred through morphine. *Share an office.*

That part of dream may have died with her, but at least Barbara could recite her pledge at the graduation ceremony as her mother had taught her. She no longer believed in heaven, but maybe her mother would know, somehow.

She fought the urge to burst into tears—or to look at the envelope again.

"What's happened?" Edita paced to her desk, eyes narrowed. Like some Slavic goddess of hearth and home, a solidness in her presence and features always reassured Barbara. Dependable, unflappable, nurturing, but fierce.

Barbara grabbed a tissue and faked a cough. "Perhaps a cold coming on. You should stay back. I don't want you to get sick."

Edita spotted the ragged edge of the envelope Barbara had torn in her hurry to get it open. She snagged the corner from under the keyboard before Barbara's hand could cover it.

"Is this what I think?" she said as Barbara made one last grab for it. "Why didn't you tell us? We wanted to celebrate with you—oh, dear..."

Barbara snatched another tissue as the tears returned, swiveling back to her computer with a sniffle. "I told you not to get your hopes up."

Edita headed Pavlina off before she began circling Barbara's desk, drawn by the sight of tears like a shark to blood in the water. "Get her a coffee from the machine. There are crowns in the top drawer of my desk. Go."

When the youngest member of their team had gone, Honza rose from his chair and strolled over. He leaned a hip on Barbara's desk and sent another pineapple figurine—this one a spinner on a stationary base—rocking with the flick of a finger.

He sighed. "Terrible news, Barbara."

Barbara struggled against more tears and waved away their concern. After acceptance into the doctoral program, she'd blazed through the coursework portion of her assignment— but after the mess at the Christmas party, she'd become untouchable. Without a fellowship or a reliable advisor, she couldn't begin her dissertation. No dissertation to defend meant no degree.

When she looked up, Edita's mouth formed a hard line.

"This is because of that jackass Tesarik," Edita muttered, glancing at Honza.

Barbara lifted one shoulder. "If I had just slept with him, it might have been easier."

"You need to file a formal complaint." Honza shook his head.

"And be *formally* blacklisted by the department?" Barbara frowned. "At least this way they will forget—eventually."

Edita set her lips. Honza looked like he wanted to speak, but at the sound of the door opening and the mute plea in Barbara's eyes, he hesitated. He sucked in a deep breath anyway as Pavlina entered.

"Honza," Edita snapped, sending him back to his desk.

Pavlina presented a cup of lukewarm coffee with the flourish of a queen's bauble at court. "Can we still do our English lesson at lunch? My interview at BioGen is next week, and I want to practice as often as possible."

Pavlina was graduating at the end of the year and was already applying to positions outside of academia. *The men are too boring here,* she informed Barbara as they reviewed job postings.

Barbara nodded, accepting the cup, and Pavlina retreated to her desk. Edita turned her back on the room, putting herself between Barbara and the others. "Bara."

Barbara looked at her ruefully.

"You are too good to that girl." Edita shook her head. "You should be charging for lessons."

Barbara's mouth tilted up of its own volition. She reached for the letter in Edita's hand. "I don't mind. I'm good with languages."

"And you are too good to be held back forever," Edita said, handing it over. "One day, you'll get your assignment."

Barbara looked down, unable to sustain eye contact as she smoothed the envelope shut. She returned it to the spot under her keyboard and nodded.

Barbara glanced at the row of little pineapple figurines on her desk. Most of the paint had been rubbed off the oldest ones. Unlike Pavlina, she didn't have a backup plan. Those three little letters behind her name would make all the difference in her chances to get a position doing conservation work. She couldn't afford to feel sorry for herself or to wallow.

Two new department requests for item retrieval waited in her inbox.

The last was forwarded from Honza with a note: *I tried, but this is a job for the superwoman.*

The nickname was as good as an apology. Barbara checked the submitting department and winced. Speak of the devil: Visiting Professor Vogel.

At the beginning of the term, an old wall had been knocked down as part of the library renovations and revealed a hidden chamber full of materials several centuries old. This kind of discovery would make careers. The role of leading the team to catalog and prepare an exhibit had been the subject of contentious politicking among the faculty and staff.

The announcement of Visiting Professor Vogel's assignment was met with a wary pleasure. His particular period of focus, the Bohemian empire during the northern Renaissance, only served to validate the importance of the find. His dissertation had become the book on post-Godswar rare human materials collection and curation.

Then the man himself had arrived and made his list of requirements, and the surprise had become consternation. A special climate-controlled room with limited security-based access, strict cataloging, rigorous materials handling standards. It might have all been common stuff from his time at Oxford, but it just served to highlight how far behind Žižkov University was in meeting the latest international standards. Nobody liked to be reminded of their flaws, and Vogel identified each with surgical precision and not an ounce of diplomacy.

Overnight, he'd gone from being a sensation to being tolerated when he could not be avoided entirely. Office gossip expounded Vogel's reputation as difficult and demanding. A small, selfish part of Barbara hoped the fuss would be enough to take the attention off her and that blasted Christmas party. In any case, she was sure her current status as a pariah would keep her entirely beneath his notice.

Since each member of Vogel's team had been handpicked, she hadn't bothered to submit her proposal for research project to him. The most she'd hoped was that a previously occupied position in the conservation department would open up in the shuffle and she could quietly slip into a fellowship. After today's rejection, even that hope waned.

Well, back to work. She called up a chat window to Edita.

I've got a hi-pri for Vogel.

Edita looked up from her monitor across the room, with wide eyes and gritted teeth. Words appeared on the screen a moment later. *Bad luck, that, but if anyone can do it you can.*

Barbara sighed. *Can you take one of my others? I'll give the boring one to Pavlina.*

Send it over.

The University was still a long way from being fully digitized, but she had to start somewhere. Barbara lost herself in department records first.

Most library patrons went through the help desk on the main floor for research requests, where a rotating team of graduate assistants helped with first level needs. Whatever they could not handle was escalated to the Reference Librarians. But requests from faculty working on special projects and department heads were sent directly to this smaller team, hand-picked for their ability to handle more complex assignments. It was a prestigious appointment, which made Barbara's inability to advance beyond it even more frustrating. With her grades, and the time logged in the special assistance office, she should have had her pick of projects.

Pavlina dragged her away from her desk at lunch. They visited their usual haunt, a basement restaurant that served cheap, starchy meals. She spent lunch picking at the plate of mashed parsnips and cream sauce bathing her cooling chicken, while Pavlina practiced tenses in English by telling Barbara every sordid detail of her previous weekend's conquest.

Usually, Barbara found her colleague's exploits amusing, if a bit outlandish, but today they served to remind her of one more area in which her life was deficient. She had no time for relationships, and the few times she'd been out she'd come home early, and alone. After that, it just hadn't seemed worth the effort.

She didn't notice the end of the day until Edita's shadow fell over her desk.

"You'll find it tomorrow," Edita insisted. "Come, let me buy you a drink."

Barbara shook her head. Mustering up a smile took more effort than she expected. "You know how I am."

"You already have a lead?" Honza laughed in amazement as he wound the light scarf around his neck.

It thrilled her to find the unfindable. It was her specialty, and everyone knew it. The one moment that she felt most herself was when she laid hands a missing item—something of value. No matter how chaotic life got, how many opportunities slipped between her fingers, she always had this.

Still, she shrugged. It would do no good to attract more attention than her reputation already warranted. "Want me to lock up?"

"If you would," Honza said as Pavlina trotted to his side. She threw her arms around his waist and chanted for a beer.

Someone cleared their throat in the doorway, and they all looked up as the head of their department tugged at his lapels. His watery blue eyes swept the room. A tidy man in his mid-sixties, the way he looked at everything, but no one directly, always set Barbara on edge. She couldn't recall if he'd ever made eye contact with her, in spite of conducting her interview for the research assistant position. "Students."

Pavlina sprang back, and Honza rose to his full height.

"Professor Novak, sir." He cleared his throat.

Their boss's gaze skated over Honza. Barbara took small comfort in knowing everybody got that treatment. Barbara rose, she'd volunteered to lock up, so she might as well deal with whatever Novak wanted. "Can I help you with something, sir?"

He frowned. "It's come to my attention that Visiting Professor Vogel is not receiving his requests in a timely manner. Who has been assigned the latest?"

Honza flushed to the tips of his ears, but Barbara spoke first. "I have, sir."

For a flicker of a moment, his gaze alighted on her before drifting over her shoulder. He huffed. "Miss Svobodová. That's surprising, given your... reputation."

Was he referring to her ability to find things, or the drama at Christmas party and the subsequent gossip? She kept her voice even. "The volume Professor Vogel requested is missing. I've been in communication with both reference and archives. I'll have it recovered, sir."

"I trust you will," he said after a long moment of marking the air around her as though trying to determine what she was by the space she occupied.

She didn't allow herself to consider what his judgment would be. She had spent too long trying to be accepted. Some days she ached to tell everyone what she thought of the fact that although she had been raised by her Czech mother and Czech was her first language, they still treated her like an outsider because her father had been a foreigner.

Today, she stuck to diplomacy. "Thank you for your confidence, sir."

He exhaled. "I don't need to remind you how important the visiting professor's work is for the University. His collection bears an enormous amount of attention from the government as well as the necromancer's office. Professor Vogel has been judged the best for the job. So we must be the best for ours."

Honza's voice deepened with gravity. "We understand sir."

After a moment of itchy silence, Honza's eyes lit with an idea. Barbara fought the urge to throw a pineapple figurine across the room at him to shut him up.

"May I suggest assigning Miss Svobodová to the collection team on a full-time basis, so that requests are attended to utilizing her superior retrieval skills?"

Too late. The project timeline was intense leading up to the exhibit. Vogel's requests were always challenging. They'd shared them in the past. What if another opportunity for a fellowship came up? Even if she was no stranger to the proposal process, writing each took time. When would she have time for the rest of her work?

Barbara held her breath, praying Novak would dismiss the proposal.

"A fine idea," Novak said at last. "I'd like to avoid this unfortunate incident again. In the future, be sure all requests go to Miss Svobodová. Miss Svobodová, you will see my office if further delay is inevitable. For any reason."

When he finally departed, they all took a deep breath.

Barbara sank into her chair and covered her face with her palms. Her nose was getting red again, she just knew it. Honza's footsteps hurried across the floor toward her desk. She held up a hand to ward him off.

He dropped to one knee at her side anyway. "I meant every word. You are the best of us."

"And you need someone else to see you work," Edita conceded. "Someone outside the department, who doesn't know about that gods-damned party…"

"The party? The Christmas party? What happened at the party?" Pavlina asked.

Honza and Edita ignored her.

"You heard Novak," Honza said. "He's the best. And rumor says he's seeking a permanent position on the faculty, gods help us all."

Pavlina bobbed her head eagerly. "And he's not terrible to look at, for all that. He's young."

"Enough both of you." Edita scowled, pushing Honza aside to face Barbara. "We all know you didn't start that business at Christmas. But blame always follows the woman. An ally would help you in the department, and maybe beyond. Getting on Vogel's good side isn't a bad idea."

Barbara took a deep, shaky breath. She blinked away the memory of Tesarik inviting her to his office down the hall from the party. His stale breath on her face, cornering her. He was old, but so much bigger than her. The distraction of Karel Broucek and another graduate appearing in the doorway as she slipped free. A few moments. Nothing had happened. And yet the trouble had started after.

"Fine. Thank you, Honza." She tried to imbue the words with a little gratitude, but came up short.

Honza studied his wingtips.

"Come on, now you need a drink." Edita tugged at her arm. "You can start making yourself indispensable to Professor Vogel first thing in the morning."

⌁

THE FOLLOWING MORNING, the paper trail for the missing book died in archives. She swore and pushed away from her desk. With various parts of the library under reconstruction, it was even more common for something to be misplaced.

"I'm off." She turned on her out-of-office message and headed down to archives.

She checked in with security, affixed her temporary badge, and headed into the stacks. Sometimes an inattentive undergraduate shelved an item improperly, so she started where it should have been. The certainty that it wasn't there pushed against her breastbone almost as soon as she moved into the collection.

She found a secluded corner of the stacks and closed her eyes. It would have been easier if she had a visual to go with the catalog data, but she was used to finding books she had never seen. Instead, she held the title, author, and edition information in her mind.

A tendril of inquiry stretched her fingertips wide. *I know you're out there, and you know I'm looking for you.* The thin sensation of familiarity tugged at her awareness. She closed her eyes and breathed deep, letting the tingle spread from her breastbone to her fingertips. *Help me out a bit, will you?*

It wasn't as though she expected it to reply. It was just that she had always had this extra sense of books, like the ability to spot old friends in a crowded room. She didn't know where it came from or why she had it. But she had to use it, that was the first rule. Disuse had done her mother in. In the end, all that unspent grace—a word less dangerous than magic—had rotted inside her. The second rule, that she must never reveal them, was a necessary precaution.

There were rewards for reporting creatures of magic to the necromancer. And thought this little trick—this bit of grace, as her mother called it—seemed hardly worth the attention, there was no mistaking it for a normal human skill. Because it wasn't the only strange thing she could do.

Combining it with her work seemed like the best path. The library was safe, full of rare and valuable books occasionally lost or misplaced in the course of study. Plenty of opportunities for her to use her grace in a way that would not attract any undue attention.

A flash of light flickered against the corner of her right eyelid. She opened her eyes and followed it to a row of offices in the back. The conservator for collections was a middle-aged man that could have been Honza's cranky uncle. She knocked, but no one answered. Urgency warred with propriety.

Urgency won. She tried it. Locked.

Barbara stared at the knob. "You should be unlocked."

She wrapped her fingers around the knob. After a moment of hesitation, the lock gave. She flipped on the light and ventured inside. At the sight of the books stacked in piles with loose papers between them, she wondered how he could find anything. She let the tingle at the tips of her fingers lead, scanning spines as she went until the tingle became a burn.

She set aside the papers on top of the stack as she uncovered her prize. The worn binding and natty edges of the slim volume indicated why it had wound up on the conservator's desk. But the paper trail that should have followed it was absent.

"You there!"

She leaped at the shout from the doorway, jostling the table. She just managed to catch the stack of books and papers before they tumbled to the floor. The staff conservator glared at her from the doorway.

"How did you get in here?"

At her silence, he repeated himself in English between clenched jaws. He crossed the room in a few strides, eyes narrowing.

That pricked Barbara's tongue into motion. In Czech, she replied, "It was unlocked."

Somewhat.

Breaking into the office of a member of the faculty was far worse than getting accosted at a Christmas party. A formal reprimand would go in her permanent record. It took her two tries to catch the badge pinned to her chest with shaking fingers. She snagged it, thrusting her shoulders back and lifting her chin. "I'm with the research assistant office."

"You don't have permission to be in here," he said. "What is that?"

For a moment, she thought he would try to snatch the book out of her hands.

Give up the book, part of her screamed. But the other part, the one that had had led her this far, refused to surrender her prize.

She tightened her grip, holding it to her chest. "Professor Novak has indicated the full force of our efforts be directed to responding to requests from Visiting Professor Vogel."

Recognition bloomed on his mottled face. He paled at the name, and she wondered at the effect Vogel had on the staff. Might as well use it in her favor.

"Research has been looking for this item for two weeks." Her voice steadied, and she lifted her the book like a talisman. "You can imagine his displeasure with not being able to locate it."

"That book has been pulled from circulation for repair."

"Strange, I didn't find the appropriate records indicating that, sir." She emphasized the title.

He drew up, sputtering. "Are you accusing me...?"

She knew she should quit now, but the conservator she wanted to be stole her tongue.

"And a book of this significance deserved its own footprint," she said, sweeping the room in her glare. "Not stacked in a pile of papers like so much rubbish."

His teeth shut with a clack. The muscle in his cheek jumped and flared.

"If you will excuse me," Barbara said, drawing herself up to her full height. She was eye to eye with his lapel. "You may wish to submit a request to the collections department to have it returned when Professor Vogel has completed his review. Thank you for your time...sir."

The conservator stepped aside to let her pass.

◆

WHEN BARBARA PEEKED into the rooms designated for the special collection team on the upper floors of the library building, she paused to admire the recent improvements. Vogel had gotten more than a few of his wishes, despite the reticence of—and cost to—the department.

The entire team was gathered in the study at the far end of the hall with his temporary nameplate in the slot beside the door. The cataloging and appraisal of the recently uncovered collection was an interdisciplinary effort, a chance for multiple programs to participate in a rare find of national significance. She recognized three graduate students from her own courses, two from the humanities department, one from forensics. The two she didn't recognize must have been the zombies. Honza was right: they did look like normal people.

The study had been converted into a classroom of sorts, with the students occupying a random assortment of chairs semi-circled around a blackboard on which a Latin phrase had been written in precise, if hasty, script. As an undergrad, she had taken a graphology seminar and found the subject so fascinating she continued her study. She noted the articulated, well-spaced letters, the 't's crossed high, and the pressure that had left chalk dust everywhere. The writer was stubborn, committed, and private.

That familiar tingle itched at her breastbone and her fingertips.

She hesitated in the back of the room, unsure of why her grace was firing now.

Professor Tobias Vogel leaned against the windowsill on the far side of the room with his arms folded over his chest. The chalk dangled in his hand. He shifted, a quick, familiar motion to push the glasses up his patrician nose before tucking his hand back into the crook of his elbow. The chalk left a streak on the cuff of his eggshell shirt.

She'd seen his photo in the press announcement. The unsmiling intensity of his gaze commanded attention, but with an unusual reserve that made him seem much older. He dressed well—if a bit like a professor twice his age. The wool vest looked tailored, nipping into his waist over the band of matching slacks.

In person, she noted a nose a touch broader and a mouth a bit fuller than the camera revealed. The warm cast to his skin made him seem to glow with health, vitality. The window at his back framed him in the weak afternoon sunlight and brightened the strands of close-cut wavy hair into shades of warm earth and honey. Though he stood motionless, there was something active in him, as though always moving, considering.

The tingle in her chest blossomed into something denser and more layered than she was accustomed to feeling from a book.

"I am waiting," he barked in English.

Barbara wasn't the only one who jumped. Her fingers clenched the book in her hands. She should have listened to Edita and sent the book via intra-office delivery. Now was not the time to make her first impression.

A desk, complete with a leather messenger bag, worn soft with use and slung over the chair back, was a few steps away. She thanked heavens she'd picked ballet flats this morning as she slipped toward it.

"Someone in this room has to have more than a basic understanding of the finer points of Latin translation? Anyone?" His voice rose as he switched to Czech. "You—in the back."

Barbara froze. All eyes in the room went to her. Heat crept up her collar. Her throat abruptly dried. She pointed at her own chest, brows raised.

"Yes, you. You're late."

"I'm sorry to disturb you, Professor," she said, keeping her address formal. "Research assistant's office. Since we located the item in question this morning, I thought it best to deliver it immediately."

His brows rose. He leaned forward, touching the frames of his glasses as if to be sure they were still there. "That was not a question. I've been made aware of your assignment, Miss Svobodová."

A jolt went through her at the sound of her name.

American though he might be, and Oxford-trained, he navigated the complex rise and fall of her surname perfectly. His Czech was impeccable. For the first time, she paused to contemplate just who Professor Tobias Vogel was.

Her grip on the book relaxed as the urge to bolt turned to intrigue.

Beneath the lenses of his glasses, eyes the colors of cold ash met hers. Her stomach filled with the languid buzzing of summer bees.

He continued to stare.

When he leaned back, his voice was as cool as his gaze. "I was assured the most efficient and skilled technician would be locating my requests for this project. I have to say it's not a ringing vote of confidence in the training of the undergraduates."

Pity filled the faces of students between them.

Heat flared in Barbara's neck, soon to make its way to her cheeks, where, no doubt even with her complexion, embarrassment would make itself vividly evident.

"If that will be all…" His attention returned to the chalkboard.

Barbara glared at the words scrawled on the black surface. Latin she had, no grace required. "It's wrong."

The weight of a stadium full of gazes would have been half of his when it returned to her.

"What you have there. 'Stamus contra malo.'" She paused, "'We stand against evil.'" It should be 'stamus contra malum.' It's a mistranslation."

The students' attention flew to him in unison, as though following a particularly gripping tennis match.

Professor Vogel lifted his chalk hand, index finger tapping his chin as his eyes narrowed in consideration. "Correct."

He did have a fabulous mouth, she considered, clearing her throat. But she wasn't here to show him up. She needed him to appreciate her expertise. He was her fresh chance—maybe a last one. And this time she would be circumspect and remember to keep her distance. She would be precise and professional and direct. She set the book on his desk with care and turned to leave. A click of recognition made her pause.

She glanced over her shoulder at the board. "The quote is from *The Phantom*, I believe. It's the motto of the Jungle Patrol. An American comic book."

Someone in the room coughed to conceal a laugh. She straightened her back, smoothing her hands on the skirt of her floral-print wrap dress. "If you'll excuse me. Tempus fugit, and all."

CHAPTER TWO

Tobias's father once told him that the problem with acting like the smartest guy in the room was that you were in constant danger of getting knocked on your ass by someone smarter with less to lose. He'd been trying to warn a twelve-year-old who delighted in showing off his intellectual prowess to the annoyance of everyone present.

At twenty-eight, Tobias finally admitted that maybe his father had been on to something.

Barbara Svobodová stalked away, her hips bouncing with the force of her stride beneath her ramrod-straight spine. Tendrils of curly hair escaped her bun with every step.

It was much better than the meek way she'd slunk into the room. The hint of bergamot had caught his attention first. It was all he could do not to acknowledge her right away. In a land of straight lines and hard angles, she was Art Nouveau with swooping, graceful curves. How a woman like that expected to go unnoticed was beyond him.

And there was nothing timid about the way her eyes glittered, even as the flush rose from her throat to the line of her cheeks. In heels, the chin she jutted out proudly as she corrected the translation would have brushed his solar plexus.

He tore his eyes back to the room of goggle-eyed students. His thoughts weren't so easily redirected.

He'd only been informed of her assignment this morning, presumably after he'd given Novak his opinion on the delays coming from the research desk. This had been an attempt to mollify him, but it galled him to no end that Barbara Svobodová was the newest entry on the list of people to be managed.

Still, something about the name gave him pause: not 'Barbora,' as he would have expected, though her last name was as Czech as it came.

Part of him rose in curiosity. The same part of him that always cringed as people meeting him for the first time after correspondence or phone conversation looked twice at his appearance. The boldest or most tone deaf even dared, "Where are you *from* again?"

He could calculate the moment they decided to accept or reject him because of their own confusion.

Be grateful, his mother always said. *At least you know right away who's worth your time.*

Now here was Barbara Svobodová, the best research assistant in the department, skilled at finding anything she put her mind to, the head of the department had announced in a tone of desperate pride, his shifty gaze sliding away from Tobias before it could fully settle.

There had been no photos in the student directory so her appearance had been a surprise. Tawny brown skin and cheeks dusted with freckles like shaved chocolate on an ice cream cone. That generous bow-shaped mouth, even tightening to a grim line, couldn't hide a plump, biteable lower lip. She was different. Just like him.

Late to the office that morning, he'd nearly collided with Professor Klisak from Archives in the faculty lounge. Since the older man was one of the few faculty who didn't seem to back up a step when Tobias approached, Tobias asked for a second opinion in the faculty lounge before he headed up to the lab. "Henri, do you know a Barbara Svobodová?"

Klisak leaned on the door frame. "Small thing. Curly hair. Very brown, yes?"

Tobias gritted his teeth. "I haven't met her."

"Excellent student," Klisak said. "Top of her class. Having some problems in the doctorate program, I hear. Personality issues."

Tobias had been the subject of enough gossip to know it when he heard it. He'd worked his ass off at Oxford to stand out and been called in to help on translations and dating of items and collections most of his peers dreamed of. He should have had his choice of teaching positions. But somewhere along the way, he'd gotten the reputation of being difficult to work with, and for. As a result, he spent the final portion of his doctoral studies traveling to threatened locations around the world to find and recover materials lost during the Godswar with a team more concerned with staying alive than keeping on his good side.

He'd seen life outside of the Necromancer Azrael's territory. How uncertain the world still was, even a generation after the Godswar. Not all necromancers patronized the arts and sciences, investing so much into maintaining the civilization of the humans they now ruled. And not all had such benign relationships with supernatural creatures in their territories.

When the offer to come home to Prague arrived, he jumped on it.

Longing for family—the sprawling, rowdy Vogel clan—was a tangible thing in his chest. He knew he'd made the right decision when he'd stepped off the plane and felt a weight lift off his chest. He took his first full breath of air in years. But deciding to come back, to settle down, meant he no longer had the luxury of disregarding the effect his personality had on people. He intended to try for a permanent position on the university faculty, but he hadn't exactly made friends since the start of the term.

Tobias had been puzzled by the first student complaint against him. The second was of greater concern.

His father had once drawn him a Venn diagram of the things it took to be successful. Three circles: Be Nice. Be On Time. Do Good Work. "You can get by with two out of three, but only just."

His work was impeccable. He was prompt to a fault. But nice eluded him.

He'd always understood words when confined to books. Languages came, if not easily, then reliably enough with practice. He'd grown up bouncing between English and German at home, and picked up Czech in school and in public through sheer dedication. Latin and Greek were necessities of his profession. French and Russian were natural expansions. Sanskrit and Aramaic were eccentric, but had proven useful a time or two. He should have been capable of a little diplomacy in any of them. Somehow when it came to social interaction, things got tangled up and made a mess of him on their way from his head to his tongue.

As a child, a stammer and the resulting attention it drew made everything worse. He'd learned to be terse because it gave him fewer opportunities to make an idiot of himself.

Say what you mean, his father urged him. *Say it simply.*

But keep a good intention in your heart, his mother interrupted.

Instead he'd humiliated Barbara Svobodová in front of a room full of her peers.

Only he'd failed in that, too. She was smart and clever. Smart enough to see the trick he'd posed to his team, and clever enough recognize nuance in the work wasn't just the translation, but the understanding of context provided by culture. Her voice shook the whole time. He would have traded the whole room full of highly recommended doctoral students for one library assistant.

He was going to have to make this right.

By the time Tobias finished his lecture and assigned reading to his team, it was almost lunchtime. One hand slid over the cover of the slim volume on his desk and, for a moment, he imagined the imprint of her fingertips underneath his. After lunch, then. He made the mistake of checking his email before heading down to the library research assistant office. Four hours after pouring through initial dating reports, team member dossiers, and ignoring press requests for interviews, he packed up his bag, locked his door, and headed to the elevator.

He got lost in the warren of halls twice before he found the office where the research assistants were kept. It was a small, cubby-like space, lined with bookshelves broken up with two rectangular windows. A portable space heater that looked older than he was collected dust in the far corner. A man and a woman looked up from their conversation by the coat rack. Their eyes widened in an expression he recognized all too well.

"Professor Vogel." The man stuck his hand out. "Honza Ruska. Lead research assistant. Such a pleasure."

"Barbara Svobodová," Tobias announced before he remembered his new commitment and took the hand. "Pleased to meet you. I'm looking for Barbara. Slečna Svobodová."

"She left," the young woman said. She was the color of fresh cream and stared at him with vivid blue eyes, contemplating him like a cat stalking a slow-moving bird. "She had a rough day. I'm Pavlina Horsakova, professor. Pleased."

Tobias didn't exactly recoil, but he released her hand as quickly as possible and stepped back. "Pleased, ah. Thank you for your time. Good evening—"

"I forgot my damned keys, again," a familiar voice said behind him. "Oh. Professor."

Tobias stepped aside as Barbara bustled into the room, wearing a short, carmine-colored hooded cape belted at the waist. The hood pooled around her shoulders and wild tangles of dark hair framed her face.

Something impossible kicked in his chest.

"Miss Svobodová," he said, aware that they were in her domain and they had an audience. "I'm glad I caught you."

She stared up at him as one might contemplate a snake to determine whether it was poisonous.

"I saw your request," she said. "I've already called it up from Archives and will have it on your desk first thing in the morning."

He shifted on his feet, trying again. *Keep it simple, stupid.* "I came to apologize."

She drew up, clearly determining the viper to be deadly. "No need, sir. I understand your frustration with the delay. I'll work harder to get your requests met in a timelier fashion." She aimed a sideways glance at the tall man, who tugged at his collar and made an in-depth study of his wingtips.

"I assure you, you have full access to my resources—" she said, pausing at her own words. The pale woman coughed behind her hand and focused her attention on her scarf. Barbara swallowed hard but pressed on. "For the duration of your work on the collection."

Tobias stared. He'd been quiet too long.

"I..." Words jumbled up in his mouth, pushing against his tongue and his teeth, but his tongue refused to work. *I will be calm. I will speak simply and clearly. I will not stammer.*

Barbara saved him with polite dismissal. "Is there anything else you needed, Professor?"

"That's all," he managed.

"Tomorrow then," she said with strained smile.

He knew an escape when it was offered. He nodded to the other two with a curt dobrý večer and stalked away.

"Good evening," Pavlina sang after him.

◆

TO AVOID a crowded tram ride home, Tobias took the cobblestone walkway along the river. The dusk air was thick with springtime, blooming things and fresh leaves and the small, furred animals that claimed the darkness.

The ruins of the old Vysehrad fortress atop the shadowed hill behind his building called to him. Only the vestiges of humanity stopped him from flinging his pack and his suit jacket on the front stairs of the building and racing into the trees.

When they came to Prague, his parents had sunk everything they had left into a shabby building on a narrow strip between the fortress hill and the river. This had been the only home he'd ever really known.

He jammed his key into the familiar lock on the building door. Home.

Each floor of the now-restored building had a memory attached: the year Chris was born, the year Mom started taking Mark to the woods on weekends, the year Issy left for the Praha Dance Academy. It had been finished and the empty units rented out by the time he'd been accepted at Oxford as one of the youngest students in the college's history.

Tobias paused at the flat on the top floor of the building. Ten years, three degrees, and a profession later, he was back where he started.

His parents insisted Tobias stay at home until he got on his feet. And given the visiting professor salary, it did help. For now. He took a deep breath.

Beryl met him in the hallway, unfazed by the wide-eyed, bristling expression on his face. He didn't know when he'd stopped thinking of her as 'mom,' only that it began the night she turned him out into the woods and let the beast claim him. Knowing she wouldn't have been able to stop it didn't soothe the sense that she had abandoned him to a wilderness in his own heart that he hadn't known existed until it dragged him in.

"Just a few hours until dark, be patient," she murmured, rocking back on her heels. "I've been calling all day. Didn't you get my messages?"

He shook his head, shrugging out of his cross-body bag and his jacket. He toed off his shoes. "I keep forgetting to turn my phone on."

"Then set up your voicemail," she said, hands on hips. "I am tired of leaving messages with the department secretary. My Czech is abominable."

He adjusted his glasses and stared down at his mother. "It's perfectly fine."

"Wanted to make sure you didn't stop and eat on your way home," she said, pausing. "Mark is here. We're doing family dinner."

Tension crawled through Tobias's chest. Of all nights. He hadn't wolfed out in weeks, and he didn't know if he had it in him to deal with his brother. His mother rested a hand over his heart. "He's changed. You both have. Give him a chance. You used to be so close, thick as thieves."

He resented how eagerly Mark took to the dual life. Intense but uncomplicated, Mark embraced this aspect of himself as Tobias had never learned to, loved it even. Tobias had fought his wolf to a draw, learned to tolerate and give it what it needed—but just.

Mark and their father were playing chess in the living room. The older man rose with a grin that was like looking into a mirror and hugged Tobias. Tobias didn't miss the flicker that crossed Mark's face at the sight of the easy affection between them. Childish as it was, he marked a point in his favor.

Their father never seemed to notice the rivalry in its many dimensions, or, if he did, he ignored it. "Stay close, you're up next. I'm about to clean your brother's clock."

Case in point. Mark frowned at both of them—he'd never gotten over his annoyance that their father insisted on speaking German at home.

Compact and muscular, Mark took after their mother as closely as Tobias resembled their father. Their younger siblings settled somewhere between their parents in feature and temperament, softening the dynamic of the rivalry. Somewhat.

"Gonna drop off my bag," Tobias said to relieve the tension. "Christof home?"

"Yo, brother!" The bellow from the hall was his answer. "Come check out this new Radiohead album."

At nineteen, Christof was the youngest of the Vogel siblings and the tallest. He hadn't yet grown into his frame, but the strength in his long limbs had increased steadily over the years.

When Tobias rounded the doorway into his room, his baby brother's lanky body was sprawled on his bed. Chris was listening to a CD, wearing baggy sweatpants and one of their father's old sweaters. He brushed a forelock of overly long, wavy brown hair out of his eye and grinned, comfortable in his skin—wolf and human—as Tobias could never be.

Tobias wanted to be mad for the invasion of his personal space, but he just couldn't hold on to it. Chris always had a way of softening the edges in situations. Releasing his wolf around Mark became much easier for Tobias once Chris transitioned.

"Where is Issy?" Tobias asked as they sat down to dinner.

"Too good for us lowly Vogels." Mark laughed. "The Academy, where else?"

Beryl shot him a look. "Isela has a seminar with a visiting lecturer from the Sur American school."

Tobias knew how reluctant she had been to let Isela attend the Praha Dance Academy as a resident student. But since the third Vogel sibling showed no inclination to transition, having her out of the house and focused on her training made keeping her ignorant of the family's secrets easier. Still, Tobias suspected it wasn't as easy for Beryl to let her go even the short distance away. He'd have to speak to Issy about coming home more often.

Midway through dinner, Tobias was itching to get out of his skin. Mark, who never kept his wolf in check enough to reach that level of frustration, delighted in verbally sparring with him. Oblivious, Chris helped himself to his third serving of mashed potatoes. Beryl slid the platter with the remainder of a roast chicken toward him, and he grunted thanks.

Tobias gave up when Mark snatched the last roll. "I gotta go for a run."

"I'm sure you do." Mark smirked at him with a knowing look.

"Why don't you go together?" Their father suggested.

Before Tobias could come up with an excuse, Mark sneered. "No can do. Got a hot date."

"Chris?" Tobias asked out of politeness.

"Saving it for the weekend, brother," Chris said around a mouth full of chicken wing. "Why don't you come with us? It's a shit ton better than sneaking around the park at night."

"Afraid you can't keep up?" Mark narrowed his eyes.

"Boys." Beryl sighed.

Tobias rose. "Thanks for dinner."

He dressed in shorts and a t-shirt, ratty running shoes on his feet. He tucked his key in his hiding spot near the garage and set out into the park. The full dark welcomed him as he jogged up the winding switchback trail, taking a detour off the main track into the denser woods before he got to the park.

Once the founding fortification of the city, Vysehrad's few ramparts and walls served as reminders of the footprint the fortress had once held. Now the ruins were a city park. After dark, it was abandoned except for the odd drunk and partying teenagers.

He slipped his clothes under a dense collection of branches, glasses tucked into one shoe.

The sharpening of his eyesight was the only thing he loved about his wolf. He'd worn glasses since he was seven, and seeing unaided for the first time had been a revelation. It was the saving grace of the transition that would have otherwise driven him mad. Each time his mind tried to panic, he returned to the glory of sight, sharper even than his human eyes could have been.

Tonight was the same. The wolf rose before he could check it, swallowing him up. Gone was the panic and disorientation. He took comfort in knowing that it wasn't as though his brain was somehow shut off. He had the same reasoning faculties as he did as a human, a certain advantage when he was a larger-than-average wolf in a city park. He kept to the shadows, running until his tongue lolled and his breath came in enormous bursts.

A scurrying motion caught his attention next and he hunted. He was full from dinner, the cooked food rich and greasy in his feral belly. Though he usually didn't hunt for sport, he imagined the large, trash-eating rats wouldn't count.

It was almost midnight when he stood on the highest part of the fortress walls, looking out over the river bathed in the wan light of the crescent moon. The wind came to him clearest here, bringing the whole city with it. He drew in a big breath, searching for the faintest aroma of bergamot and oranges. Before he could stop it the image of Barbara Svobodová appeared in the wolf mind, curious.

His ear flicked, catching the sound of a human step, and, reluctantly, he retreated to the shadows and the spot where he had left his humanity folded beneath a bush.

He slipped into the apartment shoeless, brushing his feet off fastidiously on the mat. In the kitchen, Beryl sat on the stool beside the window overlooking the park. He didn't need to ask. She always waited up for them, long after they were as comfortable in their fur as they were in their human skins.

Bathed in the thin gold light of the overhead lamp, she sat with legs folded, looking like some ancient deity. Beneath a brightly patterned scarf, a lock or two of hair spilled free, the tiny shell at the end identical to the ones she peered at on the square of velvet cloth covering the counter.

Tobias glanced at the pile of scattered cowrie on his way to the refrigerator and pitched his voice low. "Anything interesting coming?"

She sucked her teeth lightly and took a sip from the teacup at her fingertips. "Prescience isn't my gift."

"Doesn't stop you from trying," he chuckled, pulling out the containers of leftovers. They were still warm. "Can't believe Christof left anything."

"He's a growing boy," she said, returning to her shells. "You all were. Still are, by the look of it."

His belly rumbled. She laughed and slipped fluidly off the stool as though it didn't involve detangling her feet and ankles from impossible resting spots against her hips. She opened the cabinet and brought down a plate.

"It's the transition," he said, his mouth around a cold chicken leg. "Takes a lot out of me."

"It wouldn't take so much," she murmured, heaping green beans, potatoes, and gravy in a pile, "if you didn't put it off."

He shook his head and took the full plate to the microwave with one hand, while he maneuvered the bone in his teeth with the other, sucking off the last of the edible meat. His molars closed and the bone snapped satisfyingly. When he turned around, sucking the marrow around the sharp edges, her brows were up.

Shoulders hunched, he spat the bone into the trash. He jumped a little at the touch of her hand on his shoulder.

"You don't have to be ashamed of what you are."

He closed his eyes. When he turned again, she was back on her stool. She peered at her shells, cocking her head side to side as though they were a puzzle that would resolve if she looked just right.

"I see where Isela gets it from," he said, trying to lighten the mood.

Distracted, a half smile made the years fall away from her features, and her eyes came up again.

"The…" He waved his arms, pantomiming the quick twists and turns it took to get her legs in that complete, tidy lotus. "Dancing thing."

Beryl chuckled. "A yoga class or two wouldn't kill you, Tobias Vogel. You might find you like it. I started a new morning class at 6:30 on Tuesdays. You should come down on your way to work…" She paused and he held his breath, waiting for the inevitable. "There are several nice young ladies—"

"Beryl." The microwave switched off and he hurried to open it before it could finish chiming.

"From what I overhear in the dressing room, there is a serious shortage of educated, professional, handsome men in this city."

He groaned, balancing the hot plate on the tips of his fingers. "Are you running a yoga studio or a dating service?"

"You see these arms." She held them up as gracefully as a ballerina's port de bras. "Empty. I have three adult sons —"

"And a *daughter*," he whispered, lifting his fork.

"Isela's too busy courting gods to fall for an ordinary man."

He set it down with a wry grin. "Thanks?"

"That's not what I meant," she hissed. "Is it too much to ask for you to just look? You might surprise yourself. Your father and I aren't getting any younger…"

"Gods, you guys are so loud." Chris rubbed his eyes from the doorway, thin legs poking out of athletic shorts. Equally thin arms dangled from a faded Pearl Jam t-shirt—one of Mark's hand-me-downs. "Do I smell food?"

Tobias sighed and slid the plate across the counter. "Fork, or do you want to just plant your face in it?"

Chris gave him a withering look as he plucked the fork from Tobias's hand. "She giving you the grandkids speech?"

Tobias rubbed his forehead.

"You should check out the class, though," Chris said around a mouthful of potatoes. He wagged his eyebrows. "There are some girls in there, man…"

He waved his fork and gravy splashed onto the wall. He hurried to clean it up.

Tobias held up a hand. "Enough, both of you. This collection is going to be a full-time job plus. And then there's this—"

He gestured at his sweaty clothes and rubbed a hand through his hair. Flecks of leaves fluttered around him. The emotion that rose in his voice surprised him. "I need a shower. G'night."

His mother and brother stared at him: Chris, with dumbfounded surprise, and worse, his mother, with pity.

❧

BERYL GILMAN VOGEL watched the doorway long after her middle son was gone. It was impossible not to ache, seeing how lost he was in his own skin. Even after she reminded herself that his path was his to walk, she wished she could shoulder some of his solitude. It didn't seem fair that he should have to carry such an enormous secret alone.

"What the hell was that all about?" Christof muttered, filling a glass with sparkling water and drinking it down in one long slurp. A belch roared up from beneath his solar plexus. "Sorry, Ma."

She shook her head at him, and then froze as the thing troubling her about her middle son and the strange pattern the cowrie had fallen into clicked into alignment. Something was coming for him. Something big. Shadows still, too small the make out the details, but dangerous.

Christof crowded over, unable to hide his interest in her craft. He peered at the shells as she scrabbled through the drawer next to the sink for matches and a bit of incense. He started to speak, but she waved a hand for silence.

The small reed-thin curl of smoke turned green when she began to murmur a little song her mother had sung to her from the cradle. *Protection. Wisdom. Fortitude.* She contemplated the small knife in the drawer. No, too early to jump to conclusions.

Give more than you take. Offer what you must, when you have to, and never more. The tenants of her craft. Blood was always a last resort.

"Everything ok, Ma?"

She patted his hand but didn't cease chanting, casting her glance again at the doorway Tobias had exited. The shower was still running. Good. She was too far from the ocean, but this would have to do. She poured a little sea salt into the blue glass bowl and filled it with water.

"Can you tell me anything?"

"Need an offering," she muttered.

"Bowls, blue, water, saltwater, Omaaya." He fumbled the name, but returned with the bottle of white wine before she could ask.

Wise boy. Would have made a strong witch. She had been careful to hide her disappointment when she lost him to the wolf. She consoled herself with the knowledge that others of her kind were coming. Soon now, by the look of things.

Christof squinted. "That bad, huh?"

She lit the candle and took a sip of wine. "A door is opening for your brother."

"Doors are good things, right?" Christof ticked off his fingertips. "Opportunity? Change? Maybe it's cause he's back in Prague. Hey. Praha. Prah means 'threshold,' right?"

She patted his cheek, grateful always for the anchor her youngest son provided. He returned her smile with a sweetness that hadn't changed since his first. It would have been nice to have another witch in the family. One could be wolf or witch, or neither, like Isela, who was a puzzle she still hadn't solved.

And Christof never fully let go of the little things she'd taught him as a boy. Knowing the wild herbs she liked to collect, he always made sure to bring her favorites when he returned from spending the weekend at the cabin. He'd was the only one that remembered her songs, though he confused them with mantras and seemed puzzled when he was unable to find them in any of her yoga texts. Perhaps there was a little witch in him, after all.

But she could not have him interfere in Tobias's path. It might endanger them both. *Great mother, guard my son. Keep the light on his path through the shadows close around him. Long have I served you. Grant me this.*

She smiled at her baby and offered what reassurance she could. "A door is also a barrier, a gate, protection. And some barriers should not come down."

CHAPTER THREE

"Dobre den!" Barbara called a greeting over the jangling of bells hung from the doorknob.

A week after being assigned to Professor Vogel, she had never been so relieved to retreat to the sanctuary of the antique bookstore at the basement of her building. She descended the steep stairs, leaving the dusty light filtering down from the windows above as she stepped into the dimly lit shop. Tightly spaced rows of shelving cribbed from other stores snagged her coat as she passed, as if the books themselves reached out from the shelves to grab her attention.

She lifted her fingers to their contents, trailing along the spines in greeting.

She called again as she worked her way toward the heart of the shop. Shelves opened up to tables piled with display boxes of stamps, old postcards, antique photos, pins, and other small ephemera. In the back right corner of the store, blocking the doorway to the storage room, was an enormous wooden desk that appeared to have been constructed in the space, too big to have ever fit through the narrow front door or come down from the apartment building above. Stacks of newer books occupied one corner, and a box likely filled with more of the same took up the other end of the desk.

An ancient spider plant, with so many tiny offspring it looked prepared to colonize the city, cascaded over the edge of the desk to the floor. A large bound ledger dominated the remaining space.

Barbara knew that behind the desk, under a pile of papers and more books, was the cash box. No computers here, though she had begged to help install even a basic system for an inventory database. A half-empty mug sat beside the open book, a coffee tin with pens and pencils of various lengths and age at the front. No sign of the store owner.

She leaned over the desk as a rugby-ball-sized mound of calico fur and muscle leaped up from beneath.

Barbara jumped back, hand over her chest, scowling at the purring cat. "Really, Hemi. You're going to give someone a heart attack."

Still, she stroked the particolored fur, as the claws of the cat's five-toed paws flexed and danced on the wooden surface. Only females were true calicos, but with the extra toes, there was no other name for her but Hemingway, and so it stuck.

"Hello, Barbara!" an accented voice called in English.

The stockroom door opened, and an elderly woman tottered in carrying an enormous stack of condensed novels. Barbara hurried around the counter to catch the top three before they slid to the floor. The woman nodded in gratitude, and together they maneuvered the rest of the pile onto the desk.

"Hi Veronika, how are you today?" Barbara obliged her. They would begin in English—an opportunity for Veronika to practice, she claimed— but switch to Czech once her vocabulary ran thinner than her intellect demanded.

"Quite all right, thanks, and you? Tea?"

She glared into her cup as if it could be blamed for the cold, half-empty status of the tea within.

"Tired, but happy to be here," Barbara said. "I'll get it. You're busy. Book day?"

Veronika nodded, resuming her bar stool behind the desk with a little groan.

"Hip?"

The woman rubbed the offending joint. "Aging is inconvenient at best."

Barbara smiled, filling the kettle and flipping on the hot plate. She grabbed a mug, carefully measured out enough of the strong black tea Veronika preferred for two. She returned to the desk to skim the stack of condensed novels. "What a shame. *War and Peace* in two hundred pages."

Veronika patted her desk for her glasses, frowning.

Barbara touched the crown of her own head.

The older woman beamed and drew the frames down from her silver hair, perching them on the bridge of her nose. "Yes, but the students seem to love them. Especially close to finals week."

Veronika owned the building and the shop outright. But even without rent, electricity and heat must be paid and dehumidifiers run to keep the books dry, and shipping charges went up every few months. The balance between inventory worth something and inventory that would sell was often a complex negotiation.

Veronika added books to her ledger, and Barbara grabbed the light pencil used to mark the inside of the less valuable books with pricing. They worked in silence until the kettle whistled and Barbara rose to fix the tea.

She returned with two cups as Veronika finished the pile. "Want me to shelve these?"

Veronika shook her head. Switching to Czech, she said "I'm not wasting the little time I get with you these days on a few cheap paperbacks."

There was pride in the complaint. Barbara's education had begun as Veronika's assistant, first sorting and shelving, then assisting her buying and estate acquisitions. Everything she knew about assessing rare and valuable books began in this small, dusty antikvariát a few tram stops from the most beautiful library in the world.

"Come, come." Veronika hustled her and her tea to the corner tables where she stashed her newly arrived stock.

Barbara paused at a ratty cardboard carton with pastel covers and couples in unmistakable romantic embraces. "Are these..."

"Keep as many as you like." Veronika waved her hand. "I had to take the entire lot. The old biddy had a thing for love stories."

Barbara laughed, but made a mental note to go through the box later for anything she hadn't read. She really didn't need any more books, but...

"The real treasure, though." Veronika rubbed her hands together. "Come see."

Barbara's grace tingled, like her nose on the edge of a sneeze. Something was here. Something important.

Veronika stepped aside.

Valuable and rare materials had always had a curious effect on Barbara. Books, manuscript, letters, even lists sometimes twitched her bones and made the hair on her neck stand up. Years of working beside Veronika had honed it. Now she moved through the box, sorting until she emerged with a pile of seven books and what looked like a sheaf of papers that could have been a manuscript or a pack of letters.

"The rest?" Veronika asked as Barbara took up her teacup and sipped, content.

Barbara frowned, assessing the pile. "There are a couple of interesting eighteenth-century novels, maybe. But this is the good stuff."

Veronika smiled, pleased. "You have a knack."

"I wish you could convince my department head of that. Maybe he'd finally put me on a fellowship."

"You could always transfer," Veronika suggested. "With your marks and your experience, I bet you could get into Oxford or Seine."

"My French is awful," Barbara shook her head and set down her cup, her fingers still twitching. "Also, I can't afford it."

It didn't matter that her father had been a renowned underwater archeologist, or that her mother had graduated with top honors in linguistics. The benefit she derived as the child of alumni at Žižkov had been expended. She worked for Veronika, doing appraisals and deliveries to pay for her next semester's books and fees.

Her fingers stretched and curled as she slid the first box aside. Behind it was a carton nailed shut. She grabbed the nearby hammer saved for that reason and went to work on the nails.

"That's just old junk," Veronika said as Barbara began to pick through it. "Garbage for tourists."

Barbara was three-quarters of the way through the carton and convinced Veronika was right when her fingers scratched a worn wooden surface and went still.

"Hello," Barbara whispered.

She found the edges and lifted the object. It was a box the size of the original printing of *War and Peace* and made of walnut, or oak, some gorgeous hardwood with the patterned grain. But it had been fitted together in such a way that it appeared to have no seams at all. Nor was there so much as a mark to indicate the maker.

Barbara examined the corners with a frown, but Veronika announced with a pleased clap, "A puzzle box."

Barbara handed it over, but Veronika shook her head. Her hands, gnarled with age and inflammation, could barely hold the pencils she preferred for bookkeeping and inventory. While Barbara examined the box, Veronika went through her ledger, cataloging each find.

Barbara could find no entrance in the seamless edges. Gradually, she became aware of how much time had passed. The light from the basement windows had faded, and the shop was illuminated in the artificial glow of the bulbs. It was long past closing and no one had even peered inside since Barbara had come in.

"Veronika," she said, pausing. "How is business?"

"Some days are better than others. Let's pack these things you've found up. I know a dealer in Nusle. He will be able to move them."

"You know, an internet store might help you sell more merchandise," Barbara suggested as she obeyed. "Without the middleman."

"Zeman is a quirky old fool, but he's fair," Veronika said. "He's always given me a good price."

"Because he can make a better one," Barbara muttered.

"Barbora," Veronika stretched out the Czech pronunciation of her name. "That is not our way."

Barbara raised her brows, but picked up the books and found a new, smaller crate. If she were around more, she could help Veronika, even manage the online store and make connections to the collection world outside of Prague. She had the expertise, thanks to Veronika, but the advanced degree would add a title and a touch of respectability. Again she was stuck.

As if reading her mind, Veronika smiled. "When you tire of being a librarian, you come work for me. Then we will start up your internest store."

"Internet."

"And you will run the business, and I will sit behind the counter and read books all day with the cat on my lap and take money from stupid tourists."

It seemed like a pleasant way to spend an afternoon. But her heart was in the university library. They worked their way back to the counter. Veronika shooed her away as Barbara tried to take the used teacups to the back sink.

"Do you want me to take the books to Mr. Zeman?"

Veronika's smile turned apologetic. "Tonight, if you could, and take the puzzle box too. He'll know what to do with it."

Barbara sighed. She'd been looking forward to soup and curling up with a novel, but she shrugged her coat back on. She slung her bag over her shoulder and grabbed the box. "Of course."

"And stop by on your way upstairs," Veronika said, walking her to the door. "I'll have dinner waiting for you."

"You don't have to..." Barbara twisted to tug her coat free from the shelves. "Quit that, you."

Veronika laughed. "They're not going to answer, Barbara, they never do."

At the door, she tugged Barbara's knit hat down over her ears and switched back to English. "I'll ring him so he waits for you. Why don't you take a cab?"

Barbara shook her head, knowing the older woman could barely afford such a luxury for herself. "Tram's faster this time of day."

The spring evening was cool and dark, and she hurried from one puddle of streetlamp light to another on her way to the tram stop.

Havel Zeman's antikvariát shop was in a less picturesque neighborhood, but was three times the size of Veronika's. It was also organized and uncluttered. But Barbara couldn't explain the anxious sensation that rose over her as she stepped inside.

That was why she kept the wooden box in the bottom of her messenger bag as she watched him take a quick inventory of the other items and write out a note in his ledger before stacking an envelope full of paper crowns and handing it over with overly formal gratitude. His sharp blue eyes examined her as she tucked the envelope into her coat pocket. She swore she could feel them on her all the way to the door.

By the time she returned to the building housing Veronika's shop, the itchy uncomfortable feeling had vanished. Veronika was waiting, a fresh pot of goulash and an oversized glass of Moravian red ready. After fighting the customary battle over how much to give Barbara for the after-hours delivery, they sat down to eat.

Upstairs later in her own apartment later, Barbara had showered and gotten ready for bed before she remembered the wooden box in her bag. Guilt filled her. Veronika was so good to her. Other students lived six or seven to a flat, and the most interesting work they could hope for were odd-hours in the burgeoning cinema industry as extras or crew. Barbara had her own flat—albeit a tiny one–and made enough in the shop to pay for her other expenses doing what she enjoyed. She should have listened and given the box to Zeman as she'd been told. She would take it on her way home from work the following day, with an apology.

In the meantime, perhaps she could figure it out. It would be worth much more if she knew what was in it, and how to get to it.

She sat cross-legged on the bed, the box her lap. She shifted it from side to side. The contents slid and bumped against the edges with a hollow thud. Not round then. Or at least flat on one side. She shook it. The sound was low and solid, so probably not glass or metal.

A detailed inspection revealed the seams, but no locking—or unlocking—mechanism. She applied pressure at various points on the edge.

After an hour, yawning, she set it on her nightstand and went to bed.

That night she dreamed the box opened and revealed a pile of newly minted crowns inside and paper notes worth thousands. When she woke, she laughed at her own subconscious as she slid the box back into her bag.

"Full of treasure, then?" she said. "I've read that fairytale, and that always ends badly. I'm sure Havel Zeman will know what to do with you."

No one answered the phone at Zeman's shop and, when she arrived, a note on the door indicated the store was closed for a few weeks. Plan B. She he could ask around the department. Maybe someone knew about puzzle boxes and could help figure out how to open it.

When she went to sleep that night, Barbara again dreamed the box opened, and there was a single sheet of paper inside, yellowed with age and covered in a scrawling script of correspondence.

The words began to change as she read, shifting between languages as her eyes translated. It became a trifold piece of crisp white paper with a familiar faculty symbol at the top.

Congratulations, Miss Svobodová. Your application has been selected for a fellowship position in the conservator program....

◆

I'D BEEN SO LONG *in the darkness I'd almost forgotten myself. How many years has it been—a century? More? When word of the letter found me, and it became clear that I would not escape the fate of so many of my sisters, I set this great act of mine in motion. It was easy enough to spell the box, already commissioned and bound to protect the book, to keep its prize safe through the seas of time with a lure for one of the gift.*

I had not counted on the long night that began with taking so many of us. Kramer's book proved true to its name; a hammer of witches that drove so many of us to the stake, into the ground, little more than grease and ash when it was all done. Our wisdom that could not be stolen was burned, destroyed, lost.

There were precious few who stumbled on the box in the years since. None were strong enough to release me. It seemed the last of us had fallen, and that dawn would never come.

And then I felt her. The pull of her woke me, mewling from my own madness.

A sister of the blood. My blood.

CHAPTER FOUR

"Professor, Professor, I've found a book of great interest!" One of the male students shifted from foot to foot in Tobias's doorway.

Tobias was four weeks into his assignment and, as he set down his ballpoint pen, he decided to be grateful for the break from the tedium of triplicate forms instead of frustrated by the interruption. He eyed the circled date on the calendar beside the clock. This was his first time leading an entire assessment and exhibit preparation. He'd underestimated the timeline. Rookie mistake. He should have added an extra few weeks just for filling out a mountain of triplicate forms—never mind the substandard department resources.

But if he could pull this off, he'd have a strong campaign for a tenure-track position.

Challenge accepted.

He pushed his glasses into place and rose from his desk, trying to remember the student's name. "Show me, Viktor."

The other man paused, frowning. "It's Karel, Karel Broucek. Sir."

Shit. Novak's nephew. Tobias clenched his teeth. "Sorry."

Karel halted in his tracks. He could have only been a year or two Tobias' junior, but Tobias felt decades older. He looked at Tobias for a long moment. Tobias cleared his throat. "Shall we?"

In the climate-controlled examination room, the students clustered around the main table. Their faces were illuminated by the light box, their voices hushed but animated.

He noted the two zombies apart from the cluster. The other students avoided them at all costs, but Tobias had a more sanguine approach. The first was almost a hundred years old, according to the dossier, and had been a librarian for most of that. The second was a linguistics professor. Tobias had no objection to making use of their expertise. His concern was their master and the additional requirements that had come with study of the collection. As the necromancer's proxy, they could remove any item they deemed fit.

The previous week, they had taken a folio of papers preliminarily identified as belonging an alchemist in Rudolph's court. It was returned a few days later. On inspection, Tobias found it unchanged and of little interest, nothing more than a standard diary of a charlatan trying to impress an emperor with a few basic chemistry tricks.

But a second volume, an astrological chart and manual, speculated to be from the Danish astronomer Tycho Brahe, had yet to be returned to inventory. When Tobias had inquired about it, he'd been met with a blank expression. He wondered if he'd ever see it again. He imagined the same for himself, if they caught even a hint of the wolf he concealed.

The older zombie had a distant expression on his face, though his gaze appeared fixed on the book.

"Back to your work," Tobias barked, and the cluster flew apart. The zombies turned away last. "Karel."

Karel had mistaken it first for a common necrology, but a short, handwritten section turned out to be a journal of some kind written in code.

They examined the journal until just before noon. He dismissed the team for lunch. "We'll continue this in the afternoon. Book time in the lab for some definitive dating and handwriting analysis."

When they were gone, Tobias hurried the book back to his office. He dug out the small digital camera from his messenger bag.

Good, the battery was charged. He flipped on the examination light on the edge of his desk. Disregarding the pages recording names and dates of the dead, he photographed page after page of coded journal.

When he checked the clock again, a quarter of the hour remained. He prayed he would have enough time. He did a quick set of photos of the exterior, then slid his camera into his bag and returned the book to its spot on Karel's specimen table.

When the students returned from lunch, he was back at his forms, signing his name with suitable pressure to affect all three layers.

For the second time that day, a student came running. This time it was one of the women—Petra? Monika? Point two on his plan to improve student relations was to figure out a way to remember their names.

"Professor. Please come quick," she urged. "There's been a fight."

When he arrived, Karel was hunched on the floor with his face in his hands, blood leaking between his fingers to the stone below.

His opponent, the older of the two zombies, was shaking his hand. His knuckles were raw and angry. One of the doctoral students from the math department stood between them, arms outstretched.

"Professor!" Karel said, his voice muffled. "They're stealing it!"

Karel's table was empty. The second zombie slid the coded journal unhurriedly into a weatherproof specimen bag, knowing no one would stop him. Karel tried anyway, surging off the floor and lunging for the bag. The bridge of his nose was already turning purple, and the hand-kerchief stuffed below his nostrils was a lurid crimson.

The first zombie knocked Karel aside, slamming him into another table and sending a collection of letters fluttering to the floor. When Karel rose again, the first zombie met him with fists raised. They collided with tables and chairs.

Tobias adjusted his glasses and charged into the fray before blood splattered everywhere. He caught Karel around the waist, barely avoiding an elbow to his face. The wolf strength rose in him, and Tobias swung Karel off his feet as the student renewed his struggle.

"Sit down now," Tobias roared.

This time, two of the other students got a hold of Karel's arms and forced him to stay seated. The zombie backed off; he was only interested in defending possession of the book. Tobias looked down at the splattered blood on his vest and sleeves and swore. The growl rose in the back of his throat before he could tamp it down, and the room went silent.

Campus security skidded through the doors to a stop, taking in the wrecked room with heavy flashlights raised as if ready to wade into a battle.

Tobias held up a hand, wincing at the sight of the brittle old letters scattered on the floor. "It's fine. It's over. Please watch your step. There are items of remarkable valuable underfoot."

They paused, glancing down as if the stone was hot lava.

When Tobias looked back at Karel, the young man—startlingly—was weeping. "Fufshing teeves for that godsdamned necro."

The other students tried to shush him, their gazes darting to the zombies as if they expected them to drop Karel where he sat. As far as they were concerned, the undead were as bad as the Necromancer himself.

"Enough," Tobias snapped. "The rest of you collect the letters before we lose something."

He swung to face the zombies, putting his body between them and Karel.

"You are not assigned to this item."

"The Necromancer has requested access to the volume," the second said, his archaic French accent still disconcerting. "I was on my way to notify you, Professor, when the boy lost his mind."

"We need to submit it to the lab for dating," Tobias said, knowing protest was futile. "Can we delay that request—by even twelve hours?"

The first shook his head. He looked regretful. "We have our directive, sir."

"Professor," the security guard barked. "Any physical conflict must be reported and charges filed…"

Tobias removed his glasses and rubbed the bridge of his nose as the man babbled on about repercussions ranging from academic warnings to expulsion. When he looked up, the entire group of students had gone pale. Karel's tears turned to sobs. He doubted there would be any repercussions for the zombies, even if they had started it.

He considered himself lucky he got them to agree to notify him in advance of taking anything. It was the compromise he'd insisted on when agreeing to the terms. Keeping track of inventory any other way would have been maddening.

Tobias slid his glasses back into place and exhaled.

"It was an accident." He felt his tongue beginning to seize as it always did when he was dishonest. "K-k-karel tripped over the chair and fell. Must have hit his nose on the desk. Louis tried to help him and knocked his hand on the table. Right?"

No one spoke. It was weak as alternate stories went. The students exchanged glances. Finally, the older of the two zombies, nodded. Tobias met Karel's eyes.

Karel grimaced. "Over my own two feet."

The others began to nod, their gazes anywhere but Tobias or the zombies.

"I saw it," the female student who had run to get Tobias stepped forward. She forced a smile and mock-punched Karel in the shoulder. "Clumsy oaf."

Someone faked a laugh that sounded dangerously close to a shriek. The security guard stared at all of them, and Tobias returned it with steel in his gaze.

The guard backed down. "Any more trouble up here, and I call the police."

"We understand," Tobias said, turning his back. When the man's footsteps retreated down the hall, he appraised the damage. "Get this cleaned up. And take him to the infirmary. That nose needs to be looked at."

His gaze swung to the zombies. "I think it's best for everyone if you two called it quits for the day."

When they were gone, he let out a long sigh, glaring at the blood on his vest as though he could prevent the stain with a hard enough look. He looked up to see all eyes in the room on him in mute accusation.

He couldn't blame them. In their shoes, he would have seen their boss capitulating to power, supernatural or not. It didn't help that he was a visiting professor who couldn't be bothered to learn any of their names. At this rate, he'd be lucky if he didn't get thrown out on his ass by the end of the month.

He sighed and began pulling chairs back into place. Karel was escorted to the infirmary. Gradually, the room resumed the air of scholarship as the desks were sorted and the letters recovered.

Tobias assessed everything from the doorway. "I want a full report on the damage to those letters. We'll send Azrael a bill for it, and Karel's nose."

In his office, he removed his vest, grateful he kept an extra dress shirt in the storage closet in case of spills or surprise meetings. His back to the door, he unbuttoned and shrugged off the stained white shirt. The new shirt was blue, which didn't go with his tie at all, but beggars couldn't be choosy. On inspection, there was blood all over the tie, too. Damn. It was the nice silk one his siblings had given him for Christmas when he left for Oxford.

"Oh!" A female voice rose in alarm. "I'm sorry I didn't know you were…busy. I'll come back."

He spun to see Barbara Svobodová, bearing a stack of books. He hurried his arms into the shirt, tugging it closed over his chest, but she didn't seem to be able to meet his eyes.

"What do you want?" It came out terser than he intended, but it did the trick.

Anger tightened her mouth as she strode into the room. She slammed the pile onto his desk. "The books you requested this morning."

"That was fast," he blurted out in honest surprise.

She paused, mouth opening and shutting once. "I—you're my only assignment now. So…"

The moment stretched. He finished buttoning his shirt and tucked it into his waistband. She studied the floor.

"It must be awfully boring," he said. She met his eyes, startled. "Being tied to me."

The most remarkable thing happened. She smiled. The tiniest furrow appeared on her nose, a mischievous crinkle formed by one corner of her mouth rising slightly higher than the other. The unevenness of that smile, and the warmth in it, did him in. Flustered, he occupied himself with the contents of his desk, covered at the moment by his spectacularly bloodied clothes.

"It's not so bad," she said. "You do have very peculiar tastes in literature, sir."

Was she teasing him? The inexplicable lightness in his chest made him shift on his feet.

She ventured closer. "You've had a much more eventful morning, I'd guess. I didn't know special collections was a blood sport."

He had no idea where to put his hands or his gaze. The latter returned to her instinctively.

She wore yellow today, the bodice of her dress belted at the waist before giving way to the generous fabric of the skirt. It was a color he'd thought only suitable for songbirds and babies. Now it was hers. From this moment on, when he saw that color, he would think of how it set off the rich tawny brown of her skin.

The low heels of her vintage leather boots clicked on the floor as she crossed to him. Each step revealed a flash of stockinged knee between the high boot tops and the low edge of the skirt. It should not have been so deliciously tormenting. He swallowed.

It was an incongruous pairing, the delicate folds of canary and the sturdy cognac leather, and more than a little retro. Yet it suited her. She looked like a sunflower, and the matching scrap of ribbon used to tie her hair away from her face an errant petal. He wanted to pluck it, take a big whiff of her up close. Instead, he tried to focus on clearing his desk. "You heard?"

"Everybody who saw Karel Broucek on his way to the infirmary has a different story. Beware, Professor Vogel, you're gaining a reputation as quite the pugilist." She waved a hand, dismissing his protest. "Are you all right?"

He was so taken aback that anyone could think him capable of hitting a student that he almost missed her question. It was a moment before his brain caught up.

"I was the referee."

She winced. "I hope one of them has the decency to pick up your cleaning bill. Those are going to stain."

It was his turn to dismiss the concern. "I'll deal with it tonight."

"Yourself?" Her brow rose.

He shrugged.

With a husband inclined to wear his good clothes for construction, three rambunctious boys, and a daughter who wore pants out by doing the splits all the time, his mother had the herculean effort of keeping them all in clothes that fit and were clean enough. Tobias had learned the finer points of laundry from the hall matron in his dorm. Old habits died hard.

"The shirt will be easy," she said, fingers hovering above the folds of fabric still warm from his body. "But the vest. That's wool?"

He nodded.

"It will be trickier. Try a bit of white vinegar, and if that doesn't work, don't let it dry before you try a bit of hydrogen peroxide. But test the color first, it can bleach if you're not careful."

"Obscure astronomical texts and delicate fabric care. Your expertise astounds."

Barbara's eyes flitted up to his, as surprised as he was. That mischievous smile flared again.

A throat cleared in the doorway.

Barbara spun, hands clenched at her waist as though she'd been caught touching something she shouldn't. Tobias looked up, unable to keep the unhappiness off his face at the loss of her smile. Professor Novak stood in the doorway. "I understand there's been some trouble in the collections room."

"Sir," Tobias said, gesturing him inside. "Miss Svobodová, if you will excuse us."

She bobbed her head, starting for the door. Professor Novak cleared a path for her.

Tobias couldn't help himself. "Miss Svobodová."

She froze in the doorway as though his voice had been a hand on her arm.

"Thank you for retrieving my books so quickly," he said, hesitating. "And the advice. I appreciate it."

She glanced over her shoulder and, for the barest instant, that merry, bright look returned in a dazzling flash. "My pleasure. Hope everything comes out all right."

The soft clip of her heels disappeared down the hall.

Novak frowned. "What was that about?"

"Laundry," Tobias said, still a little dazed.

Novak snorted in disbelief. "Just watch yourself with that one, Vogel. She's been a bit of trouble for the department."

Interest peaked, Tobias cocked his head, unable to see how Barbara Svobodová, research assistant extraordinaire, managed to be trouble to anyone at all. He recalled how she'd stood up to him during lecture. Some men might have been put off by it, he supposed. The dinosaurs.

Interpreting his silence for a lack of understanding, Novak went on. "No one knows quite what to do with her."

"Find her a fellowship," Tobias blurted without thinking. No, he was still thinking of how quickly she thought under criticism in front of a room full of senior students. And her ability to find difficult texts was uncanny. "I can think of a half dozen collections jobs she'd have been a boon on in the research phases. How are her translations?"

"Fine. Superior, actually." The department head stammered.

Tobias was amused to see someone else speechless for once. "I don't see the problem."

"She's a bit of a personality issue," Novak said, recovering.

Tobias' brow rose. "Did she punch another student in the middle of a collections room containing an unappraised fortune in rare materials?"

The man sputtered, his face going ruddy. "She's got a reputation."

Ah, now that was something he knew a bit about. Tobias' thoughts circled back to her ramrod straight back and firm voice. Then his brain caught up with the rest of the department head's words.

"A tease, if you know what I mean."

Stillness settled over Tobias as his attention arrowed in on the man before him. The wolf roused with surprising intensity, and Tobias fought to keep his human senses in control.

Novak realized he'd said something wrong, but not what. The words kept coming. "You see how she flounces around here, in those—"

"Dresses?" Tobias supplied.

He thought back over the three-quarter sleeves and the shallow boat-neck collar that barely revealed her collarbones. The generous fabric of the skirt swirled when she had turned, no more than hinting at the round hips beneath. It seemed appropriate as far as dress codes went. What was she expected to wear to work, a nun's habit?

"...swirling and swishing around here," Novak was still talking. Tobias wondered if he'd ever just get to the fucking point. "You can't blame Tesarik, I mean, really. All year she fetches for him like a prize hound."

The hair prickled on the back of his neck. He'd met Professor Tesarik during his introductions. The senior head of collections barely acknowledged any woman existed above the neckline. He must have been her professor at some point, maybe even a supervisor. The thought made his stomach twist.

"At the Christmas party," Novak went on, "everyone has a bit too much to drink. It's all innocent, you know."

Tobias made an effort to unclench his molars and swallowed hard against the desire to take Novak by the throat and shake him until the full story came out. Whatever had happened, Barbara Svobodová had gotten the worst of it. The injustice robbed him of calm and his fists clenched. The wolf responded to the perception of threat and pricked his spine and consciousness with its presence.

He made himself take a deep breath and unclench his fists. "Did you have something to say about this afternoon?"

Novak took a step back and Tobias considered it might have come out more like a growl than he'd intended. The man shook his head as though he couldn't believe the sound. He swallowed hard enough to make his Adam's apple bob.

"Campus security came to my office," he sputtered. "And there's a student from your team in the infirmary."

Tobias rubbed his forehead. His temples ached from the effort to contain the wolf inside him. How long had it been? Four weeks? He'd turned down invitations to go to the cabin all month.

"A misunderstanding," Tobias muttered. "A simple misunderstanding."

"There will be no…action against Karel?" Novak worried his hands.

"From one of the necromancers' goons?" Tobias shook his head. "I doubt it. They got what they wanted."

The man nodded as if relieved that unpleasant business was over. "Karel's a good boy. A little hotheaded, but he does good work. I'd hate to see his career damaged because of one unfortunate incident."

The irony of his statement didn't miss Tobias. His mouth quirked and judging from the head of the department's expression, he knew it, too. Karel was a decent student, average as those things went. He didn't stand out, and Tobias intended on having a talk with him about his sloppy record-keeping in the inventory.

"As long as the Necromancer has spies in the collection," Tobias said, "there are going to be problems."

Novak straightened, seeing a small mound of high ground he might rise to. "Well, then, Professor Vogel, I expect you will manage that more successfully than you did today."

The wolf lunged into the back of his throat before he could catch the tone of his words. "Sir. Anything else?"

The man took a step backward at the clear dismissal, and his embarrassment turned to fury. Tobias watched it, wondering if he'd made a new enemy. A quick flash to Barbara's luminous smile and the curve of her cheek as she leaned in to assess the damage to his shirt banished his worry.

Tobias returned his attention to his desk. "Good day."

"A tie is a requirement of the faculty code of conduct," came the curt response.

Tobias fought the urge to throw his bloodied tie at his boss. "Understood."

He refused to give Novak the benefit of looking up, keeping his eyes focused on the sheaf of papers on his desk until the man's footsteps disappeared down the hall. When he was gone, Tobias sank into his chair, pen clenched in one hand. It snapped. He flung it across the room where the pieces bounced off the wall and the windowsill and skittered under the bookshelf. He pressed his palm to his desk before he registered a sticky sensation.

His hand, and the desk, were now streaked with ink. "Damn."

He was useless for work. He found a paper bag for his soiled clothes and packed his messenger bag, double-checking the camera tucked into the inside pocket. After locking his door, he made the appropriate excuses to the students in the lab.

His final stop was at the research assistants' office. Barbara was already gone for the day. It was for the best. He was going to come apart at the seams and, after seeing her lightness earlier, he didn't want his inability to handle his mood to bring out her bristling guard, or the cool distant shell. Still, disappointment flared as he stared at the tidy desk and its curious assortment of pineapple figurines.

"She loves them," the pale girl said as she slipped up beside him.

He jumped. "Why?"

She shrugged, spinning to place herself between him and the desk. She rested on the edge, threatening to upset a few of the little figurines when she leaned back. "Just does. It's one of her little quirks."

He excused himself as quickly as possible.

He stopped at the store to pick up the things Barbara had recommended for his shirt. The flat was quiet when he arrived home. He headed to the kitchen sink.

When Beryl came in, a knee-length cardigan over her favorite tank top and leggings, he was dabbing as Barbara had suggested. His vest already looked better.

"What happened?" she said, frowning at the sight of blood.

"Fight. My students." He sighed. The hair dusting his forehead rose and fell, reminding him he was overdue for a haircut. Great. No-tie-wearing, long-haired pugilist professor. So much for improving his reputation.

She watched him, studying his materials. "Looks like you've picked up a few good tricks as a bachelor."

Tobias put down his brush and the vest with a laugh. "Actually, my research assistant gave me a few tips."

She froze with the watchful calculation of a falcon waiting for the dove to alight from its hiding place. "Assistant?"

"Student," he amended. His tongue thickened in his mouth. "S-s-she's a student."

Beryl wandered to the refrigerator. "She?"

Tobias redoubled his efforts on the vest. Her attention settled on him, and it took all his effort not to hunch his shoulders to his earlobes. Her hand settled on his spine.

"I'm grateful someone was able to give you what I could not," she murmured. "Go for a run, Tobias."

Tobias didn't think about the book until he'd returned from his run and finished showering. Then he remembered his digital camera. He downloaded the images, then printed the best quality he could muster from the small unit below his desk. Chewing the meat from a cold duck leg he'd found in the fridge, he sat down with the coded manuscript and started to work out the key. It was almost 2 a.m. before he gave up, submitted a series of requests to research—Barbara, he corrected—and fell into a dreamless sleep.

CHAPTER FIVE

TOBIAS DECIDED that when the Necromancer returned the original journal, he would assign it to one of the students. He only continued to work on breaking the code as a diversion from managing personnel, project scheduling, and the infinite amount of triplicate forms. It was a puzzle to be solved. He was scratching an intellectual itch. That was all. It wasn't becoming an obsession. Or an excuse to have regular contact with his research assistant.

After a week without having it returned, his certainty that the book was something important and possibly dangerous grew. He wondered if the Necromancer had already deciphered the code. Every time someone passed his doorway, it was enough to make him hurry to hide the sheaf of papers under his inventory. Still he couldn't stop his attention from returning to the mystery it posed.

"Professor?"

Tobias settled the inventory over his printouts at the hesitant call.

Karel's face was a mess of bruises and bandages. One eye was swollen to a squint, the other lowered in humility. According to the infirmary report, his nose had been broken in the scuffle.

He'd wondered when Karel would make his way back. "Come in."

The student shuffled to the front of his desk. Tobias gestured at one of the chairs.

"I wanted to apologize for my behavior and my absence," Karel said.

"I'd like to pay for the cleaning of your clothes, or a replacement if you see fit."

Tobias exhaled. "That's not necessary. I'm not delighted with the arrangement with the necromancer either, but you will learn as you continue in this field, that this is often the course of things—it helps to think of necromancers as just another type of private interest. A powerful one, perhaps."

"I'm not going to continue."

Tobias sat back, stunned.

"I've decided to leave the program." Karel shrank in his chair. "I can't live with this course of things, as you call it. The items in that collection should belong to the people. Not that damned sorcerer."

Tobias pressed his glasses up his nose and prayed for patience. Those words were seditious, and Karel flung them without regard. The boy was a danger to himself, and he didn't even know it.

Necromancers made the law, and served as their own judge, jury, and, often, executioner. One step out of bounds, and the punishment could be severe.

The end of his private-sector days had come with close scrape in Indonesia. His company had been accused of violating sacred texts in the process of analysis and sentenced to execution and servitude by the Oceanic necromancer. Only a last-minute stay and appeal from Azrael had saved them. Even then, they'd been forced out of the territory with the clothes on their backs and little else.

"Are you sure that's a wise decision?" he said. "You've spent years—"

"I already spoke to Unc—Professor Novak. He's agreed to find a place for me in archives."

"Coward," Tobias snapped.

Karel sat upright, his face reddening.

"That's right. An entire collection of items no one has handled in centuries, and you want to run because you got your pride bashed in by a zombie with a good right hook?"

Tobias exhaled. Insulting Karel wouldn't earn him goodwill in the department. But perhaps extending an olive branch would—after all, the book had been the younger man's discovery. He grabbed the first entry in the sheaf of papers hidden under the inventory and strode around the desk. Karel recoiled, but Tobias slapped the papers on the desk in front of him. Karel jumped.

His eyes darted from Tobias to the papers. "What is this?"

"Look familiar?"

Karel squinted his good eye. He sat back and his bewildered stare ventured to Tobias's face.

"Stay, and help me," Tobias challenged. "Or go rot in the stacks over at archives. Your choice."

Tobias walked to the window, his back to Karel. He listened to the papers shuffling on his desk and gazed out over the rooftops. The city was greening every day, the wet March becoming a glorious April. The days were warmer and longer. His wolf was a constant presence, longing to run.

"Professor…" Karel's voice was hushed with awe. "How did you?"

Tobias turned, crossing his arms. "Sometimes it's worth skipping lunch at the bar. Well?"

Karel licked his lips. His good eye brightened. "I want in."

Tobias smiled. "The pages stay here in my office all the time. You can work at the table. I'll assign you to requisitions and equipment while you're recovering—it'll provide a good cover for you to be out of the collection room and in my office. You will not breathe a word of this to anyone on the team."

"And if we solve it?"

"You can co-author the paper." It would make the boy's career.

He'd figure out how to do that without attracting Azrael's ire later. What had his father said during their chess games? Sometimes a sacrifice must be made for the larger win.

BY THE END of the week, Tobias loathed his new officemate. Karel hummed tunelessly while he worked, gnawed on pencils, and tapped his foot. His smell, faint enough to most humans but a stench to the wolf nose, reeked of onions and old beer. And they were still no closer to deciphering the journal's code. The original still had not come back from the Necromancer. Barbara had been back and forth all week with everything she could dig up on cryptology.

As she dumped the latest load on Tobias' desk, she sighed. "That's all then."

Tobias didn't look up. "Fine, thank you."

"Want anything else? I'm going to have to order it from London, or maybe Brussels. They've got some resources—"

"That's fine," Tobias repeated.

Barbara exhaled sharply, and the strident rap of her heels on the stone floor broke his concentration. *Shit.* He'd said the wrong thing, again. He scanned the impressive stack, admiring her process by the titles alone. He started to call after her, but the phone on his desk clanged, demanding his attention.

Hours later, he rose, unable to bear Karel's presence a moment longer.

"Let's call it a day," he said in English, switching back to Czech when Karel looked at him in confusion. "We'll try again tomorrow."

Karel packed up eagerly, hurrying to join the group collecting in the hall on their way down to the cafe. Alone, Tobias threw open the window before contemplating the stack of books Barbara had left. He checked his watch. The library assistants would be gone by now.

Tobias sat down, pulling his copies of the journal from his top drawer. He could give it one more hour.

Two hours later, he was no closer when Barbara's voice startled him. "Excuse me, Professor."

He thought it was an auditory illusion conjured by his tired brain until she repeated herself. Barbara stood in the doorway, framed by the dim evening lighting from the long hall. The city was dark outside his window, and he hadn't bothered to turn on the overheads, working in the small pool of light from his desk lamp.

The perfect silhouette of her frame, curves and curly hair, woke something primitive in him. "Miss Svobodová. Come in."

The restless presence of the wolf in his chest subsided as she closed the distance. "You're working late."

The ghost of a smile tugged at his mouth. "I could say the same for you."

Her answering smile was honey pouring from a sun-warmed comb. She stood on the opposite side of the desk, sliding a book between them. "I just wanted to bring this up before I left for the night."

He found his feet and rose. He regretted it immediately when she took a half step back. With their height difference, he must seem to loom over her. "I'm sorry—about earlier today."

"You were focused." Her smile tightened, brittle now, and she seemed to fold inward.

Desperate to restore the warmth, he snagged the book, flipping open the cover. "What is this?"

"I did a little more thinking. Based on your requests, I thought this might help. It's an arithmetic book, which I know sounds off topic, but..."

He thumbed through it. Strategies for solving complex equations detailed to show patterns and highlight similarities. "It's perfect."

She clasped her hands at her waist, but did not retreat.

"You have a remarkable sense for research, Miss Svobodová."

"I took a few classes."

He laughed. The sound startled them both. Her smile eased again, and the hint of it warmed her dark eyes.

"None of it's been much help," she said, surveying the cluttered tables. "You're still here, playing secret code breaker."

"How did you..." He paused at the obviousness of the question. He thought he was so clever, hiding the pages in plain sight. Nothing would give him away like a research trail. By now everyone must know.

"You don't have to worry." Barbara's voice cut through his building concern. "The art department thinks you've found paintings, mathematics is champing at the bit to send someone up to see your ancient Greek mathematical text, and civics wants to know what private letters from Rudolf you've discovered."

She had been covering his tracks all week. Relief bathed him in a sudden cold sweat that sprung up along the back of his neck—the fear of being discovered.

Barbara pinched the edge of one lip between her teeth. "It's the thing that started the fight with Karel and the zo—undead, isn't it? So I thought, perhaps you wanted to keep it quiet. It's not good to be seen to be too close to anything of interest to the Necromancer."

Tobias could have kissed her.

She licked one plump lip and he thought how infrequently a figure of speech collided with the truth. He made himself focus on the book between them to keep from wandering along the path that urge lead.

Her ability to excel at her job did not give him permission to behave wildly inappropriately. Even if it was damned sexy.

Her job. Why hadn't it occurred to him sooner? "How about you take a look at what the fuss is all about. Maybe you'll see something I've missed."

Her eyes widened and, for a moment, he was sure she would run. He thought of Novak's words. He wouldn't do anything that would risk this moment. For once, the wolf quieted obediently. He slipped the stack of now-worn pages to her side of the desk.

Barbara stepped closer. She reached out a hand hesitantly, fingers curling toward her palm as if she was afraid to even touch it.

"Go on," he urged.

Barbara attacked the sheaf with her long, slender fingers and a butterfly touch. She ordered the stack, thumbing through them. Curiosity became fascination. She sank into the chair at her hip. He circled the desk to her side and rested his weight against the edge. She didn't seem to notice. He tried not to smile at her single-minded focus. She might as well have been the only one in the room.

When her gaze arrowed to him, he realized she hadn't forgotten about him at all. "This is a journal. Authentic?"

"Didn't get a chance to date it before the Necromancer's minions made off with it, but yes. I think so."

He watched goosebumps spring up on her arms as she whispered, "If it were worthless, Azrael would have sent the original back already, but it's been—"

"A week," He finished.

"They don't know you have this."

He shook his head once.

"And you can't break it." No accusation, just simple frustration, and surprise. "You… and Karel."

"Karel found it and I thought… if I gave him a chance, he would be less likely to file a complaint." Tobias rubbed a hand through his hair. "I know that people here think I'm difficult…anyway. He's not much help. But he thinks he's on to something."

A ripple of laughter escaped her, and he fought the urge to lean in to soak up all of that glorious sound. "I could tell by his requests."

Tobias tore his eyes away from her face to return to the papers. "Care to have a run at it?"

Her eyes widened in disbelief. He nodded. For a moment, her hands curled around the pages possessively. Then she set them on his desk and rose. Her fingers knotted at her waist again, white knuckled. "I can't. No. Thank you. But..."

She was halfway to the door before he'd recovered his wits.

"Why not?"

Barbara paused, resting her fingers on the doorframe for a long moment. She turned her head, putting her face in partial profile and deep shadow, eyes on the floor. "Good night, Professor. And good luck. I won't say anything. I promise."

CHAPTER SIX

"How is Professor Vogel today?" Veronika settled into the seat across from Barbara at the dining room table, her empty bowl pushed aside to make room for the glass of sherry.

Barbara had tried to be quiet entering the building so late, but the moment she'd released the front door, a beam of yellow light spilled over the polished squares from a door on the first landing.

Veronica's voice had called softly, "I made you a plate. Take it up with you, or keep me company if you wish."

Twenty minutes later, Barbara paused between bites of red cabbage and tasty bits of stewed boar, as her thoughts went to Tobias Vogel's stubbled cheeks and the glasses perched on the edge of his nose. She snagged a piece of bread from the bowl Veronika pushed her way, buying time to form a neutral answer. It was useless—heat crept into her cheeks.

Veronika smirked. "Has he taken off his shirt again?"

Barbara's mortification was complete. "He's an academic, for gods' sakes. He has no right to be so damned beautiful."

Veronika raised her brows, lifting her wine to her lips.

"He is my boss." Barbara protested.

Veronika shrugged. "Temporarily."

She laughed, in spite of herself. Veronika winked. That only made her laugh harder. It felt good, after the decision she'd made an hour earlier in his office. "He offered me a chance to do something incredible today, something secret..." At the older woman's prurient expression, she clarified. "Not like that, either. Really. Something to do with the collection. I can't talk about it. But—"

"You said no."

Barbara threw up her hands. "We were alone in his office, at night. And what would it have looked like to anyone—gods forbid—the head of the department come by. He dropped in while I was there a few weeks ago delivering books—in the middle of the day—and I could just see what he was thinking...I might as well have a scarlet A on my chest. And *he* assigned me to Vogel in the first place."

"You're going to cut yourself off from an opportunity because of what people may think of you?" Veronika frowned.

"Those people can make or break my career, and they won't even give me a chance," Barbara said.

"And his big secret project requires you work closely with him. Which will draw attention because two beautiful people fighting the magnetism of attraction always does."

Barbara shook her head with a wry smile. "No more soap operas for you."

She sat back with an appreciative glance at her empty plate. She hadn't stopped for lunch today. A solid meal returned her strength and her will. "He is gorgeous. He does this thing with his glasses." She pantomimed tipping them down to peer over the top.

Veronika fanned her cheeks. "A smart, attractive young man. What I wouldn't give! For me, Bara, enjoy every minute."

Barbara laughed. Before the older woman could protest, she leaped up and gave her a hug. Veronika stiffened, but patted Barbara's shoulder blades and gave her a pleased smile when they parted.

"If Vogel stays and I'm in his favor, maybe he helps me get a fellowship or writes a letter on my behalf," Barbara said. "That's enough."

After they'd done the dishes, Veronika walked her to the front door. "Don't be afraid to want, Bara. Desire is the most powerful force in the universe."

Climbing the stairs to her own apartment, Barbara admitted it wasn't just how it would look that kept her from working on the manuscript. In truth, she had known what it said almost instantly. She didn't need to translate. Words had always revealed themselves, in whatever language they originated, to her eyes. It was part of her touch of grace, and she couldn't help but use it; rule number one.

Which brought her to rule number two and why she could not work on it with Professor Vogel. Once she understood the translation, she understood the entire language: its grammar and use and colloquialisms. She was bursting with Greek turns of phrase and Latin puns she'd never be able to use because she could offer no rational explanation for how she knew them.

Eventually he would catch her doing something inhuman, and then he'd have to report her to the Necromancer.

Inside, she flipped on the light switch, illuminating the tiny entryway in rosy light. Dumping her jacket, bag, and shoes by the front door, she climbed the three steps into the narrow attic apartment. She'd chosen to focus on finding rare and valuable books, it was just safer. Because translating too well wasn't the only thing that would earn her an extended stay in a necromancer's gulag—or worse. There was also the matter of her memory.

After slipping into a comfortable pair of pajamas and pouring a glass of wine, Barbara grabbed her notebook and a pen. She took a deep breath, then used her grace to reproduce the first two pages of nonsense text she'd seen in Vogel's office from memory. When it was complete, she set down her pen and shook out her cramping fingers, double checking the accuracy. Relaxing her gaze, the text resolved into recognizable words, and she produced the translation.

She refilled her glass, cracked her knuckles, and assessed the pages before her. Pen and paper ciphers like this had long ago been replaced by computers and more complex algorithms to secure information. Most classical ciphers were easy enough to crack for even a dedicated hobbyist, but a few persisted in puzzling modern scholars. Without a decryption key, breaking a cipher could be like trying to put together 1000-piece jigsaw puzzle without knowing the final picture. The jury was still out on whether the Voynich Manuscript was truly code or just gibberish, because no one knew what the intended use of the book was.

With the original and deciphered text side by side, the patterns resolved—little beacons that flared on the pages and darkened as she scribbled them in her notebook. She crowed in delight when a linear sequence became clear. She'd always breezed through her math classes —what was math but another language?

Still, the work took time. She didn't finish until nearly three in the morning. Her pencil had been worn to a nub, but a complete key that could be used to decrypt the code was spread out before her. She double-checked her numbers and stretched her neck.

Now it was just a matter of figuring out a way to slip a large enough clue to Karel or Vogel to put them on the right track. As much as she disliked Karel, she sympathized with Vogel's desire to get on good footing in the department. And if she could help Vogel, perhaps he would be more inclined to return the favor.

The end result was all that mattered. The victory of the translation, and the gift of the text to the collection and the library and the nation. And perhaps a fellowship for her. She wasn't doing this for recognition. So why did it feel like she'd lost something.

That feeling now had a name. Veronika had said it in her apartment. Desire.

A name gave it power. She pushed aside her notes and stacked her head on her hands. Why had her first thought been to give it away? If she took Vogel up on his offer, she could claim the discovery herself. It was hers, after all, even if her methods were unorthodox. But how would she be able to explain how she solved so quickly what had stymied him for weeks? Guilt swamped her.

Don't be afraid to want.

She closed her notebook and drained her glass. As she finished rinsing and drying it, her eyes fell on the wooden puzzle box stashed on top of her narrow refrigerator. She dragged a chair over and slid the box down.

Sitting at the table, she set it before her. She rocked it back and forth, listening to the slide of the object within. It had to be a book. That piqued her curiosity more.

If only wanting it was power all its own.

Her fingers traced the edges of the box, the smooth seamless corners providing no catch for her fingertips.

Feeling silly, she thought, *Open sesame.*

She laughed at her own foolishness. But the sound caught her up short. Wasn't it bad enough that others laughed at her? Silly Barbara Svobodová, the one who overreacted to a harmless advance from a member of the senior faculty, who should have been forgiven that extra beer or two on a holiday night.

Now she was even the butt of her own joke.

She glared at the box as though it was the source of the mockery. There had to be a catch of some kind, a pressure point that would release a mechanism within. She rapped on the top. "Knock, knock, anybody home?"

She thought of Professor Novak's watery stare and every letter that had come with the same pitiful message no matter how many fellow-ships she applied for. Dreams were the language of the subconscious. The box was a perfect stand-in for her career so it was only natural her brain would substitute it. Hadn't the letter inside been obvious? She stared at the box until tears made her vision blurry. "Come on, you bastard."

Nothing.

The image of Tobias Vogel's shirtless back flashed in her memory like a beacon. The dusting of freckles across broad shoulders and the faint trace of curling hair from the small of his back disappearing into his pants. The scent of him—soap, and exertion as he examined his bloodied clothes. Most of all, his plain, unadorned gratitude, and the way he met her eyes when he delivered it. He handled interruption poorly when he was focused, and his social skills were unvarnished. But he was honest and dedicated and intelligent and she wanted to like him.

She *wanted*. Gods, how she wanted. Sometimes it felt like too much, but when she considered it, was it anything at all? Just a fair chance. And a friend. And to open this damned box.

She smoothed her hands over the wood. The words came from her own mouth as they'd been whispered in her ear. "Reveal yourself."

The box slid apart from unseen joints. Once they were open, she didn't understand how she hadn't seen them before. Of course, a hinged lid. She slipped her thumbs under the opening. The hinges complied as though they had been cleaned and oiled recently. Inside was a book. It was plainer than she's expected, the simple leather binding cracked with age. She slid it onto a cotton towel and let her fingers roam the edges.

Inside, the faded, water-stained pages made her wince before her eyes widened at the delicate handwriting. She searched the end pages and the frontispiece for a name, a date, but found none. Illustrations, once sharp, marked the edges—plants and flowers dulled into almost watercolor-like softness.

She relaxed her eyes and at once the script became a smoky, writhing mass before resettling into recognizable text. Each page was a recipe—more of an herbalist's guide than a cookbook. But interspersed between cures for boils and sour bile were more curious entries: *Reflect Harm* and *Antidote for Loveless Union.*

Henbane, belladonna, mandrake, and datura were recognized hallucinogens. And then there were words she couldn't make sense of, even translated. A *full moon under a laurel and the ichor of stone?*

Where instructions existed, they were so vague as to be indecipherable. The handwriting began to grow erratic and rigid. Beside a few were notes: *Only under the new moon. Falcon feathers not so good as hawk. Must be tailored to individual circumstances. Subject Died.*

Barbara sat back. These weren't recipes. They were spells.

A witch's book of shadows was a rare find. There were only three in public holdings—though rumors claimed there had been many more before the Godswar. No doubt the necromancers controlled any that remained.

The ones on public viewing were more almanacs and astrological or herbal treatises. Or spells so outlandish they were impossible. One toured regularly on exhibit. The second was in London, though it was Persian by origin. A third belonged to the University of Beijing.

The handwriting in hers was less showy than the one she'd seen when the touring exhibit stopped at the university in Silesian. Written in an earnest, if somewhat flourished, hand inclined to overconfidence and egomania, but detail-oriented and specific.

Barbara scoured the pages until her eyes ached. She examined the box again, this time focusing on the inside. There were no metal parts visible, nothing to give away the age or origin. She didn't know enough about carpentry to even guess at a date, but based on the way her fingers were tingling, the box—or more likely, the book—was important in some way.

If she took it to the library, she was certain it would disappear, just like Vogel's mystery journal. She hated the thought of it vanishing into a necromancer's possession, never to be seen again.

Who knew what the Necromancer Azrael did with the materials he confiscated? For all she knew, he would destroy it. A chill ran through her at the image of flames licking the fragile pages and aged binding. It would go up in minutes.

The thought made her physically ill. So much human history had been lost during the Godswar—museums destroyed, libraries burned, priceless artifacts shattered into so much dust. She'd spent her life learning to preserve the old and repair the broken, made even more valuable by their rarity. A book like this should be treasured, studied.

She went through the pages again. She made sketches of the symbols and where the handwriting changed. One spell caught her eye.

For the Granting of the Innermost Desires.

Barbara laughed—her desires were so exposed she would trip on them if she wasn't careful. She scanned the list of ingredients. All common enough—no powdered horn of a bred she-goat or eye of mandrake. A magical spell wasn't what she needed.

Barbara closed the book. The necromancers' interest in items of esoteric regard also made them highly valuable to wealthy humans who craved the danger of the illicit. If she was careful, she could name her price—and thanks to her work for Veronika, she had the connections to such buyers. That kind of money would provide her a ticket to Paris or Oxford more directly than an egg and a bit of hair.

And it would guarantee the book would be preserved.

She would do her best to authenticate it, and then sell it.

As for the journal, Karel Broucek could have it. She only wanted to build goodwill with Professor Vogel, so she'd give them the cipher's key. What they did with it was up to him.

WHAT DOES SHE WANT, my little witch? Not so easily lured with wealth or fame, this one. The times have changed. How badly I've overestimated. How crudely I've cast my net. I can feel her now, restless and so afraid. Beneath that is a power undrawn.

In my day, a witch of such sway would have been taken under the wing of an elder and tutored. Have we fallen so far? Are there so few of us remaining?

I have seen the halls of their books and learning built on the plowed-under ash of our blood and bones. These scraps they call knowledge, held so high.

It is my duty then to take her as my own. To teach her in our way and my will.

CHAPTER SEVEN

BARBARA WOKE, startled by the strong daylight streaming in the window. She shot out of bed, confusion and adrenaline racing through her. Her alarm was turned over, and the cord had been pulled from the wall. Had she done it while she was sleeping? She checked her watch. Shit.

She flung herself through her morning routine, braiding her hair and choosing the soft emerald wool sheath dress and thick patterned tights with a pair of ankle boots. She shrugged on her jacket and her book bag, sawing off a hunk of bread from the loaf by the fridge and slathering it with butter. No time for tea.

The book of shadows lay on the table where she'd abandoned it the night before, wrapped in an old towel. She could recall every page from memory. Having it somewhere protected would be best. It would keep for the day, but she'd have to talk to Veronika about storing it in the shop safe.

On her way out of the building, goose bumps sprang up on her arms. She looked up at her own apartment beneath the slanted roof. For a moment, she thought she saw a face staring down from one of the tiny windows. She dismissed it as a by-product of her own confusion. She was late.

Usually, she took the No. 22 tram to work. It took a bit longer, the rail-bound streetcar winding from the Vinohrady neighborhood to the Vltava River. She would get off by the gilded National Theatre and enjoy a walk through the narrow streets to the University library.

The underground metro was faster, the Namesti Miru station close to her building was connected to Staromeska just beside the library. It would be packed with commuters this time of day. It was also the deepest metro station in Prague. The absence of daylight and cold underground air gave her vertigo.

But she was late.

At the top of the long escalator, she took a deep breath, clutched the rubberized handrail, and stepped onto the moving plates. She tried to ignore the light sweat forming on her forehead and neck, in spite of the increasing chill as she descended. The rhythmic thumping of the metal tracks chanted her fate—*under, under, under*. She told herself she was not afraid to be underground. She just preferred being above.

On the platform, she stared out over the rails into the silent darkness of the tunnel as though she could will the train to hurry. The gust of cold air signaled its arrival. When the doors opened, she flung herself into the humid, packed car and managed to find a seat, as the train lurched into motion. The train picked up speed, swaying and rocking as it went. Her stomach pitched in a queasy weightlessness that eased when she sealed her eyes shut.

"First time?" A young man asked in accented English.

Barbara's eyes flashed open long enough to take in her neighbor, a handsome young Czech in a suit watching her with obvious concern.

"Ne." She tried to smile as she answered in Czech. "But being hurtled through the earth in a tin can isn't my idea of a good time."

He paused for a moment too long, his expression puzzled. "You're from…where? Sur America? Spain?"

"Ne."

When she opened an eye again, he was giving her a thorough appraisal. "Would you like to go out sometime? For a drink?"

Barbara stared at him in disbelief.

He shrugged. "You look foreign, but your Czech is good."

Barbara squinted her eyes shut, her jaw clinching against the bile rising in the back of her throat. "Ne."

After the next stop, he was gone. By the time she arrived at the library, she was covered in clammy sweat.

Honza took one look at her and herded her toward her desk. "Novak has called down already twice for you."

She stared after him as he hurried away.

"Took the metro?" Edita patted her shoulder sympathetically.

Barbara nodded and switched on her computer. The first, and only other time she had done it, she'd spent a half hour locked in the water closet, retching.

Honza returned with a cup of water. "Drink. You look ghastly."

"Děkuji," she said wryly but obeyed.

He watched her swallow once, hands on hips. "Now get yourself together and head up there."

Barbara paused with the cup at her lips. "That bad?"

"Not supposed to talk about it," he muttered as he helped her out of her coat. "Trouble with Vogel, of course."

She finished the water, smoothed her hair, and gave Edita a questioning look.

"You'll do," Edita said. "Good luck."

Professor Novak didn't invite her to sit in either of the chairs before his expansive desk as his secretary shut the door behind her. She didn't ask. Instead, she stood as still as possible under his scrutiny.

"I hope you don't take your reduced workload as an excuse to let your professional standards grow lax," he said. "As you are aware, this appointment will put you under consideration for future opportunities."

His lack of subtlety continued. The questions focused on Vogel— searching for a hint of a breach of protocol, or failure to comply with regulations, reaching for any lapse of conduct or professionalism. There was no mention of the fight in the collections room, probably because his nephew was involved. He inadvertently revealed that the complaints filed against Vogel had come to nothing, a fact that seemed to disappoint him.

A fierce protectiveness rose in her. If Novak wanted to undermine Vogel, he wouldn't use her words to do it.

She said as little as possible until he released her.

When she returned to her office, the others had left for lunch. She slipped the rewritten cipher key from her bag and tucked it in a book of mathematical symbolism in early Renaissance art.

Upstairs, the specimen room and lab were empty. She exhaled relief as she quickened her step. But when she rounded the corner to Vogel's office, she froze as the man himself looked up from his desk.

Was it her being generous that made it seem like a wash of pleasure crossed his face when he recognized her? The way the corners of his eyes softened behind his glasses and his eyebrows relaxed confirmed her suspicion. And there was no mistaking the smile on his face. He slid a book over the papers before him, an afterthought.

"Miss Svobodová." His smile grew.

To her alarm, the most perfect dimple appeared in his chin. She forced her grip on the book to relax. She'd planned on slipping it into the stack she'd brought up the previous day. It would be too obvious to leave it now. She fought the urge to slide it behind her back.

"What can I do for you?" he asked.

The thrum of summer bees in lavender rose beneath her sternum in response to his voice, a warm tickle of sensation. *For her? More like what she wanted to do to him. For him. With him.*

She blurted out, "You're not at lunch."

He shrugged, leaning away from the table and stretching his neck. The corded muscles stood out in the space between his neck and his collar. Was it her imagination or did he seem tired? He looked like he could use a meal and a good night's sleep. Still, his fingers drummed the table with restless energy.

She made herself focus on his voice.

"...and I can get some work done...alone." He paused. "Is that for me?"

She should lie—well, make up a different lie than she'd prepared. She could say it was for someone else, a favor for one of the other assistants since she had extra time. But facing that smile, her thoughts buzzed in the circular careening motion of bee's dance and a foolish smile formed on her lips.

"Just something." She fumbled. "It's probably...it's—how do they say —a long shot?"

He rose with loose-jointed grace. The movement, like all of his movements, had that same flexible ease, like something wild and comfortable in its own skin. No matter that he couldn't always seem to find the right word to say or when it came out it sounded sharper than necessary. When he moved, he was himself.

Up close, she was pleased to see his vest, the one that had sustained the damage from the fight, unmarked. She was used to being shorter than most people, but had he always been so tall?

Reflexively, she pressed her fingers to the curl of hair that always sprang free at her temple. Her gaze flittered north of his lapels to glimpse the pulse beating above his collar, and past the shadow of his smooth jawline, all the way up to his still-smiling face.

His chin tipped down, closing the distance between them in some immeasurable way. If she were to stretch up on her toes and reach up, she could push the glasses up the bridge of his nose with her fingertips.

"You have the most curious mind." The cool grey of his eyes softened. "A good thing for a researcher. Is that what you're studying?"

She shook her head and caught a whiff of clean spicy aftershave that tickled her nose. "Conservation. I'm interested in preservation for use and display, mostly."

"That's a shame." Color darkened his cheeks below the edge of his lenses when she frowned. "I mean, I'm sure you'll be wonderful at it, as you are this. But a mind as quick as yours could be running collections and appraisals, if not in a library, for a museum or an auction house."

There was no artifice in his praise, no search for reciprocation. His attention, fixed in those bright grey eyes, had already moved to the book. He extended a hand between them in invitation.

She bit her lip, trying to focus as she examined his palm. Like the rest of him, his fingers seemed quite a bit harder than his work required. After weeks of making out his handwriting on requisitions forms, she recognized a similar easy strength. So much confidence in the bold strokes and regular letters without the usual signs of ego. The unusual slight leftward slant—introversion or privacy—intrigued her.

When she looked up again, he studied her with the unadorned curiosity and instinctive intelligence of a child. He looked so young. He could have only been a few years her senior, but he'd gotten where she longed to be so swiftly and—from where she stood—so easily. She wanted to hold it against him, but she couldn't. Not when he was looking at her like this, as though she was the most interesting thing in the room. A puzzle to be solved.

Caught out, their gazes skated back to the book. Neither drew away.

In her world full of hidden pitfalls and traps, he was exactly what he seemed: safe.

The word burst, pulsing and warm, through her chest. She could not give him her help, but with this, he would solve the cipher easily. She handed over the book. His fingers closed as she let go and the moment of skin-to-skin contact made that warmth spread. His pupils were so round they almost swallowed his irises.

His Adam's apple bobbed. "Thank you."

The sound of footsteps and voices down the hall shook her out of her reverie. She stepped back, smoothing her hands over her skirt. "If you need anything else, I'll be at my desk for the rest of the day."

His smile faltered. In a flash, it was gone. He bumped his glasses onto his nose, then glanced at the book as he turned toward his desk.

"Professor?"

His gaze shot back to her. She faltered under the intensity of his expression, trying to choose the right words. She found that she wanted him to know he had an ally.

"Be careful. This department can be… difficult."

He nodded once, setting the book down on the pile she had brought up earlier, his attention already back on his desk. "Thank you, Miss Svobodová."

The moment she walked away and the blood returned to her brain, every second thought she'd stifled to that point came clamoring back with a shock of apprehension. He would know. He would ask her to replicate, to explain, and she couldn't because it would mean revealing how she'd discovered it. She'd broken the second rule—to never reveal her touch of grace.

"I didn't think it was possible for you to look worse than you did when you came in," Edita said when she sank into her chair.

She'd changed the handwriting and stolen paper from the math department, but the fear that it wouldn't look random enough nagged at her. Even if he figured it out she was responsible, Vogel or Karel would take the credit, and that would be it. Leaving the note had been a mistake.

Maybe he wouldn't find them before she could come to grab the book from his desk after he left for the day.

Barbara laughed, setting her elbows on her desk. "I think I'm going to need a new job soon."

"The conversation with Novak didn't go so well?"

Barbara peered between the gap in her index and middle finger. "Does it ever?"

The whole office had a slow afternoon. The only thing to do was count the minutes until the end of the day, when she could go retrieve the book. She volunteered to lock up and then headed upstairs to special collections. It was empty. Still, her heartbeat triple time as she tiptoed to Vogel's office.

He was gone, the lights off. The door was locked, but she put a hand on the knob and encouraged it to release as she had in conservation. She slipped inside and hurried to the examination table and flipped on a light. The book wasn't in the pile. She checked his desk. It was gone, sealing her fate.

◆

AT HOME, Barbara closed the door between herself and the world with a groan. Every time her mind wandered back to the book with the hastily shoved note in the back, her stomach clenched. Running the conversation in his office through her mind didn't help, either.

Her stomach swan dived toward her toes at the thought of his smile and the glasses slipping down his nose.

Did he kiss with his glasses on?

He was her boss for the duration of the project, and a faculty member, even if he was only a visiting professor. It didn't matter that he wasn't supervising her studies. She glared up at the wood-beamed ceilings. "Why, for once, can't things just go my way?"

No answer from wood, plaster, or anything beyond. The book sitting on her kitchen table caught her eye. She drifted to the kitchen counter, just out of reach, and poured a glass of wine. The world was full of things too strange to be understood. Humans harnessing the power of gods through dance and starting a war, for one. If there were necromancers in the world, then there were—or had been—other kinds of magic in the world.

Barbara finished the last gulp of wine, then poured herself a fresh glass. On an empty stomach, the effect left her facing a belligerent inner monologue. Even with her mother's touch of grace, she'd been run into a dead end by politics and academia. Why shouldn't she use every opportunity she had?

Maybe this book was a gift from the universe, to make up for the impossible position she'd been put in at every turn. She wasn't asking to be rich, or popular, or powerful. She just wanted a single door to open, where all the others slammed shut in her face.

Her innermost desire....

The second glass went down in a bitter swallow. She snatched up the book and marched to the table. It fell open to the spell for Innermost Desires. She glared at the page, waiting for the words to reform again. Nothing had changed. The ingredients list, if it could be called that, was basic. How could a short list of mundane items do anything to solve the predicament she was in?

Then again, if it was so simple, what could it hurt to try?

"I need salt." She pushed away from the table.

Salt, an egg, a hair. Items of potential. Flame, water, earth, and breath. Classical elements. Open a window.

Feeling foolish, she drew a circle in salt, unsure of where she remembered hearing that was important. She lit the candle, then fished a bit of soil out of one of the potted plants dotting the windowsill.

The incantation came awkwardly at first. She adjusted her pronunciations as she went, becoming steadier with every round, keeping her wish in mind. An opportunity. An easier path. Acceptance.

She repeated it until her eyes watered and her tongue tripped over the words. The candle flickered out in the puddle of wax. The wind from the open window stirred the salt and scattered the soil. The warm spring air smelled like rain. There wasn't even the usual tingle in her breastbone when she was onto the trail of a missing book.

Barbara sighed and rose, putting the egg back in the refrigerator and the hair in the trash. Nothing had changed.

Feeling like a fool, she closed the window and went to bed. She would start looking for buyers in the morning.

She woke in the middle of the night with a weight in the center of her chest, pinning her to her bed. Her breath came short and fast. She could not turn her head, but if she strained her eyes, she could see movement in the kitchen. A figure hunched over the book on the table, bathed in a dull glow of orange light.

Cold crept through her. Her fingers and toes twitched at the ends of her dead limbs. She tried to speak, but nothing came out. Then she was aware that the figure knew she was awake, and she did not want to see its face.

When she opened her eyes again, a woman's face, with deep-set hazel eyes and a large roman nose over her downturned mouth, was poised inches before her own. Cold terror filled Barbara. She tried to struggle, to cry out. The woman smiled and her crooked yellow teeth took on a glowing cast in the dim light. When woman drew closer, Barbara thought she would kiss her, but the stained mouth went to Barbara's ear and began to whisper.

CHAPTER EIGHT

IN THE MORNING, Barbara woke with the worst hangover of her life. As she staggered into the kitchen for a glass of water, the half-full bottle of wine seemed to taunt her. She hadn't had that much to drink, but she'd also barely eaten the day before.

Scraps of dreams slipped away as the embarrassment over the previous night's antics caught up with her. The book and the box lay where she'd abandoned them before bed. Had she really tried to cast an old witch's spell to get a fellowship? Why not ask for a million dollars and a fancy car—or a transfer to a more prestigious university and the funds to go with it?

The book was an item of incalculable value. That was the important thing.

She slapped it shut and went to grab a quick shower.

The clock above the stove chimed the hour. It was Saturday, and she'd promised to spend a few hours in the shop with Veronika. Maybe she could leave the book in the safe until she figured out what to do with it. Her stomach turned at the thought of breakfast. She'd have tea with Veronika in the shop. She tucked the opened box under one arm and wrapped the book in a clean pillowcase, locking her apartment and heading down the five floors to the basement store.

Veronika was just opening up the metal shutters when Barbara trotted downstairs. "I have to show you something."

Eagerness made her hands tremble as she fumbled to produce the box. Veronika clapped at the sight of the opened puzzle box, delighted. But her expression grew wary when Barbara set the book on the counter beside it.

"This is…important, Veronika. Where did you get it?"

Veronika eyed it as though Barbara had released a large spider on her desk. "Just part of an estate sale."

"Do you have their contact information?" Barbara asked gently. "If there's any more background I could get from them about the book, it would be helpful."

Veronika seemed unable to take her eyes off the book.

"I was wondering if I could keep it in the store safe until I figure out how to sell it. Please, it's just for a couple of days…what's wrong?"

Veronika shook her head. "I have a bad feeling about it, Bara. Things like that—maybe it was in that box for a reason."

Barbara's brows knotted. "It's just a book—"

"A book that you found," Veronika said, lowering her voice. "You and your…knack."

Ice raced through Barbara's veins. They'd never spoken about the source of her skill aloud before. She'd assumed she'd been good enough at hiding it, treating it like an accident, or a run of good luck.

Small talents like this had run in her family for generations. The shadow of her mother's warning clung to her. *There are two rules. Find a way to use your grace every chance you can, but never speak of it or show anyone its use.*

"Bara." Veronika's voice dragged her away from the well of grief she dared not peer into for too long. Barbara met her eyes. The older woman smiled faintly. "You do have the most amazing luck with these things. Go ahead. Put it in the safe."

♦

VERONIKA WATCHED Barbara disappear into the storeroom, the book in one hand, the box in the other. A late night had left dark smudges under the younger woman's eyes.

She sipped her tea as Hemingway appeared on the counter with her tail up and her fur bristling. She rubbed the cat's ear. "A good eye we'll keep on our little Bara, old girl, shall we?"

The cat rolled onto her side, and her grey-green gaze remained locked on the open storeroom door.

Barbara emerged as a pair of university undergraduates giggled their way down the front stairs. Veronika turned her face to her crossword puzzle. Barbara took the cue and went to greet them.

The world was a dangerous place, and all things magic were controlled by necromancers. She could allow no harm to come to Barbara, and so she could not risk sharing her secret. Or her concerns about the book that made Barbara flushed and glassy-eyed.

Veronika shook her head. Barbara didn't know what was good for her. While she was busy, Veronika slipped into the storeroom and opened the safe. Wincing and cursing a bit at the strain on her arthritic fingers, she changed the code and closed it, sealing the book inside. She was back at the counter when Barbara returned, annoyed.

When the customers had gone with a selection of condensed novels, Veronika wagged her pen without looking up. "You see. They sell."

"A travesty."

"Indeed."

CHAPTER NINE

Tobias's eyes throbbed as the last of the sun faded through the window. The small art book he'd borrowed—stolen—from the library and the little note scribbled inside sat open before him. Random bits of an equation, probably left over from a student's assignment tucked and forgotten between the pages. But it seemed familiar. Whatever was tugging at him remained just out of reach. The wolf snarled with the weary frustration of a long-caged animal.

The repeated knock on his door brought him back to the surface. "Come in."

"Hallo mein Kind." Lukas Vogel nudged the door open with one shoulder, a tray in his hands. "Deine Mutter hat das für dich aus der Küche geschickt."

As children, Mark and Tobias had been embarrassed by their angular, awkward father and frustrated by his insistence on speaking German to them and responding only when they answered in kind. Tobias took it for granted now, but there was no denying being multilingual had its advantages. It opened doors in his education, suited his profession, and made the acquisition of later languages a more natural process.

Saliva pooled in his mouth as the scent wafted toward him. He cleared a spot on the desk, sliding the papers under the book, away from his father's curious eyes. "Danke schön, Vater."

His father sat down on the bed, unbothered by his son's secretiveness.

Tobias should have felt silly being a grown man whose father brought him dinner, but there was something so ordinary and unremarkable about it. Beryl had given them life and kept them clothed and their grades high, but Lukas had always been their emotional center. He remained the most sensitive to all of his children's hearts.

When he gestured to the tray, Tobias knew he wasn't going to leave until the plate had been touched, so he ate. Spicy gingered greens and savory mushrooms in a thick sauce, mingling with pork stewed to dissolving softness.

"I would have brought beer, but I know you don't like to drink while you work," Lukas said in German as Tobias sopped up the last of the sauce in dark bread and shoved it into his mouth.

Tobias nodded with his full mouth. "This is wonderful."

His father rose, taking the tray with the spotless plate and leaving the glass of water. "If there's anything I can help you with, you know where to find me."

Tobias went back to work with a sigh.

After a moment, he sat back in his chair. He debated his options. Taking a book from the library had been going too far, but he hadn't had time to look at it all day and the memory of bright urgency in Barbara's face kept drawing his eyes to it again and again.

He studied the note and the book. Then he stacked them with the first few pages of his coded journal and headed down the hall. Tobias couldn't go to the math or computer science department, but maybe he didn't need to.

Lukas Vogel liked to keep his hands busy and his sons out of trouble by making repairs to the building, but he'd made a living as a software engineer. He'd even published a series of well-received articles on security and cryptography in a small journal and been invited to speak at conferences.

The door to his father's office was ajar, but Tobias knocked anyway.

"Komm herein."

Tobias eased the door open at the invitation, smiling at the telltale squeak their father had never fixed to avoid being surprised by his practical joking sons. Words always flowed easier in German. "Maybe there is something you can help me with, Papa."

His father looked up from the paper, sliding his reading glasses onto the top of his head with a delighted smile. "Ah, so it's Papa now."

Tobias winced. "What can you tell me about sequences in cryptology?"

He'd never seen his father so excited. "Seat yourself, boy. Where do you want me to begin?"

"How any way to tell if this 400-year-old document is written in some sort of code," Tobias said. "Or just a lot of gibberish that I'm wasting time I don't have on?"

Lukas Vogel clapped his hands together, rubbing his palms briskly. "I haven't had a good code to crack in a while. My group quit meeting after the necromancer's cronies raided Terrence's shop. Let's see your text."

"You were in a codebreaking group?"

"Advanced Cryptographers Social." Lukas nodded as he plucked the photocopies from Tobias' hands. "Got a hold of some old occult document we weren't supposed to. Old bone shaker sent this beautiful amazon of a woman to confiscate our entire collection."

"Jesus, Papa," Tobias gasped. "You could have been—"

"Disappeared?" His father grinned mischievously. "Rendered mute, or a walking undead? Ah, boy, are you even living if you don't tempt the powers that be?" He cackled. "Don't look like that. It's all very tame. She presented each of us with a large sum and advised us to find a new hobby. Used mine to finish the building."

Tobias shook his head, amazed. "What did mom say?"

Lukas held a finger over his lips. "I told your mother Terrance's husband wanted to retire to Spain, so they decided to close the shop. It wasn't a lie. After the raid, they did. Bought a fine place on the coast with that money. Threw a nice going away party, too."

He cleared his throat and examined the printed pages, studying Tobias' attempts in the margins. "Breaking a code is like unraveling a sweater, gotta find a loose thread—the right one—and know where to pull."

He fished in his pockets for a handful of hazelnuts, popped a few in his mouth, handed the rest to Tobias, and went on with his study, jotting down figures and bits of equations. When he got to the note tucked inside the book, he paused and sucked in a breath.

"The key, to your key." He smiled at the joke. Lukas held up the little scrap of paper. "You're on the right track, boy, wrong train, though."

"A program could do this faster, but better I show you the first time, I think," Lukas said. "You know what it is, Fibonacci?"

Tobias had squeaked through his math classes in university, and he'd never been more embarrassed than when his father ran circles around him with some equation over dinner. Still, he swallowed his pride at his father's patient smile.

"A sequence," Tobias began. Lukas's brows rose, and Tobias held up a hand. "Where a new number is achieved by adding two together, starting with zero and one."

"More or less. What makes this sequence special—aside from the fact that it appeared in India thousands of years ago, and some say it appears in the basic building blocks of nature—is that it was once a good candidate for securing information. I wouldn't use it to code the grocery list these days, even your old fool of a father can smash it—"

"Thanks, papa." Tobias drawled.

Lukas ignored the sarcasm, grabbing a paper and pencil. "But a few hundred years ago, I imagine this would have stumped all but the most determined. Of course, most of Europe was barely literate at the time."

Lukas started writing, his words as steady and sure as his pencil's stroke. "Using a sequence to create an encryption key, letters to numbers and back again. Very tricky for the day. I'm impressed. This came from your collection?"

"Yeah, but I can't really talk about it."

Lukas' eyes twinkled merrily. "Then, I suppose you and I have that in common."

Tobias stared at the equation, and the resulting row of numbers matched to the alphabet. He picked up the cipher and a second pencil and started mapping.

"It doesn't work — just more gibberish— unless my math is off," Tobias said, rubbing his temple.

Lukas appraised his work. Finally, he grinned. "This isn't Fibonacci."

Tobias shook his head. "You lost me."

"Sometimes you must tug a few threads before you get the right one." Lukas began again, scanning the note. "Let's try a little generalization called Tribonacci."

Tobias snatched another pencil from the can beside the computer. His father demonstrated the equation and slid a piece of paper at him. He kept silent except to correct Tobias' figures or provide a new sheet of paper.

When he was done, Tobias sat back in his chair, gazing at the complete solution laid out on four sheets of paper. Letters to numbers and back again. A key. He ran a test on the first few lines of the ciphertext. *In this accounting, I provide the true testimony of the accused...*

Tobias wanted to leap out of his skin, but he set his pencil down and hugged his father. Strong arms closed around him, and lips pressed to his cheek with fierce affection.

"Nice job, boy." Lukas clapped him on the shoulder.

"Vielen Dank, Papa."

"Gern geschehen mein Schätz." Lukas sat back in his chair, fingers knit over his cardigan-clad belly in relaxed ease. "Und Kind? Bring mir bitte ein Bier."

On the way to the kitchen to retrieve a beer for his father, he passed through the living room.

Beryl was folded up on her chair, watching a documentary on the nature channel. "Papa help you figure out what you needed?"

His footsteps slowed. No doubt she has sent his father with that tray just to set this in motion. It was disconcerting, and part of him resented her meddling hand in everything.

"Yeah, thanks," he muttered. "I gotta get back to it."

Her smile didn't meet her eyes. "Good luck."

⬥

By dawn, Tobias fixed a bleary-eyed stare at his hastily translated account of a junior apprentice of a favorite cleric of twice-over King, Archduke, and Holy Roman Emperor himself, Rudolf II. In what would have been an early version of a modern murder pamphlet, it detailed the case of a minor noblewoman condemned for murdering her husband and the wife of her lover. As was common for women of any social or educational deviance, she was labeled a witch and condemned to death.

It was a capricious and somewhat scandalous assignment, but one that fit with the Bohemian ruler's fascination with the esoteric—the pursuit of which troubled Rome much less than his inability to maintain a unified Christian empire. By all accounts, he was a great patron and collector of the arts, but his interest in alchemy was etched all over the city, from the Golden Lane at the castle to a recently uncovered alchemical laboratory in the heart of Old Town.

Rudolphine Prague may have been a golden era for artists, composures, and occultists, but it was just the city's latest flirtation in a long history connected to the mystical. That stretched all the way back Libuše, the Slavic princess who the historian Cosmos claimed saw the city rising north in future splendor from her seat at the ancient fortress of Vysehrad.

Though the specific vision itself might have been stolen from Virgil, by all accounts Libuše and her two sisters were witches: a prophetess, a healer, and a priestess, respectively. After the death of their father, Libuše ruled in peace until the people demanded a king. So she gave them one—of her choosing—and in doing so, birthed a dynasty that founded the city that became the crown jewel of the Bohemian Empire.

Be they truly magical, or just wise women and healers, witches made their way with little fuss until the publication of *Malleus Maleficarum* in 1482 named them a public enemy number one. The persecutions spiked around the time that Rudolph was collecting his alchemists and pondering the unknown.

This particular case earned special public interest when the convicted woman boasted openly of her knowledge of witchcraft. Much of the account was third-hand. The apprentice seemed more occupied with the surroundings than the confession: the deplorable condition of the prison, the demeanor of the jailers, and the terrifying countenances of the inmates.

When it reached the details of the crime he shifted restlessly. Born in a titled, if minor, family, the woman, Katka, had been raised in the countryside but had married well and was brought to Prague with her new, much older husband. Exposure to the court set her aims higher—a favorite lord with a young, sickly wife. She worsened the condition of the lady of the household with an herbal draught, then lured the lord to her own bed. A letter written by Katka's own husband outlining his suspicions and produced by his brother after her husband's untimely demise—by poison—proved to be her undoing.

The recording veered toward theatrical as it careened from dramatic reveal to claims of witchcraft and sorcery.

Tobias figured, at best, the bored apprentice grew inventive with his duty by embellishing a version of the condemned's confession. At worse, many trumped-up charges could be "legitimized" under confessions attained during torture.

But something strange happened midway through the account.

The voice changed to the first person, as though the woman herself had taken up the pen and began mid-sentence. Even the handwriting changed.

...*Since the time of Devin, our maiden's war, such is the way of men. And if we seek to reach for more than the baubles they cast at us, what better way to silence us than burn us for possessing the very wisdom they seek? So he will want to leave this bit out, the fool, I see it in his eyes, but to you, I tell the truth...my book will never be found by any living man. Until I burn, they will try to bribe or punish me so that they may claim my knowledge without the burden of my sex. No matter how they crow about their control, they possess nothing. Fear bars their understanding. My greatest work has been done, the ground laid for my renewal.*

Tobias lingered over the last lines.

They who claim to know all about resurrection are ignorant as babes grasping at a candle flame. They cast me into a future where I will again walk the streets of Prague, fearing no man.

Prague. Not Lesser Town of Prague, or even Malá Strana, Little Quarter, as the district south of the castle where she had lived would have been called. As though she knew that one day Praha would not just be the name for the castle, but the entire city.

Tobias set down his pencil as his alarm clock went off and stretched his neck until the vertebrae popped satisfyingly.

Should he wait to see what became of the original? Tobias could not afford to attract the Necromancer's attention. Personally or professionally, it was a good idea for him to toe the line of the demands and fly under the radar.

That would be the smartest thing to do. And he'd always been the smart guy. But the hunger to know had a hold of him and, like the jaws of the wolf, it refused to let go. This was his passion—not managing students and teaching the finer points of Latin translation and filling out triplicate forms. *This.* The missing pieces left by history and human assumption, the gaps longing to be filled, and the sense of a story he didn't quite understand.

Yet...

Tobias swept the whole assembly into his desk drawer. He needed to shower, shave, and get to the office before the students arrived. He grabbed his towel and headed for the door, but his hand caught the doorframe as if of its own volition. Pausing there for a moment, he tapped his fingertips.

His mother breezed down the hall, dressed for her first class of the day. She nodded in greeting. He bobbed his head, waiting for her to pass. But instead of continuing to the bathroom, he made an abrupt one-eighty and grabbed a scrap of fresh paper and a pencil. Bending over the desk with the towel over his shoulder, he pushed his glasses up his nose and started scribbling. A half hour later, he had a list of resources he'd need to begin and knew he'd already made his decision.

Tobias would need to be very careful when he verified this account. He stood, exhaling with the realization of how much work this entailed, complicated by the need for secrecy.

Only one person he knew was capable of the work and clever enough not to raise any red flags.

♦

TOBIAS DROPPED a note on Barbara's desk on his way to his office. When she arrived, he was pacing the space, trying to determine out how to explain the discovery.

Her first words relieved him of the burden. "You figured it out."

He grinned, unable to hide the surprise or amusement. "How did you know?"

"You look like someone just wanting to scream 'Eureka.'" An answering smile lit her face. "Also, your tie doesn't match, and I don't think you shaved this morning."

Self-consciousness struck them simultaneously. His hand flew to his chin as hers went to her neck in an attempt to cover the flush.

"I'm sorry." She lowered her eyes. "That was—"

"Accurate, observant," he finished. "Knowing how you work, I would expect no less. Close the door, if you would."

She seemed unusually disheveled. The smoothed-back strands of her hair had already begun to rebel, and there was a smudge of something—chocolate?—on the collar of her pinstriped shirtdress beneath the soft cardigan. It was also on the corner of her mouth, he noted, fighting the urge to lick his lips. She smelled like chocolate up close, over her usual orange blossom and bergamot.

His nostrils flared. He wanted to taste her.

Barbara swallowed audibly, unable to quite meet his eyes. "You needed me for something?"

Tobias bobbed his head, startled by the sudden pressure in his mouth —predecessors to his teeth growing and his jaw lengthening. It took him a moment to recognize it for what it was: the change. He'd skipped his run the previous night and apparently the wolf intended to have out right here in his office, in front of his brilliant research assistant. He had to get control of himself.

Tugging at the suddenly tight collar at his throat, he hurried to put the desk between them. He fussed with the stack of papers on his desk to buy himself time, gripped with the fear that she had seen something odd in his face.

Barbara cleared her throat. "I assume it has to do with the translation?"

A quick glance told him the flush was back in her cheeks. Worse, his ability to scent her strengthened, an overwhelming combination of human fragrances and warm female essence. Warm, fertile female.

Good gods.

Those were the wolf's senses. He was closer than he thought. Not here, not now.

"Y-y-yes." He coughed around a growing thickness in his mouth. "I, uh..."

"The book was a lark," she said. The fear tightening her voice hit him in a wave of scent. "I mean, another research assistant had pulled it for the math department, Honza reminded me, actually. So I just brought it up. I had no idea it would be helpful."

Tobias had no idea what she was talking about, as he took a deep breath and fought for control. He'd throw himself out the window before he did anything to hurt her, to scare her. And this would definitely terrify any normal woman. He took another long breath. The wolf receded. The pressure in his mouth abated. When he could look up, she was waiting, her brows lowered and eyes a little wider than usual.

" T-th-th translation turns out to be a curious account," he said, forcing his mouth to form each word. For once, he was relieved it was just his stammer he had to contend with. "I-I-I need you to do some digging, to verify—or disprove—as much of it as we c-c-can."

Her eyes lit with excitement, but none of the pity he expected. She didn't even seem to notice his stutter. She seemed relieved, as though she had expected him to say something else entirely.

"The N-n-necromancer's interest makes this..." He let the sentence go, unfinished, between them.

"Dangerous." Her pupils glittered.

The pressure in his mouth eased. "I have a list of names and dates that I need verified. I need you to look into as quietly as you can."

She nodded, coming closer. Tobias explained his research logic, and she nodded and scribbled her own notes.

They were standing like that when Karel barged in—on either side of his desk, leaning over a set of notes so closely their heads almost touched. He looked between them, mouth hardening to a long line. His brows drew down.

Tobias pushed his glasses up his nose and fought the urge to bury his notes under papers. That would be too obvious.

"Miss Svobodová, do you have the information you need to get started?" He said gruffly.

Her gaze skittered off his shoulder, to the books on the shelf behind his desk with a little nod. "Sir."

Karel refused to move out of her way, forcing her to edge around him to clear the door. The stare he fixed on her was hard and a little angry.

When she was gone, Karel shut the door firmly behind her. Tobias fought the urge to throw him against the wall and show his teeth. All of them. Instead, he sat down as if everything was normal and let Karel resume his place at the examination table with the folio of photocopied pages of the unbroken cipher.

"What's your plan today?" He drew a book on Renaissance painting over his notes. When Karel's back was turned, he slid them into his messenger bag. "More Caesar substitution?"

"That's a dead end." Karel shook his head. "I think it's pigpen."

Tobias fought the urge to roll his eyes. The boy was useless. "Carry on then."

With Karel in his office, Tobias and Barbara had nowhere to discuss her progress or what she'd found. They resorted to stolen minutes in the morning and skipping lunch to meet in the courtyard.

On Wednesday, she flew into his office, eyes alight with discovery.

It was as if he could see the words pulsing behind her lips in their eagerness to spill out. Karel glared. She paused in the doorway, glancing between them. He wished more than anything he could kick Karel out.

"Miss Svobodová," he said before she could change her mind and stride away in those incredible brown boots. "You needed me... for something?"

Her forehead wrinkled in a moment's consideration, then she brightened.

"You asked me to look into the names of women sent to the *convent* in the sixteenth century," she said slowly, brows raised.

"I did." Tobias tried not to make it sound like a question.

Disinterested, Karel returned to his work.

Barbara strode forward, her face aglow. Something tripped in his chest.

"I found a list of the clerics assigned to the documentation of their lives before their *abjuration*."

Tobias stifled a laugh at her brilliance. "Were you able to make a positive identification?"

A smile quirked her bright red lips. She was pleased with him for understanding so quickly. The wolf wanted to roll into a contented pile of fur and muscle, belly up and paws splayed.

Traitor.

"And their *apprentices*." The lipstick was new, deeply flattering and a striking contrast to the muted colors of the grey wool skirt and a silky looking pale blue blouse.

"So there is some accuracy to the claims." Tobias forced himself to pay attention. "The history department will be so pleased."

When she bent over the desk to show him the list, his eyes tripped on the sight revealed by the open top buttons of her blouse. Perfect, tawny breasts spilled over the cotton cups. He forced his gaze to the paper but wasn't fast enough. Her fingers snatched the gap closed as she reeled back in alarm. Her gaze darted around the room, unable to meet his.

"I'll continue to look into your other requests," she said, backing away. "The music department, and the exhibition request."

When she was gone, he turned his gaze back to his work to find Karel staring at him with a knowing smirk on his face.

"She pulled that one on Tesarik, too. Didn't turn out so well for him. But he's an old fart. You probably have a chance."

The wolf wanted to leap across the desk and rip the boy's throat out.

Tobias shoved it down. The savagery of the thought brought him up short.

A thread of fear roused in him. What if this was the loss of control his mother had warned him about if he repressed his wolf too long? The coldness settling into his belly at the thought drove out all distraction provided by Barbara Svobodová.

Karel laughed to himself as he returned to his useless puttering.

Tobias studied the back of the boy's neck, his vision replaced by the mental image of his teeth closing over the bony length and squeezing until it crunched.

He was going to have to get Karel out of here as soon as possible. For his own safety.

By Friday morning, Tobias had had enough of talking in code. To hell with the consequences. Karel was halfway to the exam table before he realized the folio they kept the photocopies in was gone. His gaze flew to Tobias.

"Professor?"

"We're going to have to leave off for now," Tobias said without looking up from logging lab hours. "The collections team is behind, and I need all hands if we're going to meet the deadline for the fall exhibit."

Karel's jaw fell, disbelief sputtering his words. "But I...progress...so close!"

"I'm sorry." Tobias shook his head. "There will be time after, and who knows, the Necromancer may send back the original by then—"

"This is his doing," Karel exploded. "You caved to that fucking dictator."

Tobias lowered his head and pinched the bridge of his nose. Barbara hadn't reappeared in his office all week. He should have been relieved, but the wolf was more restless than usual. Now, the pressure was back in his mouth. Hair thickened against the skin of his arms and he was glad he was still wearing his suit jacket. His shoulders felt drawn and hunched, the blades sliding down and along his ribs.

He'd wolfed out in the park twice that week. He should have been fine. Was it possible he could lose control entirely? That he would wolf out and not be able to get back his humanity?

It took every ounce of his composure and a handful of long, slow breaths to arrest the change and look up at his student. Karel stood flushed and panting, all out of words and curses, just staring at him. Likely he'd said enough things that another professor would have kicked him out on his ass. But Tobias just stared at him, too relieved that he hadn't turned into a wolf at his desk and followed his dearest desire to go for the boy's jugular.

"Are you one of them?" Karel asked.

"Undead?" Tobias barked a laugh and Karel jumped.

Tobias rummaged through the paperwork on his desk. He held up a pink carbon sheet and a smaller half sheet of notes.

"I suggest you get out of my office and see to your new assignment." Tobias extended his arm and rattled the papers.

"Assignment?" Karel roused himself and stalked toward the desk. Standing, he towered over Tobias still seated and tried to stare him down, but his eyes fell away first.

"It's a set of letters from a noble acting like something of an informal ambassador to Rudolf's court," Tobias said. "There's at least a paper's worth of research there. You'll find them in with the other correspondence. Ask Monika to give you the whole set."

Karel took the papers and strode away.

"The door," Tobias called, unable to keep the relief out of his voice.

The door slammed shut.

Tobias couldn't bother to worry about what repercussions this would have. He'd come far too close to losing himself; the wolf had never been such a unique presence before, almost taking over. He fished his phone out of his bag and turned it on. It was Friday. He meant to call Chris. But it was Mark he dialed.

The phone picked up, a cacophony of construction noise in the background behind his older brother's voice. "Toby?"

"Is this a bad time?" His voice rasped with an edge less human than it should have been.

"What's wrong?" Mark's concern was clear even on the tinny line.

The sudden burn in Tobias' eyes startled him. He closed them and rubbed his temple, keeping his voice low. "A-a-are you going to the cabin for the weekend?"

"I wasn't planning on it," Mark said.

"I-I-I need…" Tobias' throat closed, his tongue feeling like the awkward lump of flesh it always did when he had something important to say and he was embarrassed or afraid to say it.

His voice failed and a growling gasp escaped instead of his next words.

He clamped his jaw shut. The colors began to dull to grey and yellow with the occasional punch of blue as his vision sharpened and lengthened. Christ, what must his face look like?

In the background, Mark shouted something that sounded like names and a command, his voice muffled by his fingers over the receiver.

When he returned to the line, the noise faded in the background. "Will you be ready to go straight from work?"

"N-n-need clothes." Tobias said, hearing his voice fracture.

Frustrated, he slammed his fist onto the desk. His eyes widened at the crack on the wood beneath his hand. The strength that came with his transformation rarely remained in his human form. This was bad.

"Pick you up in twenty." Mark's voice steady and calm, went on in reassurance. "Und kleiner Bruder, ich passe auf dich auf."

In spite of their father's insistence on speaking German at home, Mark avoided it whenever possible. Unlike Tobias. Mark must have counted on the effect the words would have. *I've got your back.* It worked —the wolf retreated, sinking back to its restless weight under Tobias' ribcage. The tension in his body released. He rested his forehead on his fist. Salt stung his closed eyelids as the call disconnected.

He blinked hard, listening to the empty line. "Thank you."

CHAPTER TEN

BARBARA APPROACHED Professor Novak's office on Friday afternoon with her heart beating double time.

All week, her grace had driven her to distraction. She could hardly walk into the library without it pinging all over the place, recognizing books of value and importance. In Veronika's store, she'd found a box of books mislabeled that turned out to have several first editions. Her translation ability had begun to extend to spoken languages. She now wore earphones while riding the tram through the touristed sections of town to keep from being overwhelmed by conversations she once would not have understood. She fell into to bed early most nights, but her dreams left her weary by dawn.

That morning, she woke with the distinct sensation that something was going to go wrong. As she checked herself over before leaving the house, she was surprised by the outfit she'd chosen. She couldn't remember picking it out.

Her inbox had been empty, so she'd volunteered at the transfer desk to fill in for a sick colleague. She expected walking through the stacks with the long list of items to be pulled and assigned for loan to other universities would keep her busy most of the day. She never bothered to use her grace on such routine tasks; most of the books were common items not important enough to trip her abilities.

Today, she identified and located each one with almost prescient accuracy. When she returned before lunch with a full cart, the transfer

desk supervisor stared, and Barbara hurried off with the next day's list
before the woman could ask too many questions.

After lunch, when an undergrad chased her down in the stacks with
the summons to the Professor Novak's office, Barbara's sense of dread
rose.

Novak's secretary acknowledged her with suspicion, pointing to one
of the waiting room chairs. Barbara kept her face even. As the woman
turned back to her work and started to take a note, the pencil snapped in
her fingers. She yelped in surprise.

Barbara kept her eyes on her lap, biting her tongue against an apology. Had she done that?

The inner door to the office wasn't closed and she could hear Karel
Broucek's voice, "...and he's working on something secret. Something *I*
found. The book those filthy zombies took away. He's working with
them. He didn't even flinch when I...well, I lost my temper, sir, but I've
just had enough of these deceptions."

No doubt who the 'he' was. Barbara remembered Karel's speculative
glare. Indignance flared, hot and hard under her breastbone. She hadn't
asked to be assigned to Vogel, and how else was she supposed to do her
job than talk to the man, spend time with him, get to know how he
worked? And learn that he was rough around the edges but fair, and
brilliant, and startlingly awkward for all of that. It was devastating.

"Thank you, Mr. Broucek," Novak said. "All will be seen too. Now
back to your work."

Barbara looked up as Karel left the office. Their eyes met, and the dislike
in his startled her. Then she tightened her lips and gazed back, not bothering
to hide her own disgust. That idiot couldn't find his way out of the library
with a map. Here he was snitching on Vogel like a thwarted child. He looked
away first and hurried on. When she looked back, Novak was staring at her.

"Come in, Miss Svobodová."

The interrogation centered on the mystery text that only Tobias and
Karel had seen in any detail. If this had been another collection,
removing an item would have been a fireable offense. Its status, with-
drawn by their patron, left no mystery.

Novak may not have had a case to fire Vogel, but she had no doubt
he would make the visiting professor's life as difficult as possible with
whatever he gained.

She knew how that felt.

Barbara kept her answers short. No, she didn't know what her research was being used for. No, she hadn't seen the text in question. No, Professor Vogel did not ask to see her after hours or address her in an inappropriate manner.

"We are aware that there have been some issues in the past," he said, giving her a paternal smile.

Ice and fire warred in her veins. She kept her fingers knotted in her lap. "Issues, sir?"

"Difficulties," he said slowly as if speaking with a child, "with senior members of the department."

She clenched her teeth.

"If any such issues have arisen," he said, "with Doctor Vogel…"

"Professor."

"What?"

"You mean Professor Vogel. Visiting Professor Vogel."

Novak studied his hands stacked on the desk. A perverse glee struck her at the sight of him losing his temper.

"Well, we would like to know," he snapped.

Of course you would. The thought didn't feel like her own. *You'd protect your own against anything, but he's an outsider, and expendable.*

Novak went on, she forced herself to pay attention. "…We want to make sure that you feel supported in your academic advancement, your very purpose for being here."

She bit the inside of her cheek to keep from laughing. Now, he was concerned for her success?

"I understand you are seeking fellowship opportunities," he said at her silence.

She gritted her teeth and forced a tight smile. "I have applied to seven fellowships."

He looked grieved. "Perhaps something can be done to find you an appropriate opportunity fitting your goals. Conservation, I understand?"

Sickened, she was done being accommodating and deferential. "I should hope so. I have an excellent grade point average and I was at the top of my class every year of my undergraduate work. I've satisfied the doctoral coursework and then some. It's the only time in school history someone of my achievement hasn't been welcomed to an appropriate fellowship so that I could begin my dissertation."

His face went a mottled shade of overripe tomatoes.

Barbara rose. "I'm afraid I've wasted enough of your time, sir."

The moment he had used a fellowship to get her to collude against Professor Vogel, she realized how worthless it was. Silly spells were one thing. Character assassination and false accusations were a price too high. She'd rather spend the rest of her life in the cramped, dingy research assistant office than live with that stain.

"I'll get back to work now."

Barbara was proud of how calmly she managed to flee the office. She had to warn Professor Vogel. Had to let him know they knew about the book—the journal. She paused on her way up the stairs. What good could she do now, running to him?

Obviously, he suspected something, or he wouldn't have kept it a secret. He'd warned her, and if she'd had any sense she would have walked away. Instead, she had crossed the room, had leaned in close enough so she could smell the clean laundered scent and warm maleness of him. She'd been swept up in the eager smile that reached his bright, ashen grey eyes. At that moment, she had been his.

His.

She paused at the end of the hall.

It was strange being here empty-handed: no books to deliver, no note pad. All she had was herself. She glimpsed her own hands, trembling with adrenaline. He needed her for research, and if there was any more warmth in him now than after the first days, that was because she'd proven herself. That was all.

A few of the collections team members looked up as she passed the acrylic walls dividing the room from the hall. She ignored them and kept walking. The lecture room was empty. And Vogel's office door was closed. She raised a fist to knock, mesmerized by the tremble.

"He's gone."

Barbara spun on one heel, hands clenched before her. It was Elsa, the petite blonde with the round, sweet face. Barbara prepared herself for suspicion in her gaze, but the other woman smiled.

"Said he wasn't feeling well."

Barbara lowered her fist. She nodded when words failed her and turned to go. She was halfway down the hall when Elsa spoke again.

"It wasn't the first time," Elsa whispered.

She froze. When she turned back, Elsa was no longer smiling, and her eyes shone.

"You, I mean," Elsa corrected. "Weren't the first time that Tesarik..."

A wedge of helpless rage filled Barbara's throat. She rasped over it, "I'm sorry."

CHAPTER ELEVEN

MARK'S ŠKODA STATION wagon had seen better days long before becoming the workhorse for his nascent construction business. Still, Tobias didn't care that he was coated in a fine layer of dust and wood chips five minutes after settling inside. He'd spent most of the ride, hours of traffic and on winding mountain roads, curled up in the rear seat bargaining the wolf into submission while his brothers chatted idly about workouts and music.

When Mark parked in front of the tidy cabin at the end of the long driveway, Tobias flung open the back door. He tumbled into the crisp mountain air. Before he was three steps across the dirt track, he'd torn his tie loose.

"Hang on a damn minute!" Chris called, laughing, as he jumped out of the passenger seat. He yanked his t-shirt over his head and tugged open his jeans.

Mark observed from the open door of the driver's side. When Tobias looked over his shoulder, his elder brother wore a satisfied smirk.

Tobias was too far gone to care. Buttons on his vest and shirt popped and flew as the wolf tore away clothes using the man's hands. His bare skin prickled in the cold. Answering heat rose within him, and when it receded, the chilly air only ruffled the thick black-tipped guard hairs of his coat. His paws touched the dirt just long enough for him to fling himself skyward in a twisting buck.

Their youngest brother yipped and shook himself from a pair of worn blue jeans. His once-white coat had darkened with age, light shades of grey visible on the longest hairs.

They wrestled for the sheer joy of slamming their bodies against each other, yipping and snapping.

At a sharp bark, they let up, panting.

The black wolf eyed them both with his sly yellow glare. He yawned and kicked at an itch on his ear with one hind leg. The pale wolf bellied down, stretching out his forepaws to bat at his brother's muzzle in eagerness. *Let's go.*

But the yellow eyes fixed on their middle brother.

The grey wolf bared his teeth and loped into the trees.

The others followed. By the time the sun went down, they were deep in the mountains, far from the trails of men and the sound of roads and cars. The grey ran on and up, leaping rocks and protruding roots, scrabbling up steep slopes, driven by the need to keep going. The human brain settled behind the wolf and left the instinct of the beast take charge.

The pale wolf kept up easily at first, leaping and dogging his brothers as they went, before falling back as the grey showed no sign of stopping. The black wolf followed at a steadier pace and, though he did not flag, he fell back to keep his ears on the now-lagging youngest brother.

They ascended the ruins of a Celtic fortress high in the hills. The grey planted his forepaws on the stone and let his jaw hang, tongue lolling out as he sucked in the distant scents brought by thermals moving cold night air. The eldest jumped onto the rampart, threw up his head and howled. The youngest arrived last, flopping onto his side with a heaving ribcage before levering himself up and releasing an answering cry.

Tobias surfaced enough to survey his brothers at a distance, knowing them better here than he ever did on two legs.

For the first time, he appreciated the trueness of the wolf. No dissembling or politics, just ears and tails and scents—a purity of being that humanity had lost. He retreated, and the grey wolf lifted his head to let his own voice join their song.

Snapping at the pale wolf's hocks, he raced into the trees again.

The ground sloped, and they descended through the thick clusters of pine and spruce that sent their roots over the boulder-filled, soil down to thinner stands of beech and dwarf pine. The ground softened beneath his paws, and he took in the scents of other animals that had come down to the still black water. He drank deeply then shook himself, showering his brothers with silver droplets of the pristine lake.

The black looked up, ears swiveled to a distant sound. The grey lifted his nose, drawing air in little puffs.

Elk.

Yellow eyes watched him with a look that held a question: *what now, brother?*

The grey flagged his tail in answer and started after the scent. In his wake, the youngest wolf yipped in eagerness.

The course of blood in the grey's veins, hot and wild, sang with the single need. He gave himself to it and the sense of his brothers—his pack —around him. It had been too long since they had all hunted together.

As the scent bloomed, the grey slowed to a low ground-covering jog.

The three of them fanned out through the trees. The grey let his nose and his ears guide him as the low mist of the mountain valley obscured his sight. The vague suggestion of shapes, darker than shadow and shaggy from winter, dotted the spring grass. He kept upwind, circling the meadow as the pale wolf dodged ahead into the trees and the black moved along his flank, a shadow. One antler crowned head lifted—an old bull. A younger bull kept a wary distance. A cow bleated, and the answer of her calf was high and sweet.

The black wolf chuffed with the potential. But the grey didn't want a new calf.

The black made a coughing noise of surprise, but when his brother left the cover of trees and mist, he fell in at his side. The old bull scented him first and bellowed, swinging his massive head. The cow and her calf broke and ran. The young bull, not sure whether to be more afraid of his senior or the scent of predator, hesitated a moment too long.

A full-grown bull elk had certainly fended off more than one hunting attempt. The grey was no reckless pup and, after having been confined to oversized park rats, he was rusty. He felt his elder brother's approval as he cut wide of the old male towards the younger one. Untried, and still thin from winter, he would make a much easier mark.

The young bull whirled away from the mouthful of teeth surrounded by grey fur and into the snarling jaws of the pale grey wolf. He tumbled backward and sprang away from the meadow, racing for the trees.

Hunting transformed the wolves into a pack, driving their prey away from open spaces and into the dense cover and uneven ground that would cost the bull labor but earn no speed. With bursts of speed and deft ferocity, the pale wolf harried the bull first. When he tired, the black slipped into his place, yellow eyes a silent, savage menace that made the young bull elk startle from flashes of his own shadow in the moonlight.

The grey kept just off the pace. He flanked and snarled and drove, but let the other two lead the chase, conserving his strength.

Winded, the exhausted bull made his stand in a rocky gully, swinging his great horned head as rock sharpened hooves slashed at the air. The youngest and the oldest kept him hemmed in and harried. The grey went for the kill. The sharp punch of a hoof caught his ribcage. He tumbled backward in a heap, legs thrashing to bring him upright even before he hit the ground.

The bull lowered his head. His great shaggy humped shoulders rose with his charge. Still recovering his wind, the grey labored to heave his body away. A blur of dark fur and teeth shot between them as the eldest wolf launched himself at the elk and gripped a mouthful of shaggy throat in his iron jaws. The elk bellowed and spun, sending the black wolf swinging like a great furred pendulum.

It bought the grey just enough time to recover.

As the black was shaken free, the grey lunged for the exposed junction of cheek and neck. Skin gave beneath his teeth.

The elk staggered and dropped to his knees, keening.

The youngest wolf latched onto the flesh between hock and belly. When the bull went down, he scrabbled onto the elk's back. The elk shifted right into the grey's jaws and he clamped down, feeling the jugular burst between his teeth.

This, the wolf's pulse chanted with exultant fury, *this is who I am. This is what I am. This is what I can do.*

When the elk was down beneath them, the grey wolf threw up his head and called to the moon and everything beneath. *I am. I am. I am.*

Floating in a peaceful silence, the man inside the animal gazed at the stars and the darkness between and wondered at the mystery that united them.

＊

Tobias shivered awake, naked on the gravel driveway. He sat up and slammed his head into the underside of the car. It was mid-afternoon, judging by the light. Squinting, he made out the lumpy fabric of his abandoned suit in the driveway. It had rained sometime over the weekend. He couldn't find it in himself to care.

The wolf memories faded like dreams, more sense than images. Gorging on elk, then running under the moon. In the day, they slept in the hollowed-out shelter of a rotted log, curled around each other like pups. When darkness came they rose again, kings of the wild.

Two dawns. It was Sunday.

His dirt-caked fingertips probed the bruise on his chest and winced at the memory of rock-sharpened elk hoof. Ribs had been broken, without a doubt. Would a wild wolf have survived that injury? His chest ached faintly as he dragged himself out from under the station wagon. Even as humans, he and his brothers healed fast—they'd been in enough fistfights prove it.

The screen door banged.

Mark emerged with a steaming mug in hand. Showered, shaved, and dressed, he sauntered down the steps with a grin.

Christof appeared a moment later in a fresh t-shirt and his old jeans, gnawing on a piece of bacon.

Tobias' belly still felt full. The sight of cooked bacon made him queasy.

"The wild man awakes!" Christof cried, trotting ahead to crouch before Tobias. He held something out. "Here, brother."

Tobias accepted his glasses, ignoring the smear of mud his hand left on his cheek as he seated them. He wobbled for a few steps before his equilibrium on two legs returned. "How long was I out?"

When he reached the porch, Mark offered the cup. "We got back about dawn."

"Why was I under the car?" Tobias swallowed a sip. Bitter and warm with a touch of cream. Perfect. He nodded thanks.

Chris laughed, polishing off his snack and scratching the loose scab between his eyes. They'd defended their kill from a bear, and the pale wolf had taken a good swipe on the nose. "You refused to come inside. Wouldn't even change back. What were we supposed to do, drag you in by the scruff? You know mom hates when we get fur on the furniture."

Tobias looked to their older brother.

Mark wore a bit of that know-it-all smirk that Tobias had always despised. Maybe it was his imagination, but the expression was less rancorous this morning.

"You tried to bite me." Mark shrugged. "I let your ass sleep under the car. No arguing with some people."

Tobias felt the heat in his chest and his neck. "Jesus Christ, Mark— I'm sor—"

"Figured I had it coming." Mark smiled. "Never seen you so into it, though. You were all wolf."

Tobias knew what he meant. After that first uncontrollable transition, he always let himself go just enough to relieve the pressure, keeping a measure of restraint on that animal nature. But this had been something new. And it left him feeling stronger, more himself.

After all the running and the hunt, he should have been exhausted, in any form. Instead, a bladed strength raced through him. He felt as though he could pick up the car with one hand just for the hell of it, then go run down another bull elk.

Mark must have seen it in his eyes. *I told you so,* he'd have all rights to say. Instead, he collected Tobias' soiled clothes. "Chris packed you a bag. It's in the bathroom. Go get cleaned up. There's more coffee on the stove. Help yourself."

Tobias did a double take at his reflection in the warped old bathroom mirror. Behind the lenses of his glasses, his eyes were alight. His hair stood up at odd ends and wild twists. Dirt and bruises marked him in places. But that couldn't hide the changes in his body.

A lean physique came easy to all of them. He reckoned it a side effect of the physical energy expended in the transition and had been grateful, considering how they ate. Now his shoulders were wider and his arms thicker than before. He wanted to pull down the house with his bare hands and drag some of the surrounding trees out by their roots. No wonder Mark, who embraced his wolf, had gone into construction. The desire to build—or break—something pressed up against the roof of his mouth as words usually did. And it wasn't the only desire.

He flipped on the hot water and stepped under the spray.

Before he could stop himself, his thoughts went to one curly-haired library assistant, the tawny sheen of her skin like that of a summer doe. The image of his teeth at her neck, nipping, tasting, battered any restraint he attempted to muster. Spreading her wide on the mossy carpet of forest floor, blanketing her with his own body, tasting her everywhere.

He bit the inside of his mouth against a groan as he thought of her scent and the soft swell of cleavage revealed between the loose buttons of her shirt.

Damn, if he wasn't rock hard at the thought of her.

And damn if any of the reasons he should not have her made sense anymore. Those were all human constructs, human objections.

The wolf knew one thing: when she was close to him, her scent grew warm and lush. She licked her lips often, and her pupils, round and dark in the textured brown of her eyes, widened when they stood within a few feet of one another. She wanted him. The wolf found no reason to ignore the signs Tobias had willed away.

They were one and the same, though the concept still made him anxious.

When he touched himself, it was her soft curves he imagined, her throaty voice gasping his name. Release left him shuddering beneath the cooling spray of water. He braced his forehead on his arm and tried to calm the howling in his chest, calling her home.

⁂

"You good?" Mark asked as he followed Tobias out the cabin a few hours later, pausing to lock the door.

Tobias lifted the travel mug filled with the last of the coffee. "Good."

Chris tossed his bag into the back of the Škoda, on the opposite side of a bag of trash from breakfast.

Tobias stepped off the porch headed toward the car. He sniffed the air, picking up the myriad scents that made up this place, this home. Mark's eyes never left him.

Tobias met his gaze head-on. "Thank you."

Mark headed for the car. Christof took his turn in the backseat. Tobias didn't miss the worried look under his younger brother's golden brows.

"You were intense this weekend," Chris said finally.

Tobias shrugged. "I've been skimping on my changes. I needed this."

"You think? You never take the lead on hunts."

That uncomfortable roll came to Tobias' stomach and he looked out the window.

"It's about time," Mark cut in, thumping Tobias on the arm. "But next time you go for the jugular, be smart, dude. You almost got a gut's worth of antlers."

Tobias gave a fleeting grin. "Yeah, not the smartest thing I've done. I've been pretty busy at work. I'm out of practice."

"What's her name?" Mark asked. Not for the first time, Tobias wondered if he'd inherited a bit of their mother's sixth sense.

"Who?" He asked anyway.

Mark raised a brow. "Pretty busy at work never makes you smile. So she must be pretty... pretty."

Tobias looked up at the roof of the car, wondering how coffee spatters had gotten there. Then the car hit a pothole, and he was grateful the travel mug had a lid. Question answered. "I don't know what—"

"The hell you don't," Mark mused.

Chris pantomimed the joys of self-pleasure while exaggeratedly moaning.

Tobias winced at the realization of the thinness of the cabin walls—and the sharpness of his brothers' ears. "Christ."

Chris carried on in the backseat, parodying the word in his breathy groans.

Tobias leaned back and swatted him. "Shut up, you skinny little shit."

Mark laughed, wrist cocked over the wheel. "Pretty Busy got a name?"

"Fuck you, too," Tobias snapped without rancor, settling in his seat.

He felt calmer, even Mark giving him a hard time couldn't dull the inexplicable ease that had come with letting his wolf run wild.

Kilometers breezed by and Chris flopped into a comfortable sprawl in the back seat.

"She's my research assistant," Tobias admitted when he thought Chris was asleep. "Assigned to help with the collection."

"Pretty Busy is hot for teacher." Mark kept talking over Tobias' protests. "You only notice them after they start noticing you. She ask you out yet?"

"I'm her supervisor, and a visiting faculty member. There's a code of conduct."

Chris blew a raspberry at the ceiling. "Code of conduct, my ass. Chicken."

"Go to hell."

Their youngest brother always had the sharpest hearing. "Does Mom know her little scholar has such a potty mouth?"

Tobias leaned back over the seat and swung hard. The muffled contact was enough to make Chris grunt and wheeze laughter.

"Barbara," Tobias said. "Barbara Svobodová."

"Bar-baraaa," Chris teased.

"Enough," Mark said, glancing at Tobias before turning his gaze to the road. "Shut it, Christof."

Tobias' lips stuck together.

It was one thing to jack off in the shower to an errant thought or two. Admitting it, hell, saying her name out loud, made him wildly restless. He wanted to tear his clothes off again and disappear into the trees, howling. Only he suspected he wouldn't stay there. Instead, he'd be on her front doorstep, naked as the day he was born and begging to come in and lay at her feet.

The image of his wolf self curled around her ankles, nose to tail like a loyal hound, was not what he expected based on his morning exercise. It confused and unsettled him. He wanted to be close to her, to shield her with his body—whichever one she needed—and keep her warm. If she whispered his name, he would come to her side and let her curl into him. He would let her fingers settle in the deep fur of his neck. He would guard her while she slept. And their pups.

That thought chilled him. *Pups.* Whatever he and his brothers were, it came from their blood and could be passed on to others.

He shook his head, a mute promise.

He would never subject another living being to a life of fighting for control over body and mind. Never mind how the secrecy it took to maintain it would shatter most relationships. What would any normal woman say, seeing him on four legs instead of two, blood in his mouth and mud in his paws?

When he dragged himself away from his thoughts, he caught Mark sneaking glances at him.

"I know what you're thinking," Mark said, "and maybe it's not this one, this Barbara. But there's someone out there for you, brother. What Mom and Dad have, you can have it, too."

Tobias cast a look into the back seat. Chris snored, sprawled with his forearm over his eyes and mouth open. Tobias glared at the road ahead of them.

"Not me," he said. "I won't be with someone I have to hide half of my life from—or worse, bear responsibility for keeping my secrets. And I sure as hell won't pass it on."

CHAPTER TWELVE

IN BARBARA'S DREAMS, books roosted in the stacks like a great flock of birds. When she opened the doors, they rose with such a noise of flapping pages that she covered her ears. Loose papers rained down around her like shed feathers, and the horror overrode her fascination as she watched the tattered pages carpet the floor around her feet. At the end of the hall, a figure waited in the open doorway, silhouetted in the bright light beyond.

Professor Vogel?

But when she reached the figure, it was just a shadow. Beyond, light gave way to a dark cell littered with fetid straw and dank blankets. She turned to flee, and the door barred behind her was slick with something dark and wet. She looked down to find her own fists battered and torn. She woke gasping.

She'd spent the weekend minding Veronika's shop in a daze.

When she made it into the office Monday, it took her a long moment to figure out what was wrong with the desks. They had been pushed aside. Her own was crowded with books. Piles and piles of books. Library security was talking to Honza in the corner. Their conversation ceased as she entered.

Edita hurried to catch her hands, drawing her away. "Are you all right?"

Barbara shook her head, staring back at her desk. She had no idea how to begin to answer that, only that it must have to do with the dreams. "What happened?"

The men were staring at her and their suspicion made her skin crawl. Even Honza, who had always been an ally if not a friend, looked dubious. Her eyes scanned her desk. As she recognized titles, her alarm grew. Some of the most valuable books in the library had been piled on her desk. Most of them were kept under special restricted access, some requiring a several month waiting period or approval of project proposal just to view. It was impossible that anyone one could remove them all from storage in a single weekend. And the condition in which they were piled up on her desk, subject to damage by pressure and environmental exposure, was unforgivable.

As she watched, the first edition book of Czech fairytales by Božena Němcová tumbled to the floor, pages crumpling under the weight of the cover. She broke from Edita's grasp, scooping it up like a fallen child and cradling it to her breast.

"Miss Svobodová," the security guard said, hand sliding to his belt, "we must ask about your whereabouts this weekend."

"Me?" she asked, unable to hide her disbelief. "You think I did this?"

"The appropriate departments have been called to retrieve the books," Honza said. "There's been no harm…"

The man scoffed. "I had calls from half the departments in the college reporting their most valuable editions stolen."

"They've not been stolen," Edita said. "They're right here."

"On Miss Svobodová's desk," the man said, as though the case had been solved.

Another security guard came around the corner. Keeping an eye on her as though he expected her to try to make a run for it, the first stepped aside to confer with the second. After a moment, they returned. "Miss Svobodová, you will need to come down to the security office for an interview."

Edita's protest was drowned out by their insistence. Barbara was too stunned to do more than follow.

"Leave the book," the first said, pointing at her chest.

Barbara glanced down. She was still cradling the book of folktales. She handed it to Edita and tried to put on a brave smile. "It will all be sorted out. I'm sure it's just a mistake."

CHAPTER THIRTEEN

The wolf's ears registered urgency in the uneven steps rapidly approaching his office long before the speaker's worried voice reached the doorway. "Profesor Vogel, prominte, Profesor!"

Tobias set down the construction plans for the exhibit, feeling unusually calm in the face of the interruption. He wondered if Mark would take a look at the construction plans—this was his expertise. "Co ted?"

This woman looked familiar—not on his team, though he had seen her somewhere before. He wracked his brain for memory.

"Pardon me, Professor," she said in Czech. "There's a problem in the research assistants' office."

The research assistant's office. Maybe that pale, hungry-eyed one had eaten her male colleague alive. He pitied the man but couldn't figure out how that was his problem.

"I suggest you take it up with the department head who manages such matters, Miss…" The name came to him suddenly as the wolf brain connected the scent with his review of the staff directory. He didn't stop to consider how amazing that was. "Karmanova. Edita is it—archives and records management?"

The stern-featured woman looked taken aback for a moment. Some of the impatience faded from her face, but none of the urgency. "Yes. It's concerning Bara… Barbara Svobodová, your assistant."

Tobias was in motion before she finished. He snatched his suit jacket from his chair as he came around the desk. He must have moved too fast, because she startled backward as though he'd lunged at her. And he was at the door in the time it would have taken most men with sedentary jobs to stand.

"After you." Tobias insisted. "Please."

A few of the students in the collection room looked up as he passed. More than one spared Edita a speculative glance, including Karel, who looked far too smug for his own good. Tobias counted every day he didn't have a new complaint on his desk from that one as a good thing. Maybe his luck had run out. He only hoped Barbara wasn't somehow paying the price.

"Back in 20 minutes." Tobias snapped. Alone in the elevator with Edita, he forced himself to speak calmly. "What happened?"

Her composure disintegrated. Out came a wild story of arriving that morning to find the office full of books. Books no one had ordered, and no one could have gathered in two days. Tobias bit his tongue on an accusation of hyperbole, but when he reached the research assistants' office, he stared in shocked awe at the sight of before him.

The small forgotten office at the end of the hallway buzzed with activity. Whispers of "broken security protocols" and "three-month waiting list for viewing" trailed in his wake.

As Edita said, it was impossible. Even as a prank, this stretched the realms of possibility. It would have taken a team a week to find the books, to liberate them from their lockers and departments, and then deposit them here.

Then he thought of Barbara and her nose for research, and her ability to not just translate, but intuit. He inhaled a peculiar scent that reminded him of one person: his mother.

Edita met Tobias' eyes with a grim nod of confirmation. "They took her to the security office for an interview."

He started running. When he reached the security office, he brushed past the desk clerk, ignoring her order to wait.

"Profesor!" She fell in behind him. Tobias would not be handled. For once, he was grateful for his reputation.

In front of the head of the office's door, a pudgy young trainee stood, arms crossed. "You are not allowed."

Tobias stepped into his space. He was almost a foot taller and, after the weekend's physical change, he dwarfed the younger man. The man dropped his gaze, and the wolf chuffed, pleased at the submission.

For once, Tobias' tongue was relaxed and his throat open. "I need to see Barbara Svobodová."

The boy hesitated. "But this is a private interview."

"Private interviews are not allowed without the supervising faculty member." Edita huffed, red-faced and out of breath from trying to catch up, but her voice was stern.

"The head of the department is on his way—"

"Professor Vogel is her supervisor," she said, looking at him. "Or perhaps you would like him to wait here, with *you*."

The boy stepped aside. Tobias nodded once to her, gratefully. She shooed him on with one hand before returning her glare to the young security guard.

Inside, Barbara sat across from the desk. She looked composed at a glance, but his nose picked up salty, human dampness. Across from her, rising from his chair, was the security chief. Tobias remembered him from the fight in collections.

"What is the meaning—"

Ignoring him, Tobias crouched at the arm of her chair gave what he hoped was a reassuring smile. "Miss Svobodová, are you well?"

Barbara flushed and tears sprang fresh to her lashes. "I didn't... I didn't do—"

"Ok, we'll figure this out," he murmured and rose to his full height.

The man flinched, but did not back down, not so easily cowed as the one outside. "You are not permitted."

Tobias channeled his favorite professor at Oxford—an elderly fellow named Giles St. Martins. He had never been sure what position Professor St. Martins technically held in the department. There was always some conversation about his giving a lecture or a special session, but his name never appeared on the schedule. And yet, everyone deferred to him. Tobias made a study of it, but had never been composed enough to use what he'd learned—not for himself. He took a breath and made his smile as appealing as possible.

"This is a misunderstanding," Tobias announced.

The man scoffed and passed a hand over his thin hair. "Again I find you in the middle of a misunderstanding, Professor. What is it this time? She tripped and accidentally violated three valuable item policies, breaking security systems all over campus? Perhaps she hit her head on the pile of books on her desk, which is why she can no longer remember?"

Tobias ground his molars. He debated flattening the man, throwing Barbara over his shoulder, and making his escape up the fire ladders like King Kong in the old movies.

Tempting. But bound to get them both in worse trouble.

The door behind them opened and Novak charged in. Anger turned to surprise as he took in Tobias, then his eyes narrowed at Barbara. "What have you done?"

"Exactly what I had come to find out myself," Tobias said, cutting off the security chief with a little laugh. *Talk.* "Perhaps you will have better luck, as I have been met with defiance and sarcasm."

The man sputtered, sweat making his already shiny head glow under the fluorescent light. Flecks of spittle collected at the corners of his mouth. "This young woman stole—"

Tobias held up a hand. "As I was trying to explain before, this is all a misunderstanding."

Even Barbara's wide eyes fixed on his face.

"A misunderstanding?" Novak roared. "Priceless books, piled on her desk like rubbish…"

"I admit, the organization left something to be desired." Tobias shrugged. "But you did say she was the best researcher in the department. I just wanted to see how good she was."

"You…wanted…" The older man's jaw flapped uselessly.

Tobias enjoyed watching everyone else at a loss for words. He nodded. "Of course. I'm always looking to develop new talent. So I gave her a small assignment."

"Small… assignment?" The man's eyes brought to mind the pug one of the neighbors had when Tobias was a kid. Every time the dog saw him, it launched into a barking fit, eyes bulging like this. He'd often wondered if those eyes were capable of coming completely out of their sockets.

"The acoustics in this room are terrible." Tobias cupped his hand around his ear. *Make your request.* "Now, really. This is taking valuable time away from preparing my exhibit. Is there any way we can just make this—"

He waved his hands in a shooing gesture.

Both men looked at him like he was insane. Correction: everyone in the room was staring at him with doubts about his sanity. Only Barbara's mouth had a touch of lightness. He remembered the bright joy of her unchecked smile, and the fierce protective pressure in his chest rose.

Her lips moved as if to speak, but he shook his head and glared at her.

"I did expect you to follow the proper channels though, Miss Svobodová," he said. "This is just showing off."

Barbara coughed, and for a moment he thought she would burst into tears again. Instead, one brow rose. "You did say it was urgent, sir."

Tobias bit his tongue to keep from releasing the inappropriate laugh; they weren't done yet.

Novak and the head of security stared back and forth between them. "The proper requests—"

"Had not been filed," Tobias finished, he shoved his hands into his pockets and did his best to look beside himself with boredom. *Take some fault.* "That is my sin. I hate paperwork. As Miss Svobodová will attest." *Now ask for something outrageous.* "All the books are present. And being returned to their proper locations. Except for that first edition *Němcová*— that was Kafka's, no? I'd intended to ask for special dispensation to check that one out. My little brother loves bedtime stories."

Professor Novak looked as though he might faint at the suggestion.

"No, then?" Tobias tucked his thumbs into his vest pockets and rocked on his heels in unconscious imitation of his mentor. He looked down his nose at Barbara. "You'll have to send that one back, I'm afraid." He surveyed the men again. "She's got her work cut out for her, wouldn't you say? Best get off to it then, yes?"

He scowled at Barbara. When she remained still, he made a little impatient gesture with one hand.

She hurried to her feet, gaze on the ground. "Sir."

"Speaking of work," Tobias interrupted when the head of security began to sputter again. "Haven't we all better things to do than stand around heating this old storage unit?" He sniffed, glancing around the basement office before leaning in to whisper, "Ought to put in a requisition for a space heater down here. It's a wonder you aren't sick with the flu all winter."

The man paused, touching his reddened nose.

Tobias stepped aside, clearing a path to the door. Barbara took a hesitant step toward freedom. When no one attempted to stop her, she grew more confident. Tobias caught the door for her.

He paused to buy her some time, nodding officiously to department heads. "I do apologize for all the inconvenience. Dobre den."

In three long strides he caught up with Barbara, fighting the urge to settle his hand at the small of her back. He hadn't earned the right to touch her. And he certainly didn't trust himself to stop there. He was still shaking with rage at the sight of her tear-stained face.

As for the piles of books: how had she done it—and if not her, who? And why did he have that familiar scent stuck in his nose? The scent he always associated with his mother. Embarrassment kept him from lingering on that thought too long.

"I can't believe that worked," she whispered when they stepped into the elevator.

Tobias kept his stern gaze on their audience as the doors closed, trying to repress the smile pulling at his mouth. "Me either."

She stepped out on the first floor and spun on one heel to face him. A big waft of that scent reached his nose. The wolf perked up, pleased to recognize something so familiar.

"Thank you, Professor."

He shoved the button to hold the doors open. "It was my pleasure. Considering all you've done in the last few weeks. I owed you one. At least."

She shook her head. "You didn't. It was just… a kindness."

He bit his tongue on an offer to take her for a cup of coffee in the commissary. If she accepted, it might only be out of a sense of obligation, not because she wanted to. He didn't think he could bear that.

The elevator doors buzzed. He ignored it. "You might consider taking the rest of the day off. I don't know if they're going to come to their senses down there or what. Best to stay off their radar, I think, Miss Svobodová."

"Probably a wise idea," she said, snagging her lower lip in her teeth as a shy smile lifted the corners of her mouth.

Tobias couldn't look away.

She stared back and he watched the flush crept north of her neckline again. "The door, Professor."

He shoved his glasses up his nose. His whole face felt hot. He wanted to throw up his head and howl like a pup. Instead, he smiled and released the button. As the door closed, he muttered a hasty, "Good day."

"Děkuji." Her voice slipped between the closing doors and lingered with him as he rode all the way upstairs.

CHAPTER FOURTEEN

VERONIKA LOOKED up at the insistent ring of the shop bell, surprised to see Barbara trotting down the steps and weaving through the aisles toward the register.

She checked the clock. "What are you doing home so early?"

"Anyone here?" Barbara glanced around, her eyes bright with a frenetic energy that set Veronika on edge. "Something happened today. Something you're not going to believe."

Veronika listened to the whole story without showing any of her growing concern. She waited until Barbara started up the stairs before closing up the store. She had postponed calling Havel Zeman for too long.

He was the one that warned her, should she ever find any book or artifact that seemed strange, or had an inexplicable effect on things or people around it, she should call him immediately and he would see it dealt with by the proper authority. She assumed that meant he had some sort of connection to the necromancer, but found she did not want to know the whole truth. She liked thinking him as a colleague—a flirtatious old man with passable Czech, who reminded her of what it was like to be young.

In all her years, she'd never encountered a single book that met his strange criteria, though he paid her handsomely for anything related to the Silk Road and the Crusades.

Now, she could no longer ignore it.

The book was dangerous, and whatever Barbara was made her vulnerable to it.

Veronika had no qualms about the knowledge that Barbara's knack was something supernatural. It made sense, after all—more sense than a fourteen-year-old girl with remarkable appraisal skills. Over the years, she'd watched Barbara's training and natural affinity for books refine and strengthen her skill, but at its root, the ability was something not human. But she also knew how dangerous Barbara's secret was. If this book was somehow influencing her knack, it would be sure to draw the Necromancer's attention. Better to give him the book and save the girl.

The Godswar had sparked the appearance of creatures thought confined to human mythology. Some fled the conflict as humans did. The footage of an indescribable being's rampage on Tokyo that was halted by the Necromancer Denji was ingrained on her memory. He kept the creature in the garden in his palace as a symbol of his ascension.

Others, less harmless than the frightened Kriin, were not so lucky. The true monsters fed on the chaos and panic and were slaughtered. She'd once asked Havel Zeman what became of the ones who simply disappeared.

The ones who can hide do, often among us. They are forbidden to reveal themselves on punishment of death. The others who could not, or refused to... He shook his head once and lifted the teapot in inquiry before changing the subject to more pleasant topics.

Neither course was one she could stand for Barbara.

She closed the shop doors and drew the shades. Then she picked up her old rotary phone and began to dial.

"Dobre vecher, Slečna Panikova," Havel Zeman's British-accented Czech usually amused her. They would spend time flirting badly in two languages and talking business before making a date for lunch or coffee.

"I have a book for you," she said without preamble. "The kind you said you would like to see should one come into my shop."

The playfulness in his tone vanished. "When shall I retrieve it?"

"I would prefer to bring it to you," she said, thinking of Barbara's safety. She would no longer allow Barbara to make deliveries to Zeman. Not until this mess with the book was resolved. "Tomorrow?"

"Time?"

"Late morning," she said. "Eleven?"

"Fine, fine," he said, and she could hear the smile in his voice again. "May I take you to lunch after?"

He'd made no secret of his interest, but Veronika was too set in her ways to have anything more than the occasional lover. She smiled, coyness in her voice. "Perhaps."

After she hung up the phone relief filled her. *Done is done.*

She was turning to the back door leading to her flat in the building above when a shadow moved out of the corner of her eye.

"Hemi." She chided, wiggling her fingers. "Come on, you old goose. Upstairs we go."

She looked up the steps to see the cat already on the top.

Hemingway stared into the darkness behind Veronika with a shrill, rumbling growl. The cat's back arched, ears flattened.

Veronika knew better than to look behind her. She moved as fast as she could, laboring up the stairs. A cold wind blew through her, stealing her breath and bringing goose bumps alive on her arms and neck.

Someone's walking over your grave.

The first time she'd heard the English expression, she'd laughed at what a preposterous notion that was. Now the grave may as well have opened up around her. The dark, damp sensation clutched her clothes and fingertips. It dragged her backward. The steps had never been so many or so steep.

The air froze in her lungs and clenched around her hammering heart. At her age, an old heart shouldn't be subjected to so much effort. The cold was in her bones now and the air leaking out of her mouth blew puffs of condensation.

She gripped the banister with all of her strength as vertigo swept through her.

"Veronika."

At the sound of her name, she spun, back to the wall.

A figure dressed in soiled burlap emerged from the shadows at the base of the stairs. Long, matted hair hung around its shoulders and cheeks. The brief glimpses of skin were darkened with soot or dirt or dried blood, as though it had crawled out of a fresh grave.

Don't look up, she prayed. *Whatever happens, don't look up.*

"I can't let you do this." The hardness of the voice contrasted with the sing-song delivery.

Veronika tried to back up the stairs. She tripped hard and landed on her rear, feeling something important crack deep inside her body.

"She is my destiny." Had the figure moved closer, or was that just her terrified imagination? She could see the darkness behind it, the familiar shadows of the bookshelves and furniture. "She is my promise fulfilled."

Veronika tried to rise, but her body refused to cooperate.

The figure was on her before she had registered movement. The shadow of the darkened hall cloaked its face.

At a feline howl, the figure jerked up, revealing a naked, straining visage. Skin stretched over bone, lit from within, a glowing skeletal ball. A fluff of calico fur launched itself over Veronika.

"Hemi!" she gasped.

She expected the cat to pass through the apparition, for she was certain that was what it was, but cats are not of this world fully. The cat latched onto the woman's face and hair, hind claws bucking as the woman screamed.

Veronika tried to clamber up the stairs, but her arms weren't working and her fingers couldn't close and her heart—blast her heart for failing her now—kept stuttering. But it wasn't the fault of the poor organ. The ghost had done something to it. To her.

She had to get upstairs. She was never so sure of anything as she was that this woman was of the book. A witch, the old kind from whispered stories, ones who lured with promises and took more than she would ever give.

She had to warn Barbara.

The witch shouted something that sounded like a curse and tore the cat from her face, flinging it away. Hemingway landed in the darkness with a crash and a shriek.

Veronika bolted.

"That will not do, old dame." The voice hissed in her ear. Too close.

A dagger of ice plunged into her back, circling her heart in strong frigid fingers.

"I will give her all that I promise and more." The voice purred. "All that I am, she will be."

Veronika's vision swam and grew dark. *Bara…*

◆

KILLING *the woman cost me dearly. That crone would have ruined everything. It had to be done. I must recover my strength and prepare.*

That stunt in the library was foolishness. I wanted so much to show the girl her own power, but it is too soon. After so long in the darkness, impatience has made me reckless. I can't risk losing her now. I must be cautious. This chance cannot be wasted.

Let the little chit believe she is free of influence. I need to be close to her, to stay in her mind and her dreams so that she knows me, sees what I can do for her—with her.

Let her believe her own desire leads this dance.

CHAPTER FIFTEEN

BARBARA WOKE feeling as if a fog had lifted and left the world a sparkling blue and green again. The morning air rushed in when she opened the windows, a touch humid but cool in the shaded places. Winter stuttering toward spring. She picked a sleeveless navy blue swing dress with a fitted bodice and a shallow boatneck collar. A cardigan covered her bare arms for the morning chill and the office, but she was already looking forward to lunch in the courtyard with the sun on her skin. She slipped on ballet flats, shouldered her bag, and headed down the stairs at a jog.

As much as some part of her dreaded returning to work today, another part—larger than she wanted to admit—cradled a nascent excitement at the thought of seeing Tobias. She'd lacked the composure to thank him the day before.

She was still puzzled about the books on her desk.

She *had* dreamed about flying books the night before. What if the book, or the spell, somehow had an effect on her grace, turning it up?

On the first floor, she stopped at the sound of a feline moan of complaint. It was coming from the door that led down into Veronika's shop.

"Hemingway?" Barbara touched the door and jerked her hand at the crackling spark against her palm. She rubbed her fingers together. *What the hell?*

The cat yowled. She tried the door. Locked. "Veronika!"

One of the tenants from the third floor paused at the bottom of the stairs on his way to work. "Doesn't she bring the cat up with her at night?"

Barbara nodded. "I'll try her flat."

There was no answer at Veronika's apartment. Other neighbors clustered by the shop door when she returned. As Veronika had aged, Barbara had taken over simple maintenance issues and building-related concerns. They all looked to her as she approached.

She knew she shouldn't show off her grace, not now, in front of so many witnesses. But if Veronika was in trouble...

She took a breath and stepped forward. She thought the suggestion to unlock as she leaned into the door and gave it a shove. She called over her shoulder, "Sometimes it just sticks."

The door popped open and she caught herself before she tumbled down the steep stairs. Hemingway flew out of the darkness, disappearing through the crowd. It wasn't until she turned back that she recognized the crumpled figure at the base of the steps. "Call an ambulance!"

◆

"Excuse me, miss?"

Barbara looked up from the cold cup of tea at the sound of a familiar male voice. She'd called in sick to work. The authorities interviewed everyone present. An ambulance took the body away. She should be looking for Hemingway, who must have slipped out of the front door in all the commotion. Instead, she sat in a square of sun on the building's front steps with a cup of Mrs. Milanova's strong black tea.

It took her a moment to recognize the pleasant, absent-minded expression from the shop she had taken the books to weeks ago. "Mr. Zeman?"

"You work for Ms. Panikova. In her shop, yes?"

Barbara hadn't thought of the store. It should have been opened hours ago. Would have. Tears sprang to her eyes before she could check them. "Ms. Panikova is dead."

Havel Zeman's face did not change for a curiously long moment. And then, quite suddenly, dismay slid over whatever lay beneath. He patted his pockets and offered her colorful bit of silk. "What's happened, dear child?"

She took the handkerchief. A chill washed over her. "They think she had trouble with her heart last night, on her way up the stairs. Her neck was broken in the fall. I found her this morning."

Sobs overtook whatever else she might add.

She found silence at the sight of his face. He stood perfectly still, though his blue eyes moved ceaselessly, calculating. He shook himself, meeting her eyes again with that clear, piercing stare, and she wasn't sure what was worse.

"I'm terribly sorry," he soothed. "You poor thing. I had an appointment with her this morning. She was coming to my shop with a very peculiar book of some interest to my studies. When she didn't show up, I thought perhaps she'd forgotten."

Barbara looked away. For the first time in weeks, she thought of the safe. Now here was Havel Zeman, looking for a book.

It couldn't have been a coincidence.

A sick churn battered her empty stomach. Somehow she was responsible for this.

She lurched to her feet, but after being seated so long, her right leg had fallen asleep and she wobbled a bit. He reached out, and she jerked away. The cup slipped from her hands and plummeted to the steps. Ceramic shattered at her feet.

Zeman wore sympathy like a mask, and the cold blue of his eyes never left her face.

She backed up a step, putting herself at his height. "The shop is closed. For good, I think. Veronika's relatives will decide what to do with it. And the books and the building too, I suppose."

Disappointment creased his face, then a flitting smile graced his lips. He leaned in as if they shared a secret. "I don't suppose you and I could come to an arrangement? I'd just like a quick look. Maybe she left the book where I could find it? I would pay, and you could leave the money for the estate, or..."

He paused hopefully.

She recognized a bribe when she heard one. Overriding the fear that she was somehow responsible, the certainty she must protect the book gripped her.

He will take it for himself, a small voice whispered. *Steal your chance at your dreams.*

"Locked," Barbara lied. "The police locked it. You understand. I don't have a key." She thrust the handkerchief out at him. "Thank you." He reached, but she let it fall before their fingers could connect. "Forgive me. I'm just a wreck."

Zeman frowned. He made no move to recover the dropped silk crumpled amid the shattered cup and splatters of tea. He backed down the steps, hands clasped. "Please let me know about the services."

Barbara waited until he reached the end of the block before returning to her apartment for a broom to clean up the mess.

CHAPTER SIXTEEN

TOBIAS UNLOCKED the door to his office and halted. The hairs rose on the back of his neck. Someone had been here. He immediately suspected the Necromancer's zombies, but his thoughts slipped to Karel and Professor Novak a moment later.

He flipped on the lights and scanned the room. Whoever had done the search did a good job. Not a paper appeared touched and not a book out of place. Still, the reek of male musk and old cigarettes brought the wolf to attention.

His nostrils flared and he let the scent roll around the wolf nose until it triggered an association: the head of security.

Setting down his bag, he inspected the space. His desk had been rifled through, but nothing was missing. Even his personal effects—the photo of him and his siblings as kids on a rare family vacation in Austria, and a more recent one of his parents—were all in place.

It had to be connected to the journal. He was grateful he had kept the printed pages at home since he'd reassigned Karel. It had to be connected.

The journal.

Barbara.

Had her desk been searched as well? And what of the day before? He needed to see her, to assure himself that she was all right. He forced himself to be patient. She always came up as soon as she'd had a chance to settle in, usually with a notepad or a stack of books. He could set his watch by her appearance.

By ten, with no sight of her, impatience overtook him. He grabbed the nearest stack of reference books and headed downstairs.

The research assistant office was quiet. Edita looked up from her computer surprised. "Professor."

"Dobre den."

He recognized Barbara's desk. Someone had taken the time to straighten it up, replacing all the little pineapple figurines. Her computer hadn't been turned on, and no bag or jacket hung on the nearby hook.

"She's not here," Edita said pleasantly. "But I can take those if you like?"

Tobias swung his gaze back to her then down at the books in his hands. "Yes, please."

She waited. He rocked his weight from his heels to his toes and back.

"Oh, books." He handed them over but had to take the top three back when she fumbled under the weight. She set them on the empty desk in the back of the room. The frightening little pale one's desk.

"What's become of Miss…"

She smiled absently. "Oh, Pavlinka got a job with a private company —BioGen, have you heard of them?"

"Vaguely." He handed off the rest of the stack.

"Gene sequencing, science-y stuff," she said, wigging her fingers. "Increasing call for corporate librarians these days. *Information resource managers.* Turned in her notice last week, but it's been slow here so they released her from duties early."

Small talk. He was doing it.

A flare of pride struck him. His tongue hadn't faltered once. Casually he asked, "Was there anything amiss in the office this morning?"

Her brows furrowed as she considered the question. "Amiss? No, nothing like yesterday, if that's what you meant."

Tobias stepped back. One more glance at Barbara's desk. It wasn't empty. She would be back. His tongue thickened. Would asking after her give him away?

"Thank you for your help yesterday," she said, as if reading his mind. "Bara—Miss Svobodová is our best colleague. Whatever mischief occurred, she wasn't responsible."

He nodded, hoping it conveyed agreement and concern. She waited.

"Thank you," he managed, "for handling the books."

She must think him an absolute idiot. The stammer built up in his throat, and there weren't even any words stuck behind it. He spun on one heel and marched toward the door. He could feel his shoulders creeping north, all the bravado of his previous effort fled.

"She's out all week." The librarian's words stopped him in his tracks. "Death in the family. If you should have any requests, please send them to Honza or me."

He half-turned and found his voice. "I-I-I'm sorry to hear it. If you speak to her, please express my condolences."

⚓

ON SATURDAY MORNING, Tobias waited for the tram at Vyton in his best dark suit. He tugged at his collar, ignoring the few appreciative female glances aimed his way as he stepped back for the arrival of his tram. He paused before mounting the steps, again questioning why he was doing this.

Occam's razor: his mother had asked him to go.

Her weekend meditation workshop in Brno couldn't be canceled, and she needed someone to pay her respects to a former student and an old friend. So he'd put on his suit, bought the flowers, and pocketed the small card announcing the death of Ms. Veronika Panikova.

He boarded the tram as the bell announced the door closing. Fifteen minutes and a tram change later, he arrived in the neighborhood named for its history as a royal vineyard, Vinohrady.

Near his destination, he pulled the stiff, black-bordered card from his coat pocket to check the address. His steps slowed before a well-kept old secessionist building in a shade of pale canary. The subtle, neoclassical-influenced floral accents in a sunny orange contrasted with the vibrant blue street number sign matching the address on the card. The Belgická Antikvariát shop sign hung at street level, but the entrance to the basement shop was closed and shuttered. The windows to the first floor flat were open, and the sound of muted conversation drifted out as lace curtains waved against the window bars in the breeze.

He pressed the buzzer, waiting for the corresponding static to announce himself. "Dr. Tobias Vogel, a friend of the family."

Inside, people packed the flat. He searched, but no one seemed to be occupying the place of family to pay his regards. So he set his flowers by the urn with the rest and took an available seat in the front of the room.

Fear of being controlled after death by necromancers, coupled with a decreasing lack of burial space, made cremation standard practice after the Godswar. A sort of pragmatic agnosticism had done away with religious funeral services in favor of small family memorials held in crematorium halls or homes.

Polite conversation revealed his neighbors on either side to be tenants of the building Veronika had owned, and a book dealer from a shop in Mala Straná with whom she had frequently worked.

A familiar voice rose above the murmur of conversation, out of place in this solemn setting. "Shall we begin?"

The moment he recognized Barbara, it was too late to do anything but sit up a little straighter in his chair. The whole room came to attention.

She took a place before the seated mourners, the full skirt of her black dress swishing lightly below her knees. Glimpses of blue and green threads revealed by the shifting neckline of her cardigan formed the tucked head of an embroidered peacock above her left breast. They reappeared at her waist in the elegant sweep of tail feathers.

Recent tears had left her face flushed and eyes swollen. With the mass of her curls drawn into a severe bun, grief defined her features. Her gaze lingered on the urn before she faced the room.

"Thank you for coming. Veronika would have been outraged that we all got together to cry over her. In her flat, no less..." Her shaky laugh echoed through the room. "But I hope she would forgive me for not letting her passing go unremarked. She is...was...my oldest friend and my dearest, as well as being a kind employer and an excellent landlord. She will be missed. If anyone would like to say a few words about her, please share your memories."

Barbara's strength seemed to flag as she stepped away from the urn. Tobias rose. She started a little in recognition, but allowed him to steer her into his seat. The bookseller moved aside so he could take the seat beside her. They sat in silence as the people in the room came up to speak.

No one addressed Veronika, not to say goodbye or send her on her way, he noted. Instead, they told stories about her life, incidents full of humor or poignancy for her absence. She had been solitary, but she had been loved. No more so, he guessed, than by the woman holding the pieces of herself together by sheer will at his side. When the handkerchief knotted in her fingers was spent, he slipped the one from his pocket and passed it to her.

A little sniffle of thanks whispered his way made him smile.

It was torture, sitting so close without being able to do more than breathe beside her and will her some peace.

When the mingling resumed, she looked up at him. "Professor Vogel, what are you doing here?"

"Tobias," he suggested gently. One of the guests waited to speak to her, and he stepped back to make room. "Can I get you a cup of tea?"

"That would be wonderful."

He found his way to the kitchen and begged a full cup off an older woman in a floral dress. She winked at him and sent him on his way with a pat on the ass.

Barbara had assumed the family member role, accepting condolences and offering reassurances beside the urn. He stood at her elbow until she was finished saying farewell to an old client of Veronika's. She accepted the tea with an unsteady smile that made his ribcage clench.

"I'll be right here."

She nodded and turned to the next guest.

By the time the last had departed, leaving Barbara and the older woman in the floral dress, she looked spent. She stared up at him as though stunned to find him still there.

"Would you like to get some fresh air?" he asked on impulse.

It was the right thing to say, for once. Her smile, slow and weary, was full of gratitude.

"Go ahead, Bara," the old woman encouraged. "I'll tidy and lock up."

"Thank you, Mrs. Milanova. Please keep an eye out for Hemingway. I'm still hoping she'll come back."

The older woman herded them toward the door.

He'd promised himself he wouldn't touch her. But there was something so unsteady in her frame as they left the building that his fingers settled at the small of her back. The connection sent waves of heat through his fingertips and into his groin. Surprise stiffened her, but she did not move away. Her shoulder brushed his ribcage and settled there for a moment as they made their way into the weak afternoon sunlight.

Outside he let his hand fall away, but lifted his elbow. "Walk?"

A wry smile quirked her mouth as she slid her arm in his and released a little sigh.

"Miss Panikova was a student of my mom's," he said, responding to her earlier question. "She attended the seniors' class a few times a week. Small world."

CHAPTER SEVENTEEN

"Small world," Barbara echoed.

Even in grief, a small part of her responded to his arm against her own. Through layers of fabric, the contact made energy buzz beneath her breastbone and a languid warmth stretch to her fingertips. She fought the urge to see if anyone was watching them. *What would they see?*

She chided herself. His sober black suit and her grave face in the middle of an overcast late afternoon weren't exactly date material.

"You worked for her?"

"I made deliveries to private collectors and a couple of other dealers she had business with. And I minded the shop on the weekends."

"And you work in the university library. You stay busy."

"Idle hands." She gave a little laugh. "Keeps me out of trouble."

"Trouble," he mused. "Miss Barbara Svobodová, what kind of trouble could you possibly get into?"

Though his remark was innocent enough, her sinking feeling returned. The kind of trouble that left her waking up exhausted after a night of dreams, landed her in the head of security's office accused of an impossible feat, and left her with the terrifying suspicion that she was responsible for her friend's death.

Everything had started after she opened that box.

No, after she had played around with that spell. After she'd turned down the opportunity to work on his journal. She'd been so focused on building him a key, she'd barely considered the content. There had been something about a witch. What were the odds that her book and his journal were connected?

"I didn't mean to..." Tobias faltered. "Did I say something wrong?"

She made herself smile, though it felt forced. "No. It's just been a long week."

The silence grew between them. He guided her around a question-able spot on the cobblestones with the kind of awareness that belied his seemingly internal focus. She liked the quiet and that he didn't ask for the details of Veronika's death. She must have told the story a hundred times, and the chance to let her heart and her voice be still was a welcome rest.

When he spoke again, it was with an apologetic smile. His eyes went to their joined arms. "I meant to give you a break from that room, not drag you around the city. You must be tired. I should get you back."

She wasn't the only one self-conscious. Poor man. A grieving woman clinging to him like a sailor after a storm and he had no idea how to extract himself.

"I can take a tram," she said, gesturing at the stop ahead. "You must have other things to do with your day off."

She started to withdraw her hand.

"Don't," he said, squeezing his arm against his side so the gentle pressure stopped her. "Please. I'd like to see you home."

Heat bloomed in her ribcage, fragile as a spring blossom. She couldn't speak.

He looked away and loosened his grip. "But maybe you want time alone. Today must have been draining for you. I didn't realize you orga-nized all of this until I spoke with Mrs. Milanova. She said you were like a daughter to Veronika."

The last words brought a fresh sting of tears to her eyes, reminding her of everything she'd lost. She wasn't sure if any of his words were meant for her, or to convince himself, but his eyes widened with horror as he groped at his coat pockets for another handkerchief.

"It's okay," she said, lifting the one he'd already given her. "Thank you."

His hand flapped at his side. Pedestrians flowed around them on the sidewalk. She barely noticed. His gaze kept returning to her face though he seemed to want to look anywhere but at her.

She had a hard time believing this was the same man who'd stood up to two department heads on her behalf and executed a remarkable Houdini act. She'd seen him struggle before, but this was the first time he looked vulnerable doing it. Still, he didn't run. Instead, he squared his stance and turned to give her more of his full attention.

"I'm always saying the wrong thing." The words escaped him in a rush. "I don't know, how to say, what I mean…and when I do, it comes out…bungled."

He looked so distressed she wanted to reach up to touch his cheek and reassure him. "Walking takes my mind off things. Would you like to keep going?"

His shoulders softened, the confusion sloughing away from his expression. And then the most extraordinary thing happened: he smiled. She was reacquainted with the adorable dimples and the charming squint of bright eyes behind his lenses.

The crowd jostled, and she stepped—or was drawn—closer to him in the confusion of people entering and exiting the tram. They should move, but she found herself rooted to the spot, unable to do anything that might risk losing that glorious smile.

"I'd love—"

A group of young men, bristling and impatient bumped them hard. Tobias shifted to absorb the impact, and his arm circled her shoulders to steady her. "Watch it."

Two words. But the quiet force behind them made the skin on her arms prickle.

The men tumbled away with averted eyes, muttering apologies.

Tobias steered her out of the path of traffic. "Are you okay?"

She might never be okay again. But when she was with him, she felt something so unexpected she didn't know how to welcome it. He was at odds with everything she anticipated. And yet safe.

Everything almost tumbled out of her—the book of shadows, and the spell, and the something terrible she feared that had happened to Veronika because she'd tried to get the book away from Barbara. But she could think of no way to explain without revealing herself to him. It was one thing to feel safe with him on a busy street, but the presence of magic changed everything.

Instead, she nodded. "I'm fine."

Barbara found the crook of his waiting elbow and settled her palm against his forearm. His free hand rested lightly on her fingers. When the tram pulled away and the flow of people subsided, he pushed his glasses up the bridge of his nose and inclined his head toward the sidewalk.

She nodded, and they settled into stride. "It is what we do that counts more than what we say, anyway."

CHAPTER EIGHTEEN

ONE OF THE oldest neighborhoods east of the river, Vinohrady was easily Tobias' favorite. He loved how quickly it changed as they left the busier main thoroughfare for the quieter residential streets.

Within a few blocks, they would pass a new architectural style or turn a corner from a boring strip of shops to a quiet, tree-lined row of apartments street shaded by a canopy of green boughs. A well-kept building was bordered on either side by something shabbier and in need of repair. Another street featured entire rows of buildings in the pastel rainbow of those chalky mints he associated with old ladies and Easter Sunday. In unexpected places, neighborhood parks replaced a city block or filled the gap between buildings. Dogs chased balls and sniffed bushes, and each other, while their owners socialized.

With the weather warming and the days growing longer, the neighborhood had blossomed. Restaurant and cafe owners had begun setting up outdoor patios that would be filled at lunch and dinner times as the spring wore on, some just simple tables and chairs, others with whole wood plank decks raised above the walkway.

After a long, comfortable silence he asked, "What will become of the shop?"

It was easier to talk this way. Keeping his eyes ahead kept him from staring at her. The constant worry that he would make an idiot of himself or say the wrong thing faded with the effort of navigating their path. She let him lead, the tension flowing out of her arm and her fingers.

"Don't know. It took me days to track down her family. She has a distant relative in America. I took on the arrangements because she doesn't speak Czech, but property values being what they are, she'll probably sell. I suppose I'll help liquidate the shop, and maybe the new owner will negotiate new leases for all of us."

"You live in the building as well?"

"The little studio on the top floor. I worked for rent. I don't even know what I'd pay…"

The words dissolved into another one of her thoughtful pauses. He knew what it was like to need time to think without being pestered for answers, and contented himself with the view of spring leaves and the scent of bread baking in one of the apartments they passed. When he got settled and moved into his own place, he hoped it would be in this neighborhood.

She came back to the conversation on her own. "There is a will. I have an appointment with the solicitor on Monday, so I'm afraid you'll have to do without me for an extra day."

The breezy note in her voice made his chest light. "I don't know how I'll survive."

She dug in her heels. "Professor Vogel, are you teasing me?"

He allowed himself to be drawn to a stop, and his smile came easily. It felt ridiculous for her to keep calling him by his title now. They were only a few years apart in age, and if she'd gotten the respect she was due, they'd have been colleagues. "Tobias. And perhaps I am. Miss Svobodová."

She shook her head, eyes narrowing. For the first time, genuine pleasure softened her face. "Barbara."

A smile crinkled the corners of her eyes before her gaze swept the path ahead of them. They'd reached Riegrovy Sady, the broad, sweeping park on the aptly named Sunset hill, where people flocked in the summer to enjoy the days last rays. He paused in wordless question. She gave his arm another tug.

"Tell me about the plan for the exhibit," she said.

Enthusiasm had a way of overriding his nerves and he found the words came easily as they started up the path sloping up to the lawn. It seemed to be the distraction she needed.

They'd crested the hill before she slowed beside an empty bench. "Would you mind if we sat, for just a moment, my feet..."

He glanced down, noting what he should have seen before. She was wearing modest heels, classic black in suede with little blue toecaps that matched the eye feathers of the peacock on her dress. Yet she'd walked all over the neighborhood, uncomplaining.

He fought the urge to sweep her off her feet and instead dusted off the bench for her. She wiggled one foot free, then the other. Then her bare toes stretched freely, he was startled to find all that smooth tawny leg was actual skin. As flawless at it was, he'd expected her to be wearing hose.

He interlaced his fingers to keep from reaching out to take over the job of kneading the knots from her calves.

"Probably shouldn't have done that." For a moment, he thought she'd read his mind, but her attention was fixed on her feet. "I'll never get them back in."

Reluctantly, she wedged herself back into the shoes and leaned back with a long sigh. "And what's become of your journal?"

The towers of St. Vitus were just visible in silhouette before the cloudy sunset, the city draped in shadow between them and the castle. The last of the picnickers began to pack up in the coming dark, heading to the beer garden or home for the night.

The truth came out before he could stop himself. "It's the account of a woman accused of witchcraft. Rudolf's cleric was searching for her spell book when she was executed. As far as I know, they never found it. It's told partially in first person, so it must be a fabrication..." Barbara was so still beside him he paused. He wished he knew how to read her better. "What?"

She shook her head, her expression shuttering. But her fingers clenched on the bench seat, knuckles pale. "Nothing. It's just...this spell book. Does it say what was in it?"

He leaned back, studying her.

She'd been like this once before—in the security chief's office. At the time, he'd been confused to see guilt on her face. After all, there was no way she could have possibly been responsible. Not alone. He inhaled, let the wolf verify his first impression. Yes, earned or not, she was guilty about something. And scared.

"The witch, whoever she was, claims to have some sort of plans for resurrection hidden in the book," he said slowly. "Or the book is the resurrection. Sounds like necromancer stuff. No wonder Azrael was interested in it. I think I'm going to have to trunk it for a while."

"And Karel?"

The disappointment flittering across her face registered in his chest. This was what came of playing politics. If he had shown Barbara, he was half convinced they would have figured it out by now. Instead, he had wasted time sharing an office with a stinking, useless excuse for a graduate student.

"Letting Karel work on it was stupid," he admitted, "but I figured he had plausible deniability because he was the one who found it. I can't risk getting caught with copies of confiscated material or let anyone else work on it."

"The contract didn't say—"

Tobias coughed out a laugh. Even now it was impossible not to appreciate her determination. "I think I'll avoid arguing the fine print with the Necromancer, thanks. I'm holding on to this job by the skin of my teeth. I doubt I'd get tenure if he turned me into a zombie."

She put her face in her hands, a soft chuckle passed between her fingers. "You're right. I'm sorry."

"It's not fair of me to dangle it in front of you like this," he said. "But without the original, or any further record of this book of shadows existed, it's just a story. A strange one at that."

Barbara sat upright. Her fingers knotted together then unknotted—a decision made, changed and made again.

"Is everything okay?"

She held out a hand. "I want to show you something."

At the sight of that small palm turned to him, he stopped thinking altogether. The next thing he knew they were racing down the hill, hand in hand. Barbara's fingers were hot around his. They caught a tram at the base of the park, squeezing into the car already jammed with people. As the tram lurched and swayed along the cobblestone path toward Namesti Miru, he kept his feet planted and a hand on the high railing.

Unable to get a solid hold in the crush of passengers, Barbara stood with a shoulder braced against his chest.

The tram jerked, the warning bell sounding at a slow pedestrian or an inconsiderate driver. He reached for her when she tumbled sideways, catching her around the waist.

When the distance between their bodies closed, a little gasp escaped her. Arousal tightened his core as her palms flatted on his chest.

Her tongue darted out over her lips. This close, her eyes were luminous and without end. He ducked his head, hungry for the scent of her. Her chin came up and her fingers curled around his tie, drawing him closer. Anticipation raced through him. He was going to kiss her.

It was as inevitable as gravity, and he was just as helpless against it. Once he started, he would kiss her for as long as she let him, and more if she willed it, tram full of people be damned. It wouldn't be the first time most had been subjected to a borderline obscene public transportation PDA.

"Professor!"

Tobias growled at the tug on his sleeve and his arm tightened around Barbara. He tried to shrug off the hand, but it tugged again, insistent.

Barbara breathed his name, and the sound roared through him. Her hands pressed against his chest. Only her eyes, alight and desperate with a wild combination of arousal and panic, shook him out of his own stupor.

"Professor Vogel," the voice called again. "I thought that was you. Hey—oh…"

Someone was trying to get his attention. Someone from the university. He struggled for a name. Petr? Jakub? His nose was full of her scent and the wolf didn't want to let it go.

Belatedly, he realized Barbara was trying to create the proper distance between them. But, based on the way his brows rose, Jakub or Petr had already assembled the story of their flushed faces and proximity.

Tobias let her go. "Barbara, you know Petr?"

"Jakub, yes." Barbara smoothed her hair behind her ears with a tight smile. "Hello."

Tobias wished he could kick himself.

Jakub nodded slowly. "You two…"

Barbara flushed as her gaze went out the window.

"Funeral," Tobias said. "For a mutual friend."

The tram lurched to a stop, and the doors opened.

The tableau was broken by her whisper. "My stop."

Jakub looked at him as Barbara broke for the door.

Tobias made up his mind. Damn the consequences.

"I'll see you on Monday," he told Jakub.

She moved fast with those short legs and little heels, he gave her that. He had to run to catch up as the tram sped away behind them. He grabbed her arm. "Barbara, wait."

She yanked herself free and spun on her heel, continuing to stride away.

"It's just Petr," he said. "Jakub, I mean. And nothing happened."

"You don't understand." She spun on him, and the small curls that had escaped her bun bobbed against her head. "I don't have any more chances. I can't risk—" She threw up her hands and glared at him. "And you. You make me...I want—"

She shut her mouth, cheeks deepening with a flush.

He exhaled. "I put you in a bad position. I'm sorry."

Surprise washed over her face.

Maybe it was exhaustion and grief, but for the first time, he saw her, not the composed woman who she presented to the world. Every vulnerability, every fear, every desire. The last hit him like a blow to the gut. Desire. It was there, beneath the layers of resistance she'd constructed, staring him dead in the face.

He took a deep breath to steady the infernal pounding in his chest. "You have something you want to show me. I want to see it. I won't do anything like that again."

Fists clenched at her side, she nodded once and resumed walking. He hurried to keep pace. They walked side by side, not touching.

"What happened, Barbara?" he said. "Tell me why they treat you—"

"Please don't ask."

At the bright yellow building, she fished out a set of keys and started for the shop door. Inside was musty and dark. She shut and locked the door behind them, forcing them to cluster together on the small step, before leading him down into the darkness. When her fingers reached for his, he slipped his hand into hers. She guided him through the shop with the familiar ease of memory. He had very little sense of the space, and he opened up the wolf's senses to register the smells of books and tea and cat. And her. The faintest traces of her scent—oranges and berg-amot—woven through the air around them.

"Careful," she said, guiding him around the front counter.

In the tiny backroom, she closed the door and flipped on a light. He squinted in the sudden brightness. She knelt by a safe, fingers tapping over the keypad.

"Veronika let me store it here. I think it may be why she was killed."

The words tripped through his brain. "I thought..."

She swore and tried another combination. "I know they said it was a heart attack, but I can't help this feeling that it was my fault, because I asked her to keep it here."

"Keep what?"

Barbara sat back on her heels, looking at him over her shoulder. "The book."

CHAPTER NINETEEN

TOBIAS TOUCHED HER ARM. "What book, Barbara?"

Barbara settled back on her heels, fingers lax on the safe keypad. There was no point in trying again. Veronika had changed the combination.

"It's just a book," she began. "Just an old book. Hidden in a wooden puzzle box, but…"

Spoken aloud, it sounded exactly like something out of a story that ended in some ignorant mortal being outsmarted by a fairy.

The decision to show him had been driven by impulse. If nothing else, she wouldn't have to decide what to do alone. Now, the worries she'd abandoned in the park caught up with her. Telling Veronika about the book, showing it to her, had put her in danger. She couldn't risk the same for him. This was a mistake.

"Slow down." He touched the back of her hand. "And talk to me—"

A noise from the shop froze them both in place.

Barbara sprang up. "Hemi. Maybe she's back!"

Tobias beat her to the door, shutting off the light and grabbing her around the waist in a single move. Her breath escaped as he yanked her off her feet and clapped a hand over her mouth, dragging her backward. "Quiet."

As the sound resolved to footsteps, she quit struggling. More than one set, sure-footed and steady. That wasn't a cat. Someone was in the shop. She knew she'd locked the doors behind them.

Tobias squeezed her tight, and his palm slipped from her mouth. "Is there another way out?"

She shook her head, shaking.

He set her down, loosening his tie as he searched the room for a weapon. He grabbed the water kettle handle in his fist and yanked the cord out of the wall. He hefted it—thin stainless steel wasn't going to do much damage.

Then he stepped in front of her and edged them away from the door. Barbara grabbed the nearest weapon, a sharpened pencil from one of Veronika's crossword puzzle stashes, and held her breath. The footsteps came closer, accompanied by the crash of shelves and the raining thud of books hitting the floor. Barbara gasped, fear forgotten, and started toward the door with the pencil raised in one fist.

"They're destroying the shop!" she hissed.

Tobias pulled her backward. She tripped in the dark and bumped a table. They both froze. The sounds of wreckage from the other room ceased. Barbara held her breath.

The wooden floor creaked with the weight of bodies moving toward the door. Tobias stepped in front of her, teakettle raised. The door opened, and high beam flashlights swept the room and Tobias lifted an arm to block the glare.

"What have we?" the voice asked in Czech.

The tiny room was filled with three more bodies. Big men in black. Their leader kept his beam focused on Barbara and Tobias' faces as he edged into the room. A low laugh escaped him.

"Going to brain me with the kettle?" He flipped the flashlight in his hand. It was one of those heavy, industrial ones, judging by the size and the meaty thump it made as it hit his palm. "Now, this could do some damage. Let's see what you're hiding there."

"Back off," Tobias said. Only it came out with a growl that made her head snap up in alarm.

"Cool down, tough guy." Flashlight chuckled.

She got a glimpse of the other two around Tobias's arm. One appeared to have a crowbar in hand, the other a second light.

"Just want to see what you've got back there. Does the face go with those legs?"

Barbara stiffened. Tobias edged her farther away from the men.

"Supposed to be empty." One of the other men—she thought it might be Crowbar—sounded nervous. "Nobody here, he said."

"Relax," Flashlight said. "Pretty little tart works here. Reckon this is she. Catching a little after-hours time with her boyfriend. Come out, little mouse."

"I am not a mouse," Barbara said, doing her best to muster a Tobias sized growl. It came out far squeakier than she would have liked.

Flashlight agreed with a chuckle.

"Take what you want and get out," Tobias said. "We won't stop you."

"You won't," Flashlight agreed. "Trouble is, what we came for is proving tough to find. We could use the help of your pretty little bit of business back there. And then we'll be on our way."

The sound coming from Tobias' worried Barbara more than the three men in the doorway. She lay a hand on his shoulder, her voice low. "Let me do it."

"No." That was not a human noise.

"Afraid you don't have a choice," Flashlight said.

"Tobias, please," Barbara whispered.

"Listen to her, Tobias," the third man said in a voice higher pitched than she expected, tapering off into a shrill giggle.

Tobias took a step forward and Barbara clenched her fingers in his jacket. He paused. Keeping her eyes down to avoid the bright light, she took a careful step around him.

The flashlight beam slid from her toes to her face, and she put up an arm to block the glare.

Barbara affected her coolest librarian tone. "Do you mind? Your light, sir."

The shrill one giggled again. "You hear that? Sir!"

Flashlight swung his lamp and hit the shrill one in the stomach. "Shuddup."

The shrill one gagged. Flashlight swung his beam back to Tobias and Barbara, but he kept it out of her eyes.

"What can I help you locate?" She clasped her hands in front of her, ignoring the fact that Tobias still had a hold of her and wouldn't stop growling.

Even with a bit of distance between them the sound had a subsonic quality. A musky, animal smell had begun to pervade the room, one not entirely unpleasant. She kept her attention on Flashlight.

"Looking for a very old book," he said, "something special."

"Do you have a title?" She tried to keep her voice even. "Or an author?"

"Know it when I see it."

She fought an exasperated sigh. *Think, Barbara. They want things they can sell. They read the announcement of Veronika's passing and marked this place.*

"We have quite an assortment of first editions in the case to the right of the front counter," she said. "Would you like me to pick out some of the most valuable?"

Flashlight's low, oily chuckle filled the space. "Nah, we've had a look out there. You'll show us where the real treasures are kept. How about that safe, for starts?"

The flashlight beam shone on the locked safe, and Barbara swallowed hard. Crowbar edged forward.

"I think we have a problem," Barbara said, going for light but sounding on the edge of hysteria. "I don't have the code for the safe."

"The hell she don't." Shrill whined. "She's lying."

"I'm not!" Barbara squeaked. She took a breath. "I'm not. I just work the counter on the weekends. Veronika—Ms. Panikova never gave me safe codes."

"Still lying," Shrill said with absolute certainty.

Flashlight swung his attention back to her. "We have a problem then, Legs. Because my friend here has a special gift: he can tell when someone isn't being truthful with us, and I trust him."

She'd always known there must be others like her, with small graces able to pass for human skills. She'd never thought they'd be used against her. Curiosity warred with outrage. He must have to use it, just as she did. But how much could he tell? And how had he come into use for a life of crime? Oh, if only he wasn't trying to rob her, she'd love to ask just a few questions.

The shuffle of footsteps brought her attention back. Another step and the three men would be close enough to touch.

"I can't get in," she told them. "I can't get in. I tried, but Veronika changed the code, and now she's dead."

They all stopped. Flashlight glanced back. Shrill looked confused. "She's not lying, but she ain't telling the truth all the way either."

"What the fuck is that supposed to mean?" Crowbar grumbled.

"Means what I said!"

"Enough," Flashlight said. "Can't go back and say we searched the whole store if we ain't searched the whole store. See what I mean?"

Barbara swallowed hard. She supposed if she was quick, made it look like she tried a few combinations then used her grace, she could fool them.

"Maybe there's another combination I hadn't thought of."

Tobias glanced at her. She hoped her smile conveyed an absent-minded optimism. Or at least not sheer panic. His expression was impenetrable. She wouldn't have known he was feeling anything except for that sound. Something about his features had changed in a way she couldn't process under the stress. Was it the flashlight that made his chocolate brown hair seem grey?

"Do it," Flashlight ordered.

She nodded.

Tobias didn't seem to get the message. She had to pry herself free of his arm. All the while, he stared back at the three robbers as though he were calculating what grades to award them on a failed presentation. It would have been funny, except when his lips pulled back, the edges of his teeth were too sharp.

She forced herself kneel again at the safe, trying to block their view with her body. She tapped out a sequence, feeling Flashlight moving ever so closer. She tried twice. Nothing. The next time, she sent a suggestion to the keypad. *Open.* She'd only used it on door locks and drawers before, so she had no idea if it would work on something more complex, but she hadn't finished tapping out a sequence when the bolt slid and the pressure of the door swinging out nudged her fingers.

She caught it and her breath, sliding it open as she moved out of the way.

Tobias watched her intently. His nostrils flared and twitched like a dog on a scent. How strange. The flashlight beam disappeared into the safe as three men came forward. She stumbled aside, close to Tobias. His free arm slid around her waist, drawing her against him. She pressed her cheek into his lapel, inhaling deeply. The scent, warm and animal, was coming from him.

His palm settled against the back of her head, his voice dropped to a murmur. "We're going to be all right."

She pushed back to find him watching the thieves with an expression no longer quite human.

At the sound of the cash box hitting the floor and scattering coins, she jumped. They tossed out papers and Crowbar even stuck in an arm, sweeping his hand through the now-empty space. Barbara knew what they'd expected to find.

Flashlight sat back and turned his beam on her. "New plan. You come with us."

The book was gone.

CHAPTER TWENTY

THERE IT WAS AGAIN, Tobias realized. That scent. He had smelled it in her presence before, but let the uncomfortable reminder of his mother keep him from properly considering what it meant.

The lock in his brain keeping the realization apart clicked open the moment the safe door did.

The other secret the Vogel family never spoke of was that, long before she took up meddling in her son's love lives, Beryl Gilman-Vogel honed her craft. The gene that had lain dormant in their father's blood for generations was activated by *her* power. Knowing the danger of revealing magic openly in a world controlled by necromancers, she kept her craft as leashed as their wolves. But even practicing in little ways released the scent that had been part of his earliest memories.

He assumed Barbara's knack with research might be unusual, but not supernatural.

Now the scent curled into him with every breath—warm honey and spring plants—and upended his assumptions about what she was.

Nothing could convince him she'd come up with the code after being locked out moments before. From his angle, she hadn't even finished entering the last number when his preternaturally sharp ears picked up the click of the tumblers sliding free.

Barbara Svobodová was a witch.

He was still parsing the realization when the big-mouthed one with the flashlight announced his intention to take Barbara with him. The wolf lunged before his human brain could catch up. Tobias fought off the temptation to allow the wolf to take over—the risk of exposure was too great—and miraculously the wolf complied, lending him the strength and fearlessness of a wild animal defending its own.

The element of surprise was on his side.

Flashlight's throat was in his hand before the man could reach for Barbara. Tobias lifted, his suit jacket tearing, and flung Flashlight across the room.

Crowbar recovered first. Barbara screamed a warning.

Tobias blocked the swing of the metal bar with his arm as his knees flexed to deliver the follow-up body shot. His fist connected with Crowbar's sternum. The smaller man buckled, and Tobias closed with a punch to the throat.

The metal bar clanged to the floor as Crowbar went down.

Shrill swung his flashlight. Tobias kicked out, sending him sprawling across the floor.

Flashlight recovered, flinging himself at Tobias. The burlier man managed to get an arm around his throat from behind, and they both went down. Tobias bucked. It was enough to fling Flashlight back into something hard behind him, but the man's grip didn't loosen.

Tobias's windpipe closed, his throat fixed in the crook of Flashlight's elbow. He'd wrestled enough with his brothers to know that Flashlight must have his free hand locked in on the strangling arm. He could hear the others moving and Barbara screaming.

But the grip meant Flashlight had dropped his eponymous weapon.

Where the human in him knew only struggle, the wolf knew cunning. He let his body go loose, and, when Flashlight moved to adjust his hold, Tobias struck, scratching at his face and eyes.

Flashlight rolled, flailing, and Tobias took him onto his side.

Quite suddenly, Flashlight went limp. Tobias freed himself as Barbara flipped the light on. She held the metal flashlight in one hand. Blood dripped off the crumpled end. He scanned the room. Flashlight was unconscious. Crowbar was slumped again the wall, moaning. The third man was gone.

"He ran," Barbara panted. Tobias struggled to his feet, kicking the crowbar away.

She startled when he grabbed her shoulders.

"You're okay? Are you okay?" He ran his hands up her arms, turning her chin side to side.

"I'm fine," she said, wincing. "The police are on their way."

He let her go, stepping back as the adrenaline shook his limbs and color returned to his vision. Sirens sounded. He raked his hands through his hair, his knuckles grinding painfully as they began to swell.

Barbara couldn't tear her eyes from him, but it was with the panicked expression a prey animal gave a predator. The yawning pit growing in his belly doubled in size and threatened to swallow him whole.

She'd seen something. He'd scared her.

"Your arm," she whispered.

He'd blocked a blow from the crowbar with his forearm. At best, it should have been agony. He flexed his fingers, shaking his forearm. The bruising would be extensive, but none of bones were broken. "It wasn't hard. He didn't have much in his swing."

In one trembling hand, she held something out. His glasses, he realized as his vision returned to human dullness. He took them gingerly, and she let her hand fall away, clenching her skirt.

Tobias adjusted his glasses and surveyed the wreckage of the room: the open safe and the broken table, the crushed teakettle, and trembling Barbara. She looked as Red Riding Hood must have upon discovering the wolf under her granny's nightcap.

The sirens were right out front now, more booted feet and calls in Czech alerting them to police presence. She stepped closer to him but remained out of reach, facing the door. Her voice shook. "What are you?"

He shrugged and tried to smile when she glanced at him, knowing it looked ghastly. "Just an academic."

CHAPTER TWENTY-ONE

Barbara stood on her front steps in the darkness as the blue lights from the police cars bounced off the buildings and trees. She wondered if she would ever feel anything besides this stunned numbness again. The residents had come down in the commotion as Crowbar and Flashlight were taken away, the latter in an ambulance.

Mrs. Milanova had pressed a cup of strong tea into her hands, thick with milk and sweetened with so much sugar she could have stood a spoon up in the cup. But it had the desired effect: she didn't go into shock or give into hysterics.

Her eyes found Tobias.

He'd put his body between her and the threat, launching himself into a barehanded brawl—outnumbered—when the threat became an actual danger. And all the time he'd been growling.

Just an academic.

No academic she knew fought like a wild animal against three assailants. She bit down on the urge to laugh. If she started, she wouldn't be able to stop until the laughter became screams.

Barbara had embraced uncertainty when it came to the possibility of magic in the world. She knew there had been gods and necromancers that had stopped them from destroying it. As for the rest, there were things outside of her understanding, like her own grace.

Though she had never met anyone like her or seen anything overtly magical, she knew they must exist—why else would the necromancers hunt them? The man in the shop, the one with the skittery voice, had been able to identify a lie. Another touch of grace. And if there could be others like her, what else existed?

Witches, for one, if the journal she'd found was an actual book of shadows.

The memory of Havel Zeman's emotionless blue eyes and his mask-like expression of grief floated before her vision. He'd asked about a book as they stood on the steps just a few days before. Veronika meant to sell it to him.

Though Veronika had always been on good terms with Zeman, the other bookseller unsettled Barbara. Not like Novak or Tesarik—something about him made her grace shudder and shy like a nervous animal.

She'd been relieved not to see him at the funeral, though she'd sent the *parte* notifying him of the time and date of services to him, along with everyone else in Veronika's address book.

Would he have sent the men to retrieve the book? Perhaps he was connected to the Necromancer, tasked with looking out for strange old books. If so, it seemed to validate the importance of the book being more than just its value?

Her stomach lurched, and she forced down a deep breath. She had to keep it together.

The police needed rational explanations. Simple ones. They were trained to bring anything magical—even the hint of it—to the attention of the Necromancer's security team.

Surrounded by officers, Tobias stood with one hand on his hip and the other thrust in his hair. The frustration tightened his shoulders, anger punctuating the sharp short gestures as he answered yet another question. They closed in on him, and Barbara realized that something was going very wrong.

Ignoring protests from Mrs. Milanova and the officer assigned to her, Barbara stumbled down the steps, pushing her way to Tobias' side. He couldn't seem to speak a word for all his fury.

She whispered his name.

Often people reported him simply going silent in conflict. It was part of the mystique of his demeanor. She mistook it for anger at first, and then she'd seen the embarrassment in his eyes as the words jumbled behind one another and tripped over themselves on the way out. A stammer. And it would be made worse by adrenaline and the scrutiny he was under. People perceived his reluctance to speak as aloofness. Or in this case, reticence.

"Professor Vogel," she said, louder this time. He didn't respond.

She turned on the police.

"What is going on here?" she said, facing them. "Why are you still questioning this man?"

"Some things don't add up, miss," the officer in charge said, lifting his hands in a gesture to calm her. "How do you know this man?"

"Professor Vogel is the visiting professor at Žižkov University," she said, "and the reason we're still alive!"

The attention of the gathered crowd arrowed in, and she raised her voice to keep it. "Those men came in with the intent to rob the store."

The officer sighed. "And what were you two doing there?"

"Ms. Panikova passed away," she said, swallowing hard on tears. "Her niece and heir asked me to evaluate the shop for potential sale to a new owner. I work for Professor Vogel at the university, and I asked him to help appraise the contents of the shop."

A white lie. One that would protect them both.

Tobias gave a curt nod, his gaze finally on Barbara.

"We were just wrapping up when the thieves entered," she went on.

"They wanted a book?"

"They wanted me to open the safe," she corrected. "Which I did, but they weren't happy and so they tried to grab me. That's when Professor Vogel jumped to my defense and held them off while I called you."

"Three men?" one of the officers muttered, looking at Tobias.

She wanted to punch him. Mrs. Milanova huffed from Barbara's other side.

"Three men," the officer broke in, shifting under the matron's glare. "And he is one. And the one will need hospitalization from the wound to the head."

"I hit the big one with the flashlight," Barbara said. "Me."

She swung her gaze to the crowd, letting the hysteria edge into her voice as she made her plea to them. "Those men, dangerous men. Gods only know what they intended with us. And Professor Vogel... Look at his bruises."

A grumbling murmur took up.

"Miss, miss..." the officer muttered. "I'm just trying to collect his side of things."

The officer sighed, glancing at his partner.

"It's as she said," the man nodded. "Lock broken, place trashed. Signs of a struggle. And the cash box is gone. I presume it will take a few days to determine what else is missing, Miss..."

"Svobodová," Tobias' voice emerged, steady now. He took a breath. "Barbara Svobodová."

Barbara nodded, feeling the tension drain from the confrontation. Her knees softened, and Tobias caught her, easing her back toward the steps and to her seat. Mrs. Milanova blocked the police when they would have followed, a giant fury in her shapeless faded robe and floral cap. She harangued them, the crowd at her side.

"Just sit still for a moment," Tobias said when Barbara tried to rise again. "Did the paramedics check you out?"

She nodded, dizziness sweeping her. "I'm fine. But this is an outrage."

"Thank you for defending me." A smile lifted his lips, but he didn't meet her eyes. "But you should go inside. Rest. Mrs. Milanova."

The older woman came at his gentle call, letting the crowd do her work. Her face looked grave. She clucked and fussed over Barbara.

"Can you get her inside?" he asked. "Maybe something to eat? She hasn't had dinner. Make sure she's not alone tonight. In case of shock."

The matron nodded, and they levered Barbara to her feet. She didn't have the strength to resist. The last glimpse of Tobias, eyes full of regret, followed her all the way into her dreams.

CHAPTER TWENTY-TWO

Barbara spent Sunday doing her best to clean up the shop. She rescued the crushed books and moved the more valuable materials to the back room. There was no sign of the book of shadows, but she had lost interest for it. She'd spent all night dreaming she was being chased through the woods. And the sound her pursuer made was the one Tobias Vogel made when he fought in the basement.

On Monday morning, she put on her black dress, buttoned her jacket, and headed to the solicitor's office. She took the tram across the river to Mala Straná, getting off a stop early. Walking the extra distance gave the sun a chance to soak into her hands and bare legs, and for the breeze to caress the skin of her neck.

It also brought back memories of her afternoon with Tobias. The comfortable way they moved together down the street, how his hand found her back or her shoulder blades to guide her in dense crowds or around the occasional questionable spot on the cobblestones.

It was so easy to see him one way: concerned, patient, not full of words, but steady beside her. The other—she shivered at the memory of the night in the back room—the one that could lift a grown man and fling him aside was something murkier.

All the academics she knew were soft, fond of their comforts, and had no head for conflict beyond office politics. A few were fencers from their university days. But she couldn't picture a single one in a bareknuckle brawl with a couple of toughs—and winning.

And what did it mean that the sight of it had made her blood pound?

She had been frightened for them both, but had never feared harm from anyone other than the robbers. From the moment he heard footsteps in the store, everything he'd done had kept her safe. And he'd heard them before she had. She'd worked in that shop for years, knew every creak of those stairs, and still he had heard the intruders first.

She knew more than most humans did about the supernatural, but that was related only to her abilities. The rest were stories passed down from those who remembered the Godswar, stories that sounded like fairytales out of Grimm. It was impossible to tell the truth from fanciful imaginations, outright fabrications, or wild fears.

In fairytales, giants ate children, talking frogs announced pregnancies, and witches bestowed charms and laid curses. Wolves dressed as grandmothers lured innocent girls for their dinner.

She'd arrived lost in her thoughts and rang the bell for the office.

The receptionist greeted her over the intercom and the door buzzed. She let herself into the lushly appointed entryway and walked the three flights of steps to the office. The polished wooden door opened, and the receptionist waited to greet her.

Barbara followed her into the main office.

A portly older man with three hairs clinging to the top of his bare head greeted her with a firm handshake and a deferential half bow. He showed her into a comfortable sitting chair across from his desk.

"I'm delighted to make your acquaintance," he offered. "If under unfortunate circumstances."

Surprise stilled her fidgeting. "You know me?"

He laughed, rejoining his own seat and sliding a folder before him. "Ms. Panikova spoke of you often and with great affection."

Barbara burst into tears. Over the last week, she had lived in the uncertainty what would become of the shop and her living arrangements, the trouble at school, and even the mystery of what had become of the book. She could face those with only a shaky breath when she thought about them too long. It was life without slow summer afternoons in the shop pouring over the latest auction catalogs and sorting boxes from estate sales, elbow to elbow with her mentor—her friend—that seemed unbearable.

The receptionist appeared with a tissue as the solicitor rummaged helplessly around his desk.

Barbara composed herself. "I'm sorry. I thought I was ready…."

He waved a hand. "There is no rush. Veronika was a dear friend and her loss is keenly felt. This will go quickly because everything is in order. I've already spoken to the relation, a Miss Peters of Texas. There will be no contest. We can proceed with the transfers right away."

"Transfers?"

He nodded, indicating the documents on his desk. Barbara sat up in her chair.

"I, Veronika Panikova," he began, "wish to leave all my belongings, aside from taxes and necessary fees for the execution of my desires, to Miss Barbara Svobodová, to do with as she sees fit."

Barbara's heart cracked open.

He had to stop for her to collect herself again.

"Now, Bara," he continued reading aloud in an affectionate, if masculine, imitation of Veronika's voice, "you'll protest, but it's no use. You can finally get that computer database you were always begging me for. Take good care of Mrs. Milanova. She's getting forgetful and will leave the hob on without reminding. Her niece is begging her to move to the country with her family. You might do what you can to encourage it before she burns the building down."

The letter went on with instructions for all of the tenants and encouragement to move into the larger first-floor apartment. Barbara registered little of it. Then the solicitor continued with an accounting of the assets: the building, the store, all the stock, and accounts. Enough to keep the shop running, or travel, or finish her education at another university, if she sold it all.

She was by no means wealthy, and she knew how much work managing the shop and the building would be, but it was more than she'd ever had in her life.

There were papers to sign in stacks. Documents for the government and the local municipal services. Veronika's solicitor had seen to everything, even setting up appointments to transfer the business. She agreed to have him draft the new leases for the tenants, changing nothing but the name of the building owner and responsible party.

He promised to have all the completed documents sent to her the following week. He had the master keys for the apartments and the shops signed over to her.

Mrs. Milanova was sweeping the stoop when she returned to the building on Belgická. The older woman frowned. "What's happened, Bara?"

Barbara began to weep.

◆

AFTER A WEEK AWAY, Barbara was delighted to come back to her desk in the library.

The book of shadows may have vanished without a trace, but maybe all was as it should be. Or at least moving in the right direction, finally.

She was humming when she entered the research assistant office, dropped off her purse and shed the light jacket. An enthusiastic email from Pavlina waited for her, complete with a description of her new job and an invitation to lunch. Barbara was sending a reply when Edita and Honza came around the corner. Her smile faltered at their grave expressions.

"What's happened?"

"There's been a formal disciplinary hearing scheduled for Professor Vogel," Edita said. "The whole department's talking. Improper handling of materials. And Novak wants to see you again."

Professor Novak wasn't alone in his office. This time he was accompanied by the dean of the school and the student ombudsman.

"Miss Svobodová," Novak began without preamble, "this meeting is to inform you that you are being placed on administrative leave for the duration of the term."

Barbara stood up straighter, unable to hide her shock. "But I—"

He cited issues with senior faculty, including her confrontation with the head of archive conservation. "We feel your performance has suffered and your presence is a disruptive effect on the staff. It is our regret that the necessary steps must be taken."

"We've asked for specific feedback on the issues with faculty," the ombudsman piped up, looking displeased.

"But I...need this job," she said. "For a fellowship position with the department—and my doctorate."

"The department feels a separation might be wise at this time," Novak said. "You may schedule an appointment to speak with the student services office about transferring your credits to the Silesian program."

"But they don't have a conservation program," she said. "And Žižkov University's program is the best in the Czech Republic."

Whatever Novak said in response flowed around her, elusive and beyond her reckoning. A pressure built beneath her ribcage, drowning out her heartbeat and the ability to draw air into her lungs. She stood like a mannequin and let the words fall on her useless ears. When they paused in what she sensed was a dismissal she started for the door.

Her first thought was to go to Tobias. What a foolish effort that would be. Hadn't Edita said he was going before a disciplinary board? The last thing he needed was to be associated with her.

Two familiar officers from campus security stood in the waiting room of the department head's office.

"You will clear out your desk immediately," Novak called at her back.

She could feel their eyes on her. She refused to give them the satisfaction of breaking down.

In the shared office, Edita and Honza watched as she packed her personal items into a small cardboard box. When one of the security guards grumbled about how long it took, Edita snapped at him, her voice rough with emotion.

Barbara took her arm. "I'll be okay, I promise."

"We didn't know," Edita said, hugging her. "You've got to fight this. File a complaint."

Barbara shook her head, unable to look at them. She left one of her pineapple figurines with each of her colleagues, updated her datebook with her contacts, and collected her box.

She left with her chin high. She didn't need this place anymore. She had a building, and a bookstore. No one could take that from her.

CHAPTER TWENTY-THREE

Tobias reviewed the school code of conduct for the hundredth time, pausing when a shadow darkened his doorstep. He recognized Karel by scent.

"I heard you're going to need a new research assistant."

Tobias stilled and fixed Karel with a long, even stare.

The wolf had been restless after Saturday night. After letting the man control their speed and strength during the attack, the wolf wanted out. Tobias had had spent Sunday at the cabin with his brothers. When they reached the wilderness, giving control to the wolf felt less like a surrender than it once had.

After all, he healed faster as a wolf and his strength came from its presence. He would need both.

But he could only get close to her as a man. Reluctantly, the wolf surrendered to human shape to make the drive back to Prague in the back of Mark's station wagon. The need to protect Barbara became common ground.

By Monday, his bruises had faded; even his arm no longer ached. The wolf watched for her with single-minded intensity. Tobias was grateful she wouldn't be at the office. He didn't want to see her while bearing any reminders of Saturday night. The look in her eyes—nascent desire replaced with suspicion and fear—haunted him. Keeping the collection team on task after word of his appointment with the disciplinary board provided a surprisingly welcome distraction.

"You didn't hear?" Karel's brows rose.

Tobias studied the younger man as the silence stretched uncomfortably.

Karel glowered, defiant, but under Tobias' unblinking focus, his gaze lowered. The younger man's voice deflated, edging toward a whine. "She's been dismissed. Well, it's an academic suspension. But she's not coming back."

Tobias returned to the inventory on his desk, his mind already churning with what could have possibly gone wrong. He cursed his avoidance of the faculty lounge. If he stopped in more often, he might have heard something.

"This is not the time for gossip, Karel." Tobias let the wolf's voice edge his words. "I need those letters cataloged by the end of the week."

Karel spun on one heel and stomped away.

Tobias checked his watch. He had fifteen minutes until he had to be in front of the disciplinary board. He grabbed his coat, locked his office, and took the stairs in great bounds.

Barbara's colleagues looked up as he rounded the corner to the research assistant office. Two empty desks stood where there had been one. The line of pineapple figurines was gone, the computer screen dark.

His stomach dropped and the wolf rose in its place, alert and fierce. "What happened?"

"We don't know," the woman huffed, her floral perfume threaded with worry and anger. "They suspended her appointment in the library. She needs this work for her fellowship. I called her last night, but she won't talk about it."

Without another word, he turned and stalked upstairs to his appointment.

His jury and judges had convened in a conference room with a panoramic view of the Vltava River. Given Prague's rich history of defenestration, he found his desire to throw them out, one by one, until he got to the bottom Barbara's dismissal seemed somewhat fitting.

The chairs on the long side of the table facing the door had been filled by the disciplinary committee: Professor Novak, the head of his department, the dean and the head of staff, a professor from archives and conservation, and one from the history department. Judging by the security officer stationed by the door, they expected trouble.

Novak made a show of checking his watch as Tobias entered the room.

The meeting was called to order, and the grievances presented.

Improper material handling. The student complaints against him for unfair treatment. Violation of materials request protocols.

It read like a litany of minor offenses, undoubtedly ones most others had managed to overlook in their own staff. Indeed, as they were read, more than one of the other professors sat back in their chairs, looking as though they'd rather be anywhere else.

"What do you say?" Novak demanded.

His tongue felt strangely smooth and light in his mouth. He remembered how Barbara had come to his aid with the police. Even if she couldn't look him in the eye, she had defended him as if her own freedom relied on his. No matter what she thought about him, or what he'd done in that basement to those men, she refused to let him stand for it on his own.

He'd gone home thinking of nothing else but that. He'd scared her out of her mind by wolfing out in the basement. And still, she rose to his defense.

He owed it to her to get through this and get her back to her job.

They had nothing on him. This was an exercise in bringing him to heel.

But wolves didn't heel.

The wolf bristled, but Tobias answered it with a thought. *This one is mine.*

The calm of a resting predator settled over him. He turned a winning smile on each of the committee members in turn, allowing it to slide into the baring of teeth as he met Novak's eyes last.

"I am terrible with paperwork," he admitted with a guilty shrug. "Though my research assistant was taking me to task on that before she was let go. Regarding Miss Svobodová, I wasn't informed there was an issue with her performance."

Novak pressed his pencil to paper so hard the tip snapped. "This isn't about Miss Svobodová. This is about that manuscript you've been hiding and your inability to run your team."

"I failed to prevent a fight between my team members." Tobias agreed. "Impossible as I was holding office hours while the two were having fisticuffs in the collection rooms. And you know young people. It's good to see such passion for the work."

The dean looked down the table at Novak.

Tobias spread his palms. "As for the manuscript, I presume you mean item number 23-5b, Necrology. I assume your search of my office confirmed its removal, by the Necromancer's people?"

"Search?" Someone down the table muttered, brows cocked.

Novak blustered wordlessly, his face mottling.

Tobias showed his teeth. "You may note that I did manage to submit the appropriate paperwork, marking the item removed per the clause."

The dean shuffled through the papers before casting a harder look at Novak.

Tobias produced a carbon record from the triplicate form and passed it across the table. "I am in full compliance with the requirements I agreed to in my contract when I accepted the task of assessing the collection."

"The requirements...?" One of the less well-informed professors frowned.

"'All materials are subject to removal from the collection at the request of the Necromancer,'" Tobias quoted. "'To be returned at the discretion of the Necromancer. Any refusal to submit materials for acquisition will be met with removal from the team and penalty as determined by the department guided by the Necromancer.'"

Half the people on the other side of the table blanched. No one envied those terms.

Tobias tapped the glasses onto the bridge of his nose and steepled his fingers on the desk. "Regarding my assistant, am I to understand she's been removed from her position? For what cause?"

"That is not your concern," Novak said. "She is no longer under your supervision."

"As she no longer has a job, she's not under anyone's supervision," Tobias drawled. Someone at the table covered his mouth to disguise a laugh. "I'm asking why the department's most outstanding research assistant was let go without notice to her supervisor—me—who issued no concerns about her work."

And so it went. Every time they cornered him with a charge, he lunged back, quoting his contract and the school policy and turning it back to Barbara's status and her unexpected dismissal.

At the end of an hour, he remained cool and focused, hands steepled.

One of the professors across the room had nodded off. Another, he suspected, was grading a paper. Even the security guard had slouched against the wall.

"As for the incident this weekend," Tobias said, "that was a private undertaking on my own time. My contract does not preclude me from taking freelance rare materials assessment jobs. It's my specialty, you understand. Miss Svobodová requested my presence, as she was employed by the shop in question. We happened to be at the wrong place at the wrong time. An unfortunate incident. When will Miss Svobodová be resuming her duties as my assistant?"

Professor Novak snapped, slamming his fist into the table. "Barbara Svobodová is no longer part of this department."

The rest of the committee glared at him. Even the security guard reached for his baton at the commotion. Novak started to go on, but the dean lifted a hand.

"I think we've heard enough," the dean said with a weary sigh. "Professor Vogel, you may consider this meeting a warning. In the future, please comply with all university materials handling policies."

"Consider me contrite, sir," Tobias inclined his head. "Now, as to the matter of my research assistant—"

The dean dismissed him with a wave. "Student and personnel management is the responsibility of the department. Decisions made there shall be upheld. If you have an issue with the dismissal, you can file a notice with the head of staff who will look into the matter. That will be all. This committee is adjourned."

Tobias left without a feeling of vindication—this was worse. He'd done nothing for Barbara.

He kept his rage haltered until he was secure in his office with the door shut behind him. He braced his hands on the specimen table, glaring at the papers and books that all spoke of her presence. Outraged, he flung the table over, sending the contents clattering to the floor. He stood heaving over it and sighed at the futility of wrecking his own office and crouched to sort the mess.

A timid hand knocked at the door.

"Come," he snapped.

The door opened, and a petite blonde woman stuck her head in. This time he let the wolf make the connection, Elsa Westergard, art historian with a minor in archival studies who had, incidentally, eaten an almond pastry with her lunchtime latte.

Her materials assessment skills were exceptional, and she'd established herself as a reference point for the ins and outs of university policies.

"Are you all right, Professor?" she began, surveying the room. "We heard a…noise."

He rose, hands full of books and papers. "I tripped."

She frowned at the overturned table, but met his eyes. "Would you like help?"

"I can clean up my own mess, thank you."

She gave a ghost of a smile and started to back out the door. He wasn't sure he could have been more of an ass than in that moment.

Pride and embarrassment fought to a standstill, but he managed to get out the words that mattered. "I'm sorry. Elsa. Thank you, for your offer. And perhaps. Well, do you know…that is, I need to file a notice with the head of staff about a personnel issue."

Elsa opened the door and stepped in with an authority he had seen her assume many times in the collections room. "You'll need the proper form."

He set the table upright and began straightening the recovered items into neat piles. Without a word, Elsa started working from the other side of the room. He wished the floor would open up and swallow him. "You really don't have to do this…"

She handed him a stack of papers and dusted off her palms. "If you insist."

"I do." He would clean up his own messes.

"If I may?" Elsa cleared her throat and gestured at his computer. He waved her on.

As he shuffled through the pile, a requisition form for an item from special collections caught his attention. Most standard materials didn't require the form, but special collections required a faculty member signature. He'd always ignored it, and the books had still appeared. He looked at the signature.

It didn't occur to him that Barbara had done the work herself, filling out the paperwork he'd neglected. She'd made the writing look different enough from her own, but the signature was clearly not his. Another connection tugged at him, just out of reach.

He grabbed another form.

Something about the writing bothered him—aside from the wash of guilt in knowing that Barbara had covered for him. He pulled as many of the requisition forms he could find with her odd handwriting.

"Letterhead would do, but if you really want it be seen, use the form," Elsa said. "The university loves forms. Here you are."

Tobias tucked the papers into his messenger bag. First, he had to get this letter written. He smiled gratefully as she rose from the chair. "Thank you."

She nodded, hesitating at the door.

"Is there anything else?" he asked, keeping his voice relaxed.

"This is for Barbara Svobodová, right?" she said, surprising him.

"It is."

Bright spots of color appeared above her cheekbones. "She and I were in Information and Resource Organization together. I wouldn't have passed that class if not for her. It's shameful the way they treat—treated her. I...I want to help her."

"This has been a big help, thank you." Tobias gestured at the computer. "I'm going to get her back. I promise."

♠

"Welcome ho—" His mother's greeting trailed off behind him as Tobias hurried to shuck off his shoes and race down the hall. In his room, he dumped his bag on the floor and fished out the requisitions forms. He grabbed the clearest one, then stumbled over the mess on the way to his desk. He studied the firm, closely spaced letters, and the evenness between words. Even without the line beneath them, he bet they would have been as orderly as soldiers marching down a field. A slight right tilt. A familiar tilt.

He dug around until he found the note that led him to the Tribonacci sequence.

He set the two papers side by side and flipped on the study light. The answer stared him in the face.

Tobias replayed it in his mind. Barbara's hesitant face when she'd brought the book up. The night of the break-in and the lock tumblers opening before she'd completed the sequence. A sequence they both knew wouldn't work. He'd watched her try it multiple times before they'd been interrupted.

Barbara the wonder researcher, the code breaker, the witch. *It's what we do that counts more than what we say, anyway.*

He sank into the chair. The world stacked the deck against Barbara Svobodová at every turn. If something in her blood made her exceptional at her chosen field, who was he to decide she shouldn't use it?

They were alike—more than they seemed—but her secret was a boon. One perhaps safer to dismiss as luck or a fluke. Given the state of the world, it would be wise. He needed help. It was time to face the truth.

◆

"When did you know you were a witch?"

Atop her post on the tall chair near the kitchen sink, Beryl Gilman-Vogel took an enormous breath, exhaling it with a little laugh. "Is that all? I thought—oh, never mind. Damn shells have me jumping at shadows. Come on, let's have some tea."

She unfolded her legs and found her favorite teapot.

Tobias paced the kitchen with such fervor the kitchen towels rustled in his wake as she boiled water. He knew from experience it would be useless to pester her.

Being something of an enigma seemed second nature to his mother. Though ever attentive to her children's practical needs, Beryl had never been an effusive parent—the Vogel siblings had their father for words of warning and advice, and comfort when a risk turned to injury. Instead, she meted out affection and discipline with a clear eye and even hand, but largely let them learn their own lessons through experience while she pursued her own peculiar study.

With her curious "old family traditions," a funny-smelling ointment for every ailment, and the yoga mat rolled up in the corner ready for whenever inspiration struck, she wasn't like any of the other mothers they knew. She was just as likely to treat a cut with a sternly worded incantation and a piece of chocolate as a bandage, before returning to the pursuit of a perfect blend of tea for a rainy afternoon. Growing up, the siblings both adored and feared her. They had always known her devotion to them was equal only to her craft. They just never spoke of it.

The stream of hot water in her favorite teapot released the aroma of a jasmine blend with an unnerving hint of bergamot. As though she knew. "Cups, Tobias."

Obediently, he retrieved two from the stack she'd accumulated as gifts over the years. He went with the one that read, "Is there any tea in this spaceship?"

She laughed at his pick before herding him into the living room. While the tea steeped, she sat across from him on the couch and spoke as if this was a subject they discussed most afternoons.

"I've always known," she said. "My mother told me when I was small. Your grandmother—well, I'm sorry you kids never got to really know her—she was something. The women in my family, at least one, have always been witches. Some of them practiced alone, others formed up in groups. Covens. A few tried to forget who they were but were drawn back."

She poured the tea and raised her brows hopefully.

He eyed his cup, then interlaced his fingers on his lap. "Could you have ever...I don't know...not known?"

She sighed, cradling her own cup in her strong, thin fingers. "I suppose, if no one told me or taught me to use the abilities I have."

"And what if you didn't?"

Her brows twitched. "Know, or choose not to?"

"Either," he said. "Maybe if it wasn't strong enough, or you could just write it off as a weird talent."

Now she looked at him as though he'd suggested shifting into a wolf was a party trick akin to tying a cherry stem with one's tongue. He refused to let that look cow him, or force him to back down. He needed to hear her say it.

"You know, what may be taken for *talent* is usually just a lack of craft-work—practice," she said, a touch of petulance in her voice. "Often it takes an older witch, a mentor, to help a young witch hone their skills." Her shoulders lifted and fell. "With a thing like this, I think you have to use it. It isn't pretty for the ones who don't. You either embrace it, or it devours you." She sipped from her cup. "Mmm. This is almost the perfect blend."

Tobias shifted impatiently. She wasn't done yet. Nor was she clueless about what he was really asking.

His suspicion was confirmed when she met his eyes and asked, "Why do you suspect she doesn't know what she is?"

"I think she knows something, but she's afraid," he admitted. "And maybe she should be. You taught us to avoid attracting the attention of the necromancer at all costs."

"I was young, and we were new here." She frowned. "I was trying to protect you as best I could. If he came anywhere near you kids now, he has no idea what he'd stir up."

Tobias exhaled. "You can't protect us from the world."

"Maybe not," she said, undaunted. "But I can try. I always have, always will, Tobias Vogel. That's my job."

Something in his chest kicked.

She shook her head at him with a little smile. "Tell me about your witch. The one from the library."

Tobias lowered his brows at her. "How do you always do that?"

She sipped her tea and smiled serenely.

He picked up his cup as he contemplated what to tell his mother. Barbara was his to protect, but her secret was her own. He had to talk to her first, see how much she knew.

Chris bounded in, saving him from having to answer. "Pack your bag, brother. Mark is on his way. We've got some howling at the moon to do."

The wolf rose in him at his brother's summoning. Tobias thought of Barbara and a conversation they needed to have. "I wasn't planning on—"

"Go," Beryl said. "It will do you good, and whatever you have at work will hold."

Tobias looked at her for a long moment. She stared back, unblinking. Tobias looked away first. He drained his cup and rose, feeling somehow lighter and more peaceful than before.

"Thank you, Mom."

"You're welcome, son," she chuckled with exaggerated gravity. Her face lightened. "I'm here. Now go keep your brothers out of trouble. You always were the smart one."

"Ma, I'm standing right here!" Chris protested.

"Ah, but you are the handsome one."

Chris puffed his chest and grinned at Tobias. "Told you."

Tobias tried not to laugh as he leaned forward to lay a kiss on his mother's cheek. She raised her brows and sipped her tea. "Almost there. More orange peel, perhaps."

Tobias laughed, bergamot and oranges. She was always a step ahead of him. "What did you think I was going to ask you about—"

His mother shook her head. "Never mind that."

CHAPTER TWENTY-FOUR

IN SPITE of her determination to embrace her change in circumstances, Barbara spent the next two days in her pajamas surrounded by a pile of tattered paperbacks and a few bottles of wine. On the third morning, she woke up with the imprint of a book spine on her cheek.

On the wall beside the window, a framed diploma—Monika Svobodová, PhD, Linguistics—caught the morning light.

The only thing that mattered were the two rules.

She'd told herself she wanted to work in the library to use her grace safely and without too much attention. But she'd been using it in the shop for years beside Veronika. Why had she never allowed that to be good enough?

Time to let her mother's dream go.

As for the moment on the tram with Tobias—Professor Vogel—well, grief did strange things to people. She must have inflated it in her mind. He hadn't called or come by the store to check on her, and what reason would he have to do either? He'd probably been assigned a replacement before she'd been let go.

She took a shower, tied back her hair, and dressed in corduroy pants and a tank top. Then she removed the diploma from the wall and slipped it onto the top of a bookshelf. No more mourning for a door that was now closed; she would instead look to the one that had just opened up.

She paused at Veronika's apartment door, one hand on the handle.

She couldn't quite face it yet, though she could feel the buzzing of her sternum drawing her there. With a long, shuddering sigh, she turned to the shop instead.

At the basement door, she paused with the key in hand.

She didn't really need it, did she? She hovered her finger over the handle and whispered a suggestion.

The lock clicked and the knob turned. The door swung open.

Downstairs, she opened the shutters, turned on the lights, and surveyed the mess. Then she put Veronika's favorite Juliette Gréco record on and got to work.

By noon, she feared she was going to be picking up books off the floor forever. Her back ached. The shelves and scattered books were in hardly better shape than they had been hours ago.

There are other ways, you know.

The hair rose on the back of Barbara's neck. The shop was empty. No one had spoken. She thought of the library books that had appeared on her desk at the university as if by magic.

She lifted her right hand and several books floated from the floor. They followed her fingertips, swinging to a shelf and settling like roosting hens.

A shiver rushed through her.

The most alarming thing was how natural it felt. She couldn't even muster the proper shock over what she'd done. She snuck a look around the shop, worried that someone had seen her, but she hadn't opened for business and the basement windows put her at the ankle level of most pedestrians.

Taking a breath to fortify herself, she raised her left hand this time, palm up. One of the bookshelves rose upright.

"Well, bibbitty bobbitty boo."

A chill ran over her. She'd always dismissed her abilities as minor, a step outside human skills. But this was more.

She made a mental list of all the books in the shop that might have to do with ESP and telekinesis. Prescience could be considered a kind of grace. She added the witch sisters who founded Prague and Joan of Arc and Nostradamus. She may no longer work in special collections, but even students on leave could access the library. If she needed anything in special collections, Edita owed her a few favors anyway. She had to find out more about what she could do, what she was, and the library was the best place to start.

A sound at the front door followed by a familiar meow startled her out of her thoughts. She raced up the stairs. The door unlocked and opened before she could reach for the key, and a rugby ball-sized calico cat raced down the stairs.

Barbara laughed, giddy. "Hemi!"

Leaves clung to the matted tangles in the cat's fur. She purred ferociously against Barbara's legs. Barbara didn't realize she was weeping until she scooped the cat up in her arms and the calico began to lick at her cheeks.

She flicked her free hand behind her, and the door lock slid into place. "You're safe now. You're safe."

Time to put her skills to use for herself.

CHAPTER TWENTY-FIVE

TOBIAS TRIED to get in contact with Barbara for a week after her dismissal to no avail. He'd left messages with both Edita and Honza that she hadn't returned. He'd tried the shop, but it was still closed, and his voicemail got no response. Feeling guilty, he'd filched her number from the personnel department and left messages at her personal number. Still no answer.

Finally, he put on his running clothes and battered trainers and did what he always did when he felt at loose ends. For once, his mother was not perched on her kitchen stool when he left for his run. Humidity that would become standard as the days wore into summer descended over the evening. The afternoon air had been thicker than usual, the sunlight obscured by a growing layer of clouds. He snugged his laces and raced a storm out of Vysehrad and into the city proper.

Running had always been his refuge. The thing he loved most was the way it shut off his thoughts, especially when circumstances had made it hard for him to change as much as he needed. That was the beginning of his reputation as being difficult.

After regular weekends at the cabin, he understood how much he'd been missing by denying the wolf its due. He was calmer at work and what had once been a maelstrom of overwhelming scent became something he could sift through to identify useful bits of information in social interactions. He hadn't felt the stammer building in days, but his reflexes had become too sharp and it took effort to manage his strength. Once, he'd entered the lab so quietly he'd startled Jakub enough that younger man dropped the sample tray he'd been carrying. Catching the tray before it hit the ground and spilled its contents had earned Tobias even stranger looks.

Tonight, he let his speed pulse in the growing dark, ignoring a few startled gasps as he raced past.

At the base of the hill into Vinohrady, he tucked his chin and pushed his body until his lungs burned. Still, his legs propelled him effortlessly up the hill.

He slowed before a familiar secessionist building the color of an Easter mint. The shop was closed, and the windows of the first-floor apartment were dark. The top-floor windows were open, and thin strains of music drifted out as the curtains flapped in and out at regular intervals. A fan must have been running: the outside air was still and heavy, as if each molecule held the weight of a coming raindrop.

He stood at the base of the steps, chest heaving, and contemplated his next move.

He pressed the door buzzer.

Barbara's voice crackled on the intercom. "Yes?"

"I'm sorry to bother you at home," he said, rubbing the back of his neck guiltily. "It's Tobias Vogel. From the University."

A long pause. It felt wrong to be here like this, but he couldn't have made himself stay away any longer.

Correction, he couldn't have made the wolf stay away. It yearned for her with a dazzling purity of sensation he could not name. The same sensation coursed through him at the sight of his brothers in wolf form, completed him when they ran together as a pack. So far human words in any language fell short in naming it. He would wonder over an emotion unknown to humans later. For now he let it be his guide.

He stepped back, craning his neck to look up at the open windows. A small, familiar hand pulled the curtain aside and she appeared. With the light at her back, he couldn't see her expression, only the small shake of her head. She disappeared inside.

The speaker crackled before she said, "I'm sorry, this isn't a good time."

"I apologize. I tried to get in touch during business hours, but I just need to know..." His voice drifted off and he let the button go. *What? That she's a witch?*

"I no longer work for the department." Her voice buckled. Was that the speaker or something more?

There'd been no response to his request for an investigation to her termination or any of his letters.

He sighed and pressed the microphone button. "I have no right to ask you to see me, but I need to ask you about the note...in the art book."

"I have no idea what you mean." Another long pause before the speaker crackled again. "Good night, Professor Vogel."

Tobias sighed and trotted down the steps. A fat drop of rain hit him on the cheek. Great. He wiped his face on his arm and looked up. He cupped his hands around his mouth and shouted, "I'm not leaving until you talk to me. Please."

She appeared between the curtains, glancing up and down the street. "It's going to pour. I suggest you find somewhere dry."

"You didn't return my calls," he bellowed back.

"That's not my job anymore," she said, disappearing from the window.

That hit him harder than he expected. For her, he had been a job, an assignment. At first. But he had proof that it had become more than that for both of them.

He lifted his hands, cupping his mouth. "You broke the code. Yes or no?"

The curtains were flung aside with a fury. "This is a quiet neighborhood, and you're causing a disturbance!"

The rain increased. He backed under the sapling growing out of an open square of cobblestone and folded his arms across his chest.

"Suit yourself," she said. The window slammed shut.

The sky boomed once, and the clouds released a torrent of rain. Standing in the dark, soaked to the bone, he stared up at the light in her window with his jaw clenched. A few people out walking their dogs, or hurrying to get out of the downpour, glanced disapprovingly at him as they scurried along.

He planted his feet.

Goose bumps sprang up on his arms and legs, and sweat mixed with rain to form an itchy coating on his skin. He counted the droplets falling off the leaf overhead. He was in triple digits when the building door opened and she appeared, wearing some kind of long draping swath of fabric.

"Are you crazy?"

He shrugged, trying not to shiver.

"Go home," she said. "I can't help you. Not anymore."

Something broken in her voice made him stand up a little straighter. He wanted to go to her, but wouldn't risk scaring her again.

He remembered her alone in the campus security office. How had she looked on the day they told her to pack her belongings and go home? And with Veronika gone, who did she have to lean on?

"You have been helping me all along," he insisted.

"I have no idea what you're talking about."

The rain thickened, and he had to raise his voice over the roar. "Let me tell you a story about Fibonacci sequences."

"Tribonacci," she corrected before her hand flew to her mouth.

"Exactly." Tobias shifted on his feet, soggy and triumphant.

CHAPTER TWENTY-SIX

BARBARA LED the way up the stairs in silence.

She couldn't let Prague's preeminent expert on rare materials collections catch pneumonia on her porch, could she? She could barely make out the squelching of running shoes on the steps behind her over the sound of rain and her own heart.

Behind her, Tobias huffed a little sigh.

She looked back in time to see him wipe water from his hair with one forearm and almost tripped over the next step. His skin shone with the sheen of rain and the flush of exercise. Just a guy out for a run.

It was the first time she'd seen him in anything other than a suit. The old trainers, t-shirt, and running shorts made him appear younger, less distinguished.

A runner. That explained the lean, rippled legs coated in fine hair and the tight mound of his backside. Hallelujah, that. The body that had brushed against hers as she held the building door for him was more muscular than she'd expected, the water-slicked t-shirt doing incredible things to his arms and chest.

When they reached the attic stairwell, she veered off the steps to her front door. He almost stumbled into her, catching himself at the last minute in a startlingly graceful quickstep, his hands on her shoulders.

"Sorry," he muttered, dropping his fingers.

But the sensation of his touch lingered. She resisted the urge to place her hand over the imagined imprint of the contact. She unlocked the door. "There are a few more steps inside. Let me get you a towel."

He shucked off his shoes on the little rubber mat in the entryway. He didn't seem bothered by the long climb. He waited, dripping but not winded.

She hurried up the steps into the main room, glancing around in a panic. She gathered an armful of clothes and tossed them into the free-standing wardrobe, dragging the comforter off the couch as she passed and fluffing the throw pillows. She dumped it in the oversized closet she'd turned into a bedroom and closed the curtain dividing the rooms before darting into the bathroom for extra towels. When she emerged, she gave her flat one last assessment, frowning at the stack of paperbacks on the coffee table and the nearly empty bottle of wine.

Too late for that lot.

She returned to find him in a puddle in her entryway. She threw a towel at his feet and handed him a second. The sight of his biceps flexing as he dragged the towel over his face and arms made the air in the room seem thinner than normal.

She was in trouble.

"I may have an extra t-shirt that will fit you..." She took the excuse to make a second pass through the space, shoving a cork in the wine before rummaging through the dresser beside the bedroom.

When she turned around, he came slowly up the stairs, one towel around his waist over the wet t-shirt, the other patting his hair. But his eyes were on the walls. His mouth slightly agape, he did a slow turn, taking it all in.

Barbara straightened. She was a librarian, what did he expect?

She tried to see it through his eyes. No more than five hundred square feet, the attic loft had been converted to a studio apartment but forgotten until Veronika had let it to her years ago. The ceilings sloped steeply toward the center of the room, reflecting the shape of the roof, with skylights between the exposed wooden beams. The small galley kitchen with a basin sink, hot plate, and mini fridge opened up to the combination dining and living room.

One wall in the front of the building had a little dormer window that formed a natural alcove from inside. She'd turned that into a reading seat, though most of the place was set up so that any spot was a good one to curl up with a book. The walls were lined in shelves, and all of them packed with books.

She wouldn't be embarrassed or feel small. Least of all with this man.

His eyes found hers again and there it was, the dimple that undid her every time it appeared with that rare, brilliant smile. "Pineapples."

"Pineapples?" she stammered.

He reached out and tapped a grinning cartoon caricature on the nearest bookshelf. With arms extended on a round base, it rocked a few times, appearing to wave before settling. "You have a lot of them."

"I like them," she shrugged, feeling the tension ease out of her shoulders. "And everyone who knows me keeps their eye out for them. Veronika gives me one every year for my birthday... well, she did."

Barbara blinked hard to ward off the tears.

The smile faded from his face and was replaced with concern. She shook her head, unable to bear the reminder of how comfortable she'd been with him. How safe. Bringing him up here was a terrible idea. There wasn't enough room for her to change her mind, and no way of keeping a safe distance from her attraction to him.

"Barbara—"

She held up the bundle of clothes she'd retrieved before he could finish. They would wait out the rain and she would figure out how to get him to let this go, and then he would go away and she wouldn't have to see him again. "You can change. Bathroom is that way."

◆

TOBIAS EMERGED from the bathroom after wringing out his soggy clothes and doing his best to make himself presentable. The old Žižkov University gym shirt stretched tight across his chest and the dark gray sweatpants were too short and hugged his butt in uncomfortable places.

Thank goodness his brothers couldn't see him. Mark would never let him live this down.

The kettle whistled and Barbara pulled it off the burner. "Would you like some tea or coffee?"

"Coffee," he said, "if you have it. I'm not much of a tea drinker."

She moved into the kitchen, pulling open the cupboard and rummaging through the contents.

"Ha!" She emerged victorious, holding up a crumpled foil bag just bigger than a deck of cards. "I had a dinner party a while back, must be a leftover." She gave the contents a little sniff. "It smells fine."

From where he stood, the contents smelled like the petrified remnants of what might have once been coffee, but guilt at barging into her apartment made him bite his tongue. He would drink the stale coffee, by the gods, and he would like it. Or put on a good show. He owed her at least that much.

Barbara resumed her rummaging until she dug up a cone drip apparatus and a paper filter.

He waited, hands behind his back, unable to resist the temptation to stare at the contents of her bookshelves. Professional interest gave way to amusement.

Alongside a thorough collection of classic literature and books on library sciences were hundreds of novels: romance and pulp science fiction. He recognized titles he and his brothers had stolen from their father's office as kids.

At the counter, she poured hot water with the precision of a chemist in the lab. Her brows knit low as she peered into the cup. Curious, he relied on his wolf senses at the next inhale, and her magic bloomed as the coffee took on a warmer, fresher scent. He fought the urge to tell her to stop using her abilities for something so insignificant—that he wasn't worth it.

His throat closed on the words. That scent was a part of his childhood and the surest way he knew he was loved.

She moved on to her own cup of tea, and the scent faded, leaving behind the rich chocolate and nut aroma of coffee and the lighter leaf and flower scent of the jasmine green. The scents came closer, and she rose on her tiptoes to see what he'd pulled from the shelf.

"*Dragon's Island*," she said, waggling her eyebrows. "'*She was a century ahead of her sex.*'"

He laughed, setting the book down to accept the cup she offered. "I read this when I was nine or ten, I think."

"It wasn't his best. That was—"

"*Darker Than You Think*," they finished in unison.

She took a sip of her tea, focusing on the shelves. He lifted his own cup and took a cautious sip, followed by another. He stared into the cup, amazed. Pulp science fiction and delicate laundry and a cup of coffee that tasted like something grown, roasted, and poured from heaven.

He must have made a sound because her eyes darted to him before returning to the shelves. The fearful optimism in them almost undid him.

"I mean, *Dragon's Island* is recycled from *Darker*," she murmured. "You can pretty much tell from the first chapter. It's just more science fiction than horror. And the ending's more optimistic."

"This is the best cup of coffee I've ever had."

Her eyes, wide and round, shone in the light. For a moment, he thought he'd said the wrong thing, but when the corners of her mouth bunched and the bridge of her nose wrinkled, he knew he had said it right. He would do whatever it took to make her look at him like that forever.

◆

BARBARA TRIED to keep her gaze anywhere but his Adam's apple bobbing as he drank.

His face had been too lean and sharp in the dark on the night of the robbery—inhuman. She considered the book he slid back onto the shelf. Shapeshifters. Wasn't that the plot of *Darker*? Necromancers and touches of grace were one thing. But humans that transformed into animals? That was just outrageous.

When he looked at her again, all she could think of was his breath, light on her mouth, and his arm on her waist on the tram before the robbery. The way he kept her from being jerked around like a rag doll and set his body between her and the thieves in the shop.

He set down his cup and drew a plastic pastry bag from his pocket. As he gingerly unfolded the damp papers within, dread blossomed rotten petals in the pit of her stomach. A second piece of paper—the familiar pink carbon copy of a special materials requisition form—had been tucked inside.

He caught her hand, placing both in her palm. His fingers were still warm from his cup and he closed them around hers briefly, trapping the papers before letting her go. "Please, tell me how you did this."

He lifted his cup and took a long sip.

She examined the triplicate form and squinted up at him. "You have to press hard or the information won't make it through to the carbon copy and the records department gets testy if they can't read it."

That dimple flashed again as he tapped the notebook paper. "And this one."

"What are you doing out running on a night like this?" she challenged, setting the papers on the bookshelf. "You should have known it was going to pour."

"I needed the exercise," he said, redirecting. "Leaving aside for a moment that you should have refused my requests without the proper forms, the handwriting is the same. I know you broke the code to the journal, Barbara."

Panic tightened iron bars around her chest.

All the way up the steps, she was convinced she could somehow talk herself out of this. Hearing him say it, the commitment and confidence in his voice, made it real. Forged signatures on paperwork were the least of her worries. Now she could lose everything—she could be made to disappear, her whole life erased.

What would become of the shop, and the building, and Hemingway, and poor old Mrs. Milanova?

She forced a laugh. "Really, Professor—"

"Tobias," he corrected, a gleam in his eye that was as unfamiliar as it was intriguing as he edged closer. "Though my siblings call me Toby."

"How many?" She took a step back, her shoulder blades and rear bumping against the bookshelves.

He blinked, head cocked in confusion. "How many what?"

"Siblings do you have?"

One eyebrow arched over the top of his frames. "Two brothers and a sister."

"Older, younger?"

"Both." The line of his mouth swept up in a subtle curve.

She swallowed hard and tore her eyes away from the faded Žižkov University logo stretched over his pectorals. "Do they all live…here?"

"In this apartment?" The reappearance of his dimple set her focus whirling like a top. "No. Where would I put them with all the books?"

Laughter bubbled up her throat before she strangled it. "The books add insulation."

His smile flared before deepening to something more intense. "Barbara—"

"In the city." The words left her in a rush of startled air, cutting him off.

He planted his hands on his hips and stared up at the ceiling with a long exhale. When he met her eyes again a perplexing warmth unraveled her resolve with every breath. He huffed.

"My entire family lives in Prague. My parents are retired, though my mom teaches yoga in her studio. My older brother works in construction and has his own place in our building. My younger sister has basically lived at the Praha Dance Academy since she was twelve. We're lucky if she comes home for dinner once in a while. I'm convinced my little brother is never going to leave the nest. My turn. Why did you let me think I solved it?"

A vast chasm opened at the edge of her toes and threatened to suck her into its depths.

"Well, you did, didn't you," she said weakly. "Once you had the key."

"The key that you wrote." The timbre of his voice rolled through her, raising the fine hairs on her arms to attention. She snagged her lower lip in her teeth in helpless response. A shudder swept him, visible when the sleeve edges of his t-shirt quivered. "Codebreaker."

She swallowed hard. "I picked up a stray request for Edita. From the math department. I opened this book, and I just saw it."

"The key?"

She nodded and pressed her lips together. That wasn't a lie, not exactly.

"But you only saw the journal for a few moments."

"I have a good memory." She crossed her arms over her chest.

His eyes narrowed. "Eidetic?"

She shrugged. It wasn't unheard of. It was a bit like being a pitch-perfect musician—rare, but not impossible. Time to change the subject. "My turn. Tell me how you knew how to fight those guys in the shop."

"My brothers and I fought a lot as kids—hell, even Issy can throw a punch. I learned a few tricks. What did you do to the safe?"

Barbara's heart skittered against her ribcage. Not that. She wasn't ready to talk about that, maybe not ever. "How did you get strong enough to throw that guy across the room?"

"I work out on the weekends." He smirked, and his shoulders rose and fell in mockery of her shrug.

She stepped into his space a half second before she realized what a mistake that was. This close his eyes were the color of ashes banking a flame. She'd mistakenly thought that by getting him to confess what happened in the shop that made him look non-human, he wouldn't be able to betray her, not without risking whatever secret he guarded. Belatedly she realized didn't want to gain leverage. She wanted to trust.

"You threw him *across the room*." Her voice sounded breathless even to her own ears.

All the humor fled his face as he set his coffee cup down on top of the papers on the bookshelf. "I was afraid they were going to hurt you. I couldn't let that happen."

She tilted her face up, unable to resist the gravity of his gaze. She licked her lips nervously, and his gaze flickered, fixated for a long moment on her mouth. He shook his head, rubbing his palm over his chin, and stepped away. That step left every nerve in her body singing the loss of closeness to him.

His chin met his chest. "I promised I wouldn't."

♦

TOBIAS WAS in so much trouble.

Barbara was alight with a wary desire even as confusion pinched a line between her brows. The combination was intoxicating.

"After what happened on the tram," he ground out. "I promised I wouldn't do anything like that again."

"Like what?"

The words escaped him as though pursued by the wolf in his chest. "Try to kiss you."

Shy charm swept across her face. "But, Professor, it was I who tried to kiss you."

That sealed it. Whatever this was, whatever she was, he was there for it, and for her. But it didn't matter what *he* wanted. He took a breath, considering his next words carefully. "Is that what you still want?"

A litany of words escaped with her next exhale.

He laughed. "Come again, please."

She cleared her throat. "'Stand tall, wear a crown, keep your sweetness on the inside: like a pineapple.' It's what my mom always said to me when people treated me differently, or stared, because of how I looked. She found it on a postcard. She died when I was 14."

His breath tangled in his throat.

"It's why there are so many pineapples." Her voice shrank with her next words. "I picked them up wherever I found them, and then my friends, my colleagues, caught on to it, and it just became a thing. But I never told anyone why before."

Bottomless russet eyes stared up at him, eyes he could lose himself in.

"If you still want… to kiss me, I want that too."

Kiss her? Hell, after that, he wanted to wrap himself around her so that nothing could touch her with malice ever again. She may not wear a crown, but he would make her his queen if she let him.

She exhaled and lay one small hand over his heartbeat with a sad little smile. "It's okay if you change your—"

"Be quiet." It came out sharper than he'd have liked. But he couldn't have her doubting herself—or him. Not for one moment.

Her eyes widened, and she tried to pull back, but he was faster.

He swept her up as though she was spun gold, surprised to find her solid and warm in his arms—not fragile at all. The lines of her soft, curving body fit against him so well. They were made for each other. It left him wondering how they'd managed to avoid this for so long.

It took every bit of restraint to be tender, plying his lips to hers as he would touch a priceless manuscript.

That first touch was everything: the summation of his excitement, the hope for what he might find, a test of the resilience of the materials at hand. It would tell him how to proceed. Whether he would require delicate instruments and velvet touch, or if it would tolerate more confident handling.

The mouth that met his exceeded his wildest imaginings.

They clacked teeth as she rose to meet him in eagerness. A smile tightened his lips for the sheerest instant and then he gave himself over to convincing her she was in the best care.

The smallest sensations overtook him, the swell of her lower lip against his, the way hers parted when he gave her breath and stayed that way when he returned for more. The warm, wet depths that opened to his exploration, and the tongue that met his.

Desire tasted like the sweetness and tang of forest honey, and the green tea that lingered in her mouth.

Nothing in his experience prepared him for the instant, overwhelming sense of belonging. Or the desperate yearning when they parted. He needed her like he needed his heart to pump the blood through his veins. He may have started it, but he couldn't help feeling like she had possessed him in a single sweep of tongue and soft lips.

At the sight of her mouth, glistening and swollen, a sudden painful pressure rose his groin, and he bit down hard on a moan. Her lashes swept away her cheeks, revealing the thin bands of her irises, flecked with lighter bits of hazel and edged so dark they were almost black.

"I hope you didn't think a few dozen pineapples would change my mind," he murmured.

CHAPTER TWENTY-SEVEN

"THIRTY-TWO," Barbara whispered, adding when he paused, bewildered, "pineapples."

Whatever response he might have made was lost in the next kiss. Her arms swept up around his neck, committing herself to contact with the improbable reality that was Tobias Vogel.

Sometime in that next, interminable claiming, he'd braced one hand against the bookshelf over her head. She hadn't noticed a release of support. Instead, his single arm had made up the difference by gripping her against him like she was the last flotation on a sinking ship.

The shelves crowded into her shoulders, back, rear, and calves, but the sensation was distant. More pressing was the enormous trembling man in her arms. Every unforgiving inch of him conformed her body to his.

The trembling undid her, the vulnerability a tender contrast to his strength.

The surrounding arm loosened just enough for his palm to draw her spine away from the wooden shelves, skimming her shoulder blades and her low back. His brows drew down. "Still okay?"

She pushed up onto her toes and reached for the mouth that had rendered her so senseless. It was good of him to help her with the height difference, she considered, when his hand slid to the base of her rear and he lifted her off her feet altogether. She gasped at the casual power in the movement; her legs parting and seating his erection in the junction of her thighs as his mouth closed the distance to hers.

The tingling flooded her ears, the tickling warmth stretching lower and making her limbs full and heavy. The dim awareness of him pushing off the bookshelf and his hands at the base of her thighs, securing her legs around his hips before the unsteady stumble across the room.

"Table," she muttered into his mouth, waving a hand behind her in what she hoped was a valid directional gesture toward the miniature farm table at the wall between the kitchen and the living room.

The wooden edge took her weight, but his height left him arched over her.

His hands skated up her hips to her waist before his palms curved over her shoulder blades. She was sure he could feel the wild beat of her heart through skin and bone and cloth. His fingertips slipped along her nape, stroking the tiny hairs with feather-light brushes that robbed her of the ability to draw more than a shallow breath.

The slopes and angles of his back and shoulders rose against her fingertips, firm like the spines of books on a shelf. He was, she delighted in discovering, warmer to the touch than any man she'd ever been with. He smelled of rain and coffee and the faintest trace of sweat from his run. Beneath it all was a familiar scent she couldn't name.

He still hadn't brought his hands from her shoulders, kneading them with an unmistakable strength as his mouth moved to her jawline and the column of her throat.

Maybe he just needed a little encouragement.

His shirt came off under her insistent fingers, and a groan tore from the depths of his chest.

She slipped her hands down to the waistband of the sweatpants and over the firm mounds of his ass. Gods, it was the most perfect, firm thing in her palms. She couldn't help it; she gave it a hard squeeze, hoping it served as appreciation and an invitation.

Tobias gripped her shoulders hard, drawing her back. His breath came in pants and, with distance between them, the sight of his lightly furred chest and the line of dark hair beneath his bellybutton disappearing into his pants transfixed her.

Her name strangled in his throat, a plea for mercy.

She strained forward to lick the salty skin beneath the shadow of his jawline.

He growled and she drew back, eyes wide. He immediately looked chagrined, like a puppy caught chewing a shoe. She pushed hair off his forehead with her finger tips. It had gotten longer in the last few weeks, but unkempt looked good on him. It reminded her of hot chocolate, with threads of honey in the thick waves.

"You need a haircut," she teased to break the tension.

At his distress, she regretted even that. She pushed his glasses back up his nose.

"I like it," she said, threading her fingers through the back to tug him closer. "You look...wild."

This time the growl sounded softer, more inviting.

His hands settled at her hips. He closed his eyes, and she realized that his trembling had increased at the contact. When her fingertips followed the curve of his ear, he leaned his head into her touch but did not speak.

"Is something wrong?"

He shook his head, but his eyes sealed shut and he turned his face away from her. Her heart did a free dive in her ribcage, sinking desire with it and leaving behind a seashell's echoing chorus of why he wouldn't want her.

And yet.

How dare he show up soaking wet with his big gray eyes devouring her every move like a hungry animal. Did he think he could just come into her apartment demanding answers, and bring her to her edge with a few kisses and that caveman grab and carry then walk away when she reached back? If he rejected her now, she was going to kick him out of her apartment, bare-chested in the pouring rain, pneumonia take him.

"I haven't ever..." He forced the words between gritted teeth. Ashen eyes blinked open, staring into her with such naked uncertainty the breath caught in her throat. "I want you so much."

The ache broke in her like waves on stone. "I want you, too. I want this."

He kept her hipbones cradled in his palms but without the previous urgency.

She understood what he meant by feeling like he couldn't say the right thing, no matter how hard he tried. So she said what she meant. "Don't stop now."

His eyes flew to her face, the desire in them breathtaking. He kissed her, long and hard enough to leave her light-headed and struggling for breath.

He nipped at her lower lip, working small wet kisses along her jaw to her ear with the words. "It's just I've never...been with...anyone."

The words came together in her head slower than any ever had because by then his mouth was on her earlobe, teasing it with his lips. Understanding splashed like cold water on her skin.

She drew back. "You what?"

He sighed and pushed his glasses up his nose. He was as pink as spring roses. He didn't speak, and she realized he was struggling with his stammer.

She prayed for control. "*You* are a virgin?"

The blood raged in his face, and he coughed with the thwarted attempt to speak.

Barbara realized what was happening a moment too late and reached for him, but he pulled away, finding his shirt.

"This was a m-m-mistake," he said. "I didn't c-c-come here to—"

"Oh no," she said, flinging herself off the table and grabbing at the length of cloth in his hands before he could sort it into a neck and armholes. "You don't get to run away from me after *that*."

She bit down on her tongue in an effort not to laugh, but it was so unbelievable.

"You can't expect me to believe," she breathed, "that you...you're..."

He whirled on her. She expected anger. Not confusion. Hurt. Her laughter died.

"An inexperienced boy?" The words fired out like a machine gun before slowing again. "This is all w-w-wrong."

She grabbed his arm, digging in her heels and flinging herself backward. She wasn't strong enough. All she had were her words. "You make me want to come just by kissing me."

He froze, shirt forgotten in one hand.

"It just doesn't seem possible," she said. "Because you're so good at...that."

He sighed. "I-I-I didn't say I'd never kissed a woman or made out. I don't need this"—he gestured at his crotch—"to make you come."

The stark admission sent a shiver through her. She swallowed hard. *Ooh la la.*

His nostrils flared as if he was scenting her desire. "In fact if *that's* what I was depending on, I'd say I was doing it wrong."

Swoon.

She stared, trying to decide if this meant she would be taking advantage of him—or corrupting him irreparably—if she asked him to prove it.

He swept his free hand through his hair and it stood up at odd angles. "I haven't ever wanted this...with anyone...like I want you."

"Are you abstaining?"

His laugh stuttered on embarrassment. "Gods no. I was just... busy. With work and school."

Part of her understood that. He was one of the youngest professors on the Žižkov faculty, visiting or otherwise. She'd done the math—he'd completed his doctorate at the age most started their programs. That took more than intelligence. It took single-minded focus and dedication. But...really?

Disbelief colored her words. "Too busy to get laid?"

His shoulders heaved in an enormous sigh. He tugged this shirt down over his head, and part of her mourned the loss of the view.

"I'm just trying to understand how a man like you..." she said, waving her hands.

He flushed again, eyes rolling upward. "Like me?"

"You're smart and unbelievably sexy, how is it that somebody hasn't seduced you?"

"It's complicated." He shook his head, but his eyes found hers again, sliding up her body with undisguised longing. "But you..."

"Me?"

Hunger flashed in his eyes again.

"You're one of the sharpest people I've ever met, Barbara Svobodová," he said simply. "And you're so fucking beautiful I can't breathe when you walk into a room. You challenge me, even when your voice shakes, and you're so brilliant at it. I want to be with you. Right here, right now, in whatever form that takes." A little flush colored his cheekbones. "I just want you to know, if we get that far, what you're dealing with. Because if I'm an absolute disaster the first time, that's why."

Tension fled in an extraordinary mix of relief and affection.

She crossed her arms over her chest, fighting for a stern expression, as she stepped backward. "Are you asking me to grade you on a curve, Vogel?"

He lowered his brows, every bit the serious and dedicated student. "Ideally, Professor Svobodová, I was hoping it would be an open book exam."

"I don't know what you're used to at Oxford..." She hummed, tapping her lip as she narrowed her eyes at him. "Here at Ziz U, we have rigorous standards."

"Did I mention I was top of my class?" He approached her slowly, but with unmistakable intention. "Every class."

She stepped out of reach, and it took all her composure to mock a frown. "It appears that some of your education was neglected."

Her rear hit the table.

He kept coming, sliding a hand to the tabletop on either side of her thighs. "I'm a quick student." A shiver raced through her when his mouth brushed her ear. "You won't regret it."

"I don't expect I will." She bit the inside of her cheeks, but the smile broke anyway.

She fisted her hands in his t-shirt and dragged him down.

A handful of kisses later, his shirt was on the floor where it belonged. This time, she straddled his hips on the couch, settled on his lap, and did her best to kiss him as close to orgasm as she was. Which wasn't easy when he got his hands under her tank top. The brush of skin on hers was transcendent.

He stroked her back, trailing the pleasant scrape of nails up the length of her spine.

Ripples of building pressure reduced her to arching and groaning, her fingers in his hair. He cradled her breasts in his palms and brushed the hard pads of his thumbs over her nipples until she ground herself down on him, leaving them both gasping.

He gripped her hips hard, eyes wide and almost panicked. "I'm not going to make it if you keep this up."

He wasn't going to... she almost laughed. "Let's just relieve the pressure."

Before he could protest, she slid off his lap to the floor between his legs. He groaned, trying to stop her, but her hands found the length of him and she sank her teeth into her lower lip. His eyes went hazy with arousal. "I can't. You haven't…"

"We have to start somewhere."

He was hot and hard and salty in her mouth, and the sound that tore from his chest sent a shudder of pleasure between her thighs. He rubbed her neck and shoulders, wordless cries overtaking him until the heat of him boiled over and he went so taut he almost bucked himself out of her mouth. The only sound he could make was her name, begging, pleading.

He was still shaking when he dragged her up onto his chest. He cradled her, rocking and stroking her spine as his breath tickled warmth along her ear. "You are…"

"Experienced."

"That, too," he said. "Amazing."

She laughed, palm splayed over his chest to savor the feel of his pounding heart.

That she could reduce a man this strong to a twitching wreck was a powerful sensation. He never quit stroking her, under the long robe hanging at her elbows, over her thighs and hips, tracing the angles of bent knees and her curling toes.

"I don't suppose you tucked a rubber into your running shorts."

"Between my keys and the cipher a mysterious research assistant left me in an old book," he said, brushing his lips over the curve of her ear. "You have a stash somewhere?"

"Alas," she said, shivering.

She pushed his glasses back up his nose and started to lift herself off his chest, but he held her fast. "Now I get to demonstrate my skill in other subject areas."

"Other—" Her words became a shriek as he swept her off the couch with dizzying power. When he wrapped her legs around his hips, he grunted pleasure.

His mouth hovered over hers. "Do you have a bed in this closet?"

It was her turn to flush. "It's in the closet, actually."

THE CLOSET. Tobias followed her finger toward the little alcove behind the curtain. He shoved through, too fast for her word of warning, and his knees hit the bed and sent them both tumbling onto the mattress. He caught himself on his elbows to keep from crushing her.

She glared up at him. "I tried to warn you."

"You did," he agreed, dipping low to taste the sweet salt of her mouth. "I was in a hurry. Also, I expected more of a room."

She freed herself, wiggling away from him in the dark. She found a little switch on the narrow table nestled between the edge of the bed and the wall. A band of golden light bathed the room. Somehow she'd wedged a bed inside, allowing the main room to be a library and sitting room, and make this tiny apartment seem bigger. She'd draped the ceiling in a myriad of colorful fabrics, a few of the longer pieces trailing down the walls.

The wolf recognized a den when it saw one and approved heartily.

He fiddled with the edge of a saffron linen. "Cozy."

Her gaze fixed over her shoulder. "It's a closet."

He scanned the room again, the plush collection of jewel-toned pillows in sensual textures, the cobalt blue duvet, and, even here, a stack of books piled close to the light. The room resembled the inside of a many-hued cocoon. Her sanctuary. He wiggled up on the bed, pinning her to an enormous electric pink fuzzy throw pillow with his chest.

"It is yours," he said, between kisses. "And I love everything about you."

The word slipped out. His heart stuttered in his chest for one terrifying second. He fought the urge to slap his palm against his forehead. One blow job and he'd proclaimed his love. He'd spent enough time trying to ignore Mark's sermons to Chris about how much women seemed to like a challenge. Here he was throwing his heart at her feet at the first opportunity. He could hear Mark now: *nice one, smart guy.*

Distract her. He slipped his glasses off and set them on the nightstand table.

"Won't need those where I'm headed," he said with a wink.

She was laughing when his mouth slipped over the tight pebble of her nipple. The left. She was more sensitive on the left side; he'd discovered that with his fingers. He wanted to see if it extended beyond her breasts and the tissue-soft skin of her throat.

By the time he reached the inside of her left hip, her breath came in ragged gasps. She threaded her fingers into his hair. The scrape of her nails on his scalp almost undid him. He parted her, rendered breathless by the full, slick depths of her arousal.

He swirled the dampness around the swollen core of her heat until her back bowed. He slipped a finger into her, two, and her voice broke into wordless moans. She bucked when he lay a kiss on the inside of her right thigh, then on the left all the while stroking.

He gave up with a little grin and let his mouth join his busy hand.

She shattered, quenching the long thirst that brought him so far at night, in the rain, searching for answers.

He rode the long waves of pleasure with satisfaction he'd never known.

In the past, this infrequent exchange, with much less affection, had been enough to tide him over. Now, just as roaming the park did not compare to nights in the primeval forests, it only proved how inadequate anything else would ever be again.

CHAPTER TWENTY-EIGHT

IN THE MORNING, they took turns in the narrow shower, Barbara laughing as she fried eggs to the sound of his elbows and knees banging against the walls. Her laughter faded at the sight of her towel wrapped around his waist, the still-damp hip bones emerging above the thin cloth, and the bulge in the towel's front. Sometime before dawn, there had been a delightful repeat of the previous night, but release only left her longing for more. The buzzing began in her chest at the sight of him, tender and warm and ticklish against her ribs.

He rubbed a second towel over his damp hair, squinting like a mole, and sniffed. "Something's about to burn."

She dropped her gaze in time to rescue the eggs. When it occurred to her to wonder how he'd known, he'd disappeared into the bedroom with his clothes.

He emerged dressed in stiff running clothes and wearing his glasses.

She set the plates on the wooden table and went to the counter for coffee and tea. When she returned, he'd put both plates before him. She set the cups down and he grabbed her waist, dragging her onto his lap.

"Too far," he said, sliding a fork across the table to her fingers. "You, all the way over there."

Given the size of her apartment, it was impossible to be too far away from any other thing in the room, but she liked the sentiment. When she bowed her head, his lips closed over the soft skin at her nape in a kiss more tender than hungry.

Midway through breakfast, he spied a square of expensive paper in the stack of mail next to the window.

"What's this?" He plucked it, sipping at his coffee with a contented grumble.

"Invitation," she said around a mouthful of toast. "It's the annual book appraisers' ball in Vienna. Veronika was on the VIP list."

"How did she manage that?"

Barbara glared at him. "Veronika was a respected bookseller. Her father served on the original guild committee that started the ball. She even goes every few years...went."

His hand settled against the curve of her neck as her voice faded. His fingers squeezed, thumb kneading. "It's addressed to you."

She bobbed her head. "Veronika's solicitor notified them of her passing and the transfer of ownership of the shop. And this came to me."

"Slečna Barbora Svobodová and guest."

"They spelled it wrong."

"They spelled the Czech way. How did you come to that spelling?"

"The Czech is a variant." She lifted a finger imperiously. "Barbara. Feminine of the Greek *Barbaros*."

He coughed. "Is that how I look lecturing?"

"Only when they don't keep up with you."

He pressed his mouth to the skin warmed by his palm. The gust of his exhaled laughter tickled her collar. "Foreigner. Stranger. A traveler from a distant land. From which we also have 'barbarian.'"

She snorted. "In use, anyone judged uncivilized or primitive—so, anyone who didn't follow the customs or speak Greek or Latin."

"Snobs didn't know what they were missing. Uncivilized can be fun." His teeth closed lightly on her shoulder with a little growl. "Common root with *barbaras* from Sanskrit—stammering."

Her eyes slid closed when his hand settled on her thigh. "That's more a play on an inability to speak the language. Bar-bar-bar."

"Ah, onomatopoeic hypothesis."

"It shows up in English as 'babble', and maybe even the German—"

"Blabla." His voice rumbled through her as his fingertips probed the sensitive skin inside her knee.

If he didn't stop, they would stagger right back into the closet and get very inventive. His hand left her thigh, arm circling her waist to draw her close.

It was too easy to feel safe with him, protected. She'd ignored his slip the night before, but the word drifted back to her when the moment of arousal slid into something deeper.

Love her.

He had no idea what she was capable of—maybe even getting her mentor killed. Guilt scored her ribcage, making it hard to breathe.

"Ground control to Major Barbara," he said, rocking his knee beneath her. "Did you hear me?"

"Not a word," she confessed, moving the subject back to safer grounds. "My mom favored your translation. She loved the poetic. A reminder to be of the world and not root myself too deeply in one place. And Barbara is also found in Spanish. My dad only spoke to me in Spanish as a kid."

He laughed. "That must be a dad thing, then. Mine still insists on German. Yours?"

"He died when I was nine," she said. "He was an underwater archeologist. He came to dive the Hranice Abyss and met my mom at a lecture. Caves were his specialty but they're dangerous. His luck ran out."

His amusement evaporated as his arm snugged around her and his chin settled against the curve of her shoulder.

"It turned out he'd signed a contract with a necromancer. No one knew—he'd been claimed before we could see the body. As far as I know, he's out there somewhere. Undead."

Diving in the service of a necromancer.

She couldn't bear the sight of those earnest gray eyes fixed on her with unflinching sympathy. She busied herself scraping a bit of egg off the plate with the crust of bread.

He pressed his lips to her temple. "I never believed in a calling until my sister, Isela. Even when she was little it was like she had this music, that only she could hear, running through her veins instead of blood. When she was eleven, she was invited to attend the Academy. It turns out she has a gift—something few humans and even fewer dancers have."

"She's a godsdancer?"

"She graduated last year," he said. "But she's already gained some pretty impressive patrons."

The ability to call on the power of gods through dance had plunged humanity into a catastrophic war. An allegiance of eight powerful necromancers ended the war in exchange for total control, but let humans maintain their ability to call on gods for less ruinous favors under strict regulation.

Successful goddancers entertained a status akin to athletes or minor celebrities. They were admired and feared and occasionally hated for their connection to the supernatural. The Praha Dance Academy trained many of the best.

"My mom is terrified we'll lose her, between gods and necromancers," he said. "Maybe we already have."

She shook her head. "You can't accept that. Hold on to her, in whatever way you can, no matter what this makes of her. If my dad came home tomorrow… none of it would matter."

She did not cry. She'd done that enough alone in her bedroom, after weeks spent watching her mother stifle her gift and surrender to a broken heart. The ache was old now, a it's shape and bulk in her chest familiar as the handle of an old suitcase.

But lighter when Tobias' arms closed around her, and his mouth moved against her hairline. "You're right, it doesn't."

When she drew back, her gaze swept his damp, sleep-tousled hair, and the glasses askew on his nose. She started to adjust them, then frowned and rose. "Give me those."

She withdrew a tiny screwdriver from the top drawer in the kitchen and squinted at his frames. A few quick twists to the lax screws that allowed the nose pieces to give and she handled them back.

"Try that."

He slid his glasses on, nudging them into place. When he lowered his chin, they stayed put. If she'd deciphered the Voynich manuscript while he'd been sleeping, he couldn't have looked more impressed.

"The screws just needed tightening." A tingling warmth blossomed in her ribcage, honeybees and lavender blossoms.

He squeezed her waist. "Your list of talents grows, BB."

"Bebe?"

"Beautiful Barbara," he elaborated.

"That's Terrible, Tobias," she wrinkled her nose.

She liked being able to kiss him whenever the urge struck. Glasses or none. When she let him go he blinked owlishly a few times, grinning.

He waved the invitation. "You should go."

"It's tomorrow night."

He shrugged. "I've seen your wardrobe. You have a gown somewhere."

"I need to open the shop, and I still haven't taken care of Veronika's apartment."

"It's been almost three weeks, neither of those things can wait one more day?" One brow sketched upward. "You could make some contacts that would be useful as you take over the shop."

The trip would also take her mind off the university and her dismissal.

Vienna was a few hours by car, and she loved the city. Plus, someone had emailed the shop inquiring about an estate appraisal in Holašovic. A quick side trip, and who knew what she might find?

But balls were for dancing, and dancing was for couples. She held her breath.

Getting out of the city would give her a chance to get to know him better, to decide if she could tell him the truth. If she made the wrong choice, she'd risk her life, not just her future. And that knowledge could put him in more danger—more than he had already assumed when he kept copies of that journal. More than perhaps whatever secrets he still hid. She wasn't the only one with something to lose, or gain, by risking trust.

She plucked the card from his hand. "I suppose I should see if Honza from research is free."

Tobias tensed, his shoulders drawing up, but he dropped his chin once. "If that's what you want."

She snorted. "That's not what I want, you silly man."

"It's your decision who accompanies—"

"Do you have a tux?"

"Tailcoat, even."

"Fancy." She scanned the invitation again with raised brows. "Come with—"

"Yes."

"That easy?"

"Absolutely." He paused. "We'll take the train?"

She smiled. "Leave the transportation to me."

CHAPTER TWENTY-NINE

TOBIAS DOUBLE-CHECKED his razor and shaving cream before tossing the toiletries case into his weekend bag and giving his dress shoes one last pass with the brush. Once the shoe tote was secured in his garment bag, he flipped his wrist and glared at his watch. One hour to go. Despite spending the last twenty-four obsessing, he still hadn't figured out how to talk to Barbara about his wolf—or her magic.

After a sleepless night, he'd given up and gone for a run that required four legs instead of two.

He'd raced the river until the lights of the city gave way to the night sky. What better way to earn her trust than to reveal his own vulnerability? Maybe then she would confide in him. And if she didn't know about her own magic—or didn't believe it was more than luck—he would be proof that such things existed. He just needed the right moment. And the words.

When he returned home around dawn, he tiptoed into the kitchen and buttered a baguette before packing it with cheese.

"You forgot this," his mother yawned, sliding the deli paper package across the counter on her way to the kettle.

"Water's hot," he said before she could turn it on, and shoved the entire mess of prosciutto into his haphazard sandwich.

She set about mixing her morning tea blend. "What are you doing up so early?"

He swallowed, shrugging. "You? You don't have an early class on

Saturday."

Surprise lit her face, and he regretted how self-absorbed he'd been since he returned.

The kettle steamed, and when she nodded, he poured water into her little pot. "I p-p-pay attention, even if it doesn't seem like I do."

"I know you do, Tobias," she said with a small smile. "Where are you headed?"

He returned to his sandwich.

"I saw your tux bag on the door last night."

He bought time chewing and swallowed, trying to sound casual. "Looking at books, and then a ball in Vienna."

Her brows rose. "A ball."

He wanted to grin like a maniac at the thought of having Barbara Svobodová all to himself for thirty-six hours.

"A work thing," he said around a mouthful before more questions came. "Should get packed."

He was humming a waltz as he retreated to his room. The tune died under the indecision of what to wear. A suit was the safe choice, but he didn't want to remind her of work, or the funeral. And a road trip gave him an opportunity to be casual. And not soaked running shorts and t-shirt casual. He decided on slate gray slacks and a pale blue button-down shirt. He fished a thin merino sweater out of his closet and shook loose an argyle tie.

"You gotta lose the tie, man," Chris said from the doorway.

Tobias jumped, spinning on his younger brother with bared teeth. "Don't sneak around like that."

Chris ignored him and sauntered in. He leaned against the desk and almost knocked over the stack of books. "Don't you ever do casual?"

"This is casual," Tobias said, gesturing at the slacks and the shirt.

Chris squinted in question.

Tobias sighed. "No jacket."

"No jacket." Chris rolled his eyes. "For fuck's sake."

He shoved off the desk and shouldered past Tobias to get to the wardrobe. He emerged, flinging a pair of chinos at his older brother.

"Untuck the shirt and lose the tie." Chris stalked out of the room.

Tobias sighed. He shucked out of the slacks and into navy chinos. He tossed the tie on the bed.

Chris returned, holding out a pair of shoes.

Tobias grimaced. "No fucking chance."

"Casual." Chris waved the expensive-looking athletic shoes at him.

Tobias tugged off his wingtips. "They're probably too big, knowing your boat paws."

"They're last year's," Chris said. "Issy snagged them for me from some exclusive Academy thing, but they're too dressy. I wore them once."

Too dressy. The boy considered a long sleeve t-shirt formal wear. But the shoes were comfortable. Tobias looked at himself in the mirror. Untucked, relaxed. Chris circled behind him, dropping a hand on his shoulder. "Not bad, brother."

Tobias rolled his shoulders and touched his glasses, though they stayed in place after Barbara's simple adjustment. The image of her pinching her lower lip between her teeth as she narrowed her eyes and fiddled with the tiny screws sent a shock of longing through him. "Thank you, Chris."

His younger brother succeeded in looking only a shade smug.

Tobias checked his watch. Thirty minutes.

"Hey, Chris," he said as his brother headed for the door.

"Yo?"

"Uh... is there any way I could get a..." Tobias floundered. "T-t-that is, maybe a c-c-couple. Just one. If you have one...h-h-handy."

Chris did him the distinct courtesy of not smirking as he left the room. His benevolence was ruined when he returned to stand proudly in the doorway and opened his left hand. A strip of foil packets accordioned from his palm to the floor. "Should I grab a few more?"

"Hey, boys, your laundry is taking over the—" Their mother paused behind him, took one look at the condoms, and kept walking. "Christof, I expect you to fold your clothes today."

"Yeah, Ma!" Chris yelled, winking at Tobias.

Tobias snatched the foil packets and landed a solid punch to his little brother's shoulder. Chris lunged, and they mock-wrestled until Tobias's glasses clattered across the floor and his breath came in heavy pants.

"You are a fucking infant," Tobias growled, retrieving his glasses and straightening his shirt.

"I'm not bumming rubbers off my kid brother," Chris countered. "So the librarian. The hot one?"

"She's no longer with the library," Tobias said, guilt twisting in his chest as he shoved the condoms into his bag. He threw his wingtips and the cardigan in for good measure.

He'd gotten no response to the letters he'd submitted on her behalf.

The offices of the head of department and the head of staff stonewalled every inquiry. The part of him that held out hope that she would be reinstated bristled with the reminder that what was happening between them would be a violation of school's policy.

"Does she make you happy?" Chris asked in a rare moment of seriousness.

The smile that rose in answer came unbidden.

Chris slapped his shoulder. "Then it's all good, cause I know you're gonna make her happy." He pantomimed a hip thrust.

"Would you get lost?"

Chris saluted and moseyed from the room.

"Hey, Chris?"

"Yo?"

"Thanks."

"I got you covered, brother." He laughed. "Literally."

Tobias grabbed his bag and headed for the front door. Unable to resist, he plucked a scarf from the hook and wound it around his throat. With a deep breath, he checked his watch and jogged down the stairs. Five minutes.

As he stepped onto the sidewalk, the sound of a car rounding the corner caught his attention. A sleek ebony Citroën cabriolet with chrome trim pulled in at the front of the building. The car looked like the earthbound offspring of a spaceship from a pulp sci-fi novel.

Barbara emerged from the driver's seat, and he forgot all about the car. He'd never seen her in slacks before, and these had been cuffed at the ankle and hugged her legs and ass in all the right places. She wore a loose, thin sweater and a floral scarf. A little straw boater tipped jauntily over her curls. He swallowed hard and tried to regain his equilibrium.

You're beautiful, and I'm a werewolf probably wasn't his strongest opening.

"What do you think?" she asked, rounding the car to approach the curb.

He took a moment to realize she was talking about the car, and he tailored his response. "Nice."

"Hey Toby, you forgot something."

Chris jogged down the front steps, the garment bag over his shoulder. He slowed at the sight of Barbara and extended his hand. "I'm Chris, the younger brother."

"Barbara." She slid her fingers into his palm, and Tobias fought the urge to growl at his brother.

Tobias recognized that lady-killer grin. He grabbed for the garment bag, but Chris slipped sideways.

Chris whistled, long and low. "Beautiful." He glanced over her shoulder at the convertible. "It's in great shape."

"It belonged to an old friend," she said. "I don't know much about it, but she loved it."

Chris edged a shoulder in front of his brother before Barbara, dimples crinkling.

She looked around him to snare Tobias with a mischievous grin. "Should we get going… Toby?"

The little mischievous smile she gave sent warmth to his toes.

"Absolutely." He hooked the garment bag and grabbed his brother by the scruff, dragging him backward. "Thanks, Christof."

The path clear, she stepped toward Tobias and slipped an arm around his waist, claiming him and their connection. The touch, confident and familiar, made him feel ten feet tall. He took in the elegant sweep of her brows shaded under the hat, the crinkle at the corner of her eyes, and her mouth curving in a luscious arc.

Chris cleared his throat watching them with arms crossed over his chest and a shit eating grin. Before Tobias could speak, he waved them away. "Nice to meet you, Barbara."

She leaned into Tobias's side and hummed a response, ignoring his handsome little brother entirely.

One arm around her, Tobias slung the garment bag over his other shoulder and steered them both to the car.

"Don't forget to pace yourself," Chris called as they pulled away from the curb, taking advantage of the open top to shout after them. "Stay hydrated. Be safe. Wear your seatbelts!"

Barbara laughed.

"I'm so sorry," Tobias groaned. "He's—"

"It's ok," Barbara said, reaching across the seat to squeeze his knee. "You really should put on your seatbelt."

Relief and amusement warred over Tobias' tongue, so he did as she asked. When her gaze skated over him a rosy gold flush lit her cheeks.

She grinned. "Are we that obvious?"

"Does it bother you?

She snuck another look at him with a little head shake. "You?"

"I'm terrible at hiding things. Especially when they're important to me."

She didn't answer, but once they settled into speed, she slipped her hand from the gear shift and found his. Their fingers slid together, resting on the bench seat.

They left the city behind and, with the top down, the wind flapped around them, carrying a flood of scents from the passing scenery. It was all he could do to keep himself from sticking his nose over the window frame.

Did you know wolves can smell about a hundred times better than humans?

With the wind, talking was almost out of the question. That was probably a good thing.

She drove like she did everything, with fearless competency. Driving had always been an activity he'd found a nuisance. He did it as infrequently as possible and, judging by any passengers unfortunate enough to be in his care, not very well. With her hands on the wheel, her eyes scanning behind the dark glasses, lips pressed together attentively, he felt, well, safe. It was astonishing.

As the city fell behind them, the car hummed along as though happy with the excursion.

"Music?" She asked after they'd left the main highway for smaller roads.

Ever heard wolf song under moonlight? "If you like."

She slipped a CD into the aftermarket radio. Based on her style, he expected a funky instrumental or jazz. What came out was a shocking clamor of guitars and drums under tortured vocals that made him sit up in his seat and look at her again.

She turned the volume down. "What's wrong?"

"Nothing," he said, tugging his collar.

"You are a terrible liar." She smiled and pointed her gaze out the window. "It's grunge. American. I thought you'd like it."

"You'd like my brother," he countered. "The other one, Mark. He was eight when we came to Prague and had somehow already acquired terrible taste in music."

"You pick next," she said, and waved a hand at the glove box.

Next came after a brief stop to consult the map. While her finger traced the connecting routes, he contemplated if this was the moment.

They were in the middle of nowhere. What if she reacted poorly? He turned his attention to the radio. He couldn't even picture what acceptance looked like. Maybe he'd wait until they reached the hotel. He swapped CDs.

When she started the car, the light strains of Dvořák rose under road noise.

"A bit on the nose, don't you think?" she asked with a grin.

Speaking of noses, remember how I knew those guys were coming before we heard them? I need to tell you—

At the memory of her face after the robbery—the fear in her expression—the words escaped him.

She must have misunderstood his silence. She leaned over, braced her hand on his knee, and planted a kiss on his mouth. The sensation of full lips and the warm slide of her tongue rendered him speechless. Hallelujah for bench seats. He grabbed her waist, hauling her out of her seat to straddle him. When she was able to draw in a gasping breath, she purred and ground herself against him.

He captured her mouth again, loving her little squeak of surprise. After a bit of exploratory pawing, his fingers cupped the sheer lace over the full round globes of her breasts. He slipped the strap over her shoulder and peeled one cup away, rewarded with the warm skin spilling over his palm and her soft cry of pleasure. The heavy pressure in his groin beat with the steady rhythm of his pulse as she rode him, clothes a tantalizing barrier.

A car zoomed by, startling them both.

"Not like this," he panted. He helped her clamber back into the driver's seat as she tried to straighten her clothes. Hot dark eyes fixed on him, and swollen lips curled into a smile.

"You have a lot of requirements," she said with a laugh. "No wonder it's taken you so long—"

This time he lunged for her mouth, pinning her to the seat.

"I want you," he said after a starved breath. "And I want it to be right. The first time. After that, all bets are off."

She wiped the lipstick from his mouth with her thumb and straightened her hat. "Let's get going, shall we? Check-in is at four."

CHAPTER THIRTY

DVOŘÁK WASN'T her first choice for a road trip, but it had a certain appeal as they wound their way along the narrow roads and through sloping tracts of land between tiny villages. The colorful melodies reflected the tree-blanketed hillsides and long stretches of farmland. Like the land itself, the contrasts balanced and complimented one another. She let the music and the landscape distract her from the puzzle of Tobias Vogel.

It was getting more and more challenging to hold on to reason in his presence. Each time he kissed her, touched her, looked at her with all that want, her ability to logic fell away.

Remember rule number one.

"Tell me more," he said. She tensed until he finished the sentence, "About the estate."

"A descendant reclaimed old property," she said. "Plans to make a boutique hotel out of it. He found a small library in storage. Lots of these old villages were all but abandoned, until after the Godswar. In the last twenty years there's been a significant repatriation of Czech descendants from the American Midwest in the countryside."

"I don't remember much, but the West Coast was flooded with refugees from the eastern conflict zones. Resources were scarce, jobs worse—even a generation later. People took whatever opportunities they had. My family qualified for repatriation because of my dad. But there were more jobs in Prague."

"I did a paper on language in Bohemian towns bordering Bavaria.

There were a few Vogels in my research with quite the reputation as hunters and gamesmen."

Tobias fidgeted. As had become a familiar habit since they'd set out, he started to say something, but seemed to change his mind.

Before she could ask, he spoke. "My dad loves genealogy. I'm sure he could talk you to death with all the old crests."

There was so much love in his voice she tore her eyes away from the road to catch a glimpse of his face. Affection transformed his expression to something vulnerable and startlingly fierce.

"Were you away for a long time?"

"The better part of ten years aside from a few holidays and special occasions."

"They must have missed you."

The sweetness of his smile was infectious. "I missed them, too."

She focused on the road again and hummed the next measure of movement without thought. He squeezed her thigh.

"I thought you didn't like Dvořák."

Even without being near her ear, his voice sent a shiver along her spine. Or maybe that was his palm, feathering a fraction of an inch upward as his fingertips began to stroke her inseam.

"I just said it was a bit on the nose for an academic on a road trip to a ball in a classic European cabriolet."

"Don't forget our stop to do a spot of rare manuscript appraisal," he said in his best posh accent.

She laughed.

His lips brushed at the spot where her jaw met her neckline, just below the ear. "I'd hate to ruin my image. I suppose it's a good thing I didn't let you debauch me on the roadside."

"Driving," she gasped.

Tobias sat back, withdrawing his hands, but wearing a satisfied grin. And tugging at his pants.

An hour later, they pulled up at the gates of a sizable farm estate bordering the village green of Holašovic. The village had been around since the Middle Ages, swapping back and forth between German and Czech populations. Now overgrown and in disrepair, this had been one of the main estates. The gabled roofs and blunt, squared-off buildings were an impressive example of historic southern Bohemian architecture. The boarded-up windows and crumbling façade betrayed a lack of care, but the whole estate possessed an unflappable feel. *Time batters me, yet I stand*, it seemed to say.

The smaller house was in better condition and occupied, the sign of a future.

A tall, bronze-colored dog rose from the porch and wagged its tail with a few half-hearted barks. At the sight of Tobias, the dog quit barking and stood still as a statue. It whined once and then bellied down in its bed with flat ears and a low whine.

Tobias watched the dog warily. His smile was smile too bright and forced. "Guess he doesn't like me."

The owner came out onto the porch. Barbara stepped forward, but Tobias hung back until the man joined them in the driveway. The dog didn't stop whining until they were out of earshot, and, based on how Tobias kept glancing back, maybe he still heard it. They left the car charging and followed the owner to the garage.

Tobias helped with the heavy doors. Her grace lit up, fingers tingling. Barbara stepped eagerly into the darkness.

The owner flipped on the light, revealing an old worktable stacked with books and crates. Barbara went to work.

Tobias hesitated, so overwhelmed by the volume of materials he seemed unable to proceed beyond commenting on the conditions of the unpreserved papers and books.

Barbara let her grace guide her, checking her finds with glances and briefly paging through books to confirm the quality before starting a smaller pile. After a moment, he seemed to notice and examined the items she'd set aside. He made a sound of surprise, but she didn't pause in her work. She let the strength and the steadiness of the warmth in her fingers guide her, cocking her head to listen to the tingle in her breastbone a time or two as she contemplated the next crate.

The owner drifted to Tobias's side. She registered the low hum of voices: the owner's questions, Tobias explaining and verifying dates, periods, contents of the materials she'd selected with increasing confidence. After a while, she realized both men were watching her—the owner with consideration and Tobias with unchecked delight. She shook her head a little and went back to her work.

When their host had left them to it, Tobias brought another box to her elbow. "Where do you want this?"

She cocked her head. Yes, something there. Noting of major note, but worth attention. "Why don't you have a look?"

He settled it beside her, prying off the nailed lid. "Christ, what a mess. I need gloves, and we should get a team down here."

"What team? What funding?" she murmured under her breath. "Look for the value. It was the first lesson I learned with Veronika, and the hardest. We can't save it all, but what we can sell, we can preserve."

He was quiet so long worry crept into her. Maybe he thought she was only in it for the money. She fought the urge to explain how badly she wanted to save everything, how hard it was to reconcile her twin worlds: academia and business. How one could absorb a few bad choices, while the other could not.

"We?" His mouth tipped up.

She flushed.

He flipped through a page and paused. "How do we decide?"

She looked over his forearm into the box. "Know the market and the customers, and sometimes we just take a chance. I've got a collector for almanacs and anything related to weather, so pull that one. Is that a hymnal?"

An hour later, she set down a big leather portfolio, carefully sliding a single sheet free. "Professor."

Tobias joined her, chuckling. "I think we're past...wait, is that—"

Barbara hummed, her suspicions validated by his instinctive response. The single illuminated sheet was done in delicate in pink and mauve with darker script. She sniffed the edge of the page, tested the flex gently over her finger. "Vellum leaf, sixteenth century—"

"Fifteenth," he corrected quietly, accepting the second pair of gloves she held out.

She squinted, sometimes her ability to translate interfered with her spotting the finer points of the original text. "You're the expert."

"Where was this?"

"Tucked in among some old art sketches," she said, lifting the portfolio. "The leather preserved it excellently."

"Barbara, this is worth..."

She shook her head, sternly. "It's only worth what a buyer would pay."

He nodded, and her composure broke with a grin.

"Yes, this is...very important," she admitted.

He lifted the portfolio, as if expecting to find others. "Amazing. How did it get in here, I wonder?"

"Who knows?" She laughed, then sobered. "Often people don't know what they have. Or something is passed down through families as an heirloom and the true significance is lost."

She rocked back on her heels, grinning. "Once we found a copy of *Tales of Sir John Mandeville*, translated to Czech. Fifteenth century from Prague. It had this wonderful green cast. Stuffed in a cello case full of clothes. The commission paid for most of my books and supplies for a whole year."

That dimple had reappeared in his chin, and a slow-moving fire filled the space where her breath should be. If he wasn't careful, she was going to kiss him for looking at her like that. She cleared her throat. "We should get back to work. Let's put this back in the portfolio for transport. It's served well enough so far."

He held out the portfolio with a look of contentment so deep she forgot how to speak any language at all with the sheer magnificent transformation. She focused on slipping the page carefully back inside as her heart chipped away at rules, one beat at a time.

It wasn't unreasonable to need someone to trust. She would tell him the truth. Maybe then he could find his way to sharing his secret with her.

CHAPTER THIRTY-ONE

SILENCE HAD ALWAYS BEEN a comfortable place for Tobias, but there was something new about the kind that settled over the rest of their ride to Vienna. Instead of filling the empty space with aborted sentences and uneasy shared isolation it wove something immutable between them. Maybe it helped that they stayed in physical contact the entire way— fingers intertwined, a brush of knuckle agains cheek or jaw. When she reached for the radio he brought the inside of her wrist to his lips instead. The sound of her breathing and the pulse of the blood in her veins was all the music the wolf needed. Her answering smile turned the hunter into a lupine ball of fluff inside his ribcage.

They reached Vienna at dusk, but since arriving at a ball before nine was out of the question, they ate a quick dinner in a restaurant close to the hotel. To the porter's dismay, they brought everything up to the tiny room dominated by a single bed.

When Barbara paused in the doorway, Tobias cupped her shoulders and drew her back into his chest.

"We can get a second room," he murmured, ignoring the ache that accompanied the thought of spending another night away from her.

She spun on him, and the hope in her eyes banished his worry. "Not a chance."

She kicked off her shoes and disappeared into the bathroom, humming.

He stared after her, trying to make sense of the feeling that some internal resistance had gone out of her in that garage. She had to know how much she had revealed of her own ability. And showed more control and finesse than he'd expected. Working alongside her, he'd witnessed her sheer expertise in appraisals. She'd managed to bring the two into alignment, skill honing power.

When she came back, he would ask her. Or tell her.

She returned, pressing a towel to her cheeks and neck with that pleased, secret smile, and his voice failed.

He started to pick through the boxes.

"What do you think, Professor?" She tossed the towel on the table and wrapped her arms around his chest. Cool, damp fingers slipped beneath his shirt. He sucked in a breath and did his best to focus on the book in his hands.

"This is a common manual on herbal remedies, late 1800s, but someone added illustrations, the details of which are exquisite," he said, lifting another volume. The moment hovered and he took a breath, gathering his courage. "What you did back there…"

"Was unorthodox."

She hadn't tried to hide it, or distract him, just did her work. Maybe she was trying to tell him, in her own way. Why couldn't that be enough? He needed to hear it aloud.

He slid his hands over hers, trapping her. "How does it work?"

Her cheek settled in the gap between his shoulder blades. Her words vibrated through the wall of muscle and bone and into the most vulnerable part of him. "They find me. The important things. Precious things. I've just been refining it. School helps with that."

He tugged on her wrist, dragging her around his chest.

"It's why you're so good with lost books." His mouth brushed her cheek.

She shivered.

His lips slid along her hairline to her ear. "You opened the safe without a code."

"I just made a suggestion." Her breath hitched. "I'd never tried it on a lock that complex."

"Did the key to the cipher reveal itself, or did you see the translation first and work your way backward?" He took her earlobe in his teeth.

She shuddered hard. "Not translated. I understood it."

He released her ear and rocked back, pinning her between his thighs.

"And you led me there," he said. "A trail of breadcrumbs. You're more than my clever, brilliant researcher—you're a mastermind."

The morning of the stolen books loomed in his memory. Maybe they had more in common than he originally thought. Without the ability to express itself freely, maybe her ability was just as unpredictable as his wolf.

"You stacked those books on your desk, just not on purpose. Is the power getting away from you?"

She tried to bow her head, but he cradled her cheeks in his palms. Her hands splayed over his chest, unable to pull him closer or push him away. Her lips trembled as she fixed them together.

She shook her head.

"I've seen things like this before."

The searching in her gaze undid him. "Like me?"

The words fought up his throat. *We're alike, you and I. Something lives inside me and I can't always control it. A beast.*

This moment would crash to a halt. He couldn't bear to watch fear replace the heat and want in her eyes. He spoke over the gravel in his throat. "There's no one like you, Barbara, and I would never let anyone hurt you."

He released her. Made a show of checking his watch. "Now you deserve the opportunity to stun the Viennese booksellers. We should talk later." He hooked his garment bag on his way to the door.

"Where are you going?"

"I'll get dressed in the gym," he said. "A little trick I learned living in a building with a bunch of guys. Meet you in the bar, say eight-thirty?"

He left her staring after him. As soon as the door shut, he grimaced, pounding his forehead with a fist. Like a coward.

LATER, in the hotel bar, Tobias couldn't say why he glanced up when he did. Was it the scent that preceded her, or that his body knew her presence as a vine opened its petals to the sun? It meant he was watching the door when she rounded the corner. He witnessed the way her chin rose from her chest, and her shoulders settled into that self-possessed bearing that marked her every entrance into a room.

Stand tall, wear your crown, and be sweet inside.

The sweetness defined her, even as she strode forward as though it *were* a crown and not a delicate collection of gold floral strands that held her curls away from her face.

Her dress had been conjured from the same textured darkness as a primeval forest lit by a waxing moon. The dropped collar revealed more of her skin than he'd ever seen outside the bedroom—long bare lines of her neck and shoulders. Emerald velvet flowed over her breasts and down her arms to the elbows in tapered sleeves. A subtle band of gold brocade cinched below her sternum. The rest of the bodice clung from ribcage to waist, belling into a skirt that cascaded over her hips to the floor. When she moved, a generous slit exposed a glimpse of leg and her dancing heels.

She could have been the muse for a dozen Mucha paintings. If she were a season, it would be spring—the lush, verdant nights and the brilliance of dawn through wet leaves.

Around the teeming lobby, glances became stares and conversations tapered as she passed. Tobias rose. Her eyes flew to him with all the familiar, mischievous warmth, and they shared a smile. Her mouth was a plump, vibrant red, like cherries. She slipped her hands into his as he skimmed his lips over either cheek.

"Stunning."

"Not so bad yourself, Professor." He gloried in her fingers, smoothing the lapel of his tux, casually possessive as if she were aware that many eyes following them were for him.

They got a taxi to Hofburg Palace, and then they were swept into the crowds entering the great hall. The invitation granted them seats at a table near the dance floor, a treat that would give them a place to rest their feet between dances. They had a prime position for superb views of the performances.

Tobias had accepted suffering through formal events since he'd been fitted for his first tuxedo. But this was different. Watching her was more pleasing than any of the pageantry. Everything amused her, her glass of champagne forgotten as she took it all in. Once in a while, she met his eyes in delight over the spectacle of a dress or the traditional dancers. At last, the ropes descended as the traditional 'alles walzer' opened the dancing to everyone. The dance floor became a swirling mass of color and texture.

He rose, presenting his arm. "You didn't think we were just here to watch?"

CHAPTER THIRTY-TWO

THE HALL WAS a jewel box of color and sound, from the sumptuous literary-themed décor of oversized books as table centerpieces and wall hangings made to look like illuminated pages, to the rainbow of elegant gowns and jewelry. Glasses of champagne glittered in the light, and the scent of goulash warming for the midnight fare filled the air as they made their way to the dance floor. It was hard not to gawk at everything, and Barbara second-guessed the simple green velvet gown amid so much more ostentatious finery. But Tobias' eyes strayed from her only to guide them around the dance floor, and his steady gaze reassured her that she'd made exactly the right choice.

He certainly knew how to waltz. And he looked crushing in tails.

"My sister taught us all," he explained when they took a break from the dance floor.

She glanced up to see high rosy flush dusting his cheekbones that wasn't just exertion.

"The dancer?"

"The one and only," he explained, sweeping her gracefully aside as another pair of partners bumbled past. "And she's a brute of a teacher, let me tell you. She carried a stick with Christof."

A snort escaped her. "Why am I not surprised?"

Between dances, he escorted her while Veronika's solicitor introduced her to acquaintances and contacts in the dealer world. Most were male, all quite a bit older and more than a few did a double take at her, even as they reached for Tobias' hand with eager respect. *Herr Doctor Vogel*. Each time he deferred quickly to her as "the proprietor of Vinohrady's most respected antikvariát," but the double standard burned.

One of the local shop owners sidled up to her with a glass of champagne. The woman was everything Barbara loved about Vienna, timeless and refined in a way that didn't seek to impress anyone and still managed to be the most notable thing in the space. "Is that *the* Doctor Vogel in the role of your shadow this evening?"

Barbara accepted the glass. "He's a visiting professor at Žižkov University."

The woman's mouth twitched in amusement. "An assistant of mine took a seminar with him in grad school. I heard he breathes fire and eats graduate students for breakfast."

Barbara took in her date—tall and aloof and so handsome it made it hard to breathe when he looked right at her. As he did at just that moment. He gave her a secret little smile and lifted his glass before returning to his conversation.

"Only on Tuesdays and Fridays," Barbara said, raising her glass in response.

When she returned her attention to her companion, the woman smiled knowingly. "Now, tell me how you're making the transition. I understand you worked with Veronika for many years."

After the final dance, Barbara took off her shoes and slipped on a pair of comfortable flats when Tobias retrieved their coats. Throngs of people filled the courtyard on the hunt for taxis and hired cars.

"It's a few blocks," Barbara said.

"Fifteen or so," he muttered.

"Longer than a run from your place to mine?" she teased.

Moonlight soaked the old stone and the entire city glowed with it. Their breath formed small clouds in the early morning air, and Tobias slipped his jacket around her shoulders. The warm scent of aftershave and salty male settled around her. She tucked her cheek to her shoulder and breathed in deep. When her eyes opened she found his gaze fixed on her face, something so powerful and unreadable in his expression, she almost looked away. Instead, she tucked herself against him, settling against his ribcage with a little sigh.

"You *do* have a have a reputation," she mused. "Fire breathing and eating undergraduates."

He snorted. "Only on Wednesdays and Saturdays."

"Oh dear…"

Warmth suffused her ribcage when his dimple made a bashful appearance. "I was jo—"

"I got the days wrong," she giggled.

The laughter wouldn't stop. She wrapped her arm around his waist, holding on for dear life.

"Does it ever get exhausting?" she asked, after they'd sobered enough to continue. At the question in his brows, she went on, "That people see you as something you're not, and judge you for it?"

"You tell me." At her silence, he squeezed her shoulders.

Her laugh sounded strangled to her own ears. "It's a house of mirrors where none of the reflections resemble who you actually are."

"And you've paid a much higher price for it than I ever have." He pulled her to a stop. "It's unfair. I want to tear the whole place down to the foundation to make this right."

"And where would you work?" She laughed shakily.

"Maybe I could get a job at an antique book shop, know any that are hiring?"

"I don't think I could afford you."

"Are you sure? I'd hate to have to go the competition."

Her brows rose. "Blackmail. How ruthless."

Tobias sobered, taking her hands again. "My dad always says, find the people who see you, and keep them closer than anyone who doesn't."

"I like your dad very much." She hated that tears made her voice wobbly, but his thumbs slid along her lashes too tenderly to make her regret them.

"I promise to see you, exactly as you are, as often as you let me."

Her chin rose as his lowered. He tasted like champagne and the faintest hint of goulash from the midnight meal.

"But don't tell everyone about me, okay?" he whispered when their lips parted.

She offered a hooked pinky finger. "Promise."

He snagged it with his own, squeezing it tightly against his chest. It should have been playful, a childish gesture, but the intensity of his eyes burned the remaining laugher from her chest and left her breathless.

I would never let anyone hurt you. How badly she wanted to believe that promise.

She nodded once, accepting, and sealed it with a kiss.

Wrapped around each other, they limped on bruised feet to the hotel room. Barbara eased onto the edge of the bed. Tobias toed off his shoes and shrugged out of his tux jacket.

Barbara had never been so tired, and the idea of curling up in the bed with a big, warm man and sleeping the next few hours away seemed like heaven. But first, getting out of her dress. It had taken her and a helpful member of housekeeping staff to get her buttoned into the thing in the first place.

She twisted her arms behind her back. Strong hands squeezed her fingers. "Let me."

Silence descended, as textured as a favorite blanket. The words that needed to be said were spent, leaving the ordinary magic of proximity. Tobias unhooked the buttons one at a time, his fingers caressing the delicate fabric. She sighed with relief. He smoothed his hand over her shoulder to the velvet of the bodice.

Thoughts of sleep dissolved as her blood began to sing in her veins.

She took him in over her shoulder. The loosened tie, top buttons undone, wearing only shirtsleeves and the vest.

He crouched at her feet, scooping up the velvet edges and cupping fabric between his palms and the skin of her legs as he rose.

The combination of tenderness and heat set her trembling.

He closed the gap between them, steadying her with his body. She tucked her elbows so he could maneuver her arms from the sleeves. He turned away, laying the dress over the chair at the desk and smoothing it with one hand before returning to her.

The nearly backless dress hadn't left her many options for underwear. A friend in the theater department had shown her the wonders of double-sided tape and strategically placed petals. Since velvet showed whatever was beneath, she'd splurged on a silky thong from the lingerie store Pavlina always talked about. He took her in with eyes wide and hungry.

He knelt at her feet again, and this time she rested her palm against his shoulder at the tug on her ankle. One foot slipped free of the simple canvas slipper before he moved to the other.

When he rose, his Adam's apple bobbed as he skimmed his way past the swells of her breasts, pausing to thumb her covered nipples. "Can I?"

She nodded. With the kind of individualized attention reserved for the most fragile papers, he attended to the adhesive. She winced when the last bit came free. He rubbed the sore skin with his fingertips before lathing the dark peak with long, wet kisses.

"Better?"

A grunt escaped her.

She attacked the buttons of his shirt, and then the waistband of his pants until hey stood skin to skin with the barest bit of fabric between them. His fingertips traced the back of her arms as he breathed into the mass of her upswept hair.

He moaned. "I want this to be perfect."

She laughed and slid her arms around his waist. "I hope not. Leaves us no room for improvement. Are you sure this is what you want?"

"I've never been more sure of anything."

"Then stop thinking and kiss me."

⁂

THE NIGHT HAD BEEN WONDROUS, and the image of her in her shadowed emerald dress like a hidden jewel amid the ballroom's finery would be one he treasured forever—second only to the way she closed her eyes and trusted him as he guided her around the dance floor. Both a distant third to walking arm and arm in the Vienna moonlight, the sound of her laughter making him prouder of himself than any degree or award.

And now, this kiss. Nothing gentle, no hesitation. A clash of open mouths and tongues, suggesting the warm wetness he might find elsewhere. He tilted her onto the bed, pinned her between his thighs, and kissed her until his brain shut off.

She thumped his shoulder with one small fist, dragging in a hard breath when they parted. "Where are they?"

What were words? What was speech? Could they just kiss more and talk later? She shoved again and he rolled obediently aside as she wiggled out from under him. "Where. Are. They?"

Oh, that. "Top pocket inside my bag."

She leaped off the bed and scampered across the room, returning with a train of foil packets and arched brows. "Ambitious, are we?"

He flushed. He should have just torn off one and hidden the rest. He wanted to make it so wonderful for her. Now he seemed like a maniac who expected to pound her brains out as many times as possible.

Before he could squirm away, she straddled his hips and sat on his thighs. "You're thinking again, aren't you? I know an excellent way to shut that big brain right off."

"But I..." he breathed as her fingers slid around him, "I might not... And you..."

"Have had a whole night of foreplay," she said. "I'm ready, I promise."

First, he discovered, she was *so* ready. Second, what he'd believed about the sensations he'd encountered with his hands and mouth paled in reality to the actual pressure of her body around his. He wanted to beg her to go faster, but also to slow down so that first enveloping never ended.

She paused halfway, licking her lips with a hitching exhale.

Tobias reached over his head, gripping the headboard to keep from grabbing her hips and thrusting deep. He tried to keep his voice light. "Everything good?"

"Good is rather an understatement, don't you think?"

He laughed as she settled on him with a little sigh and pleasure burst across his eyelids, wild colors swirling in infinite directions. The weight of her body, the slick press of her soft thighs on the jutting bones of his hips, the way her inner muscles quivered. His fingertips curled around the soft rise of her ass, pressing into the taut muscles in her lower back.

He scrambled for something, anything, to help him fight off the coming release. He wasn't aware that his lips were moving until she laughed softly. The muscles clenched around him and he groaned.

"Are you reciting the Dewey?"

His eyes popped open. Mistake. From his position propped up on pillows against the headboard, her breasts rose and fell with her uneven breath at his eye level.

He started at the 800s. Philosophy and Theory. Miscellany. Dictionaries and concordances. "I'm trying to..."

Her eyes were glazed and bright, lips parted in a smile.

A heady thick sensation like sun-warmed honey unfurled in his chest and slid to his fingers and toes.

Her chin tilted to the slightest angle, a question in her eyes.

He nodded.

When she began to move, nothing else mattered but the slow rock of her hips accommodating his girth. Her expression drew him, the gradual coming undone with a searching hunger. It seemed unreal, being inside her body. Feeling her this way. And that she might be overcome with it. As overcome as he was.

Her hand flew to the headboard beside his head, gripping. Close enough for him to press his mouth to the inside of her wrist, to suck the skin in his teeth and nip at her pulse. A little cry escaped her, and her body clenched on him.

The instinct to roll her beneath him and give in to the animal rising in the space where his brain used to be took the remains of his control. Every rock of her hips sent him deeper, triggered a corresponding pulse of heat. When he sucked one brown, pebble hard nipple into his mouth, her other hand flew to the headboard.

His restraint snapped. He gripped her hips and arched into her. She wailed something resembling his name, but all he heard was the *more* part and he'd be damned if he didn't know how to follow instructions. Release cracked through him like thunder. He opened his mouth and let it groan free. Her head dropped back, a long deep gasp and accompanying shudder answering his.

The remains of her strength slid away, leaving her draped on his chest, fingers flexing on his shoulders and breath hot in his ear. He tried to speak, but his voice failed him. Strands of curly brown hair caught in his stubble, and her eyelashes tickled his neck. All the air in the room seemed to have gone into their lungs during the act, and nothing remained now. They gasped like survivors of a shipwreck who'd swum the impossible distance to shore, hand in hand.

He tried again. "That was—"

"You simply must have the last word," she laughed, and stole the rest with a kiss.

TOBIAS SLEPT LIKE THE DEAD.

Barbara had fought her way free of his long, heavy limbs to call down to the front desk to extend their checkout time. When she curled up beside him again in the bed he stirred only to wrap his body around her with a happy grumble and resume breathing into her nape.

Based on the empty foil packets on the nightstand, they'd earned the extra rest.

What he lacked in experience, he made up for in zeal and a willingness to take instruction. A good student, indeed.

She slipped out of bed and into the shower. The hot water soothed skin raw with sensation. She let it sluice her body for a few extra moments, praying for clarity. A spot in the center of her chest pulsed with every memory of his touch, his body, his eyes on hers. The ache spread, curling along every fiber of her being. Greedy desire claimed the part of her attached to reason.

She wanted.

And the little voice asked why she should't have him. He was hers for taking. It was in his eyes. Every time she opened hers, she found him focused on her face with fascination and devotion.

The promise that she would think of nothing beyond this weekend, these moments, eroded with every whispered endearment. She wouldn't be able to go back to not knowing the way his body rode hers through release. The sticky tangle of limbs, the way his hair curled when it was damp with sweat, and how he clenched her as if nothing but the two of them mattered.

She wanted more.

Except. A few times while they'd slept, he'd woken her with inhuman noises—a soft whine, a lower-pitched rumble. After each, she recalled his face in the flickering darkness of the basement during the robbery. The long ears, too many teeth, the strength. The way he'd fought—like an animal—and shaken off the damage he'd sustained. She studied his sleeping face, searching for clues. She'd shown him her abilities, answered his questions. What was he hiding from her?

When the shower door opened, she jumped, startled.

Tobias appeared, sheepish and disheveled. "I'm sorry I didn't mean to scare you. I just wanted…"

It certainly didn't hurt her ego to have a man tongue-tied and staring at her as he did. Doubt fell away under that raw display of longing. Exhaustion faded. Her pulse leaped. Without his glasses, his features seemed sharper and more dangerous. His nostrils flared. It was like he could sense how aroused she was.

A shiver raced up her spine.

He'd kneeled before her last night, sometime between round two and four. Even on his knees, cradling her in his palms, there had been nothing of the supplicant in that gaze.

She needed to keep a clear head.

"All done," she said, rallying a smile as she started to slip past him.

His hand splayed over her belly, kindling the smothered flames. "Do you have to go?"

◆

BARBARA WAS TOO QUIET. As she packed the last of her belongings, the pale yellow sundress swirled around her thighs, the cardigan molded to her back and breasts. Tobias felt lightheaded watching her, so he made himself focus on zipping up the garment bag. He wondered if he'd ever get used to the rush of pleasure at the sight of her. She'd matched his appetite until well after dawn, and then again in the shower.

But her stifled yawns gave away a lack of real sleep. Exhaustion also exposed the wariness in her eyes when she looked at him. The small furrow between her brows kept deepening.

"I can drive today," he suggested. "If you'd like?"

"Sure."

The knock signaled the arrival of the porter, and he cast a last glance around the tossed room before opening the door. The smell of sex filled his nose, and he hoped it was his wolf sense and not as obvious as he feared. The porter loaded the hand cart, giving Tobias a long approving look, and he fought the urge to growl at the man.

Oblivious, Barbara checked her purse and snugged the little straw fedora over her curls. He cradled her shoulders as she looked around the room. The day before they had stood the same way, on the precipice of something unknown. In those early morning hours, they had leaped, hand in hand, and found the stars. Until dawn's light revealed the true distance remaining between them.

When the porter had started down the hall, Tobias grabbed her hand, holding her back. "Bebe?"

Her brows tilted in question, the nickname lightening the corner of her mouth for just a minute.

"Glad we came?"

She laughed and tilted her cheek up. "Ecstatic."

He pressed a kiss to the skin over bone. He let her go to sweep their garment bags over his shoulder. "If you need a date for next year, I'm free. Letting you know in advance."

This time, the face-crinkling smile he loved blossomed. They followed the porter from the room, arms around each other. Next year, and every year for the rest of their lives, he hoped.

But first, he needed to tell her his secret.

As the kilometers stretched, leaving Vienna behind, he found himself unable to speak the words. He tried half a dozen times, ending in laughter and awkward flirtation that seemed to leave her a little less settled every time.

Her blood was a talent, a gift that she wielded in service of a greater good.

His was something savage to be kept caged. Another truth settled over him as he turned it over in his mind. He and his brothers and their mother lived with the risk of exposure every day. Their father knew about it, but what of their sister, who knew nothing and had worked so hard to build a career for herself? Surely she carried the wolf gene in her own blood—perhaps that would be enough for her to be guilty by association or relation?

Sharing his secret would risk the safety of his entire family. He'd tear out his own heart first.

CHAPTER THIRTY-THREE

ONE THING TOBIAS VOGEL did not excel at: driving. Early on, Barbara decided the best thing to do was sleep. At least she wouldn't see whatever did them in coming. She roused herself as the city lights brightened the car and, in the moment before uncertainty came rushing back, she reached for him. He squeezed her fingers.

In front of his building, he shut off the engine, lingering. "Thank you again. For this weekend. It was... wonderful."

"Thanks for making me go," she said, trying to convince herself it was only exhaustion that made her eyes sting, not the weight of everything still unsaid between them. The sounds in the darkness, the teeth, the growl.

They climbed out of the car together.

On the curb, he curled his fingers and brushed her cheek with the back of his hand. She couldn't meet his eyes.

His brows knit together as his thumb swept the skin beneath her lashes and came away wet. "Please, Bebe, don't—"

"Is this your librarian?" They both jerked at the voice from the steps.

A young, brown-skinned woman descended the building steps with the thoughtless grace of one who had honed the art of their own movement. Up close, she was smaller than Barbara had expected, the mass of curly dark hair piled on top of her head adding an extra few inches to her slim, muscular frame. But the family resemblance was clear when an identical dimple appeared in her chin.

She stuck out her hand. "I'm Toby's little sister, Issy."

"Not so little," Tobias said. "Barbara, this is Isela."

She and Tobias had almost the same eyes, though hers were a shade earthier.

"Nice to meet you."

Tobias tossed her his bag, becoming a big brother in a heartbeat. "Why don't you quit flapping your jaw and make yourself useful? Take this upstairs. I'm just gonna say goodbye."

She stuck out her tongue. "I *am* making myself useful, Tobias Henry Vogel. My seminar got canceled, so I came over—thanks for the voice-mail guilt trip you left me, by the way. Mom overreacted, and now she and Chris are making a big dinner." She bestowed a serene smile on Barbara. "She sent me down to see if Barbara wants to join us."

Tobias looked to be wrestling the impossible burden of his own tongue and settled on glaring at his sister.

Ignoring him, Isela made her appeal directly. "We've all promised not to ask you anything about work...or your weekend." She lowered her voice. "Did you have fun? Isn't Toby a good dancer? He was the easiest to teach."

"You did a fine job." Barbara laughed. She leaned in to whisper, "He's an excellent lead."

Isela gave Barbara a smile that would make an audience rise to its feet with applause before lowering her brows at her brother. "Come on. It's just Mom and Dad and Chris, and me. Mark's working late."

A coded look passed between the siblings. He gave Barbara a helpless shrug, but she didn't miss the hope in his eyes.

She smiled at Isela, but her eyes stayed on him. "Sure. We drove straight back and I'm starving. I'd love dinner."

The nerves started as soon as they mounted the stairs, Isela bounding ahead in that glorious dancer's run that belonged on a stage.

Tobias caught Barbara's hand in his own, drawing her back. "If this is too much—"

"I'd love to meet your family," Barbara said cheerfully. "And I *am* hungry."

His smile warmed her to the core, banishing her worries about the things unspoken between them for a moment longer.

The old building had been well loved. Barbara paused to take it all in. "This is gorgeous."

"Our parents bought the building when they came to Prague," Isela said. "They've been restoring it ever since. As soon as we could hold a paintbrush or a tool, we all helped. But Toby got out of most of the work because he was so smart, Dad let him run books and do the ordering."

"The Vogel compound." Tobias waved his arms at the surrounding lobby. "How does that song go? 'Check out anytime you like...'"

"Nobody made you move back in with Mom and Dad." Isela rolled her eyes at him. "You could have said no."

He snorted.

"Isela did her barre exercises with a paint can and a mop handle," Tobias told Barbara, ignoring his sister's growing scowl. "Until she kicked over a full can of periwinkle blue Beryl wanted for her studio."

"It's called a battement, not a 'kick.'" She groaned in outrage. "I thought Papa was going to have an aneurysm."

"It was the last can." He grinned.

She winced. "And they were out."

"And so were you, after that." Tobias laughed. "Demo only from then on—trash runs and sweeping. Free to battement dust bunnies all you liked."

"Shut up, accountant." She shrugged and admitted to Barbara, "Mark was the only one of us worth our salt when it came to the work, this is all him and papa and isn't it lovely?"

As they mounted the stairs behind Isela's constant stream of conversation, Barbara let herself be lulled into the quiet that settled over her. She hadn't noticed how loud and busy her own thoughts had become. Padding up the stone stairs and surrounded by the pale walls, a deep calm washed over her. The constant buzz subsided. She sighed.

Tobias squeezed her fingers.

The top floor was a spectacular home of its own. Isela sprang ahead to announce her success.

Barbara slipped off her shoes in the entryway and waited for Tobias to set down his belongings. She glanced into the expansive sitting room overlooking the tree-lined cobblestone path along the river and the more industrial, business-oriented Smichov neighborhood on the opposite bank.

"Ready?" Tobias asked, his voice tight.

"It will be fine." She stretched up on her tiptoes and brushed her lips against his stubbled jaw. "Pineapple."

He grinned and tipped his chin down to press his lips to hers. "Sweet."

When she settled onto her feet, she saw Isela leaning on the doorframe, a little smile on her face. Barbara let him go, feeling heat flushing her chest. His palm settled in the curve of her spine and stayed there.

"Don't, Issy," Tobias warned.

"You guys are adorable." Isela lifted her hands in a helpless gesture. "that's all I'm gonna say, I swear."

Isela grabbed her hand. "Come in."

In the living room, Barbara gave a crooked smile to the familiar figure sprawled on the couch in front of the TV. Christof waved. "Good to see you again. Both of you. In one piece. You must not have let him drive."

Tobias snorted. "Thanks for the vote of confidence, little brother."

When their father entered the room from the hallway, a newspaper tucked under his arm, Barbara was struck by his uncanny resemblance to Tobias, down to the sweater over collared shirt and tie. Aside from the grey hair and the slower step, they could have been carbon copies.

The older man offered his hands as he brushed her cheeks with his own. "Lukas. Willkommen, Barbara."

"Dad, Barbara doesn't—"

"Ich bin sehr langsam," she said haltingly. "Aber ich kann ein bißchen sprechen."

Lukas beamed, drawing her into a hug as he spoke slowly in German. "I'm so pleased to meet you."

The pleasure of the warm welcome undid her. She swallowed hard. He gave her another squeeze before releasing her.

The door to the kitchen swung open.

"Christof Douglass Vogel, you better not be watching—"

"Yeah Ma, coming." Chris flung himself off the couch with admirable agility but didn't manage to turn off the television in time.

This woman could not possibly have adult children. With flawless walnut skin, only the dreadlock escaping from the scarf on her head with silver at the roots gave an indication of her age. She tucked it behind one ear as she fixed the taller, younger man with an unmistakably maternal expression.

Chris moved fast, vanishing into the kitchen.

She pivoted to take in the rest of the room. She moved like a dancer, palazzo pants swirling around her calves, wrap top hugging her waist.

Something in Barbara snapped to attention when their eyes met, the older woman's presence reverberating like a tuning fork pressed against her sternum. She almost rubbed the spot, feeling for a point of contact.

The woman's serene face settled into the natural creases of a mischievous smile. "I'm so glad you're joining us, Barbara."

Barbara hoped she wasn't staring, or gaping, but in the end, she wanted to do both.

"This is my mother, Beryl." Tobias narrowed his eyes.

Over their mother's shoulder, Isela rolled her eyes. "Mom, don't go all kooky. I promised we would be chill. You're going to scare her off and Tobias will go back to being grumpy all the time."

Lukas sighed, fighting a smile. "Sprich bitte nicht so mit Deiner Mama."

"Aber Papa." Isela's protest died at his lowered brows. "Sorry mom, you're just so intense all the time."

"Isela," Lukas chided almost succeeding at hiding a chuckle.

Oblivious to the exchange, Tobias' shoulders had drawn together, his cheekbones reddening.

"I-I-I am n-not grumpy all the time," he muttered.

"Pretty grumpy," Chris called from the kitchen. Isela nodded.

"I know where you sleep, ingrate," Tobias shouted.

Lightness expanded in Barbara's chest, the urge to weep turning to laughter at the comfortable affection between all of them. "Thank you for inviting me."

Beryl closed the distance between them, arms open. It was like being hugged by a tender grizzly bear. The strength and warmth in the other woman's arms infused her, softening any remaining worry.

"You are welcome in our home, and safe." The words were plain-spoken but monumental.

Home. This is home. A tightness Barbara hadn't known she held in her chest released.

Beryl didn't let go until Barbara did, giving her one last squeeze. "Don't mind us. We've never been normal."

Before Barbara could ask what that meant, Lukas touched her elbow, his German careful. "Do you play chess?"

"I used to be pretty good," Barbara said in kind.

Tobias shrugged when she glanced back, hands in his pockets and smiling. "It's your funeral."

Isela bounced to his side and rested her head on his shoulder. She gave him a nudge.

He bumped back hard enough to make her catch herself in a little plié. "Dork."

After being destroyed on the chessboard, Barbara and Isela curled up on the couch, flipping through a collection of photo albums. Tobias and Lukas bent matching heads over the carved pieces, speaking so softly in German it took her a moment to realize they were ragging on each other. Listening to Tobias, she heard a new ease he lacked in English or Czech. All the measure and abruptness of his tone vanished. He was charming and funny, even to her imperfect ear. From the kitchen, the conversation between Beryl and her youngest son reached a laugh.

As the weekend caught up with her, Barbara softened into the overstuffed couch and allowed her attention to drift, anchored by Isela's cozy warmth.

"Hallo!" They all looked up at the call from the entryway.

Isela's face shadowed before she smiled. "Mark must have finished early. Let's see how this goes."

Where Chris and Tobias inherited their father's height and long limbs, their elder brother had Beryl's compact frame and dark brown skin. Issy rose to give her oldest brother a peck on the cheek. His bright copper-colored eyes roved the room, pausing on Barbara.

Only the brush of fabric on her shoulder clued her to Tobias' approach. She jumped a little, startled by how fast he moved. He focused on his brother with matching intensity.

Chris poked his head in from the kitchen, dusting his hands on his apron. "Mark, did you get the bread? Markus?"

Mark tossed him the bag from the bakery without breaking his stare. Before disappearing into the kitchen, Chris sent a warning look to his brothers. "Don't make me get Mom."

Mark's gaze settled back on Barbara. "So, you're the girlfriend."

"This is Barbara," Isela said brightly, "Tobias' friend from the university who happens to be a woman."

Barbara offered her hand.

His grip was cool and firm, his gaze assessing as it moved from his brother's face to hers. Tension radiated out of Tobias at her back.

"Nice to meet you," he said. "I'm the jerk older brother."

"I see," Barbara said, maintaining eye contact. "That's quite a mouthful."

Isela laughed and tugged her oldest brother's arm. "She's good."

Mark gave a crooked smile, releasing her hand. "It's just Jerk, for short."

His eyes narrowed when he took in Tobias, missing nothing. "We missed you this weekend at the cabin. How was Vienna?"

Tobias leaned into Barbara, and she feared they wore identical goofy smiles.

"Ah ha," Mark drawled. "I'm gonna need a beer."

Dinner centered a massive spread of food and resembled an Olympic sport. Long after Barbara was reduced to sipping water to relieve the pressure of a full belly, the three brothers continued to clear plates. Her stifled yawn became a laugh as Beryl refereed a brief dispute over the last of the dumplings. Her brows lifted, and Chris released his grasp of the plate to Mark's smirk.

Barbara rose to help clear the table with the others, but Beryl took her arm. "This is why I have children. Come, let's get to know each other."

Beryl poured two glasses of wine and led her into the sitting room before the massive windows.

"You've been alone a long time," Beryl said after they praised the view and the city.

Barbara was surprised by her own reaction. She should have been alarmed or at least bothered that the woman was so invasive. Instead, a wave of relief at being seen and understood flooded her.

"I know what it's like," Beryl said. "I'm lucky to have Lukas, my boys, and Isela. They keep me grounded. Who does that for you?"

She thought of Veronika, and Beryl touched her arm. "I'm so sorry for your loss. She loved her store and her books, and you a great deal more than both."

Grief tied complex tangles in her vocal cords. "You knew her well?"

"Not as well as I would have liked," Beryl said. "These guys kept me busy, but as they grew up, I visited her shop once in a while. And when I opened the yoga studio, she was one of my first regulars."

"I must have seen you in the shop sometime," Barbara wondered, searching her memory. "And now... with Tobias at the University. We've been a degree or two apart. That sounds silly."

Beryl squeezed her arm. "We're all connected, Barbara. It's just a matter of timing. The more connections, the more grounded we are. Staying grounded keeps us safe. Especially those of us who are not common here."

A little sparkle in her eye made Barbara shiver and come alert. Her instinct said Beryl meant something deeper than the color of their skin.

Tobias joined them, wariness in the gaze that bounced between them. Beryl asked about Vienna and the drive, and Barbara registered something more unyielding in his voice when he spoke to his mother.

The exhaustion became impossible to fight off.

"I should go," Barbara said. "It's been a long day."

Her goodbyes to the family ranged from Isela's wholehearted embrace to a firm handshake from Mark. Beryl came last, and she hugged Barbara with a strength that made her breath catch.

"You have our kinship and our protection if ever you need it," Beryl whispered. "All you have to do is ask."

On their way out, Lukas handed Tobias a set of keys. Tobias led the way down the stairs holding Barbara's hand. The door above closed behind them.

On the next floor, he paused, jingling the keys. "Not subtle, my dad. But come on."

The empty apartment occupied half the floor with views mirroring the flat above.

Barbara gazed out at the deep boughs of spring trees just visible at the bottom of the windowsills. "It's yours?"

"They want me to take it." He stood with hands on hips in the middle of the living room.

"Are you planning on staying after you finish the collection?"

It wasn't hard to imagine the place full of books and smelling like his aftershave. She started down the hall, counting three modest bedrooms.

"I didn't realize how much Prague felt like home until I was away," his voice followed her down. "When I started there were rumors of a position opening up in the department. But who knows now? I haven't exactly made friends."

She winced. "I heard about what you did at your hearing. And filing that complaint with the head of staff on my behalf—"

"I meant my team. As for Novak, what happened—what they did—it isn't right, Barbara. I won't stand for it."

She shook her head, fixing her stare out the window to avoid shedding the tears that sprang to her eyes. "It was for the best. The shop takes so much time, and I'm digitizing inventory and making real inroads with an online store. It will keep me busy. Too busy for school, maybe."

Despite her new commitment to the store, the ache of her dismissal lingered. She still wasn't sure giving up everything she'd worked for was the right decision.

"I won't slide into position on the faculty knowing what they did to you."

"The school is lucky to have someone of your caliber. You could use that to make an impact. Make sure it doesn't happen again."

"I won't give up," he said. "I promise you that."

"You should."

"Why?"

Because then whatever this is can't be.

They'd crossed the Rubicon on her couch two nights ago. Vienna had only cemented things. If they reinstated her tomorrow, this would end. Or she would have to give up everything she'd worked for to keep him. She wasn't strong enough to contemplate either future out loud, so she changed the subject.

"Why do you call your mom by her first name?"

The question came to her before she could check it, curiosity stifled after hours of being among the family who had seemed so otherwise at ease with each other. Even Mark, prickly as he might have been, obviously adored their mother. Only Tobias's affection for her seemed tempered with distance.

"It's her name." The smile seemed as forced as the laugh that followed. "Just always have."

He shrugged, and the deep breath that followed was full of unspoken words.

At the car he couldn't seem to let her go, stroking the backs of her arms, and gathering her hands in his. When she raised her chin, he cupped her cheeks and laid a kiss of such shattering tenderness on her mouth, her eyes stung again.

"Give us a chance," he said, a catch in his voice. "Give me a chance. Please."

CHAPTER THIRTY-FOUR

MARK WAS GNAWING the end of a baguette while checking his phone when Tobias returned the keys to the ring beside the stove.

The knotted expression in Barbara's brows and the shadow in her eyes haunted him. This was uncharted territory—relationships, and the way sex complicated everything. When they were in the same room, he could hardly think for the roar of blood in his veins. Every time they were together, the sensation grew stronger. All he wanted was to be curled up around her body.

She wasn't as blinded by libido as he was. He was hiding something, and she knew it.

"Gods, they're shameless," Mark said, grabbing his third beer. He offered one to Tobias.

"Thanks, no. Who?"

"Dad." He gestured at the keys. "And Mom. Sending you to that funeral."

Tobias froze. He took a deep breath, bracing his hands on the counter. Mark watched him, calculation darkening his bright copper eyes.

The corner of his mouth tipped up. "Didn't put that one together, eh, smart guy?"

The growl rose in Tobias, but he bit down on it. "Explain."

"Mom knew that old woman for years, probably watched that girl the whole time, and you walked right into it. The two of you. Ten-to-one, she's got no idea either."

"Toby she is so sweet!" Isela trotted into the kitchen, her smile dying with a quick glance at their faces. "What are you two—"

"I thought that was Jerk to you." Mark cut her off.

Isela glared. "If it walks like a duck and talks like a duck."

"Ducks quack, bird brains," he snapped. "If you're going to be a miniature Mom, at least get the saying right."

Tobias stared at him. "Why are you such an asshole all the time?"

Isela crossed the room to Tobias' side and touched his arm. "Toby, Mom only wants—"

He snatched his arm away. "Don't."

"Don't you yell at her," Mark barked. "Your dumb ass walked right into Mom's meddling, that's not Issy's fault."

Isela looked between them, rounding on Mark. "You're mad because no one wants to subject some poor woman to you by meddling on your behalf."

"Of course you take his side." Mark rolled his eyes, laughing. "You're not around anymore to know which way is up, Miss Fancy Pants. Too good for the rest of us."

She stepped back, eyes wide and shining. "Now it's poor big brother? Who loaned you the money to start your business, Markus? You don't approve of what I do or how I live, write me a check now, you jackass."

Beryl stormed in. "That's enough, all of you."

"Tell this miserable old turd to stop trying to destroy everyone else's happiness!" Isela spun on her heel and fled, her breath hitching to sobs.

Beryl rounded on him, then glimpsed something in Tobias' face and paused. "You have something to say to me?"

Tobias shifted on his feet, jaw clenched.

Mark relaxed against the counter, one arm crossed over his chest, and drained half his beer in one long pull. He looked less satisfied than Tobias expected, considering his success in ending the evening on a sour note. Their mother's looks weren't the only thing Mark had inherited. He'd been a thorough study of her ability to meddle, but seemed only to create chaos.

"Go ahead, Toby," Mark urged, his voice low and taunting. "You've always been the one who tries to get along. How far is too far? When do you stand up for yourself?"

Tobias was no longer the boy fleeing the monster in his blood by burying himself in his studies. He'd made a fragile accord with the beast. An incredible woman had turned the light on in the dark corners of his life, but now doubt soured even that.

"Did you send me," he began, unable to look at Beryl, "to Veronika's funeral intending for Barbara and I...?"

She sighed and flipped on the kettle. "I didn't know she was your research assistant."

He groaned, closing his eyes. He pounded the counter with a fist. "Ma, really? Why are you always meddling?"

"You see!" Mark crowed

"Shut the fuck up, Mark."

For once, their mother didn't chastise either the curse or the nick-name. She fixed her eldest child with a look that held less censure than it should have, in Tobias's opinion. "You should call it a night. Apologize to your sister."

Mark scoffed.

Her expression hardened. "Go."

He snagged his beer and shoved off of the counter, then grumbled his way out of the kitchen. Beryl watched him, a sadness in her face so great Tobias almost regretted his anger. Almost.

"He always puts himself on the outside," she said. "He's the only one of you kids I don't know how to help."

And then she said something like that.

"Maybe you should stop trying to help so much."

She sifted tea into the pot with a little shrug. "Being your mother doesn't stop. And what's left for me to do once you're able to feed and clothe yourselves? That's when the hard work starts—your happiness."

"My happiness isn't your job."

"I know." She sighed. "But you'll understand when you have a family of your own. Children."

Something deep in his chest shuttered, tumblers of a great lock shut-ting. With lightning-sharp clarity, he saw why he'd avoided romantic relationships and sex for his adult life. "I don't judge you and Dad. I'm grateful for everything you've done for us. But if there's a chance that I could pass this on, I won't take the risk."

"Tobias," she murmured, shaking her head, "it's not a fatal disease."

"No, it's a curse," he corrected. "I growl in my sleep, mom. And whine. Like a *dog*. How's that relationship going to work?"

He laughed, hearing the edge and bitterness clawing up his throat.

"If you go out with your brothers every couple of weeks..."

He shook his head. "Since I've been doing that, the wolf is getting stronger. My senses are changing, my strength. I'm healing faster. I have to resist the urge to catch things that fall at work or carry things that should be too heavy. How am I supposed to hide that in my own home?"

She was quiet for a long moment, pouring two cups of tea and letting her fingers dance on the rims of each. He scented the spell now. The same scent he'd picked up in Barbara's coffee. He folded his arms over his chest.

She sighed. "I admit, based on what Veronika told me about her particular talent, I suspected Barbara was different, so I paid attention. But I didn't interfere. I wasn't going to. But she's alone in the world now, Tobias. It's a dangerous place, given what she is."

She held out the cup, a peace offering. He raised a brow.

"It's just tea," she said, then admitted, "and a little charm for calm."

"A charm?" His eyes narrowed.

She held up a palm. "I've never done anything with my abilities to affect the thoughts or actions of you or your siblings. It goes against the vow of my craft."

He refused to smile at her put-upon expression, but he took the cup. "The night of the break-in, I almost turned fighting off those guys. I scared her."

"If you could explain at a safe time when her life isn't already in danger..."

Tobias closed his eyes, thinking of his aborted conversations in the car. "If I tell her about me and then you get hurt... I won't risk your safety."

Her teacup touched down with uncharacteristic force. "Mark isn't the only one carrying too much. Don't take that on. My choices are my own."

He bowed his head and leaned toward her. "I'm sorry, Mom."

"I'm sorry for meddling." Her hand settled on his shoulder. "I only want you to have a full life."

Tobias locked his jaw, sealing in another counter argument.

"Your hair looks nice a little longer." She brushed the strands back from his forehead.

The calm spread through him, soothing the aching places no painkiller would touch. She smiled, but he sensed the subject wasn't closed. "What else, Mom?"

First time in years, she looked troubled. "Tobias, there is something untapped in her, something powerful. She has no training, no coven. It makes her vulnerable."

"I'll protect her," he vowed. "I can do that—s-s-he doesn't need to know about my..."

He shook his head against the word that rose in him: *beast.*

SO MUCH POWER *in this one, barely tapped. Laboring in the old crone's shop is a waste of our considerable talent. She who would have betrayed me, submitted me to those lords of death for their judgement. I have bigger plans for you. Starting with the halls and stone of those arrogant pricks who bid and dismiss you at their whim. It pains me to see another sister pressed under the heel of such men.*

And the were. In my day most were vermin—diseased and lawless—a corruption of the grace in their blood. I will not have you suffer under his influence any longer.

Their halls of knowledge will be the avenue to our glorious future. Why should all that information remain under their control?

CHAPTER THIRTY-FIVE

THE PHONE RANG as Barbara scanned the email of a collector inquiring about the illuminated manuscript leaf.

A week after returning from Vienna, she had almost finished adding listings for the rarest editions in the shop to the website. She'd already sold three to buyers who'd seen them online. At this rate, the computer system would pay for itself in a few months.

She turned away from the computer screen, wishing more than anything she could turn to Veronika with a smile and announce the sale. But Veronika's empty chair reminded her that would never be possible again.

Barbara still hadn't worked up the courage to clean out Veronika's apartment, never mind contemplate moving downstairs.

Hemingway leaped onto the counter, butting her head against Barbara's chin. The phone rang again. She swallowed her grief, checking that the shop was empty before wiggling her fingers in invitation. The handle floated off the base and settled in her palm. "Antikvariát a Belgická."

"Slečna Barbara Svobodová?" Sounded official.

She straightened, fingers frozen on the cat's ear. "Ano."

"Vodičkova, with the office of the head of staff at Žižkov University," she continued in Czech. "I'd like to schedule a meeting."

Hemingway tapped her wrist with one furry five-toed paw, and Barbara resumed stroking her. "I am no longer with the university."

"An examination concerning the circumstances of your separation has been conducted and we would like to share the findings."

Barbara sighed, unable to keep the bitterness out of her voice. "Can't you just send me a letter?"

The voice on the other end lowered. "It is our policy that investigation issues are handled in person."

So they could lay out whatever spurious argument they'd used to justify firing her?

After how hard she worked, toeing every line they set before her, leaping over every obstacle, the humiliation of being escorted out of the building like a criminal choked her. Blindsided, she'd never even had a chance to respond. Now she wanted to tell them what she thought of their bullshit process and her dismissal. Perhaps she'd lodge her own complaint.

Anger burned bright through her veins. The papers on her desk began to smoke. She yanked her fingertips away, wide-eyed. The outline of her fingers had been singed into the paper.

She stared at her hand. She'd been using her bit of grace all week, more than ever and in new ways, but it had never manifested like this before.

"Miss Svobodova?" The voice on the end of the line echoed distantly.

"Yes, I'll be there," she said, startled by the chill in her tone.

Even an hour later, she couldn't stop sneaking glimpses at her hand. Try as she might, she couldn't recreate that heat. She wasn't sure she wanted to. Her touch of grace had always seemed so harmless, helpful even. This was something destructive. Dangerous. A fire in the shop could be catastrophic.

Tobias called as she was closing for lunch. She knew should be thinking about whatever it was he was hiding from her. But the sound of his voice lured her away from worry, stirring that warm honey bee tickle in her chest. Though they'd talked on the phone during the week, he was as busy preparing the exhibit as she was getting the store online.

"Did you hear anything?" she asked, after telling him about the call.

Doubt weighted his voice. "No one said anything to me. Do you want me to go with you?"

"I can handle this," she said, scooping up Hemi and turning off the lights.

He made an unhappy noise, but didn't argue. Instead his voice lightened with a subject change. "If you don't have plans tonight, could I take you out for dinner?" He rushed into the empty space before she could answer. "The Matylda is nice in the evenings. The bugs might be a problem. Perhaps the Dancing House. Or the Žižkov Tower. I can call for a reservation."

A few days apart made her restless for his presence. Maybe not just his *presence*, either.

They could do fancy restaurants anytime.

"Why don't you just come over and I can make us something?" She glanced at the listing for a new Chinese food restaurant that delivered.

"Are you sure?" he asked warily. "I want to do this right. We're together now, yes? I'd like to be."

"You are doing it right," she said. "But I'm inviting you over. I close up at seven."

She locked the store a few minutes early and raced upstairs with the cat to clean up her apartment and get ready. Just after seven, her buzzer rang. She hit the button to unlock the downstairs door.

He appeared at her flat with flowers and a bottle of wine. He looked breathless, and his eyes were bright with hope and mischief, his hair tousled on his brow. He'd tucked his jacket over his bag, and the bright green shirt sleeves set off his grey eyes.

"That was fast." Barbara laughed.

His cheekbones flushed rose gold. "I ran."

She couldn't help it, she folded into his arms, craning up on her toes until he lifted her off her feet to kiss her soundly.

They were interrupted by a screeching crash from the kitchen and a low feline growl. Hemi crouched on top of the refrigerator, her back arched and tail lifted, claws scraping the metal.

"What on earth is the matter with you?" Barbara tried to coax her down, but the cat refused. "Hemingway!"

When Tobias approached, she yowled and flung herself along the cabinet tops, disappearing out the open door.

Barbara sighed. "Ever since the break-in, she's been...weird."

Tobias smiled uncertainly. Maybe he didn't like cats?

"I'll just go put her in the shop tonight," she said.

When she returned, he'd uncorked the wine and found a vase. She stroked the plump heads of the unopened peonies. They would be magnificent in a day or two.

"What's for dinner?" His brows rose as he peered at the hotplate.

Barbara laughed. "I thought I'd call in a takeaway order from the Chinese restaurant around the corner. That way we could focus on... other things."

The intensity of his gaze jellied her knees. "Call it in."

By the time she'd finished, he'd yanked off his tie and vest. He swept her off her feet and onto the kitchen table. "How long do we have?"

"Twenty-five minutes." She laughed as he rucked up her skirt.

He checked his watch and took off his glasses, sliding to his knees. "Let's not waste it."

Nineteen minutes later he left her shaking on the kitchen table. He rose, whistling, grabbed her keys, and headed for the door.

"Back in ten," he said. "To finish what I started."

She raced to her room to change. Eight minutes later, she was tossing a robe over the sexiest bit of lingerie she owned and tugging at her curls to shape them into some semblance of order when she heard Tobias crash into the apartment, bearing bags already beginning to show signs of leakage within.

He kicked the door closed behind him. "How much food did you order?"

"I was at your family dinner the other night," she said, reaching for the belt of her robe. "I've never seen a carcass picked so clean."

"The Vogel boys can eat." He laughed, setting the bags down on the counter and turning to her. Laughter was replaced by a long hungry look that had nothing to do with food. "Leave it open. What on earth do you have there?"

She released the belt, revealing the creamy chemise.

The sunny lemon yellow, made of water-thin silk, clung to her. His breath quickened as she stepped toward him. She wanted to do unspeakably dirty things to him just for looking at her like that.

The words escaped him in a rush. "'*Each time, you happen to me all over again.*'"

"Wharton." Blood burned to her face. "What a romantic you are, Professor."

She grinned as he cupped her cheeks to draw her close.

"How do you like your takeout?" He traced the shape of her mouth with his lips, sending currents of need down her spine. "Plates or straight out of the carton?"

Her fingers found the buckle of his belt. "Cold."

Later, she shrugged on her robe and retrieved her slippers while he pulled on pants and his unbuttoned shirt. They carried the food and the wine to the roof. She spread a tattered blanket as the last of the daylight faded and the stars made a bashful appearance. He ate like a starving man, long after she retired to nurse her wine.

She leaned back on one elbow, amused. "Didn't you get lunch?"

"I forgot," he said, offering up the last of the wontons. "Meetings for the display all day. How's the shop?"

She shuddered and waved him on. "Busy. I had three calls for estates and offers on some of the things we brought back from Holašovic. What about your journal?"

He shrugged. "I've had to set it aside for now. The Necromancer's people haven't returned the original, so it's not part of the collection and that's all I have time for these days."

She shook her head, and the words escaped before she could catch them. "Do you ever wish…you hadn't seen it?"

He frowned, a furrow between his brows. "Never. It's a clue. It helps us paint a bigger picture of what life was like, what people were like. Even if it's a fabrication, it tells us a story about the way events were recorded and what was considered scandalous or of note. Even if I never see it again, I know it's out there. That it exists."

She nodded, though he hadn't entirely understood her question. Of course, he didn't know about the dreams or that foolish spell she's cast from the spell book. Innermost desires.

Is your power getting away from you?

She considered what she'd done in the shop and the little ways her grace had changed in the last few months. That had all started after she found that book. At first, it had seemed wondrous. But she'd almost set a fire with just a touch today. Maybe Veronika had been right to separate her from it. Wherever it was, Barbara wished it good riddance.

When the bottle was empty and a good many food cartons relieved of their burden, Barbara and Tobias stretched out on the roof.

They joined slowly this time and, as he settled between her thighs under the blanket of night, for the first time it wasn't urgency that drove them. Wine softened everything to a comfortable blur. He moved inside her with leashed ardor, his eyes on her face, hands on her breasts and her shoulders.

"Stay with me." The words, spoken when she would have closed her eyes and rode the wave building to a crest, brought her back into her body with a jolt.

She found him instead, and their noses came into alignment, shared breath ragged. Sweet and salt mingled on her tongue.

His hand rose to her thigh, bracing her under the slow resurgence of his body. She made out his voice over the hazy warmth consuming her. "I'm yours."

She became a million pieces all at once, mirroring the stars overhead with a long sigh. He kept his rhythm the entire time, his eyes on hers, and only when the crest receded did she feel his rise. Her body tripped again, joining him with breathtaking speed, and this time she did close her eyes with a guttural cry as his forehead pressed into her collarbone and he buried himself deep.

"Stay," she asked as they came down. "Please."

"As long as you'll have me," he whispered.

In the morning, she watched him wake when her alarm buzzed. He snorted at the tail end of a snore and blinked like a mole.

"Already?" Tobias groaned, pulling her close.

"Again?" Barbara wiggled her hips.

"It's as inevitable as dawn," he drawled, kissing her nose and rising. "But if you give me five minutes to take care of some business, I..." He glanced at the clock and swore. "I'm sorry, Bebe, I gotta go."

She nodded with a little sigh. One of the luxuries she hadn't counted on about losing her job in the library was a later start to the day. She didn't open the store until ten. "You shower first."

She made coffee and eggs while the shower ran. Something inside her had settled last night on the roof, soothed to restive peace. There were truths he could not yet speak, but in every movement, in every act, he was hers.

For now, as she watched him dress in the previous day's clothes, snugging the tie around his neck with a little grin, she knew she wanted this. She wanted him. She was happy with her work and the shop. There would be plenty to keep her busy. She sent a little prayer of thanks to Veronika and handed him a steaming mug.

He kissed her first. "I used your toothbrush. I hope you don't mind."

"I'll get you one today."

The look on his face—as though she'd promised his favorite dessert at every meal for the rest of his life—made her heart hiccup with glee.

"And you should probably leave an extra shirt or two here," she added as casually as possible. "I can make some room in the wardrobe."

He froze. "You're sure?"

"Just don't expect me to iron." She winked.

"Deal."

They ate in a hurry, and she snagged his plate and cup on his way down the stairs to the front door. He tied his shoes, rechecking his watch. "What time is your appointment?"

She'd forgotten all about it, and her smile slipped. "Half past eleven."

He rose from his laces to draw her to him. "Can I call you after?"

"I have to run an errand while I'm out," she said, unable to keep from smiling. "Toiletries. But I'll be in the shop for the rest of the afternoon."

He brushed a thumb over her cheekbone and his lips to her forehead.

"How about we go out for dinner tonight? Somewhere nice. We can talk. Not just..." He waved a hand.

She rested her hands on her hips. "Bored, already?"

"N-n-no way." He froze, his face drawn in horror. "I-I-I just..." He took a deep breath, gaze roving her face until it locked on hers. His brow sketched an arch over the frames of his glasses as his eyes narrowed. "If we're in public, it will keep me minding my manners. Maybe I can keep my hands to myself for five minutes."

When she gave up fighting the laughter, he snatched her up against him so fast she gasped before their mouths met.

It was her turn to blink owlishly when he lowered her feet to the floor. She met the satisfied glare of a man sure of his prowess. His voice rumbled through her. "I miss the sound of your voice when you're not screaming my name."

Heat flushed her chest and neck. The insides of her thighs tingled with warmth. "Get out of here while you still can, Professor."

After a hot shower and another cup of tea, she dressed for the day in her most conservative outfit, a high-necked shirtdress, and ballet flats. On her way to the university, she checked on Hemingway, refilling her water dish and food bowl. The cat was back to purring thunder on from the sunny patch under the window, no worse for wear.

"If I have my way he's going to be around for a while, Hemi," she advised the cat. "You'd better make your peace."

When Barbara arrived at the head of staff's office, the secretary introduced herself and led her inside.

She paused for a breath at the sight of the head of staff, the university dean and Professor Novak. The latter's look of discomfort was its own reward.

In the offered chair, she perched on the edge and crossed her legs at the ankle, tucking them beneath her. She smoothed her skirt and picked at an imaginary piece of lint to hide the the the way her fingers shook.

The head of staff was a severe-looking woman in her late forties, her coifed blond hair threaded with silver. She explained that, after reviewing the case and the volume of letters written supporting her excellent work in the field, the decision to put her on leave had been reversed.

"Volume of letters?"

The head of staff slid a folder across the desk. Barbara flipped through them: Edita, Honza, a past professor or two. Tobias Vogel. Over and over, his name signed neatly above the print and his title. Pages. One a day, since she'd been dismissed.

"You may resume your duties in the research librarians' office on Monday," she said. "You have also been awarded a fellowship in the conservation department with Professor Klisak."

Klisak hadn't had any openings this term. She'd been told he was retiring and no longer supervising doctoral candidates. She was too stunned to respond with anything but affirmation. There were handshakes all around, and even Novak made an apology that sounded more sincere for the presence of the dean and head of staff. Barbara left the room in a daze.

Everything she'd reached for so long was back in her grasp. And the shop?

You saw how they looked down at you at the ball while shaking the hand of that professor of yours.

But it could be like in Holašovic—she'd proved herself, beyond her grace—

Come now. Why settle with a little shop, when you could have an entire library?

When she reached the research assistant office, Edita and Honza were both thrilled. It wasn't until she stood before her empty desk that she realized what else she'd have to give up.

"Honza, I'm sure you meant well, but this is the wrong volume," Tobias said from the doorway.

He faltered, the book forgotten in his hand.

Just the sight of him made a tickle of warmth shine at her fingertips, but instead of going outward it shot in, threading delicate tendrils around her heart. He was fresh air and sunshine and lavender blossoms.

She'd found him, and been found in the process.

And she would have to give him up. She stifled a gasp.

"Barbara." He closed the distance quickly. "What's happened?"

"Professor Vogel." Her tongue tripped on the formality, well aware that Honza and Edita were watching and that her face was not as composed as it should have been. She put the desk between them as her eyes darted to their audience. He hesitated, but took her cue and stood still.

"Wonderful news," she said, trying not to make it sound like an accusation. "I've been reinstated."

He couldn't mask shock, but he recovered quickly. "Of course you were. As you should have been. Will you be returning to the collection?"

"I'm beginning a fellowship with Professor Klisak. I'll be half time in research, and half in conservation."

She watched him register the information, the slow nod, and the way his jaw flexed closed on words they both knew could not be said here.

"Congratulations, Miss Svobodová," he managed. "Good to have you back."

"Your complaints started the whole process that exonerated me. So, I owe you...an enormous debt of gratitude."

He shook his head and swallowed hard, his mouth a tight line. "I'm glad to hear the matter has been resolved in your favor. As it should have been."

She wondered if the entire room could hear the desperate beating of her heart.

Honza broke the silence. "Sir, I'm sorry about the book. I must have misread the form."

Tobias forced his gaze toward the younger man. "It's possible I filled it out incorrectly. Thank you."

"I'll get that to your office this afternoon," Honza murmured.

Tobias stood, as if unable to remember how to end the exchange. His eyes found her again. "Bebe—"

Funny how a word so meaningless to everyone else in the room arrowed right through her, slicing the last of her resolve clean away. There were too many tears to swallow, too much emotion to fight back. Six steps and she could be in his arms.

Edita entered her field of vision, breaking the dizzying intensity of his gaze. The next step put her between them.

"Professor," Edita began, another harmless word but layered with a warning.

Tobias straightened. Hs snapped out a terse, "Good day."

When he was gone, Barbara sank into her chair. Honza hurried to the stacks to retrieve the requested volume, oblivious.

Edita spun on her. "What happened between you two?"

"Everything."

CHAPTER THIRTY-SIX

Tobias jammed the buzzer impatiently.

"I'll be right down," Barbara's voice sounded distant.

It's the intercom, he told himself. Don't make it more than it is.

That morning, he'd met for the first conversation about an ongoing position at the university. Afterward, he'd enlisted Isela and her well-connected Russian dancer friend to get him an impossible table at a restaurant overlooking the Charles Bridge and the castle. When he thought about a future in Prague, he couldn't imagine one without her in it. It wouldn't have mattered if the Necromancer himself had arranged for Barbara to come into his life. The wolf didn't give a tinker's damn about how they'd met, as far as it was concerned, she was theirs now.

Forget the toothbrush, he would say. *Move in with me. I can't imagine the big drafty flat without you and your piles of genre novels and your insane cat. Though the cat scares me a little.*

No, too soon. He didn't want to scare *her.* But by Christmas, perhaps. First, furnishings. At least the basics.

He'd been almost humming when he'd discovered the wrong book on his desk and headed down to research.

The sight of Barbara's face, pale and on the verge of tears, standing over her old desk brought the wolf to the front in a heartbeat. The news didn't fit the stricken expression on her face. It took him a long moment to understand what it meant. They might not be working

together any longer, but school policy prohibited student-faculty relationships.

Tobias spent the rest of the afternoon strategizing.

What to say. How to say it. When would Barbara graduate—six
months, a year, tops?

He made a list of weekend getaways that would take them out of the
city and away from chance encounters. He rehearsed in front of the
mirror in his office, practicing the words until his tongue didn't trip over
itself in his hurry or desperation.

But when she opened the main door of the building, the words
vanished at the sight of her eyes—enormous, luminous, and already
damp. She wore the same severe black shirtdress. It was a shame: she
belonged in yellows and golds, reds and turquoise, colors that brought
out the dusting of freckles on her cheeks. Black muted her natural glow.

She curled into his arms as if drawn. He tucked his chin over her
crown and took a big whiff of her: bergamot in orange blossoms and the
faintest trace of grief.

A crack formed in his ribcage, drawing everything he'd prepared to
say into it.

"I made a reservation." he began anyway.

She shook her head, blinking hard. "Can we go for a drive?"

"Whatever you like."

She pulled the Citroën from the musty garage at the back of the
building and onto the narrow cobblestone streets. They drove north,
crossing over the river toward the Troja estate and vineyards. On the
spot overlooking the river, she pulled off the road and parked. Her
hands clenched the wheel.

"A single letter, I'd understand, but you wrote every day," she said.
"Tobias, why?"

He dredged up a smile, rubbing the prickle of a day's growth on his
chin. He should have shaved. What an idiot. As if she wanted to go to a
nice restaurant with his shaggy face. "You needed a champion. I wanted
to be him."

She encircled his fingers, drawing them into her lap, and slid across
the bench seat to his side. Her voice shook. "All day I've tried to figure
out how to make this work."

His voice strained. "Barbara—"

"I've spent my whole life pretending to be untouchable." She choked on the words. "Not letting anything get to me. To spend the next year and a half acting like you don't mean anything? Hiding and sneaking around, hoping people don't see us... I won't stand on the other side of the room from you at department events like a stranger. Not anymore. Tobias, I love you."

His arguments evaporated in the wake of her words. A crystalline tear fell into the folds of her skirt. Her ragged little gasp speared his heart.

"This is everything I've worked for," she said. "And I'm so close, I can't give up now."

He could push, insist they risk everything. And if they were caught? Putting himself between her and her dreams would make him more a monster than the wolf ever had. He'd promised not to let anything hurt her. He hadn't known it might include himself.

He slid a hand to the back of her neck and gave the taut muscles a squeeze. Then he buckled down the ragged ache in his chest and let her go. "You're back where you should have been a year ago. I will always care about you. That won't—ever—stop. I want the best for you. And that is this."

He smiled when she met his eyes. Her lower lip trembled.

"We take a break." He shrugged, assuming that Professor St Giles confidence he'd always envied. Knowing it this time for the act it truly was. "The time will fly by. What if we promise to revisit this after you graduate?"

"I won't ask you to wait for me."

"You're not asking," he said. "And after a lifetime of waiting for you, a year and a half is nothing."

Only he hadn't known her scent before, or how she felt wrapped around him. He had survived ignorant of the visceral joy of her welcoming him into her, the soft sound of contentment she made when he slid home.

A year and a half without being able to touch her, to fall asleep beside her, might kill him. The time, or the wolf, would. It didn't care about department regulations. They'd laid the kind of claim on one another that was not put aside. No amount of running with his brothers was going to make up for her absence.

Barbara would go on to find her own cohort—peers and colleagues.

Beyond school, the world of booksellers would open to her with opportunities she couldn't yet imagine.

Lovers. Ones who knew how to court her, make love to her, whose tongues didn't get stuck on their own words. Maybe even ones who would earn the approval of that terrifying cat.

Ones without monsters living under their skins.

The thin, craven voice crowed with relief that he would never risk her rejection of the wolf inside him. She'd made the decision for him. He would focus on his career with his family secrets safe and his heart intact.

After the exhibit, he would pursue a permanent position and set down his roots in Prague. He'd move out of his parents' building. Get a sunny flat in Vinohrady, near the park, and fill it with books. He would publish a few papers about the collection and work follow-up exhibit and interdisciplinary work if he could get the other departments to go along with it. He would be too busy building a career to go sneaking out of town on weekends, eat Chinese food on rooftops at twilight, or lose sleep in her arms.

He clung to that voice. Damned if he would let her see how much the fear of losing her shook him.

"Let's put it—put us—on hold. Deal?" He glanced at his watch, desperate to stave off the return of her tears. "Now come on, we're only a little late, maybe they'll hold our table. You reclaimed your place in the department. We should celebrate. We can practice being... whatever we're going to have to be to get through the next year and a half."

They made the drive in silence.

At the restaurant, the food clumped like sawdust in his mouth, but he forced each bite down under the weight of her too-perceptive gaze. He focused the conversation on transitioning back into academia. Klisak would be a good advisor; he was fair and thoughtful and seemed delighted to be assigned a fellow as bright at Barbara. He suggested a few students he thought might be good working in her shop part time.

"I won't need them," she answered slowly.

Relieved for an excuse to put his fork down, he stared at her. "How are you going to manage—"

"I'm not." She met his eyes, and he saw the liquid shine pooling over her lower lashes before her gaze darted to her plate. "I've decided to sell the store."

"But you've done so much work, with the database and the listings," he said.

Her shoulders rose and fell in a shrug that ended in a slump. "I can't do both, and this is what I want."

His mouth moved over words that wouldn't come. Finally he managed to strangle out, "But Bebe, you love—"

"The shop was Veronika's dream, not mine." Her hand clenched on the knife, knuckles white. "Not mine."

She set her knife down, smoothing her open hand over the tablecloth with a long deep breath. Her voice lightened, but didn't lose its wobble. "Why would I want one dusty old shop, when I can have a whole library? This is where the real work happens, right—the funding, the scholarship. Not just what we can buy and sell."

"It's your decision," he murmured.

After dinner, he stood on her doorstep, hands in his pockets, and tried to figure out the right thing to say to end it. She stood a step above him, making them almost eye to eye. Barbara's hand settled on his cheek, meeting his gaze.

A mix of gratitude and anguish made her eyes churn again as her mouth pursed hard to avoid a frown. "Thank you."

He managed a smile and tucked a curl behind her ear. *I love you. I don't know how I'm going to live without you.*

"Good luck, Barbara Svobodová. Not that you need it. I'll see you at school."

He would, every chance he got. Just to make sure she was all right. And then he would watch her fly away.

"Can we…" she asked, looking at his mouth. "It's cruel to ask. I just want to remember. Once more."

In an instant, he knew what she wanted and that a kiss was a definitively lousy idea, because he couldn't be sure he was strong enough to walk away after.

No, he wanted to beg. *Let me pretend like I can leave without my heart and be fine.*

Instead, he tipped her chin up and, when their lips met, tasted salt of her grief. The hard lump in his chest shattered into an explosion of sharp edges that pressed against his ribcage with every breath. He pulled back with a groan. Unable to sustain his resolve, he backed down the steps.

When the door closed behind her, he swiped the blur from his eyes with the back of one hand and started running.

He ran until he feared his heart would burst. Too late. He came to himself in the dense undergrowth of Vysehrad fortress, heaving. Then he surrendered to the wolf and silence.

CHAPTER THIRTY-SEVEN

BARBARA FOUND no reason to hold off tackling Veronika's apartment any longer. At least she would have an excuse to have a good long cry that she could tell herself wasn't connected to watching Tobias Vogel walk away.

He'd tried to support her with his swift and cavalier insistence on waiting. As though he'd put his life on hold for her. Still, he took her to an expensive dinner and toasted her success. If not for the hollowed-out look in his eyes, she might have believed him.

Instead, she tore the last bits of both their hearts out on the stoop. Just for kicks.

The kiss had been a mistake.

Now she would remember forever what she'd given up. She would bury the nascent dreams for her own future to preserve history.

She blinked back tears. Not yet.

Cold and dark greeted her in Veronika's apartment. Twice the size of her own with a good-sized kitchen, the apartment looked onto the quiet street below.

The plants had withered on the windowsills, in spite of Mrs. Milanova's regular watering. Barbara regretted not coming down sooner. Veronika always talked to her plants. She said it made them grow.

She exhaled, swiping her cheeks on her sleeve.

She turned on the lights and plugged in the record player. The Juliette Gréco record spun and the needle crackled, finding the groove.

Feeling foolish, she walked along the windows, touching leaves and softened tendrils, explaining Veronika's absence.

Then she settled into sorting. The temptation to use her grace rose, but she tamped it down. It didn't belong here. She wanted to touch everything with her own two hands, to say goodbye. Still, she was unable to stifle the slight buzz of activity in her chest—likely from Veronika's personal collection—as she worked.

She set aside a few things for herself and organized the rest to offer residents of the building. Whatever remained would go to charity. It was midnight when she made it to the bedroom.

Painted an incongruously cheerful blue, the bed faced the big bay windows with lace curtains. Up with the dawn, Veronika always boasted. No better time to start the day. Framed photos covered the wall next to the bed, but the rest of the walls were lined with books. Barbara stared at the images of young Veronika. Her mother and father at their wedding. Veronika and her school mates. Amid the shelves in the store, reading beside a stack of books. Teenage Veronika on a horse, beaming.

Startled, Barbara recognized her own face in a new image, tucked into the corner of the framed photo of Veronika's father standing before the Citroen with a puckish grin.

Veronika had found the camera in a box from an estate. The roll had a few images left. She asked Barbara to look up from entering inventory at the counter.

We can't waste film, can we?

The photo captured her awkward smile and frizzy hair held away from her face with an old scarf. Pencil in one hand, book in another. But it also revealed her happiness. For the first time since she'd lost her mother, she had a purpose, a place. A home.

The first sob tore free with a harsh cry. The next collapsed her knees. Barbara curled up on the bed, and the tears came in force.

She must have fallen asleep because when she opened her eyes again, a hand cradled the back of her neck.

"Tobias?" she breathed, sitting up.

But the hand was too small.

The room was empty. She blinked away the stickiness in her eyelashes as the record spun, silent in the empty apartment. Folded over her knees, with her feet on the floor, she contemplated the aching, hollow cavern of her chest.

She'd tried to honor her gifts, to make the best choices. She'd gotten everything she wanted. And somehow lost anyway. Maybe this was the price of a grace like hers—no contentment, no ease—just constantly searching for the next thing of value, the next thing she would have to give up.

Her parents, Veronika, Tobias. The book.

The book and that spell. She'd given it up too, hadn't she—just stopped looking, left it to the whim of the Necromancer and that meddling old woman. Let fear and suspicion make her afraid of her own grace, because it had done something unpredictable. Dangerous.

Pah, what was dangerous? A thing was only dangerous when one doesn't understand it, control it. Nothing in that book has been a danger to you girl. It's only given you exactly what you asked for.

Barbara rose, entranced.

The voice in her head wasn't her own. And her fingertips tingled. She followed the pull to the closet and tugged the chain attached to the light bulb. In the top of the closet, she found rows of hat boxes. One box in the back remained out of reach. On tiptoes, she rose and hooked it with the tips of her fingers, surprised at the weight as it slid against the shelf. Records, perhaps, or documents.

When she grasped it, a jolt ran through her. She knew what was inside before she stumbled back into the bedroom and lifted the lid.

The book of shadows.

Sparks arced off her fingers at the connection, but for the first time, the familiar buzz was accompanied by needles of pain. Relief came quickly after, then a flare of anger. How could that old woman have tried to keep it from her? It was hers, by rights.

She closed up the apartment and ran back upstairs, clutching the book to her chest.

That night, she dreamed she was turning the pages and reading the secrets of the universe. When she woke with a fuzzy head, she could remember nothing, but she stroked the book cover. "You're home now. Everything's going to be fine."

CHAPTER THIRTY-EIGHT

BARBARA DUMPED her bag and her keys onto the kitchen counter with a sigh. The slow ache building in her temple all day reached a steady, pulsing throb.

One month in, and she had to admit the truth: going back to the library had been a mistake. Delighted to be her doctoral advisor, Professor Klisak assigned her to manage the conservation efforts for special collections. It was an unprecedented level of responsibility and ideal for her dissertation. And she loathed every minute. She'd known at the end of the first week, but stubbornness held her firm.

She'd given up Tobias for the book and this dream. She contemplated the closed shop and the interested buyers waiting for her response.

She clenched her teeth as the thought of the book stirred a longing in her.

"I will not open it," she promised. "I will not turn the pages."

She'd taken the box off the top of her refrigerator and set it on the table before she knew she was moving. The pull of the book grew stronger every day. When she slept, her dreams were restless and full of dark figures and shadowed whispers. All would be found in the book. If only she would use it. So far she'd resisted casting any more spells, but the compulsion to do so only grew stronger.

In her few moments of clarity, she knew she should put it in the safe, or back in Veronika's apartment. But it wouldn't let her.

She clutched her own hands. Dinner first. Shower. Sleep.

She gasped, yanking her fingers away from the box. They shook.

Her fingertips rubbed together, sparking. Just to turn a page or two. She couldn't remember her last meal. Food first. She'd forgotten to stop at the grocer on the way home—again. She combed through the pantry. Spaghetti noodles, a packet of dried soup. She hadn't had time to shop all week, but this was getting desperate. She could order in. First, tea.

She flipped on the water kettle and rummaged through the cupboard for tea and a mug. Tomorrow was a big day. She made a report at the weekly department meeting and fielded questions from the other department heads. She needed to be sharp. The meeting. Her new role in the small department made avoiding Tobias impossible.

Professor Vogel.

Every time she gave the update, he sat at the other end of the table without looking up from his paperwork. He seemed thinner and more tired, but the exhibit opening approached. She heard his team was pulling uncharacteristically late hours and he drove them on with sheer will to make the deadline. But there were no more complaints filed, and the rumor mill dried up with lack of fodder.

Once, she'd gone up to the floor where the collection team was housed after hours, thinking she'd just slip into his office for a few moments with the excuse of dropping off some paperwork. Instead, it seemed the entire team was gathered in the glass-walled specimen room —minus the zombies and Karel Broucek. The tables had been cleared, and they lounged on the chairs and surfaces with paper cups and coffee mugs filled, she presumed, from the bottle of beer making its way around the room.

Tobias leaned against the counter, waving the bottle on when it came to him. He was in the middle of telling a story. And they were rapt. Or maybe it was a joke, because he reached a point and the group broke into titters and guffaws. Tobias pulled off his glasses and wiped his eyes, shoulders shaking. He grinned at them, dimpled and content.

From her position, resting shoulder to shoulder with the shy art historian, Elsa caught Barbara's eye with a smile and made a little beckoning motion with one hand. Barbara shook her head, backing away— but not before Tobias lifted his head and looked straight into the shadow where she lingered. Even without his glasses, his gaze fixed directly on her and his smile buckled. Recognition warred with something more powerful on his face.

Barbara fled.

When the water kettle on her counter went off with a small click, she found herself at the table with the book of shadows in her hands, flipping the pages. She didn't remember removing it from the box or opening it. But no power on earth could make her close it again.

You want a look? Let me show you how you may get what you want.

The title of the page before her: "Seeing that which is not present."

A bowl of water, a chant. Without hesitation, she cast. Finding herself staring at her own reflection in the pool of water after a few minutes with no result, she stumbled to bed. Maybe now the book would let her sleep in peace. It seemed quieter after she had worked a spell or used her grace in some new way.

When she closed her eyes, she rose from her body, traveling through the walls and out over the city. This was no peaceful soaring. It lacked any joy of weightlessness or flying. Her vision whirled with the dizzying speed and loss of control.

She stopped at the building below the Vysehrad fortress. Some kind of protection placed on it blocked her progress inside. Beryl.

Barbara clung to the windows, searching.

Tobias sat in a little room, hunched over the tiny desk. He was so still she assumed he had fallen sleep working. When he stretched his arms over his head and rolled his neck, she realized his stillness came from the intensity of his focus. She strained to see the source of his attention through the window.

The journal. Printouts of the photographed pages spread out before him, and the translation in the notebook below, made in his uniform handwriting. She pressed her fingers to the glass, longing to be close enough to touch him, to smell him. She looked forward to the agonizing moment of passing him in the collections meeting each time. Once she'd even leaned in to breathe him in.

Each time you happen to me all over again.

He looked up and toward the door as Beryl appeared in the doorway, her expression concerned. He looked over his shoulder, through Barbara, and she shivered. Her eyes flew to Beryl and the older woman looked straight at her, her face taut with anger. She mouthed a single word. *Go.*

The power behind the word flung Barbara backward as though she'd touched a live wire.

Mummy doesn't want you near her precious son anymore? See how threatened she is by your power. Your strength. Our strength.

She woke up back in her body and stumbled to the toilet retching.

Spent, she flipped on the tap and sat down in the shower, letting let hot water run over her until it turned cold.

When she looked at herself in the mirror the following morning, something had changed. She saw herself at a distance—washed out and pale, darkness growing beneath her eyes—and there was something unfamiliar in the face staring back at her. She hurried to dress and went to work.

The library was in an uproar. She felt the familiar squeeze of panic on her windpipe from the morning the books had appeared on her desk. She walked as though she expected the floor to give under her feet with every stride.

But Edita grabbed her arm in the hall, eyes alight with the fire of news. "They caught Professor Tesarik stealing from the library. They found valuable books in his possession."

Barbara's vision swam and she stumbled a half step. Edita dragged her to a couch in the library lounge to fill her in. Tesarik has been caught trying to sell the stolen books. An anonymous tip revealed conversations with dealers and collectors for library property.

"Anonymous," Barbara said, a curious tickling sensation in the back of her throat.

She'd forgotten her previous night's dream until this moment.

In it, she sat in a bar across from a woman whose face she shouldn't see. She shared the whole story about the party and the consequences over a bottle of wine.

The woman shook her head. *Once we controlled knowledge and they've never forgotten, even as they covet our bodies. We will make him pay. Watch.*

"Bara?" Edita said, cutting into her memory. "Are you going to faint?"

This is just the beginning. It is our time now. They will all be made to pay for their crimes.

"No." Barbara forced herself to her feet. The thing welling inside her wasn't silence, but another consciousness with a desire and voice of her own.

She had to get away before it took control.

Half running, she found the faculty office. Professor Klisak was gathered with the rest of the department faculty members. She barely registered Tobias among them. But he moved toward her as she swayed on her feet.

"Another time, perhaps, Miss Svobodová," Klisak said.

She shook her head. "I have to tell you now. I have to go. I quit. I don't want this."

The light flickering in Tobias' eyes in a way that made her realize how empty they had been in the intervening weeks.

She tore her gaze away from him. "You will have my resignation by the end of the week."

CHAPTER THIRTY-NINE

THE OTHER FACULTY members shook their heads as Barbara fled,
returning to their conversations. Tobias stared at the doorway a moment
longer. She seemed fevered and frantic, her clothes hanging from her
frame.

"The flu." Tobias shrugged at Klisak's surprised expression. "A
couple on my team are down with it. Best let her sleep it off. If you'll
excuse me, I'm afraid I've got to go back to work."

He paused long enough to collect his things. In the research
assistant's office, Edita stood beside Barbara's desk, an abandoned
pineapple figurine in her palm and deep lines bracketing her mouth.
"She left them all."

"I'll find her."

At home, he didn't bother call out a greeting on his way to his room.
He wrenched out of his tie and jacket, shoving a change of clothes into
his weekend bag. As an afterthought, he stuffed the photocopied pages
on top.

"Your friend, Barbara, is in trouble," Beryl said without preamble.

"You know?"

Tobias traded dress shoes for the athletic ones Chris had loaned him.

"I saw the minute she walked into my house," she said. "I tried to
invite her to safety, but she's all bound up in shadows and can't see a
way forward."

"Why didn't you say anything?"

She folded her arms over her chest. "You would have believed me? I'd hoped being close to *you* would keep it at bay until you two figured out how to ask for help."

"I'm going after her." He rose, shouldering his bag and bracing for an argument.

She stepped aside. "I'm not stopping you."

Flummoxed, he paused.

"You just need to understand what you're up against," she warned. "You'll need more than research to fix this. It will take all of you."

"You mean the wolf."

Wolf. Had he ever said it out loud? To name a thing is to know it. To know it, the beginning of understanding.

Not a monster. Or a beast. A part of himself.

The words were the end of running through the darkness and going nowhere. His foot settled on a path.

Beryl smiled and, through her concern, lightness touched her eyes for the first time since he'd come home. "Do you know, your grandmother warned me away from your father?"

Tobias frowned, wondering what had brought on the change of subject but certain she would manage to tie it back somehow. "I thought Grandma Rose loved dad?"

Her shoulders rose and fell.

"Once, there were many more of us, and the wolf-skinned preyed on man and animal alike. My kind served as shepherds and they were our greatest adversaries."

Tobias's grasp of the world around him slid again. His hand found the doorframe, something to hold him steady, all the while his heart went on thumping *Barbara, Barbara.* "You fought?"

"Me, personally?" she laughed. "No. The war ended generations ago, humans burned us both, so it didn't much matter in the end, and the world changed and left all of us behind. After the Godswar, the necromancers codes kept us all in line. But your grandmother knew he carried the wolf and there was no telling what would happen when our lines crossed."

"You had us, raised us, knowing—"

"Nothing is certain, in this world, not even blood," she smiled, a weary promise. "Destruction is carried in the seed of every creation. The only thing we control is our choice." The graveness faded from her face a heartbeat later. "Have you met your father? He's got a marshmallow for a heart. Won't kill a spider if it bites him. I'm the one you kids had to watch out for, and we both know it."

He smiled, in spite of everything.

"Grandma Rose saw that quickly enough," she said. "And now we know what can happen when wolves are raised knowing love, or witches are abandoned to the world."

Witches. The word settled between them.

She touched his arm. "The other night, something with her face tried to get into the building. Whatever is riding her is old and dangerous. I didn't want to risk hurting her, so I sent it away."

"Can't *you* help her?"

"If I could have built up trust, perhaps," she eyed him pointedly. "But she loves you. She trusts you. Wolves were such a powerful adversary because your nature is resistant to our craft. You can reach her, and your wolf can protect you against it."

She followed him to the door.

He halted, unsure of what to say next. When he didn't pull away, she settled a hand on his cheek.

"Take her to the cabin," Beryl said. "We are in our greatest power when we follow creation and she can draw on the natural world to defend herself." Her expression hardened. "She's always been stronger than she knows. Whatever's got its claws in her needs her to submit to its will. Don't let her forget who she is, and how much she has to lose if she surrenders."

◆

BARBARA DIDN'T ANSWER her buzzer. Tobias waited on the step, pacing between jabs at the bell. The front door opened, and Mrs. Milanova appeared in a blinding floral muumuu and carrying her broom.

Her brows lowered as she blocked his path. "You don't come around anymore. Why is that?"

"It's complicated," he said with the ghost of a smile. "Do you know where I can find her?"

Mrs. Milanova stepped aside, opening the door and worry clouded her face. "She came home too early, wouldn't say a word."

Tobias charged up the stairs. Her door swung open at the touch. The shambles of her small, tidy studio greeted him.

"Hello?"

No answer. Empty. Then he remembered the roof. He turned the corner outside her apartment and took the stairs in threes. Her keys dangled in the lock. He pulled them out and stepped onto the roof.

Just a few weeks ago they'd lain right here under the moon, making promises with their bodies that their hearts would be unable to keep. The glare of sunlight on the roof turned the day bright and hot.

He squinted. "Barbara?"

She stood at the low wrought-iron railing at the edge of the roof. Her skirt billowed around her, her hair floating behind her on the breeze.

"Hey, Bebe."

She spun on him. "Not me."

Her features jerked with a puppet's uneven motion. A chill washed over him. It seemed impossible that Barbara had found the spell book hidden by a witch 400 years ago, until he considered what it truly was. The name of the condemned woman in the journal came to his lips. "Katka?"

The knowing smile pinched her face as she twirled along the narrow edge, singing. "Clever wolf. Did Mother help you figure that out?"

Barbara's body pitched and rolled like marionette in the hands of an amateur puppeteer. Revulsion gripped him, but fear of what would happen if she slipped froze him in place.

"I see you for what you are." She executed a wobbly about-face and stumbled off the short ledge onto the safety of the roof, moving toward him. "I'd offer you a place at my side, but I think you will not take it. You want this foolish chit tied to her tiny desk. Slaving away at the whim of men like yourself, who think so much of their learning and their cocks. Such a shame, such a waste. I have much better plans for her. Bigger."

"The bookstore?"

"Why would I want one dusty old shop?" she cooed in a mockery of Barbara's tear-strained voice. Her mouth widened in a rictus grin. "Tesarik was only practice, Professor. Walk by my side. Step aside if you must. But stand in my way and I will make your life hell before it ends."

She'll need you to remind her who she is.

Ignoring the urge to recoil as she drew closer, he looked into her eyes. "You are nothing but a parasite. Bebe, if you can hear me—"

The witch cackled, but the muscles twitched in her cheeks dragging the smile off her face. He lurched forward in time to catch Barbara as her body went slack. She clutched at his lapels, disoriented. "Tobias?"

He swept her off her feet. "Welcome back."

"How did I get here?"

"Long story."

He stopped in her apartment long enough to assemble a few changes of clothes and locate her travel bag. In the bathroom, he found her toothbrush, and a second, still in plastic, sitting on the shelf.

He paused at the sound of her shuffling around the other room but her step was her own, if slower. When he returned she sat, folded over her legs, on the couch.

He scanned the bookshelves and the tables for anything resembling a four-hundred-year-old book of shadows. "Where is it, the book?"

"I dreamed it." She listed, as though drunk or losing consciousness. "It told me what the universe is made of, but I can't remember the words. I saw my father, swimming in the coral, deep in the caves. I have a way to get him back."

Tobias stared. Break the contract of service with a necromancer? He'd never heard of such a thing—especially for one who had volunteered. But if the witch was trying to lure her, what was to stop it from offering impossible feats to encourage her to open up to it.

Fuck it. If the book was still here somewhere, maybe getting her away from it might be the best idea.

He forced a grin. "Let's out of town for the weekend."

For a moment she was lucid again. "But the library…"

Slinging her bag over one shoulder, he wondered how a few changes of clothes could be so heavy. "Trust me, with all the drama at the school, I don't think anyone will miss either of us. I want to take you someplace special."

He found the car keys and tossed her a sweater. "You're gonna need this. It still gets cold at night where we're going."

He didn't give her a chance to argue, helping her into her shoes and closing the door behind them. At the bottom of the stairs, her head lolled against his shoulder and he managed to catch her before she collapsed. He shifted her into his arms and came face to face with Mrs. Milanova.

He froze. This was going to take some explaining.

"I packed you a picnic," she said, hefting a plastic bag. "Something to keep you for the road."

"How did you..." He let the question die and dipped Barbara lower so the matron could deposit the bag into the woman's lap. "Thank you."

He started for the garage. Halfway there, he spun on one heel, wobbling under the weight of his burden. "The cat—"

She waved him on. "I'll feed that dreadful creature."

"Oh good, it's not just me," he exhaled. "Thanks, Mrs. M."

In the car, Barbara drifted into the kind of deep sleep that made him pull over twice to check her breathing. He questioned the wisdom of this as the road narrowed and dimmed under the cover of trees. Maybe she needed a hospital. But the deepest part of him realized no doctor could do anything for her.

By the time they reached the cabin, the sunset had taken the warmth of the day.

The shadows deepened between the trees, covering the clearing. The wolf stirred in him, recognizing the surroundings and anticipating a run. Tobias wouldn't risk having her wake up alone in a strange environment.

For once, when he quieted it, the wolf's presence settled.

The cabin seemed emptier without his brothers—isolated and defenseless. If something did go wrong out here, how would he help her? He exhaled; he'd have to trust his mother was right about nature giving her some fortification. Maybe when she woke up, they'd go for a walk in the forest.

Tobias started a fire before bringing her in. She didn't even stir when he laid her on the sofa. He dragged a blanket over her and retreated to the kitchen. Lost, he pulled out the photocopied pages and his own note-book and continued to work on the journal.

Now he understood the bias of his first read. Without the assumption of the narrative as a fabrication for public titillation, he noted the absence of the usual markers that characterized such tales. No claims of bargains with the devil, or names signed in great books promising souls.

Katka's vast self-assurance in the final pages was still present but, this time, he also recognized the depth of her knowledge. Without train-ing, learning by trial and error, she became skilled enough to imbue a book with her soul and create a way to transfer it to another witch.

Tobias cursed himself for not bringing Barbara to his mother at the first hint of her magic. He had chosen the blinders when it came to his mother, and now Barbara might pay the price for his willful ignorance.

"Where are we?" Barbara sat up, tucking her legs beneath her.

He recognized the warmth in her gaze with relief. Not the witch, then. Maybe the distance had severed the connection.

"Thought you could use some fresh air," he said, kneeling at her side. "I missed you."

The flush came to her cheeks a moment before tears caught in her lashes. She slid off the couch and into his arms where she belonged. His whole body shivered in relief. They held each other, rocking and breathing each other in and when she looked up, she seemed more herself than she had been in weeks of meeting rooms and casual encounters in the department offices.

"Are you hungry?"

A rueful smile curled her lips. "Starving."

He rose, taking her with him, and deposited her on a stool at the kitchen counter. He swept away his work, tucking papers into a drawer. He wanted nothing to threaten this fragile moment between them.

There would be time enough to deal with Katka.

"Good of Mrs. Milanova to pack us a lunch," he said, reaching into the bag. "Er... dinner."

He brought out a loaf of bread, catching the pained expression on her face.

"What's wrong?"

Her lips stretched over her teeth in a grimace. "Mrs. Milanova's not known for her culinary skills."

He examined one plastic container, filled with an ambiguous brown stew. "She's an old-school babička—every vegetable will be cooked within an inch of its life, but it can't be that bad."

He sniffed and reeled backward, slamming the lid shut. He set it down on the counter with a little shudder.

"She lost her sense of smell about five years ago," Barbara said, wincing. "Stroke."

Boiled potatoes packed the next carton. The last contained some kind of fish. He walked straight to the front door, opened it, and pitched the stinking mess out into the night.

When he returned, Barbara pressed her fingertips to her lips, unable to hide the amusement bubbling to the surface. It reminded him of the old days, and he'd open another hundred containers of dubiously prepared food to see that look.

Her stomach rumbled.

"Right." He laughed. "We can fry the potatoes."

He returned from the refrigerator with a hunk of butter and a jar of homemade jam. "Toast."

He ransacked the pantry and came up with two tins of meat. Barbara wrinkled her nose, and he put them away again.

"We have some game in the freezer out back," he said, trying to sound casual. "Venison sausages, or some boar."

She looked around, taking in the cozy cottage. "Is that what your family does up here, hunt? Mark is probably good at it."

Tobias thought of his elder brother swinging from the neck of a bull elk like a furry pendulum and smiled. "Something like that."

She sat in silence, watching him slice bread. They ate as he fried up the potatoes in hot oil with salt, and heated sausages. He watched her finish her entire helping, sliding the last of his to her before he took their plates to the sink. He did the dishes to the sound of the fire crackling.

When he looked up she was her wiping her cheeks as she stared into the fire, an indiscernible expression on her face. He inhaled and let the wolf sort through the scents of old oil, dish soap and burning wood to the more delicate aroma of her grief and sharp twinge of anxiety.

He set down the dishrag and slipped his arms around her from behind. "We're going to figure this out this together."

A shaking sigh left her as she sank into him. "Gods, I've missed you. I didn't think this would be so hard. How much I..."

He didn't need her to finish. The sensation of her absence and the disorientation of seeing her walking around alone hounded him. The wondering if she was suffering, sad, lonely. The deepest fear that she was just fine without him.

"I promised not to let anything hurt you. I intend to keep it."

She twisted in his arms and her mouth crashed into his. When they pulled apart, it was her turn to wipe the skin below his eyes, staring in wonderment. "Still?"

The worry in her voice shattered his heart. "I'm yours, Barbara Svobodová. I always was. I just didn't know it."

Unshed tears made her laugh husky. "That's just because I'm the first woman you—"

Tobias stopped her words, pouring all his longings and pent-up need into the warm connection. He nipped her lips, caressing the line of her spine with his fingers. A wave of dizziness floated over him with the rush of blood away from his brain. He ignored that for the moment, focusing on her dreamy, soft expression as her eyes cleared again.

"I think you exaggerated your innocence," she whispered against his temple. "You had a lot of experience in doing other things."

He grinned and nibbled her neck. "What other things are you talking about?"

His tongue darted out to taste her pulse. She shivered.

"Well, kissing," she said. "And necking. And dining in…"

Her words shuddered to a halt as he grabbed the skin of her throat in his teeth and pulled. She sucked in a breath, molding her body to his. Her thighs parted, enveloping him, and the thin folds of her dress did nothing to block the heat radiating from the core of her. Everything in him wanted to be deep inside her. Judging by the way she tugged at his collar and ground into his erection, she was amenable.

She will need all of you.

Whatever that meant, he couldn't keep his secret from her any longer.

He pulled away, capturing her wrists and pinning them in her lap. Time to find courage.

She sat up, breathing heavy between kiss-swollen lips. "What's wrong?"

The terror rose under his breastbone, not unlike that first time the wolf had claimed him. Only this time the beast did not push itself to the front, but pressed behind his ribcage, a warm and not uncomfortable fullness. He tugged her to her feet.

"I need to show you something."

He grabbed her sweater on their way outside. When the cold hit her, she let go of him to shrug it over her head, puffing out a visible breath and shivering.

"It's freezing. Where are we, the Alps?"

He laughed. "Šumava."

She sent a searching, nervous gaze into the uninterrupted darkness of trees. "Where are all the other cabins? This is wilderness. What kind of animals live out here? We could get eaten by something."

He laughed. "You will get eaten if you play your cards right."

Barbara flushed, grinning as she reached for him. He caught her hands, holding them against his breastbone. She must have felt his heart racing, her gaze turned up to him, alarmed.

"I promise it won't hurt you," he said. "If you get frightened—too frightened—you can go into the house. He—we—won't follow you. I promise."

The fear met confusion her eyes.

Best not to delay and let her anxiety build. He'd experienced how awful that could be firsthand.

"You knew something wasn't right about me." He tugged off his shirt as he put distance between them. His fingers shook, undoing his pants. "I wanted to tell you so many times, but I couldn't make the words come out."

He held out his glasses last.

She flinched but reached out a hand. He deposited them without touching her, and then he took a step back.

"This is the best way, for you to see for yourself. To know that whatever's happening to you, you don't have to handle it alone."

All right, you big hairy beast, let her see you.

CHAPTER FORTY

THE AIR SURROUNDING HIM SHIMMERED, but the details eluded Barbara. One moment a man and the next, the most massive wolf she had ever seen, as though every inch of adult human male changed form without any loss of mass. If he stood on his hind legs, he would have towered over her just as he did on two feet.

His coat was the impenetrable shade of a gloaming forest. The shadowed tips of his guard hairs gave way to the creamy moonlight of his throat and belly. Chocolate and grizzled hair shaded the mask around his eyes and the saddle marking on his back. He would have been invisible on a winter hillside, amid dormant branches and snow drifts. At first, the sight of him in the open triggered something ancient and terrified in her hindbrain that registered only a predator.

But his eyes, pale earthy gray, remained the same. Familiar.

She dropped to her knees with a gasp before him, reaching out. The wolf flinched, lowering head and tail, and the sight of the magnificent animal cowed broke her heart.

"Tobias Vogel," she ordered. "Come here right now."

He came, crouching to make himself look smaller, less dangerous. His belly dragged the ground. The ragged double-time beat of her heart quickened. He wiggled forward the last few feet, chin on his paws. When he swallowed, the muscles in his jaw flexed. Enormous. That jaw could break her thigh bone without effort.

She hesitated as she reached out, her fingers curling back, and he cringed. The muscles beneath his coat tensed, sending the hairs erect as if he prepared to fling his body away.

"Stay," she ordered. "Please."

She reached, and her breath caught. The long whiskers on the end of his muzzle brushed her fingertips. Until that instant, she might have thought it a dream, or a hallucination.

The contact ignited a warm, tugging weight in her belly and the sparks that lit when the hairs brushed her fingers brought only warmth and a delicate tickle of bee wings and lavender blossoms.

He shook his head as a few errant flickers of dancing light settled on him, bouncing off his dense coat and back into her.

Knowing there were other things in the world—bits of grace and necromancers and witches—was one thing. Touching something she'd thought impossible changed everything. And she had never seen something more strange, more mysterious, more beautiful.

Wings of possibility unfurled around her heart, expanding her chest.

In protecting them from gods, the necromancers had also cut them off from the wonder of a world that contained magic like this. The hunger to know everything about this world, and her part in it, overcame her.

When he didn't pull away, she buried her hands in his heavy coat. The simple contact banished the last of the chill. A wall of muscle ran beneath the fur, every bit of him a hunter. She scooted closer, ignoring the soil beneath her bare knees until they touched the ends of his forepaws. His claws raked her skin. He tried to withdraw, but she grabbed two handfuls of his coat and latched on. "No, you don't."

His jaw fell open, a pink speckled tongue rolling past canines the length of her thumbs.

She continued to explore him, watching for any sign of the inhuman behind those too-familiar eyes. By the time she reached his belly, she had surrendered her fear. If he wanted to, he could have her by the throat before she could decide to run. Instead, he panted softly. She caught a whiff of salty, fried potatoes.

A strange wash of arousal passed over her. The wolf whined, and his nostrils flared. His gaze fixed on her, puzzled.

"You kind of turn me on, a little," she said. "I don't want to do anything strange... I just. All this fur, and you inside somewhere."

He chuffed and his tongue lolled again, ears flicking as his great plumed tail swept the ground.

"Don't laugh at me," she scolded, touching his long forelegs and the bony slopes of his paws.

She slid her hands over them and, when he lifted one, she flipped her palm over. He settled the rough pads against it. Her palm disappeared, fingertips just visible around the edges of his claws. He dragged his paw down, leaving a trail of soil. His tongue slipped over the skin of her hand, the warmth making her squirm.

"How do you hide this from everyone? Does chocolate make you sick? Do you get fleas?" She met his gaze. "I have so many questions."

The skin around his mouth drew back, exposing a fearsome array of teeth, but his expression was placid. Amused.

Impulsively, she threw her arms around him, burying her face in the ruff of his neck. His swallow bobbed beside her collarbone and his chin pressed against her back.

"Tobias Vogel, you are extraordinary, and I love you," she whispered. A strangled whine rose from his chest. "I'm not special like you are. Not like this."

He made a sound between a growl and a bark. When she rocked back on her heels, he pounced.

She shrieked, more in surprise than fear, as he knocked her flat, planting his paws on either side of her head and glaring down. He dropped to his belly, his ribcage pinning her to the ground and shook his head.

"It was my turn to say the wrong thing," she laughed. "I understand why you need to keep the secret, but you should never be ashamed of this. Did you think I wouldn't..."

He withdrew, hanging his head.

Now she charged. She shoved at his side. He didn't move. She pushed again, and he had the decency to rock sideways, though she was positive he did it make her feel better.

"You thought I wouldn't want you because of *this*."

His eyes darted to hers and away.

"Oh, you big dumb..." she said, flinging her arms around his neck. "Wolf. Wolfman. Man-wolf. Are you a werewolf? What do I call you? It doesn't matter. I love you despite your foolishness."

The longer, stiff hair tickled her nose, the denser, softer fur beneath radiating heat. For a long time, they breathed like that, hearts beating against one another.

She rose, dusting off her knees.

He circled her legs and sat down at her feet. His tail curled over her toes, and he pushed his snout into her belly.

"We playing Little Red Riding Hood?"

He chuffed a laugh and looked out into the forest. She followed his gaze, shuddering a little at the dark. He snorted again, and his back rose under her palm. When he stood up, her elbow bent under the support of his spine. What could she fear, she wondered, with him at her side?

"Lead on."

He guided her through the gloom, his body a substantial warmth, the brightness of his coat collected moonlight in each clearing. Perhaps it was the waxing gibbous moon hanging above the treetops, or the fear-lessness the presence this impossible creature lent her that gave the night a dreamlike quality. But instead of leaving her confused and exhausted, the surreal peace settled deep in her bones and spread to her fingers and toes.

She leaned on him and, when the traveling got difficult, she slipped onto his back and he carried her.

They could have walked for hours, for days, without ever leaving the night wood, but at the end of a long climb, they came to a set of ruins. She recognized the orderliness of cut stones, and the square angles of the walls protruding between the overgrowth of roots. The trees thinned out, and the moon bathed everything in silver light. The wolf lifted his head and loosed a great spine-tingling howl. She sank to her heels at his side and leaned it his warmth, inhaling his animal musk. Her eyes shut.

She woke, sensing the arrival of daybreak in her chest.

At some point, she'd coiled into a ball and been wrapped in heat. She snuggled into the solid wall of fur-covered muscle that might be his shoulder or haunch. A cold nose pressed against her leg. She yelped.

The cradle of fur resolved itself when his head rose, and silvery eyes stared down at her, squinting in humor.

She tried to glare and failed. "Are you going to turn back, or do you have to wait until a full moon?"

Before she'd finished asking, a human man sat beside her. Her man. He shivered. "It's cold. And I don't have any clothes."

Truth. He was covered in gooseflesh and fully erect.

She pounced.

He rocked back against the root-covered ground, laughing and wincing as she hitched up her skirt, thighs on either side of his hips. His laughter only lasted until the first touch of her slippery heat.

She rode him in an animal silence, fixed on the planes of his face, her fingers digging furrows into his shoulders as day broke cold and bright around them. When release took her, he closed his eyes, shaking.

She gasped when he slid free and took himself in his hand, spending his release in the dirt.

He sat up, arms braced on his knees, head hanging. It took all her concentration to rise, sweeping the earth and twigs from his back and laying a kiss between his shoulder blades. "Thank you, I wasn't thinking—"

"Let's get back." He rose abruptly, and took her with him. "I'm going to change and carry you, is that okay?"

She nodded, the words stuck in her throat. All the distance that had closed between them was back, for no reason she could discern.

They arrived at the cottage mid-morning. Barbara stared at the tidy roof shrouded in mist and the first shafts of sunlight until she was sure she wouldn't weep in front of him. When she turned around, human Tobias gathered his clothes, fastidiously brushing off the dirt.

He didn't meet her eyes. "You take the first shower."

◆

WHEN TOBIAS EMERGED from the bathroom in a fresh t-shirt and sweats, Barbara's tuneless humming ceased abruptly and she glanced at him with a hesitant smile.

The way things ended at the ruins left a sour burn in the pit of his stomach, sullying the sheer pleasure of her response to him. She'd been delighted, overwhelmed, and awed. Most of all, she *saw* him. Even in the wolf, he recognized him. The scent of fear vanished. She'd talked to him as they walked, explaining things about her family and her past, her voice like music in the dark. When he caught her fingers in his teeth for silence, she crouched at his side, stroking his head and waited. She trusted him as much in deep wood as on the ballroom floor.

She'd followed his gaze into the gloom without another word. A moment later, a family of lynx appeared: a mother and three kittens, jogging down the deer trail ahead of them, their tufted ears bouncing.

Barbara clapped her hand over her mouth with delight. When they were gone, she squeezed his neck and breathed into his fur, "Thank you."

And in the morning, waking up and curling into him, he hadn't been able to resist her warmth, her softness. The wolf hadn't cared. This was what bonded things did—find each other and mate and raise their young. He'd almost forgotten his promise to himself, and he hadn't been graceful or considerate when he'd remembered.

"I don't think I've ever seen you in a t-shirt that fits," she said lightly, turning back to another round of buttered toast.

"It's a big weekend for firsts then, I suppose," he said, wrapping his arms around her.

She stiffened. "Is everything okay?"

He nodded, spinning her around and drawing her between his thighs. "When I hit puberty, I started wanting to chase things—animals—and dreaming. I didn't understand what was happening to me. With Chris and Issy so much younger, our parents worried the more people knew, the more dangerous it would be. So even though Mark came into his wolf almost two years before me, they kept it secret until my time came. Beryl—mom—brought us here. I hated every minute. It took years to accept that side of me, and I'd never welcomed the wolf before last night."

The resistance went out of her.

Tobias took another breath, willing himself to continue. "Y-y-you made me feel—like what I am isn't a curse."

He squeezed her, and she tucked her cheek against the hollow below his collar.

"But there will always be a part of me I have to hide. It's a half life. I'd never want a son of mine to live like this."

Barbara drew back in time for him watch the dream die in her eyes. "Or a daughter."

She pressed her face against his shoulder. Hers did not shake. Her breath did not catch. But the soft whiff of salt, like a distant sea accompanied his next inhale. For a moment, they stood in shared grief, mourning what never would be.

She sighed and rubbed her face in his chest, tipping her chin up. "It doesn't matter."

He laid a kiss on her brow, sealing his eyes shut and pretending she meant the words. "I love you, Barbara. I never stopped. I never will."

She laced their hands together and walked him to the bedroom.

She stripped down. Then she laid him on the bed and drew him to her. When he could bear being apart from her no longer, he covered himself and gave himself over to the cradle of her thighs and the heat of her breast.

His own sounds came as if at a distance, the pants and groans more animal than human. Her nails bit his back. He sank his teeth into the skin of her shoulder. She bucked, tossing her head back, and bared her throat. The taste of her pulse beneath his tongue, the sweat on her skin, the surrender. When he came, he roared her name, hands fisted in the sheets and driving himself deep.

It wasn't until her fingers cupped his face that he felt the wetness on his cheeks.

"Maybe it's not a half-life at all," she whispered. "Maybe it's twice the life."

CHAPTER FORTY-ONE

"No more toast," she announced when she joined him in the kitchen after a hot shower. She tucked the ends of a towel around her damp hair. "We need real food. Can you go bring back a deer or something?"

He laughed around a mouthful of bread, offering her a bite of jam-slathered toast. "Fourteen percent."

She chewed, her brows drawing together in question.

"The hunting success rate in wild wolves. And we didn't have a pack to learn from. Maybe with my brothers, but I think we'd have better luck driving back down to the restaurant in the last village. Why don't you wave your wand or wiggle your nose?"

She swallowed and touched her chest with the tips of her fingers. "Me?"

He shoved the last of the bread into his mouth, dusted off his palms, and settled them on her hips, drawing her close. Little kisses accompanied by a night's stubble tickled the skin at her jaw. She shivered and curled into him. This was what it was to feel safe, protected, treasured.

The joy of being together crashed against the despair of knowing the decision he'd made to be the end of his line. A family of her own hadn't been a priority, but she'd always imagined it part of a distant someday. After seeing Tobias with his sprawling, affectionate clan, that someday had begun to take shape in the back of her mind.

"You asked me why I call her Beryl, instead of mom." He waited until her gaze rose to his again. "I blamed her."

"Because she brought you here the first time?"

He shook his head. "My dad is a carrier, but he's never wolfed out. And it shouldn't have expressed in us, except because of what my mom is…"

"What she is?"

"She thinks her power activated the gene. Mom's like you. My little witch."

Hearing him say the word out loud did strange things to her. To be named.

But what was being a witch in a world ruled by necromancers? All that she knew of witches were fairy tales and historical accounts of village healers and wise women condemned as evil. That was all humans were allowed to know.

"And now?"

"Now I realize what an ungrateful little shit I was," he said. "She was trying to protect me—to protect us all, and to give us the best chance to survive in a world that has no mercy for people like you and I."

He rose and guided her to the stool he'd been sitting on.

He withdrew the photocopied pages and his own notes and slid them in front of her. "You should read this."

She sat down, drawing the crumpled-edge pages toward her. Another piece of bread buttered and soaked in jam, appeared at her fingertips. She ate and sipped the cup of tea that followed.

After a while, the weight of his gaze crept into her awareness. "What?"

Amusement lifted his brows. "You haven't even looked at my translation."

"I don't need it," she said, thoughtlessly. "I can see it. It's like the words reform in my brain and I understand them."

It was a relief, not having to hide, the same kind that filled her on waking up to his snuffling in his sleep when she remembered the wolf. She'd slipped into her own dreams again, comforted with the knowing.

He smiled then and she saw the admiration in his face, though he kept his voice light. "That's convenient. Read. Then we can talk more."

When she was finished, she sat back, wishing she hadn't eaten the last bit of toast when her stomach rolled. A low pulsing ache started behind the bridge of her nose and spread behind her eyes. She blinked hard against the desire to lay her head on his chest and weep uncontrollably.

Tobias roused from staring broodily into the fire to look at her, worry carving a line between his brows. She saw the wolf now even in these simple motions, the graceful movement before he came to perfect stillness again. He folded his arms and nibbled at his index finger.

"You think it's real," she murmured. "You think she picked me, because I'm like she was. A witch."

"The books, the locks…the universal translation thing. Do you think those are just party tricks?"

"I thought they were just what they were," she cried. "Little touches of grace, like my mother's and her father's. Something I could keep busy working in a library all day. This, this is…"

"Mom said it's a matter of training, and that you're stronger than you know."

The book of shadows was her confirmation—she'd cast those spells.

Pain stabbed behind her left eye, a pulse of pressure as though something was trying to break through. "Beryl sent you to help me?"

He shook his head. "I promised I wouldn't let anything hurt you, and I mean to keep that promise. If we could just find the other book, maybe we could break her hold on you."

The pulse sped in her veins.

Barbara walked into the living room, ignoring his call for her to wait. Instead, she rifled through her bag and returned, bearing the book wrapped in a towel. She set it on the counter, plucking the corners away without touching it. Now the cover appeared malignant. How had she thought it harmless?

"When did you…"

"When you were in the bathroom," she confessed. "I couldn't leave it behind. It called to me. *Is* calling to me. I hear it everywhere. Except it's not so loud here, and I couldn't hear it at your house at all."

"That's because Beryl's got both locked down with wards," he said. "Nothing comes in or out that could do any harm to anyone within."

He paused at the implication, and she met his eyes.

The hollow darkness rose inside her. And she'd brought it inside.

"She—Katka—needs you. She's not as powerful as you are, just older."

"The books," Barbara whispered, feeling the bile rising. "Tesarik."

"She moved those books and screwed Tesarik, but she used you to do it." He told her about encountering the witch on the roof in her body. She recalled almost nothing of the time after she fled the university. What memories remained floated like dreams, vague and without substance. It sent chills through her. How often had the dreams and the increasing sense that she no longer recognized herself in the mirror been the signs of someone else inside her?

"Your mom should have helped you learn to protect yourself, or at least warned you."

Why would she have? No guide came with her grace and, even in her wildest moments considering her mother's gifts, she would have never imagined her with powers like this.

A buzzing of angry bees thrummed in her skull, tiny rat paws scrabbling at the base of her neck, the cool heavy pressure of a reptile on her shoulders, and a resounding crack, as though a great egg had shattered.

Who is he to judge the line of your mothers? The voice slithered into a far corner of her mind, tugging at her. *Wearing the skin of an animal is not even the beginning of power like ours.*

She pressed the heels of her hands to her eyes.

The voice had found her. She pushed back, mentally resisting, but the pressure swelled.

"Bebe, what's wrong?" Tobias tried to catch her.

She yanked away. "You don't know anything about my mother."

He held up his hands, watching her warily. "Beryl said being in nature would support you, give you something to draw on to protect yourself. That's why I brought you up here after you quit school. You weren't yourself."

No, she hadn't been. Except in one regard. "I quit because I was done. However this ends, I'm not going back."

He stared at her. "But you've worked so hard—you can't just quit."

Awareness sank, tumbling back from the sound of his voice, deciding for her. Denying her.

He'll deny you everything, the voice whispered. *Your dreams, your progeny, your line. This is the danger of men. Once you give yourself to them, they assume ownership. Possession. You need no one, girl. Not anymore.*

This time when the pressure surged, her resistance buckled.

"We've got to destroy this thing." Tobias rose, eyes on the book. "It's screwing with your head. You don't know what you're talking about."

They reached for the book at the same time.

No more.

Her fingers connected a half second before his. The needles lanced up her arm as the book gripped back, rooting into her as surely as her hands closed around it. Hands that were no longer her own.

When Tobias touched it, the book flung him away.

He howled in pain, shaking, as energy coursed through him. Hers. She had done that.

She screamed his name, but nothing came out. Her lips had been sealed.

The witch stepped forward in her body, gazing down at the broken man. Her hands lifted, preparing to send another jolt into him.

No! Barbara screamed, throwing all of her will at her limbs.

The hands jerked back to her side.

Fine, the witch snarled. *But he won't get in our way any longer.*

Her left hand came up, sketching a symbol in the air before them. The handles ripped themselves from the cabinets, forming manacles and pinning his wrists, neck, and ankles to the floor. Tobias groaned, gasping as the bar around his throat tightened. Then her body spun and he passed out of sight. She swept his work off the counter and cradled the book of spells against her breast.

As she passed the fire, she hurtled his notes and the photocopied pages into the flames.

She stalked out of the room, snatching the keys from the table beside the door. It took too long for Barbara to understand the slow, steady chant of the witch's words.

No. No no no.

The echo of her own wail bounced back at her as the witch built a wall within her own mind, stacking brick by brick until she was contained in a windowless tower. She beat her fists against the wooden door, screaming. The stench of burning wood and fabric reached her.

Every cage had a door.

Tobias. She summoned every ounce of will, every bit of ingenuity and desire.

She glimpsed herself in the rearview mirror as the car bounced along the gravel. The gaping mouth, skin stretched tight over cheekbones, eyes narrowed in anger were those of a stranger. Behind the car, plumes of smoke rose through the break in the trees.

The witch was a terrible driver. But that kept her attention on the road and the car, and not on Barbara.

Barbara flung herself forward as the Citroen bounced onto the paved road. She tried to recall the weight of her own hands, the curve and flex of her fingers, the cups of her palms. The texture of the steering wheel pressed against her skin.

She jerked hard, and the car rocked over the center line.

The witch countered. The Citroen swerved across the two-lane road. Barbara tried to get control of her feet, reaching for the brake.

A horn blared, and she looked into the oncoming headlights of a battered old Škoda station wagon. The witch took advantage of the distraction, yanking the car back on to her side of the road.

"Now, you learn your place," Katka snarled.

Barbara tumbled backward.

Her strength failed. The play for the wheel had taken everything she had. This time when the walls came up around her, they soared overhead, a pinprick of light at the top and the sensation of being deep within the earth.

Barbara folded, shuddering in the endless cold.

CHAPTER FORTY-TWO

TOBIAS GAGGED IN THE SMOKE. His eyes streamed. He'd tried changing twice, but each time the bar on his throat made it impossible. He didn't know if it was the magic or the physical restriction, but after a lifetime of fighting his wolf, the irony of not being able to change to save his own life didn't escape him.

Even his strength was no match for whatever magic she'd used to pin him to the floor. His struggles faded as the fire robbed him of air to breathe. The image of Barbara's horrified face as her body moved against her own volition swam in his vision.

He surged, fighting.

He should have just thrown the damn book in the fire. But he'd trusted the wards were strong enough to protect her here. Maybe they would have been, but he'd let the witch inside when he'd brought Barbara here.

No time. He focused on one limb. Just one. Willing everything into his left arm, he pressed up, calling the wolf. Tendons and muscles strained against the bone. The manacle shifted.

Come on, you monster, we're the only chance we've got.

The wolf responded with toothed desperation.

This time, the metal groaned. One more surge and the end popped off the floor. His left arm slid free, leaving skin along the rough metal edge. He reached for the bar at his throat. Maybe if he got that loose, he could change and the wolf's paws could slip clear of the remaining manacles.

Flames crept across the ceiling and flakes of ash rained down on him. Embers danced over his skin. His vision dimmed through his watering eyes, and every breath only worsened the burning in his lungs. He got his fingers around the neck bar and pulled. The wolf pulled with him.

Together they drew on every ounce of strength.

There was no more air. His limbs began to tingle, blackness edging at the corners of his vision. Something hot fell on him, but no pain registered.

Fight, Barbara, fight her. Don't let her win. You're stronger than she is. Don't ever give up.

Something crashed in the other room.

He coughed, blinking. "Bebe?"

"No, you fucking idiot." Eyes appeared over a soaked rag tied around his head, bright yellow instead of their usual copper. "It's your jerk of a brother. Crowbar!"

He snatched the metal bar flying toward them out of the air. A moment later, Chris appeared, pale eyes wolf-bright over his makeshift mask. "Hey, smart guy. Looks like it's Handsome and Strength to the rescue."

He tied a damp rag around Tobias' head. The cool eased his burning throat.

The crowbar screamed against metal beside his ear, taking a layer of skin, but the pressure vanished.

"I knew that chick was trouble," Mark grumbled, popping the other manacles loose. "She tried to run us off the road on the way up."

Tobias surged, but only got lungs full of hot, smoky air. Chris dragged him back into the colder current on the floor, wheezing with laughter. "Don't talk shit about his girl. He's going to kick your ass. Here."

He dropped Tobias' glasses into his palm. Tobias groaned when one lens popped out.

"It's not looking good, shitheads." Mark crouched, shielding Tobias's face with his upper body as sparks rained over them. "We're surrounded. Best chance we got is to make a change and hope the wolves can protect us. You in, or you going to stay here and enjoy your little roast?"

Mark slapped his cheek. The sharp sting brought the wolf up with a blaze of clarity.

"In." Tobias snarled over the length of his elongating canines.

Mark bared a matching grin. "Good choice, smarty pants. Christof. You're up."

Chris shifted, untangling from his clothes. He whined and coughed.

Tobias bobbed his head, transfixed by the bent frames in his hand. "Go. I'll follow you."

Mark grabbed his glasses and tossed them into the fire. "I didn't bail on a hot date for you to crap out on us at the last minute. Change now, or I'll drag you out of here by the throat."

For a moment Tobias feared he wouldn't have the strength. But the only strength in the transformation had been control and restraint. Becoming the wolf took nothing more than letting go.

The wolf shook himself free of clothes.

Mark shouldered against him, pushing toward the door. Chris led, yelping as sparks and burning floaters struck his coat.

Blisters formed on the pads of Tobias' paws. His legs wavered. The black wolf bit the ruff of his neck, hauling him like a pup.

The pale wolf crashed into the door, knocking it off its frame. Fresh air only added fuel to the fire. Mark shoved Tobias clear, yelping as he went down in a wave of heat. The flames roared, singeing their tails.

Tobias twisted, sinking his teeth into Mark's neck.

Chris turned back and got a hold of the other side. Together they dragged each other away from the fire.

Tobias rolled onto his side next to the car, watching the flames devour the cabin. He'd hated this place as a kid, and all the loss of control it represented. But for a little while, with Barbara, it had been a sanctuary. Watching flames eat the rafters and lick out of the windows filled his chest with a pulsing ache.

Chris sat in the dirt, bare skin streaked with burns and soot, arms around his knees. Mark stayed wolf, belly down on the gravel. He barked.

"Gotta keep moving," Tobias said. "We wolf it."

Chris looked at his brothers. "What about the car?"

"We'll tell them we were out hiking when the cabin burned down."

Tobias staggered to his feet and fell. He was a wolf again before he hit the ground, landing on all four paws. The black wolf shook himself before nipping at the youngest brother still sitting in the gravel.

Chris swatted at him. "Fuck off. I'm coming."

The three wolves jogged into the trees. Tobias led, pushing them harder than he knew he should. Mark limped to the rear. Tobias circled back, torn.

Mark snapped at him. *Go.*

But Tobias set his shoulder against his brother's. The forest thinned, and road noise grew closer. It would get more dangerous from here. They would be traveling in the open, in the fading daylight, through fields and villages.

Three wolves the size of small bears would not be unnoticed.

Chris, singed and weary, sprawled in the dirt. Mark licked the oozing pad of his hind paw. Tobias herded them both under cover of brush and circled back to the edge of the clearing, keeping watch. His breath no longer wheezed through his lungs, and his eyes had stopped burning. They would heal fast, recover enough at least to make the journey. Nightfall would come in a few hours.

He ignored the tug in his chest that pressed him to keep going, toward Barbara. Katka wouldn't hurt her; she needed Barbara too much.

She needs you—all of you.

And he needed everything he was. That meant the wolf. And the wolf needed the pack. His brothers.

He drifted in and out of a light doze when the tap of a horn roused him before dusk. A substantial gray Sprinter van pulled off the road, slowing. Tobias yipped to his brothers, emerging as the van skidded to a stop.

"Mom?" He stumbled to human feet limping over the uneven ground.

She flung the back doors open. "Clothes are in the car. Everybody in."

The wolves flopped onto the van floor with heaving exhalations. Tobias tugged on a shirt and a pair of sweatpants as she closed the back doors. He jogged to the passenger side and climbed in as she resumed her seat behind the wheel.

His mother fished around in her purse with one hand and produced his spare glasses.

He planted a kiss on her cheek. "Thanks for the save, Mom."

"Oh, it's mom now?" She smiled as she put the van into gear and swung out onto the road. "Now hold on."

Tobias had to grab the door handle to keep his seat. His brothers pulled clothes from the pile in the back, sliding across the floor.

"Easy on the gas, Ma," Mark called. "No seatbelts back here. Hey, pro-tip, smart guy. Put on yours."

Tobias obeyed.

Chris flipped him a bottle of water. Tobias drank deeply as his youngest brother attended to his eldest's burned places with the first aid kit. Mark, irritated by either the inconvenience of injury or a stubborn bottle cap, scowled. Gratitude clogged Tobias's throat. Both men looked up as one and, for a long moment, the three stared at each another. The constellation of their relationship realigned itself in a single instant.

Chris rolled his eyes and went back to applying the paste to Mark's foot. Mark ripped into the pack of sausages with his teeth. Tobias had never loved them more.

"Hey, Strong and Handsome," he said, his voice rough as he wiped his streaming eyes with the back of his hand.

They looked up again, Chris amused, Mark annoyed at the interruption.

"Thank you."

Chris saluted.

"Shut the fuck up and eat," Mark said, heaving another pack of sausage at his head. "Healing takes calories, and I can see your ribs from here. You're going to need fuel to burn once we catch up to your girlfriend."

Tobias settled back into his seat as he ripped open the package. His stomach was raw with hunger, bread and potatoes exhausted long ago. When he looked over, his mother had her eyes on the road, but the smile softened her expression.

"What?" he said between bites.

"You're doing great."

He snorted, scowling out the window. "Not sure how almost getting my brothers killed after a dead witch tried to burn me alive in our cabin qualifies as great. You need to set the bar a little higher."

She grimaced. "That part could have gone better."

"And Barbara," Tobias said, hoarse with desperation. "I couldn't stop her from taking over Barbara."

"I woke up with a bad feeling. That's why I sent your brothers after you. Thought you might need a little help getting her back."

"If that's what you want." Mark clambered up to the space between seats. Tobias turned on him, but he held up his palms. "She pinned you to the floor with the drawer handles and left you in a burning building. That's all."

"She's *possessed*."

Mark shrugged. "They always have an excuse."

Their mother sighed, glaring over her shoulder at him. "Where did I fail you, Markus?"

"You're perfection, Ma." He leaned forward to kiss her cheek. "Nice save, by the way. How did you know where to pick us up?"

"Tracking spell," she said. "You've had one since you were nine. Couldn't let you get into more trouble than I could get you out of."

Chris howled with laughter, rolling across the back when the van hit a curve. Mark threw his half-empty water bottle at him. "So, we find the girlfriend—"

"Barbara," Tobias corrected.

"Bar-ba-ra. With the booty."

Tobias swung at him. "Were you checking out my girlfriend?"

"She does have a nice, round—"

"Boys!" Their mother barked. "I'm going to run this van off the road. That's enough."

"Yeah, Ma," Mark said, before hissing, "like a ripe peach."

Tobias swung and missed.

Chris shoved between them, elbowing his way to the front. "What'd you tell Dad?"

"Isela had an event tonight," she said. "I sent him. Keeps them both out of the way while we clean this mess up. Tobias, I need to know everything."

Tobias' cheeks got hot, but for once his tongue didn't trip him when he spoke. "She *is* my girlfriend—I mean, after Vienna when we—"

"Put it here!" Chris lifted his fist.

"The boy has become a man," Mark drawled. "Popped your cherry, huh?"

Their mother held up a hand. "That's the one part I don't ever need to know about from any of you."

"How do you expect these damn grandchildren you're chasing after us for?" Tobias coughed, laughing.

Chris tugged his elbow. "Did you use the whole pack or what?"

"Christof Douglass Vogel," Beryl said, but laughter crinkled the corners of her eyes. "That's enough."

Tobias sighed. "Sorry about the cabin, Mom."

"Sorry about the forest and the birds and the squirrels and the deer," Chris muttered. "But fuck the boars. They're assholes."

Speechless, Beryl exchanged a questioning glance with Tobias.

"He got chased one time by a cranky old male," Tobias muttered. "They *are* dicks."

She raised her brows. "The fire won't burn past the foundation. We can rebuild."

"The last time a woman claiming to be my girlfriend tried to kill me, that was definitely her way of breaking up," Mark said idly.

Three sets of eyes turned to stare at him.

Tobias frowned. "Exactly how many times—"

"I don't want to know that either," their mother interrupted. "You see why I have a tracker on him? Just tell us the witchy part this time."

Mark and Chris settled within hearing distance, and Tobias told them about the journal and the translation that led him to Barbara's magic, then the disappearing book behind the robbery. And the moment on the roof when it had been Katka, not Barbara, behind her eyes. And then thinking they were safe in the cabin only to have her slip in and flip the tables on him.

"I was close to untangling how she did it, I think. And maybe how to stop her."

"Burns up his shit," Mark said idly to their youngest brother, "and tried to kill him. Make notes for the next time some pretty smile with a nice ass gives you the time of day."

Chris' blondish brows rose. "Noted."

Their mother rubbed her temple with a sideways glance at Tobias. "You see why I'm pinning all my hopes on you?"

"Ma, we're right here." Chris objected.

She ignored him. "Every time Barbara cast a spell from the book, it opened the door a little wider. As she grew confident in her own powers, used them, it sped up the process. And now Barbara's no longer in control. Any idea what she wants?"

"The library, I think," Tobias said. "Maybe the whole university."

Chris sat back on his heels. "She wants to take over your school? Who is this nerd witch?"

"And we don't just give it to her because?" Mark grimaced.

"She possessed Barbara." Tobias scowled at them. He rocked restlessly in his seat, staring out the window. "She was executed for witchcraft—"

"I thought she killed her husband," Chris said, nudging Mark.

"And her lover's wife," Tobias said. "Not the point. Look, she's executed in 1593. Rudolph's been in Prague for a decade as Emperor, and the whole royal court is obsessed with art and science and philosophy and astronomy and alchemy, a lot of which was considered pretty woo-woo at the time. Meanwhile, the Catholics and Protestants are trying to gain control in the country—basically competing for the hearts and souls of the masses. Witchcraft had been tolerated mostly, but once things start heating up, the ability to identify and stop witches became a way to prove the 'efficacy' of doctrine to superstitious villagers who can't read or write. Ergo, witch hunts."

"Am I supposed to be on the murder witch's side?" Mark said doubtfully. "Because…"

"She's off her rocker, okay." Tobias exhaled. "But maybe she also has a little magic, and she starts teaching herself—or finding others who will show her— strengthening her craft. She gets caught and someone catches on to the fact that she's not just a social climber with enemies but a *real* witch, and Rudolph's cronies try to con her out of her book of spells, then burn her anyway."

He shuddered at the memory of being pinned to the floor with the house burning around him.

"You know how long it took to die by burning?" Tobias said. "Long enough to really think about all these rich assholes talking about science and building centers of learning and trying to turn lead into gold. Meanwhile, in the villages, they're burning anyone who skips church. So in her—admittedly criminal—mind, what does she want?"

"More rich asshole murder, I'd guess," Mark chimed in. "Too bad they're all dead now."

"Anyone know the year Žižkov was founded?"

Chris grinned. "1864, Professor."

Tobias looked down at the university t-shirt. "Nice try. That was the year ŽižU split from Charles. It's a trick question. Originally they were one, and guess who was a major patron of the university during the heyday of stargazing and spell thieving?"

"Rudolph and Co.?"

"Exactly."

Mark sat back with a sigh and opened a granola bar. "You couldn't have just said revenge."

"She doesn't want revenge," Tobias said. "She wants control. Barbara was basically blacklisted by the university, then they fired her. We heard nothing for weeks about her case and then suddenly they call her in and reinstate her, like that." He snapped his fingers. "The witch ran Tesarik out, and I bet Novak is next, then probably me."

"She did try to burn you alive." Mark shrugged. "I'll buy it. But what's the plan, if taking over the university is endgame?"

"Who cares?" Chris mused. "She keeps burning up shit and showing off and she's going to get Azrael's attention, and then she's toast. Again."

Quiet settled over the car. Mark nodded once.

"I don't care what happens to Katka," Tobias said, resolved, "I promised I would protect Barbara. I'm getting her back. But this isn't your fight. I won't risk—"

"For fuck's sake, haven't you figured it out yet?" Mark snapped. "We are your *family*. We do this together. So quit trying to get all the glory."

"What he said." Chris jerked a thumb at Mark before whispering, "Isela loves her. She'd kill us if we let her stay a witch puppet."

Their mother gave him a sidelong look and a smile. "It'd be nice to have another witch around. We're not unlike wolves, you know. We do better with others than on our own. Is it all right if I meddle this time, just a little?"

He exhaled a laugh. "Please. I'm out of ideas. But we can't hurt her. Barbara is in there somewhere."

"Great, stop a five-hundred-year-old witch who will try to kill us all without hurting your girlfriend," Chris said. "Check and check. Anything else, Tobias?"

"She's four hundred and change..." he corrected.

Chris threw a water bottle at him.

Their mother chanted as she drove, her fingers dancing over the steering wheel in a set of symbols. When she sat back, the car steered itself.

"Navigation," she said to three sets of staring eyes. "I set a tracker on her when she came for dinner. Hand me some water."

Chris complied. Mark looked admiringly at her. "You're ruthless, Ma."

"What's the plan?"

"She's headed to Vysehrad," she said after a moment. "Of course. Libuše's seat. Perhaps Katka is of her line and thinks she can tap into her legacy. Good."

"How is that good?" Chris snorted. "Powerful witch gets super-charged at a sacred site, and we let her go there."

"Because she's not the only one that can draw from the site," she said, pleased. "It's why your father and I bought the building so close to the park. That's where we stop her."

"You're planning to take her on," Tobias spoke into the sticky silence. "Mom, this isn't good fortune charms and injury rehabilitation balms."

She blinked at the three of them, laughing with bared teeth. "You think all I've ever been was your old mother meddling for grandkids?"

Tobias looked away, abashed. He'd given so little thought to what she might be capable of outside his own sense of betrayal over the years. Everything he knew about her changed when he considered how often, and in how many ways, she must have kept them safe.

She touched his chin. "I reckon I can make Katka wish she had stayed in her book. And once I separate her from Barbara, Tobias, get her as far away as possible. Possession bonds work best with proximity. It will be much harder for Katka to get back into her at a distance. Especially if she's busy defending herself. And she'll be vulnerable out of physical form."

"You watch Toby's back." Mark turned on Chris. "Stay close and don't do anything stupid. Let him fight the big fight, whatever it will be."

"What are you gonna do?"

"I'm staying with Ma," Mark said. "And don't anybody say a fucking word."

Tobias and Chris started shouting immediately. Mark silenced them with a snarl.

"Tobias, you're supposed to be the smart one," he said. "We don't know how Azrael finds out about other magic. Maybe he's got spies around town. Maybe it's that tall, scary-looking dude in the fancy suits. All I know is, if Mom takes on the witch, there are going to be fireworks. And if Azrael or his people show up, somebody has to make sure Mom gets out. That's me."

She took a breath, but Mark growled again. Chris nodded.

Tobias smiled. "Not one word, Mom."

In full darkness, she backed the van into an abandoned access point near the base of the fortress. Tobias hopped out and ran to the back, throwing open the doors. The black and pale wolves leaped out, clothes piled beside the empty water bottles and food packages.

Beryl caught Tobias with his shirt in his hands and reached up to cup his cheeks.

"Every parent hopes their children will go out into the world and do something noble," she said. "Help someone, save something, fight for something bigger than themselves. You've exceeded my wildest dreams, Tobias. I'm so proud of you."

"It's not goodbye, Mom," he said, kissing her cheek. "I'll see you later."

She nodded, and her finger sketched a symbol on his chest, above his heart. Energy rushed through him. His senses expanded; his strength returned. He wanted to howl and tear something apart.

"What was that?"

His mother smiled, took his glasses, and slid them into her pocket. "Only a little mother's love. Now go get your girl."

She turned to close the door, and when she looked back, he had joined his brothers, paws scratching the gravel. "Don't jump the gun, no matter what it looks like. I'm going to have to lure her, and that may mean making her think she has the advantage. Go."

CHAPTER FORTY-THREE

SOME DAYS, Beryl felt every moment of her fifty-four years. Raising four children between two countries in uncertain times had a way of doing that to a body. But her craft had always sustained her through the worst. On days it seemed time might best her, she found the faith to call back *not today*.

She prayed for the courage to shout one more time. She hoped today that courage would be enough.

The fading light of sunset cast the gothic spires of the St. Peter and Paul Basilica in sandy pink and shadow, a monument of one religion—but not the first to mark this spot as sacred. The magic flowed under her feet, undulating beneath the cobblestone from the heart of the hill.

She tapped that energy now, sending her request deeper than she'd ever dared.

A call for assistance. A call to arms.

She wasn't the only one drawing. One familiar—the sunshine and green branches of the woman who'd captured her son's heart. The other, like aged wine, forgotten and now breathing again. Both native to this land, and the older one a truer descendant of Libuše than Beryl could ever be.

Beryl was a foreign magic and hybrid: the great powers of west Africa sundered by the horrors of life in chains, rewoven with the indigenous threads of the new land. Her magic had no native soil, not anymore. She carried it in her arms with her children and her hope, twisted into the locks of her hair.

Images, movement, and intuition had always guided her magic. To practice was to step into the void, arms outstretched, heart open with the faith that the path would appear.

In this new land, like the generations in whose footsteps she followed, she adapted. New spells, new herbs, new dangers. And books. So much of the magic of this land had been bound in pages, stuffed between board and rendered harmless—or near enough—until spoken aloud.

Vowels, consonants, accents, all the words articulated just so.

What a headache.

She had never considered herself a woman of words, and that had created a chasm between her and her most cerebral offspring. She had not understood Tobias, who seemed absent of even his father's empathy, stuck between walls of iron reserve and rapier intelligence.

But Barbara had, and Beryl loved her for it.

For them, Beryl would risk herself. Even if she fell, they would have each other. Barbara would take her place, drawing the others and completing the circle Beryl started when she made her own vow to the magic in her blood: "Four for the directions, four for protection, made whole by bond and bound by love."

Now she prayed her twenty years exchanging breath and blood with this air and this earth would be enough for the land to recognize her or, failing that, her intention to free the young witch and fall on the side of righteousness over legacy.

Being of this land might give Katka the advantage in the end.

A risk she would have to take.

No point in mentioning that part to her boys. They did worry so.

Safety nets are for circuses, as her mother used to say. *Magic is for those who refuse to let fear of falling keep them from flying.*

Now, Beryl pressed her hands on the broad church doors and marveled at the passage of time since she'd first stepped into this space. Had this night been set in motion by that day, the spiral moving outward through the years beyond the two women who found each other before the painting of a saint?

Friendship was another kind of bond.

Veronika had not been a constant presence, though a welcome one.

When Beryl had opened her studio, Veronika came often for class. After one, she mentioned a strange girl, a curious creature with an unusual nose for valuable books, skittish as a whipped horse and as bright as the first star of the night. She'd asked Beryl for advice—how to befriend her, to determine if she was safe, and to provide for someone too proud to admit she needed help.

Beryl whispered a little prayer. *Old friend, help me to save this girl.*

And then she walked inside.

The power needled against the wards she'd imbued in her clothes and her skin. She reinforced them with a burst, and the resistance eased as she pushed through the thick air. Light flared inside the church from the altar, setting off the gold in the walls and making the frescoes dance as it flickered.

She walked toward the altar steps, pausing briefly to nod at the painting of unruffled old St. Genevieve.

"You have someone that does not belong to you, witch," Beryl called as she approached the crossing, summoning the strength that made her voice ring across the church. "And in the name of the light, I demand her release."

The glow resolved itself and Barbara spun, her body jerky as a marionette on strings. Revolted, Beryl fought the bile rising in her throat. A spell like this violated every code any coven held dear.

The familiar warmth of each of her boys hovered on the edge of her perception.

She remembered the oldest two as children, dancing in the motes of light, staring in awe at the gold. For a moment, they stood hand in hand as they hadn't since they were toddlers, and she had smiled watching them. Now they numbered three and stronger than they had ever been.

"I meant you no harm." The voice belonged to Barbara, but even the tone and phrasing had changed. "I'll even overlook how you've sullied your line with the blood of vermin if you join with me."

Beryl laughed. "Those days are dead, old woman. A lot has changed."

"Am I to fear a lord of death?" The witch snorted, descending the steps to the open space between them, within a few feet of Beryl, but just out of reach.

This close, the stress in Barbara's face was clear. The muscles tensed and strained, as though not in full cooperation with the voice speaking through her. Good. The girl was still fighting for control. There was more than a chance.

Katka had the book in the cradle of her right arm. Everything depended on being able to separate them.

"This is their world now," Beryl said coolly, clasping her hands at her back to hide the twitch of her fingertips. "And they will crush you, as they crushed our sisters after the war. None together were strong enough to stand against them."

"Cowards," Katka sneered. "All of you. You deserved to be crushed. Stand against me at your peril, witch."

Beryl didn't speak the words of a formal challenge; she didn't announce the lineage of her craft or acknowledge the rules of combat—Katka had violated those codes the moment she had taken over Barbara.

The rules were forfeit.

Instead, she cupped her hands, summoning the force of the air chilled by stone, and flung a charge of energy between them. Barbara's body fell back against the railing under the force and buckled. The book slipped free and tumbled to the stone floor.

The witch jerked to Barbara's hands and knees. The lights flickered and waned as Beryl drew on the electricity. She hurtled lighting, striking between the girl and the book. Katka recoiled as Beryl sprang. Beryl grabbed the book and rolled, feeling the muscles in her back strain. Katka's hand clamped on her thigh. Beryl gasped with the strength of her opponent, swinging hard with the book.

It hit Barbara's temple, knocking her back.

"Now!" Beryl screamed as Katka lunged again.

Mark galloped from behind the altar, teeth bared. She tossed the book, not pausing to watch him snap it out of the air.

Beryl went down under the other witch's weight. She managed to get to her back. Katka knelt over her, her mouth open in a scream of rage, her body stiffening as the witch drew on the power of the sacred ground for one final blow.

Beryl didn't waste time trying to defend herself. The protections she'd been weaving into her skin since her initiate days would hold, or they would not. She grabbed Katka's wrists, dragging her closer as she spoke the words of the invocation.

The summoning became a litany, chanted over and over.

The younger witched stopped fighting, limbs shaking with suppressed motion.

"No, Beryl." The voice became familiar again. "Save yourself. I can buy you time."

Beryl smiled into the raging face. Only her eyes, wide and wet with tears, revealed the young witch within. "Veronika warned me that you would be too stubborn to ask for help."

Barbara fell back, surprised. Beryl doubled her efforts, knitting her call to the memory of spring green and sunshine until she lost connection with her own body, only power and will remaining.

Barbara arched with one ragged shriek as the spell yanked the burning orb—Katka—out of her. The girl collapsed. Beryl rolled to her knees and staggered to her feet over Barbara's prone body. Her eyes stayed locked on the light zigzagging around the altar, palms spread as she crafted a bind with thought and intention. *Keep fighting, Barbara.*

The light flinched as the craftwork expanded away from Beryl, but the energy wasn't meant to capture it. It melded with the walls, spreading and forming a protective boundary. The light screeched, flinging itself against the border, but it could not pass through as it did the objects in the room.

It turned back on them, as Beryl knew it would.

This time she drew the energy trapped in the room and raised a shimmering wall infused with the solidity of stone.

Katka crashed against it and fell back, screaming.

"Tobias, you're up." Beryl bared her teeth. Grizzled fur brushed her leg and she braced herself against the onslaught as she kept Katka from her target. "Go."

With Barbara away, Beryl turned to the task at hand. Time to put down a crazy old witch. She cracked her knuckles.

"She made no bargain with you," Beryl said, sliding the little knife from her belt. "And you will answer to me."

If there was a better moment for the power commanded by a blood spell, she hadn't known it. Consequences be damned. She slid the blade over her palm. The sting flashed—a sharp, bright thing, as the bead of maroon rolled free. She dropped to one knee and pressed her palm to the polished floor.

"On the souls of my mothers, I summon thee to right the wrong done by this false practitioner. She has robbed one of our sisters of her agency and violated the vow of the coven to protect the vulnerable. Come now, judge of all matters, holder of the balance, great Mother to us all."

The torrent of power she expected never came.

"You fool." The erratic light resolved itself into the figure of a woman, her dark hair blowing, face pale and eyes bright with twisted with madness. "You come to my house, call on what is mine? I am a child of Libuše. My foremothers ruled in this land when yours were crossing an ocean in chains. I will bleed your tainted whelps dry before you die, witch."

The black wolf pressed against Beryl's side. Beryl gave her eldest son a wry look. "That didn't go as planned."

A low growl settled in his chest.

"She talks a good game," Beryl agreed. "But the world needs one less foul-mouthed old hag."

A bolt of energy sent her sprawling. She gasped, rolling away, and flung up another shield to block the next.

Even a hedge would have been better than sitting in the open like a ninny, she chided. *Getting rusty, old girl.*

With a flick of the wrist, she sent a swirling mass up from the floor. It solidified into a block of hewn stone, trapping the spirit within.

Mark whined.

"Go now." Beryl snapped at him and turned her attention to binding the stone with wards. "Get the book out of here. Tell Tobias. Tell him that the source is the key. Tell him…It's not over."

CHAPTER FORTY-FOUR

THE PROBLEM with losing his clothes every time he shifted was that he would need to have a convenient stash of clothing everywhere—or end up, like he was now, running naked through a church carrying an unconscious witch.

The pale wolf racing behind saw the humor in the situation. Tobias could hear his huffing laughter as they ran. "Not funny."

The wolf yipped and dashed ahead.

It was a little funny.

Tobias pushed through the doors to the empty vestibule.

Barbara stirred in his arms, clutching at him. "You're alive. What are you doing here? Why are you—oh?"

His eyes weren't so great without his glasses, and it was slow down or risk falling with her. Tobias dropped to the stone floor, dragging her onto his lap. Her arms locked around him, and tears streaked his bare chest. The pale wolf circled them both, whining impatiently.

She stared in wonder, shivering. "Chris? Is that you?"

He opened his mouth in a wily grin and sat down beside them, lending them his warmth.

Barbara burst into tears. "I'm so sorry. I tried to stop her, I did. I didn't know—"

"I saw you in there, fighting. But we have to keep moving."

The black wolf appeared out of the darkness, bearing a familiar book in his teeth. Tobias grabbed it as his brother rose from four legs.

"What are you doing?" Mark speared them with a glare. "You're supposed to take her *out of the church.*"

The doors slammed shut, locks sliding home. Mark swore, throwing his body at the door. The same shock of power that had leveled Tobias in the cabin hurtled Mark backward. He rolled to his knees, snarling and yellow eyed, tufts of fur reappearing at his elbows and throat.

Chris winced. "Too late."

Oblivious, Tobias cradled her face in his hands, inspecting her. "Are you all right?"

Barbara laughed hollowly. "Me? I almost killed you."

"Lucky for him, he has us," Mark said, scowling as he paced the entrance. Each time he reached out, a blue arc hit him, and he snarled back at it.

"What's the backup plan?" Chris asked when Mark rejoined them.

Tobias sat back as all eyes settled on him. "Me?"

Mark jerked a thumb in Christof's direction. "Handsome." He lifted a finger indicating himself. "Strong." Then he slowly aimed it at Tobias. "Smart. Ma can't hold her forever, and she said to tell you the source is the key. You're up."

"The source?" Tobias shook his head.

Maybe with his notes and the journal, he would have been able to come up with something. But with Barbara finally in his arms, all he could think about was ripping an old book page from page until she was free once and for all.

"She's too powerful." Barbara's voice rose, but she kept her eyes fixed on her own hands without looking at any of them.

They all realized why at the same time.

"It seems like the safest place," she squeaked, her gaze darting up to Tobias before ping-ponging around the ceiling. "You're all so very...naked."

Chris wheezed laughter behind his fist.

Tobias whacked him. "Shut up, you hyena."

"No time to be shy, baby," Mark drawled. "Sure you picked the right Vogel?"

The wolf snarled in Tobias chest, but Barbara clapped a hand over his bicep and glared at Mark. "Who hits on their brother's girlfriend?"

Tobias and Mark looked at the youngest Vogel.

Chris held up his hands. "Hey, now. Toby doesn't date, and you don't bring your girlfriends home anymore. When would I even—hey!"

Barbara giggled until a little coughing snort hiccuped out of her chest. "Unbelievable."

Mark's slow laugh came with a genuine smile aimed at Barbara. "If you don't get turned into witch puppet and then squashed like a bug by a necromancer, you'll fit right in. Now focus. You and Toby are on the inside of this thing. We need a plan. Fast."

Barbara nodded. "The book, the book is the key. It's the source, right? It's where she came from."

"We end the book," Mark reasoned. "We end the witch."

"But she's not in the book," Tobias said.

Mark spread his palms with a shrug. "We get her in the book, and then we end the book. Yes, or yes?"

Tobias froze, working over the logic. He slapped Mark on the shoulder with a wild grin. "Yes."

"How, exactly?" Chris finished.

"It's draining being non-corporeal," Barbara sat up, trembling with excitement. "The only way she's managing so well is she bound the energy of this place. But sustaining that fight with Beryl is costing her. She's going to need a physical host, and soon."

"And we need to keep her from heading back to Barbara," Tobias said.

"Which is why you were supposed to take her the hell out of here," Mark snapped. "To stop that from happening *again*."

"What if we don't stop her?" Barbara exhaled. "Each time she transfers takes power. If we force her to jump twice, in a short period, there might not be enough of her left to fight."

Mark's gaze narrowed in approval at Barbara. "Oh, so *you're* the smart one."

Tobias squeezed her fingers. "I just got you back. I'm not risking—"

"This is the best chance we've got," Barbara whispered. "We let her back in and then make it so that I'm no longer an option, so she has to transition again. That will burn her out. Beryl's too strong, and Katka wouldn't dare try to jump to her. She'll go to the book. She'll have to."

"What do you mean, no longer an option?" Tobias ground out.

"You have to kill me."

◆

"It's a good plan," Beryl murmured from the doorway.

The waves of power flagged beneath her skin, Barbara noted with concern. She was no longer as vibrant as she had looked when she walked into the church.

The fear that coursed through Katka at the sight of the older witch had given Barbara hope, and built courage atop it. When the first tendrils of Beryl's spell had reached her, she had gripped the stones of the oubliette Katka had built around her, forcing handholds where there had been none, and hauled herself toward the distant scent of lavender and sunshine.

Now, Beryl swayed a step. Her hair had come down in the struggle. The silver in her meticulously twisted locks had barely reached her chin jawline before blending with the darker hair. Now silver streaked their lengths halfway down her back.

Barbara stood, wrapping her arm around the older woman. Mark caught Beryl's other elbow, easing her down to a seat.

Tobias glanced at the doors behind them. "How did you stop her?"

"Seal of Solomon," Beryl said, looking a touch smug. "I figured she's arrogant enough not to bother learning much about the craft outside of the home, so maybe a thousand-year-old West Guinean trick would keep her busy for a while. It's based on the legend of Solomon's ring—the design meant to dizzy and confuse demons trapped within. Big hit at the solstice party before you all were born."

Barbara gaped. How had Beryl known such a thing? Who taught Beryl? Where could one learn? The questions, and hunger for answers, overrode her fear. Barbara couldn't help herself—she hugged Beryl hard enough to make the older woman smile.

"Welcome back," Beryl squeezed back, but her former strength was gone. "I can stop your heart. Just for a few minutes. Long enough to get her to jump again."

"We're not killing Barbara!" Tobias shouted.

The terror in his eyes ripped into her. She remembered the horror of watching smoke billow in the rearview mirror, knowing he was trapped inside.

Barbara laced her fingers with his and tried to put on her most reassuring expression.

"I read about this kind of spell, there's something like it in the book." Her gaze swung uncertainly to Beryl. "It's not a real death, right?"

Beryl's smile didn't reach her eyes. "It's not a true death. Sort of like limbo. I will call you back but you must answer. The pull of the afterlife can be great. Your will to return must be stronger."

"This is insane." Tobias bit out the words.

Beryl's gaze locked on the door, troubled by something beyond. "Out of time. Mark."

"We do this now before she comes up with anything else." Mark nodded, and the long hairs of his ruff stood on end.

A moment later, the yellow eyes of the jet wolf glimmered in the dark where he had been sitting.

"Or before the Necromancer busts up the fight," Chris said, dropping to four paws.

Only Tobias remained human. "I won't do this."

Barbara flattened a hand over his heart. "Wolves are resistant to our power. It's why she had to trap you and try to burn you alive."

His jaw flexed, unhappy, but he nodded.

"Then stay with me as long as you can," she said. "I promise, I'll come back if I know you're waiting for me."

He swallowed thickly, but a moment later, wolf fur pressed against her palm the heartbeat steady beneath. She rose, facing Beryl.

Beryl took her shoulders. "You are a brave young woman."

"And a foolish one." The pressure of unshed tears stung Barbara's throat. "This is all my fault."

Beryl cupped her cheek, drawing her eyes back. "There is no crime in wanting more for yourself and using everything in your power to get it. It is the only way we accomplish great things. But sometimes we lose our way. You stepped off the path. That is all."

The weight slid from Barbara's shoulder under the woman's warm gaze.

"Now the hard part—I need physical contact with you to stop your heart once she's inside. She will not want you too close to me, for obvious reasons. I need you to distract her, and I have an idea."

Beryl leaned in close, whispering, and Barbara let the words flow into her. She wouldn't need to remember. When the time came, they would be ready.

Finished, Beryl exhaled wearily, but her spine remained straight with determination.

The gray wolf pressed Barbara's thigh with a whimper of uncertainty. She cradled the book and rested a hand between his ears. "I'm ready."

As they walked to the doors, she took Beryl's arm. "Thank you for everything."

Beryl smiled. "It's 'see you later,' not goodbye."

The moment they cleared the doorway, a brittle ache weakened her knees. The same malignant sensation behind the whispering voice and the dreams that left her wrung out.

They made it halfway up the aisle before the tremors forced her to stop. The light quit its erratic darting, and she felt the witch's attention shift to her.

"Be brave," Beryl whispered. "Let's finish this."

"You can have me: I won't fight you. Just let them go, please." Barbara lifted her head and took the final steps, leaving Beryl's side to step forward alone.

Not alone. Tobias moved between Barbara and the light, his hackles up, his teeth bared.

"What are you doing?" she hissed, trying to push him away.

But the wolf refused to back down. The light slammed into them both.

CHAPTER FORTY-FIVE

WHEN BARBARA OPENED HER EYES, she and Tobias stood in the oubliette. Her heart flung itself to a gallop at the sight of the familiar walls.

"Where are we?" Tobias stood, running his hands over the featureless stone.

No handholds this time. Even the pinprick of light was missing. Tremors rolled through her.

Trapped underground. This wasn't a prison. It was a tomb.

"How far down do you think—" The sob of desperation cut off her words. Her stomach twisted.

Tobias threw himself at the stone, pummeling the walls with his fists and his feet as he shouted. The sound bounced back in a chorus of echoes.

Barbara covered her ears and rocked, trying not to vomit. She sank into a ball in the center of the room, tucking her knees against her chest.

Spent, he leaned his forehead against the wall, his spine hunched. "Maybe that was not my brightest idea."

She opened one eye as he put his back to the wall and slid to his heels, thumping his head against the stone.

He pushed his glasses up his nose and met her gaze. "I promised I would protect you. You, who even without a coven or training are powerful enough to free a 400-year-old witch. And I can hardly admit what I am."

Tobias wore the suit she'd first seen him in. The silk tie that had been stained with blood from the fight in the collections lab. His hair was short.

How did he have his glasses?

She clambered to her feet. Vertigo twisted her balance, and she stood splay-legged as a foal, measuring each breath carefully to keep from losing control. Her hands shook as she pressed them to the wall. None of the cold, weeping damp she expected. She looked back at Tobias.

"You can't protect me." Barbara whispered.

"I have no idea what I'm doing."

She rubbed her fingertips together, letting the dawning truth settle into certainty.

"Neither do I, Toby." She dropped to a crouch before him. "But I know that you can't protect me against myself."

Tobias stopped rocking his head against the wall. "What?"

"She knows I'm afraid of being underground because of my dad," Barbara said, tugging at his shoulders to get him to his feet. "And she's using it against me by putting us here. But she's in *my* head."

"But it looks—" His nose twitched, wolf-like. He exhaled sharply. "It doesn't smell."

"Because it's not real. She can use my memories to trigger my fear, but she can't make them real because we're in my head."

His nostrils flared and the bones in his face shifted subtly beneath the skin, rendering him identical to her memories from the night of the robbery. It was impossible not to see the wolf in him, the wildness within turning intellect to cunning.

To protect her.

She smiled to herself as love for him—wolf and man—slipped warm tendrils of weight inside her ribcage, grounding her. "Desire is the strongest force in the universe."

He cocked his head in a lupine expression of confusion.

Fur tipped his ears now, and the length of his hair had gone black-tipped with grizzled grey roots.

She reached out a hand and his slid around it, like metal filings to a magnet, soft fur ticking her palm as she locked their hands together. "I got myself into this, and I'm going to get us out."

Their eyes met. Even his eyebrows were fluffy and growing more like the animal than man.

"Whatever happens, I love you, Tobias Vogel. You and your hairy friend. Never forget that."

Still clasping his hand, she began to chant the words of the spell Beryl had given her. As the image expanded around her, the walls fell away and left them momentarily blinded by sunlight.

She squinted, recoiling from the sudden brightness.

Tobias sucked in a hard breath.

They were back in the church. Sun filtered through the windows, dust motes sparkling in the air, as shafts of light illuminated the interior.

In all her years, she had never been inside the small basilica in the daytime, and she was struck as mute with awe as Beryl had been on the day this memory was made. The bright sandstone walls were adorned from floor to ceiling with blossoms and bunches of ginkgo, bordered by gilt accents.

At the corners, enormous winged women with broad, glowing halos held up the ceiling, their hair and robes streaming in shades of red and gold. Geometrically spaced stars over a cobalt background covered some smaller sections of the arched ceiling. Others bore rows of blossoms and feathers and ribbons.

"Mom?" Wonder in Tobias's voice softened the word.

Barbara followed his gaze.

A brown-skinned woman in her early 30's stood in the center of the aisle, wearing jeans and tennis shoes, her shoulder-length dreadlocks sticking out from beneath her knit cap. The cries of the baby in the chest carrier softened to whimpers as her small, puckered face eased. The woman bobbed, a smooth, automatic motion, and the baby made contented chirping noises.

Barbara felt it as if it were her body moving under that warm living weight, heard the woman's thoughts as her own.

Beside her, Tobias made a sound of disbelief as two small boys walked past him, heading up the central aisle. The younger of the two was reed-thin except for the soft baby face and sported a truly outrageous pair of glasses. The older was no more than ten, but he clenched his brother's hand as they stared at the sunlit church.

With a glance at her boys to make sure they posed no immediate danger to the serene interior, the woman began a slow circuit of the perimeter.

The baby quieted against her, settling into sleep and she almost wept with relief. In the few months since they'd arrived, none of them had gotten much sleep. And the days were so long, trying to keep three children occupied until the next attempt at bedtime. At regular intervals, she questioned their decision to come here, only to remind herself that there really had been no choice. Not given her family's unique situation.

But here, time seemed to stretch to proportions almost magical in length and intensity.

The energy tingled her fingertips first, rising up through the ground, soaking into her, imbuing her with a sense of peace and calm. She made a small tapping motion with her fingertips against the baby's spine, over her own heart, acknowledging with gratitude the gift received. In response the calm, blossomed into celebration, recognizing her for what she was and welcoming her.

The figure in each of the long frescos adorning the pillars had been painted in the Art Nouveau style synonymous with the city itself, thanks to Mucha's prodigious work. Their tranquil faces held none of the torment she associated with the usual depictions of saints and martyrs.

The image of a woman reaching for a child, who in turned offered an armload of leaves to a young deer, drew her. She puzzled at the name below the figure.

"You recognize her?" A Czech woman in a matching cloche and skirt suit approached Beryl with a smile, her blonde hair cut to what had been a stylish bob twenty years ago.

Barbara let out a soft sob that neither woman noticed.

"I don't even know what that word spells," Beryl said wryly.

The woman pronounced the name in Czech. "In English, Genevieve."

"Thank you."

"Veronika Panikova." She offered a hand.

"Beryl Gilman-Vogel."

"Do you know, about Genevieve?"

Beryl smiled ruefully, shaking her head. "She just looks peaceful, and that's enviable when you've got kids."

"They are yours... all of them?"

"Would you like one?" Beryl drawled as the boys began to rouse themselves from their fascination and return their attention to one another.

Veronika winced. "You are a stronger woman than I. Come by my book shop when you have time. I have books in English, and a few children's books. I'm sure I have something about Saint Jenny here."

She handed Beryl a card.

Beryl considered it, and her gaze flicked to Tobias. He'd had to leave so many books behind. She spoke slowly to keep her voice steady. "Thank you, but right now there's not a lot of time for reading—or money for it, for that matter."

"And what do you do, here in Prague?"

"We've only been here a couple of months." Beryl sighed as Isela stirred. "Back home, I used to do some graphic design work, when I could find it, and taught a little yoga at the senior center. But these guys keep me pretty busy right now."

A familiar, weary longing filled her chest, making the next breath a challenge.

She swallowed hard, tapping her fingertips again, this time against each other in a backward circular rhythm, hoping to bring back that sense of calm, and purpose. The tingling resumed, strengthening in answer.

"I see." Veronika watched her carefully, but with none of the suspicion or judgement she'd experienced on the playground or riding the tram.

Beryl tried a smile. Veronika returned it. But knowing her boys, they'd be restless soon. She had to keep them moving, or they'd take it out on whatever the nearest surface was. "I should go," she said, "before they kick us out."

Veronika shook her head. "They've seen much, much worse, I promise. What do you say to a trade? My English was good once, but I'm out of practice. Come by. And I can find you a few books. Do they like stories about rocket ships, your boys?"

"My eldest, Markus, will *only* read if there's a rocket ship involved," she said. "But the little one, with the glasses, that's Tobias. He'll read all day if I let him. And he loves rocket ships and robots. Like his dad."

Barbara recognized the consideration in Veronika's face and the decision. "He's come to the right country. Do you know we Czech invented the word 'robot'? Our very own Karel Čapek in 1920."

Beryl tucked the card into the pocket of her jeans. "I didn't know that. Thank you. Nice to meet you."

Beryl sought out the church often in the following years, sometimes just to sit in the sunniest pew and let her mind rest. She always visited St. Genevieve, searching for some clue in that tranquil face for guidance on how to put up with the inane amount of bullshit the world could throw at a person.

Barbara almost laughed at the tone of the thought, so clearly straight from Beryl's mind. She hadn't understood what Beryl meant when she promised a memory snare, but this was wondrous. Like being the dreamer and the dream.

Katka rose from the first pew, dressed in widow's black. "Very clever, little witch. The stronger the memory, the tighter the trap, but it will only hold me as long as you can hold on to it."

Rage turned Barbara away from the vision. "You killed Veronika. You tried to steal my life from me."

"What were you using it for?" The witch sneered. "Your job in the box? You were content to be a worm in the mud before I came."

Tobias's grip tightened on her own.

Katka looked over her shoulder at him. "And you fucking wolves. In my day, no witch worth her salt would consort with a two-skinned creature." She sneered. "He isn't worthy of you, little witch."

Tobias laughed, but it sounded like a snarl. "I may not be worthy of her but, if she'll have it, my life is hers."

Katka cocked her head, a knowing smile on her face.

"Do you want to see what comes of the life you tie to this witch?" She didn't wait for an answer. She waved a hand, and a garden replaced the right section of pews, overgrown with green things and redolent with the scent of blooming flowers.

In the garden, an older version of Barbara wore her yellow sundress, with a wide-brimmed hat shading her face that she recognized from Veronika's closet. She kneeled on a blanket, laughing at something. When she opened her arms, a boy of no more than eight ran into them. He bore a striking resemblance to the chocolate-haired boy wandering toward the altar. The older Barbara swept him onto her lap, tickling him until he wiggled like a caught fish.

A third Tobias strode through the grass, a boy and a girl—twins—balanced on either hip. His daughter had her mother's freckles. His son had her curly hair. Their son.

Present Tobias staggered back a step, unable to tear his gaze from the scene before them. His hand fell from hers.

"She knows what you're afraid of," Barbara whispered, reaching for him. "She's trying to scare you. Like the oubliette. It's a lie."

"Didn't your mother warn you, boy?" Katka said. "The gift of prescience is given to descendants of Libuše."

"Shut up," Barbara screamed.

Katka ignored her, addressing Tobias. "Ah, but you know the truth. That is your future if she walks away today. Anything for hers, eh? Even passing your tainted blood onto a new generation of mongrels."

All around them, the sunlit church began to fracture. Barbara fought to maintain the image of Beryl's past, but her eyes kept traveling to their future. She tasted desire on the back of her tongue like a spell begging to be spoken. The memory of the sleeping infant's weight, soft and solid and so real on her chest. Beryl's memory. Would her children be witches, like her? Weres, like their father? Both?

Tobias met her eyes, a question. She stepped away from him, toward the sound of Beryl's chant and the distant sensation of the older woman's hand wrapping around hers. She needed a little more time. So she let the words come: a diversion, a distraction, and the truth. "I hoped I could live without a family of my own if I had you. But I think… I think I can't. And if you stay with me, that will be our future, and your sons and daughters will live with the wolves in them. She's right."

Stop Katka. It was the only thing that mattered. She prayed she'd given Beryl enough time.

Her heart stopped.

Katka's scream of fury tore through her. Barbara clapped her hands over her ears. When it was done, she blinked her eyes open. She and Tobias stood in a blank grey space. No walls. No sensation of being underground. Just emptiness.

"Where are we now?" Tobias took a step before spinning back to her. "And where is she?"

"It worked," Barbara said with certainty. "I can't feel her anymore."

Beryl's voice rang in the distance. *Come back. Come home.*

Light bloomed before them, and she shielded her eyes. From the light emerged two women she recognized first with her heart. They held hands, waving to her.

"Maminka? Veronika?" She started for them, but Tobias grabbed her wrist.

"Remember what Mom said," he whispered, waiting for her eyes to find his before continuing. "This is death's pull. If you go to them, you don't come back. Your will to return has to be stronger..."

Barbara stopped, a hand on her ribcage. Her chest ached as the slivers of her shattered heart cut deep.

Life. She had to want that.

A life at the university? To hang a diploma on the wall beneath her mother's. A piece of paper wasn't a connection. She had memory for that. Beryl had shown her that power.

The alternative was a future she hadn't even been able to dream for herself because she'd been so fixed on living life to honor the past. She looked into the light, squinting at the two familiar figures, now holding hands. *You don't have to choose. You never had to choose.*

Perhaps.

But she could not make a choice that changed his future.

♦

BERYL'S CALL rang again in the emptiness and after a lifetime, Tobias recognized the demand of a parent expecting to be obeyed. Full of love and edged with fear. Calling them home.

How much time did they have? Could they be trapped here? And what of the Necromancer? Certainly all that commotion with the witch had tripped an alarm somewhere. He had to be on his way.

It didn't matter.

None of it mattered. Mark and Chris would have to look after Mom. Because he wasn't going back without Barbara.

Still Barbara hesitated. "That future..."

Nothing could have prepared him for that. Retreating came automatically: the flinch anticipating the blow. Only this time the wolf lunged back, howling in exultant fury at a future fully realized.

We are.

"Look at me." Tobias took her face in his hands. He kissed her cheeks, her lashes, her brow. She stared above his head, the heartbreak glistening at the corners of her eyes. "Bebe. Please."

He caught the tears with his thumbs and his own vision blurred. This time the words he needed were right there, waiting for him to catch up. A good thing, because the sound of her voice cracking with apology for revealing the truth of her desire shattered something in him.

He'd promised not to hurt her, and he'd failed by letting his own fear close off possibilities.

No more letting fear make the decisions. No more running away, hiding from what he was. Not when she saw in him a future that big. Not when she looked at him as she had in the oubliette the moment before she'd broken Katka's cage—full of hope and power.

"You turned the lights on." He let the words rush out of him and when he tripped over them in his hurry and impatience he shunted aside embarrassment and kept on. "I've been stumbling around in a dark room my whole life, frightened of all things I thought I could make go away if I refused to see them. You showed me the gift of my wolf. You know what I felt when I saw that future?"

When her gaze skated off his, he caught the tiny tendril of hope curling in their depths. The wolf pressed against his breastbone, scrabbling at his ribs, urging him on. *All right you big beast, I'm doing my best here. Calm down.*

"I saw love," he whispered, tipping her chin up. "Did you see how much they—we—how much we loved each other? Why fear any future with so much love in it?"

Now he could hear it—a distant rhythmic pulse growing louder, stronger and faster, determined to survive.

Her heart.

"But you didn't want—"

"I didn't want what I had, but everything is different now. We know what's coming, we can prepare them. They'll have their uncles—though that may be a mixed blessing." He laughed and wiped his own eyes. "And a grandmother that will smother them. And you. A powerful witch for a mother who will protect them, no matter what comes. I want everything in that future—especially you."

"I won't close the shop."

He laughed. "Thank gods. You were magnificent in Vienna, and I'm not talking about the dress. If it wasn't for the shop, you would have had an inbox full of job offers on Monday morning."

Barbara looked back at the figures. "And I want to finish school. Somehow."

"I think I have an idea about how we can do that." He raised a brow in question. "Trust me?"

She laughed, a sweet sound full of relief. "What are we going to do about Hemingway?"

He held out a hand. "We'll figure something out. Come on, Bebe. Let's not be afraid to want anymore."

CHAPTER FORTY-SIX

BETWEEN THE WEIGHT pinning her to the floor and the face full of fur, Barbara struggled to breathe. She thumped the solid body above her. Tobias shook from nose to tail, transitioning to free her.

Mark threw an altar cloth at him. "Make yourself decent."

While his hands were busy, Barbara slipped away to join Beryl, standing over the book. It lay still, as innocuous as an old volume could be.

The older woman looked up with a wan smile. "Thanks for bringing my boy back."

"Beryl, when did you meet Veronika?" Barbara said, her voice ragged.

Beryl cocked her head, puzzled. "Veronika was a student in my class. That must have been how we met."

"You don't remember coming here with the boys when they were small?" Barbara asked, the whole story came to her as she spoke, as though it was her own. She paused; it couldn't be. "St. Genevieve? Robots and spaceships?"

Beryl smiled at the odd question, but showed no sign of recognition. "Isela did a report on the artists in school before she left for the Academy. I brought her up here for the first time. I think."

"The memory," Barbara gasped. "You lost it when you gave it to me."

More than watching it play out, Barbara had felt how much the moment meant to Beryl. That had been the turning point, the touchstone she returned to time and again as she carved out a life in this new home. What had Katka said—the stronger the memory, the tighter the trap?

Beryl sighed softly with realization, and the grief on her face broke Barbara's heart. "Must have worked, then. You gave me just enough time."

She slipped her fingers around the older woman's and squeezed. "I'll tell you everything. It may not be the same, but at least you'll know."

"I'd appreciate that," Beryl said.

The book at their feet rocked and flapped open.

Barbara jumped, but Beryl gave it a long, searing look.

"Stay put, hag." Beryl made a gesture with knotted fingers that stilled it again.

Chris peered over their shoulders, holding a blue velvet cloth embroidered with little gold stars around his hips with one hand. Barbara was pretty sure he'd snagged it from the Madonna and child.

"Man, she doesn't give up easy, does she?" he grumbled.

"We must destroy this book," Beryl sighed. "I have to maintain the dampening spell on the church to keep the Necromancer from sniffing us out. I'm going to need you for this, Barbara."

Barbara hesitated, curling her fingers against the energy crackling in her palms. She felt, more than saw, Tobias move toward her, but Beryl held up a hand.

"What is it?" Beryl smiled as though there were no necromancers or possessed books needing to be dealt with.

Barbara looked into her own palms, searching for the answer to a question she didn't know how to ask. The well of power Katka had unbound surged in her. This was so much more than what she had known in the library, or the shop. And the last time she had tried to use it—

"I hurt people," Barbara whispered, unable to look at Tobias.

When she met Beryl's eyes, she saw recognition in the older woman's steady gaze.

"You were dabbling."

Barbara flinched as if the words had struck a blow.

"Mom," Tobias murmured.

Beryl ignored him, her eyes never leaving Barbara.

"You've learned your first lesson in the hardest possible way," Beryl said, and her tone softened the words so they only stung a little. "You had no goal, no purpose, only raw desire. You were throwing a penny in a well without making your wish. It opens up the door for all manner of things to slip through. That's how Katka got control. You must learn to balance both: want and control. Intention."

They all froze at the sound of ringing too clear and high to be that of a church bell.

"Necromancer?" Mark tensed.

Beryl shook her head once. "Something old, though."

As one, they drew close, putting Barbara in their center. In spite of the danger and uncertainty, Barbara had never felt so safe.

The scent of age and incense faded beneath the bloom of crushed laurel leaves and stripling birch, spring grass and hops as something more primal than saints and angels filled the space.

"Here we go again." Chris grunted, dropping to his paws with a huff and a sigh. He shook hard, the blue velvet puddling beneath him, and showed his teeth.

"Easy, Cujo." Tobias' voice became a lupine rumble.

Mark gave their mother a worried look before his features transformed into the eldest wolf of yellow eyes and midnight fur.

Barbara knew what he saw. Beryl had given so much tonight; it showed in the slacking of her facial muscles, the ashen underlay of her vibrant brown skin. Practice and habit kept her spine tall and her shoulders back, but her grace now clung to her in tatters, no longer emanating from her like a shield. Even still, she nudged Barbara behind her shoulder, the intent to protect clear.

Barbara met the dark wolf's eyes with shared understanding.

Light lanced up from the floor from the grooves between the stones. This time, it spread, illuminating the entire church until every wall and fresco shone as if lit from within. The angels raised their trumpets, and the painted saints all looked toward the light, their faces expectant.

The wolves drew close.

The heat crackled in Barbara's palms and raced up her wrists to her forearms. Desire. Control. Intention. She would protect the people who had refused to abandon her in her greatest need.

She flexed that intent. The wood railings and pews groaned in response. Lavender and sunshine rose in gusts of spring air over her shoulders to surround the pack and the older witch. When their eyes met, Beryl nodded. "You see."

Individual shafts of light collected above the altar, taking human shape. The face was too bright to make out features, too transparent to be more than a suggestion.

The light dimmed, and a high voice filled the space. "Peace, sisters. I mean you no harm."

Beryl inhaled and her spine stiffened as a new essence unfurled before them.

Barbara recognized it immediately from the memory of the church, the same strength that had reached toward Beryl with joyous recognition. "Libuše?"

The light flickered, acknowledgment. "May I?"

Beryl stepped back as the great light passed through the altar to approach.

Mark lowered his head but didn't stop growling as the unearthly figure stopped leaving a good distance between them. The book rose toward to the light, thrashing.

"Your grief is great, daughter, and not unearned," the figure mourned. "But your greed leads you astray."

The book howled, straining at its bindings. The sorceress stretched a hand out over the aged leather. The light flashed with blinding radiance, and when it dissolved, tiny bits of glimmer floated to the floor like ash.

"It is done," Libuše said. "The name of our lost daughter is written on my heart and will not be spoken again."

Beryl slipped to one knee. Gentle pressure pushed Barbara aside as the light passed through their defenses and cradled Beryl's shoulders, lifting. "Rise, sister. It is I that should kneel in gratitude."

Beryl looked up, startled.

The light took a woman's face, the suggestion of features forming a smile. "A daughter of my lineage violated our sacred trust and, when you called on me, I was silent. Still, you fought for our path. You honor your mothers, Beryl Gilman-Vogel, and the divine to whom we are all but children. My obligation and my blessing are yours. This is your home now. The blood you spilled here is your claim. Rebuild your coven and preserve our teachings."

Beryl's hands, cradled in light, rose. An opalescent ribbon sealed the jagged red line on one palm and faded into her skin. Beryl gasped, her eyes lit and shining like jewels. The exhaustion sloughed away, the locks of her hair floated in the residual glow, silver returning again to black.

Libuše addressed the wolves. "I never knew you could be so beautiful."

Chris preened, Tobias huffed stiffly, and Mark refused to lower his eyes.

Her glow flickered with a nod. "Witch and wolf are bound now by a power greater than old animosity. I anoint you sacred guardians of both our kind. Wherever you go, the wild places will restore you in your hour of need. Your strength and speed increases, and your line will live long and be exalted among those of the Mystery."

The wolves lifted their muzzles and the glow dusted their coats and eyes like the twinkling of starlight. The hearts of the men shone in their chests with each beat. Tobias' forehead butted her palm, and she met his eyes. The grey glittered, full of promise.

A warmth fell on Barbara's face, the perfume of crushed laurel leaves settling around her. She lowered her eyes and would have gone to her knees, but the light caught her, lifting.

"I owe you an apology, daughter," Libuše said. "You were a child in isolation."

"Not alone," Barbara whispered. "I had a friend. Veronika."

The words lodged in her throat, and Barbara didn't feel the hot tear on her cheek until the light brushed it away, cooling and soothing.

"Your mentor is safe now. My court needed a woman of words."

Barbara's tears became a cough of joy. Libuše cupped her shoulders. "I see why she favored you. When I saw this future, I dreamed not of spires and roofs, but this. You were the hope through the shadow that followed my reign. You have a fine teacher now. Learn well, and become greater than even I. This is your destiny."

The great sorceress took in the wolf pressed against her thigh. "This woman has chosen you, wolf, to knit her legacy against. Do you also take her?"

Barbara flushed, but when she looked back, Tobias stood beside her, unafraid. He faced the light, bare as the day he was born. "I want nothing more, Great Lady."

Barbara swore the sorceress winked.

Libuše brought their hands together and lay hers on each of their shoulders, forming a circle. "You will protect her, honor her, respect her, and raise her children to the light."

"With all that I am," Tobias vowed.

"And you, daughter," Libuše said. "Is it your will to protect him, honor him, respect him, and bear his children, leading them in our nature?"

Barbara couldn't see through her tears, but she searched for Tobias' face anyway. "When he's ready."

She squeaked when he dragged her close, his laughter warming her hair as he pressed his mouth to her brow.

She lowered her chin to nod. "Joyfully, lady."

Libuše's glow flared. "There is no greater bond than your promise to one another. Be blessed, children."

She wove ribbons with her fingers, leaving streaks of that opal shine on their eyes, throats, and hearts, binding their hands together. The angels blew their horns, releasing a great shower of petals and ginkgo leaves in celebration. Libuše returned to the altar, pausing to sketch a symbol on the brows of the remaining wolves.

The light dimmed as she went leaving behind a woman, in wool and fur, her reddish hair braided into twin plaits looped behind her ears. Two others stood holding hands at the altar: one blonde and sunlit, the other raven-dark and pale. Their free hands extended in welcome to their sister. Libuše looked at the living witches and wolves over her shoulder and lifted a hand. Then she completed the circle and they vanished.

The fading ring lingered a moment longer, the sound echoing too high and pure to be a bell. Tobias slid his free arm around Barbara.

"Were we just married by the ghost of a thousand-year-old witch?" he whispered, shivering.

She shrugged off her sweater and handed it to him. "Let's call it a very formal engagement."

EPILOGUE

"Papa, Ich habe Angst."

Tobias halted in his tracks. It didn't matter that he could hear his brothers calling in the distance. It didn't matter that the wolf inside him was pressing against his ribcage, begging to run loose.

The hand pressed against his trembled, fingers clenching with strength beyond a boy's years. Tobias could smell the wolf thick in his blood. Isaac had always been the studious one, as much like Tobias as he had been like his father. And he was younger than Tobias had been when he'd come to this place.

"What do you have to fear, Schatz?" He gazed at his son with all the patience in the world and a smile. "Lila is waiting for you. Thyme too. And your uncles."

"Everything ok?" Barbara called from the porch, warming a mug of tea in her hands. "Toby, do you want me to..."

Standing in the doorway behind her, Beryl spoke, "Come now, leave them to it."

Her words were for Barbara, but impossible to keep from the sharp ears of wolves.

Barbara held her ground. Tobias met her steady gaze. *You don't have to do this alone*, she promised. *Never alone.*

His heart suddenly seemed too big for his ribcage. He nodded.

Barbara came down the porch, drawing the length of her braid out of the way as she tugged the cardigan over her shoulders. The dark twist, feathered with rebellious curls, hung to the small of her back. Haloed in the light of the fading day, she glowed, the shine of a few silver strands streaking her temples making her look otherworldly. She stole his breath every time.

"Mama." Isaac hugged her.

Tobias wrapped his arms around them both, snugging them against his bare chest.

Isaac shivered. He was tall for his age, long limbs even smaller and thinner out in the cold of the fading day.

"You'll be warmer as a wolf," Barbara said cheerily, rubbing his bare shoulders. "All that fur was made for a cold spring night like this. You'll see."

Isaac hung his head. "I feel it inside me. It's so strong. What if I can't come back? What if it doesn't let me go—the wolf?"

"Lila has always come back," Barbara said.

"That's just Lila," Isaac exhaled sharply.

Tobias knew what he meant. His niece (the older of twins by two whole minutes, as she liked to remind everyone) was the most stubborn, determined, wily person he'd met—human and wolf—much like her father.

Tobias took his son's shoulders. "You are not separate creatures—you and your wolf. That eagerness you feel, that's you. That strength—that's yours. Together you are more than you would be apart. Do you want to come back?"

Isaac looked at him, alarmed. "Of course. I have a test on Monday."

Tobias bit his tongue against a laugh.

Barbara tipped her chin up and made an intense study of the magenta framed clouds overhead, amusement in the curving line of her mouth and the gather of skin beside her eyes.

"Then you have something important to get back to," Tobias said, unable to steal his gaze back from his beautiful wife. "It helps to have something to come back to."

"Ok, I'm ready." Isaac sucked in a breath. "Oh, man. What's she want?"

"Mama!" Octavia called from the porch, bouncing on her toes and oblivious to the fact that they never touched the wood. She held a ball of light in the palm of her hands, two of her younger cousins dancing around her in glee. "I did it, come see."

"Just a minute, baby, I'm talking to your brother," Barbara called before sighing in relief. "Great grace, at last. If I heard that incantation one more time…"

"I heard that!" Octavia sang gleefully. For a ten-year-old witch, she had remarkably sharp hearing.

"Toes on the floor," Barbara said. "Rule number one: no levitating until you can break Solomon's Seal."

"Ma!" Octavia groaned.

"Come back in here, you scalawags," Beryl called, herding them inside and giving Barbara a wave. "Tavy, let gramma show you the key to old Solomon's trick."

Barbara sighed, one brow raised. "We wanted this."

"More than any other future." Tobias kissed her temple. "You are a patient teacher, Dr. Svobodová."

"This is why I only teach seminars and special sessions," she laughed, a warm throaty sound that still sent a shock of desire through him.

Another night he would take her out into the woods for the long walks that usually ended in them returning by dawn, picking leaves and bark out of her hair and, once or twice, a splinter in an unfortunate location.

They had many such nights to look forward to.

Tonight belonged to Isaac. Tobias drank in the sight of his son. "What do you think? The moon is up soon, and Lila wants to try her teeth at a hunt. In?"

Isaac took a breath, squeezed his mother one more time, and let her go. He met Tobias' eyes, a glimmer of wolf already shining in them. "In."

Tobias clapped his shoulder with a grin.

"That's my boy." Tobias shivered and rubbed his hands together. "All right. The wolf is in your bones and your blood. All you have to do is let it out."

Isaac hesitated, and his hands lingered at the towel around his waist. "Mom—are you gonna watch?"

She spun on her heels, hands over her eyes, and tried not to laugh. "Absolutely not. I'm just here to take the towels inside, so they don't get wet overnight. Oh, wait," she spun again. "Your glasses!"

She held out a hand, and Tobias dropped his into her palm. Isaac's joined them. She slipped both into the pocket of her cardigan and put her back to them. Tobias looked at his son. "Ready?"

♠

BARBARA SPUN at the sharp bark. A familiar grey wolf swung his tail once, pale hairs at the root of the long black tips rustling in the motion. He flexed his spine and shook. The grizzled markings that made him blend into a forested hillside in winter rippled over muscle beneath. He had grown more solid with age, and his eyes of smoldering ash were lovely as ever amid the mask of chocolate and grey fur.

Beside him, the adolescent male wolf wobbled on four oversized paws, searching for his balance. On four legs, her son was every bit as beautiful as his father. His charcoal coat, nearly black, bore his father's markings surrounding a luminous set of pale brown eyes. He stared back at her, a look of wonder and recognition in his gaze.

"Go on, you big pup," she said. "Run."

Isaac took a step and tumbled into the big wolf with a yelp.

Tobias chuffed softly, a laugh. He clicked his teeth once, lightly tugging the young wolf's ruff to steady him. Then he lifted his chin and loosed a long cry that made the hair on her arms stand on end. A moment later, an answer came from the north, near the ruins.

The young wolf's ears and tail lifted, excitement rippling his coat. He looked back at her once, jaws wide, then bounded toward the sound. Each leap brought him more steadiness, balance, power. By the time he reached the tree line, he was all wolf with the boy tucked safely inside.

"You too," Barbara whispered to the wolf that remained, wiping the tears from her cheeks.

The wolf circled her and came to rest against her hip. For a moment, his heat pressed against her belly and thighs. She looped her arms around his neck, breathing in musk until the tickle of wolf fur made her sneeze.

She released him. "See you Sunday."

And he raced into the trees.

♠

If you enjoyed *Binding Shadows*, check out the Grace Bloods series at
www.jasminesilvera.com/books

THANKS FOR READING

Reviews help other readers find their next favorite book. Please consider recommending it to a friend or leaving a review wherever you purchased this book.

Interested in more Vogel Brothers?

Read the first chapter of Conjuring Moonlight at:
www.jasminesilvera.com/conjuring-moonlight-sneak-peek

ACKNOWLEDGMENTS

It feels strange to thank a city, but since Prague and its mysteries continue to spark the 'what-ifs' that become stories, expressing gratitude seems like the only proper thing to do.

Early readers Lucie Greenidge & Beth Green provided invaluable insights into college life and other odds and ends (cell phones, student jobs, takeaway) in the Czech Republic in the 90s. Any deviations from the factual are mine.

Thank you to the Somebody Just Pooped crew for being a launchpad for all of my visits. Nina, Caroline, Sarah, Shannon, Pennie, Geoff & Sasha—you are a special kind of magic that makes Prague feel like home no matter how long I've been gone.

Helping to excavate plot buried in my meandering love for a city was Bethany Robison. Thank you for seeing right through to the heart of the story and lighting the way, handhold by handhold, to the top.

Tasha L. Harrison, The Book Brander, and Lopt & Cropt Editing thank you for making this book beautiful.

Outside of these pages, thanks to Eva Moore, who stood up to rescue me from my own desperate babbling and made a lifelong friend. From OSRBC to NYC to OGG: you know all the best places to hang out and are a damn fine roommate.

Thanks Dee J. Holmes, Sara Lunsford, and Kelly Charon for sharing the joy of the Canadian Standoff and of falling *into* chairs. Destroy that video.

Hat tip to Lin Lustig, Kitt Masters, Elle Beauregard, Chris Henderson-Bauer, Melora Francois, and Alexis de Girolami — midnight pizza mavens—your gif and track changes game is the stuff of legend.

I owe Clarion West an enormous debt of gratitude for putting me on the path to living a dream, and the workshop board and staff for keeping me busy in the meantime. Thanks Misha Stone and Claire Scott for proving libraries is where all the fun stuff happens and inviting me to the party.

The unwavering confidence of my family is the shore from which I sail into the wild seas of story. Thank you, Scholzovas and Silveras, for keeping the fire burning for the row home.

Finally, readers: you have my eternal gratitude. You made it through three Grace Bloods books and kept asking—but what about those *brothers*? You are as persistent as a first-page typo, and way more fun. I hope you find Toby and Bebe's story worth your tenacity.

This one's for you.

ABOUT THE AUTHOR

Jasmine Silvera spent her impressionable years sneaking "kissing books" between comics and fantasy movies. She's been mixing them up in her writing ever since. A semi-retired yoga teacher and amateur dancer, she lives in the Pacific Northwest with her partner-in-crime and their small, opinionated human charge. She is the author of three books in the Grace Bloods series: Death's Dancer, Dancer's Flame, and The Talon & the Blade.